DISHONESTLY
YOURS

Also by Krista and Becca Ritchie

ADDICTED SERIES

RECOMMENDED READING ORDER

ADDICTED TO YOU

RICOCHET

ADDICTED FOR NOW

KISS THE SKY

HOTHOUSE FLOWER

THRIVE

ADDICTED AFTER ALL

FUEL THE FIRE

LONG WAY DOWN

SOME KIND OF PERFECT

DISHONESTLY YOURS

KRISTA RITCHIE
and
BECCA RITCHIE

BERKLEY ROMANCE
NEW YORK

BERKLEY ROMANCE
Published by Berkley
An imprint of Penguin Random House LLC
penguinrandomhouse.com

Library of Congress Cataloging-in-Publication Data

Names: Ritchie, Krista, author. | Ritchie, Becca, author.
Title: Dishonestly yours / Krista Ritchie and Becca Ritchie.
Description: First edition. | New York: Berkley Romance, 2024. |
Series: Webs we weave ; 1
Identifiers: LCCN 2023046665 (print) | LCCN 2023046666 (ebook) |
ISBN 9780593549551 (paperback) | ISBN 9780593549568 (ebook)
Subjects: LCGFT: Romance fiction. | Novels.
Classification: LCC PS3618.I7675 D57 2024 (print) |
LCC PS3618.I7675 (ebook) | DDC 813/.6—dc23/eng/20231107
LC record available at https://lccn.loc.gov/2023046665
LC ebook record available at https://lccn.loc.gov/2023046666

First Edition: July 2024

Printed in the United States of America
1st Printing

Book design by George Towne
Interior Art: Spider Web © Sveta Aho/Shutterstock

To our mom & dad
For always believing in us

One

Phoebe

People say you choose your friends, but my friendship with Hailey Tinrock never felt like a choice. We clung to each other because we were told to, and then it became survival. And now—together—we're leaving our families behind.

At midnight, the motel room stinks of stale cigarettes and a microwaved burrito from its previous resident. Yellowed stains bleed into the cement walls and ceiling tiles. Five-star accommodations right here. *Luxurious.*

It's definitely not the Ritz-Carlton, and I've already become a roach murderer. I've counted four cockroaches so far, killed three with a rolled *Forbes* magazine that Hailey had been flipping through. She ripped off the cover with the roach juice to keep reading. I watch as the last one skitters into an air vent. It was smart to run away from us.

He knew what was coming.

As I plop down on the lumpy mattress, it lets out a warning screech but supports my weight enough. I appraise a box of poison—sorry, I mean *hair dye*. My scalp burns like I scrubbed it with sriracha and chile flakes.

"It says to wait thirty minutes," Hailey tells me, sitting cross-legged on the disgusting plaid chair in the corner. Her wet hair hides underneath a plastic cap, the color processing. She's wearing only an oversized black tee that says HEXES ON MY EXES, knee-high socks, and jet-black lipstick.

I'm not shocked she's painting her nails the same inky color.

Hailey dresses like she's someone who could stab you while she's sucking on a cigarette, but her favorite movie is about sisters working at a small-town pizza joint and falling in love so, *so* slowly. I can't sit through ten minutes of *Mystic Pizza*, and Hailey watches it every weekend like it's her bible.

She also has *zero* exes to hex. Just a laundry list of one-night stands and short-term flings. Our lifestyles aren't compatible with long-term relationships.

At least not real ones.

Hailey doesn't recheck the instructions on the hair dye box. I trust that she remembered the info on the first read through. Photographic memory and all.

I'd be envious if she weren't my best friend and didn't use her beautiful brain to bail me out of a million and one tragic scenarios.

"Are we sure they didn't make this stuff out of jalapeño paste?" I force myself not to itch, but yeah, I kinda scratch and wince. *No self-control.* "It feels like fire ants are exploding on my head. I've never even heard of this brand." I rotate the box to stare at the front. "Vivid Value Color. What's our plan B if our hair starts falling out again?"

"We shave our heads," Hailey says, like it's the obvious solution. She blows on her wet nails, and I try not to mourn my hair. Would I actually shave it?

Yes, I'm all-in with her.

Would I tear up?

One hundred percent.

Would she?

Probably not, considering she shaved her head when she was sixteen. Now that she's twenty-four, it's regularly chopped at her shoulders in an edgy cut.

At the moment, I'm restraining myself from doing a full-fingernailed scalp massage. *Do not*.

She can see my struggle. "We didn't have much to choose from at the gas station, Phebs."

"I know." I sigh, trying not to complain. We might be the same age and she might be the one figuratively behind the wheel, but I'm the one dead set on protecting us and keeping us from struggling.

When Hailey came up with this idea in Carlsbad, we had just trekked away from a multimillion-dollar beach house in the pouring rain. All façades dropped—we didn't call for our personal driver in his Bentley to take us "home."

We just slipped out. Without splendor or attention.

Almost like we never arrived.

It'd been a little past one a.m.—you don't forget things like time when it's one of those days that stay with you. Or in this case, one of those nights. After a long, barefoot trek with our heels in our hands, we sat at a bus stop, thinking we could escape the rain while we waited.

We didn't.

Carlsbad's bus stops have fancy white *pergolas* as roofs. So rain slipped through the slats of wood and wet our hair and our flowery Oscar de la Renta dresses we just purchased this summer. Her dress was embroidered with poisonous white oleanders. Mine was threaded with delicate pink tulips.

Hailey was silently crying. I could tell, even in the storm. She's an ugly crier when it's not faked. Her whole face was scrunched, and her reddened eyes looked touched by the salt of her emotion, not the sky.

Dark mascara streamed down her cheeks, and I clasped her hand tighter while my knees jostled. *From the cold*, I wanted to believe.

I was just cold from the rain.

"Phoebe," Hailey choked out. "I-I don't think we should do this again." She tried to catch my gaze.

But I stared at my lap. My dress was riding up, and a trickle of blood on my thigh became exposed to the elements. The rain washed away the crimson streak in a blink.

Just a millisecond. That's all it took before it was gone.

"We're leaving California tomorrow," I reminded Hailey. "It'll be okay." I was ready to get the hell out of there. To start the next job.

It's always about the next job, bug, I heard my mom's voice in my head.

Hailey turned more to me. She squinted at me through rain and tears. "What if we don't?"

"Don't what?" I blinked through confusion.

"Don't go to Seattle."

To the next job, she meant.

My stomach tossed like it had earlier that night. I glanced back down at the inside of my thigh, expecting to see more blood, but it really was gone.

Now she squeezed my hand. The desperation in the strength of her fingers clung against my heart. "We could retire, Phebs."

"We're *twenty-four*. I don't think we're in a position to retire." I held my Hermès purse over Hailey's head as an umbrella, so the rain would stop pelting her face.

She looked simultaneously thankful and distraught.

We weren't trust fund children with loaded bank accounts, but growing up, we'd experienced wealth like we were daughters of neurosurgeons and tech moguls. A Bugatti for two weeks. Penthouse suite at a five-star luxury hotel for a month. Two-grand rib eye with shaved black truffle for dinner.

There were times the fantasy would pop, and we'd reconvene at a Holiday Inn like regular middle-class folk, but only for short moments. One night or two.

Our lives were always fantasies, and our parents taught us how to construct them and then rebuild when they started to crack.

Money would flow in heaps and go out just as fast. Be flashy enough to maintain appearances but not enough to cause attention. Wear the designer dress. Drive the car that'd elicit your neighbor's envy. Pick up the thousand-dollar tab once to show you can.

Insulate yourself in the "right" social circles.

When we became adults, things shifted a bit. Instead of playing with private school kids at some rich family's mansion for an afternoon, I could now attend an exclusive nightclub with VIP bottle service. Or the strip club that B-list celebrities frequented.

Only, I wasn't just partying the night away but seducing someone out of a few grand. Felt a lot different than batting my eight-year-old innocent eyes at the unsuspecting elite.

The marks tended to be affluent assholes, and as a kid I liked to believe we were Robin Hood—stealing from the rich, giving to the poor. But we weren't. We just gave to ourselves, and I was mostly a prop for my mom's long cons. There to give her backstory—sometimes as my doting mother, other times as my kind aunt or selfless guardian—more credibility.

By the time I was a teenager, I was no longer a shill. A prop. I had more responsibility and a bigger role to play. Long cons were always the bread and butter that kept us thriving. Short cons were like practice and a way to travel from A to B: conning someone out of a hundred bucks in sixty seconds, short-changing a cashier.

Anyway, after all our families did to live this *fabulous* lifestyle, my savings didn't see much reward. It was never about saving money for some brighter future.

We were supposedly already living the "brighter" future. Our line of work is ethically and morally questionable and bor-derline corrupt, but it's not like we robbed banks. Most of the time, we just . . . tricked people. Into believing our fantasies.

Our lies.

But still, I listened closely to Hailey at that rainy bus stop like I *understood* what she was saying already. Even if the concept seemed far-fetched.

"*Retiring* is the wrong word," she whispered, but no one was around us. Barely any cars zoomed past our stretch of road. "More like . . . starting over. Like *really* starting over, from the beginning." Her mascara-smudged eyes were plead-ing with me. "Phebs." Her voice fractured. Despite her goth wardrobe and her unapproachable aura that radiated toward strangers, I'd seen Hailey cry plenty of times in our lives.

She cried over a turtle she ran over.

She cried when Romeo and Juliet died in the 1968 film.

She cried and cursed after breaking her pinky in a door-jamb.

And now she was crying from the fucked-up Carlsbad job.

I hated seeing her this distraught. Tears of my own threat-ened to rise, and I was trying—God, I was *really* trying to see what she saw. A way out? I'd never considered it.

I never wanted it.

"We can do the normal thing," she said. "The way that normal people do."

I couldn't see.

I couldn't see. "Hails—"

"We can. I *know* we can. We don't have to keep doing this. We *don't*. You and me—let's leave together."

My eyes stung, and I looked around for answers that I still couldn't see. Not like her.

"Inertia," she whispered a life-changing word into the rain, one that swung my head back to her.

My pulse raced. "What?" I breathed, thinking I heard her wrong.

"*Inertia*," she said more certainly, more forcefully. "I'm invoking *inertia*."

Inertia: an object will continue at its current motion until some force causes a change in its speed or direction.

She was unearthing a childhood pact that we buried like a time capsule. If someone invoked the word *inertia*, then whatever road we were taking, we'd have to change course together. To change course was to do the opposite of what our parents wanted for us, and that felt like the ultimate rebellion.

We never wanted to be alone when contesting them.

It felt isolating and devastating to stand against the indomitable forces that were our mothers. So the pact was born to ensure it'd always be the two of us against the world. It was an unbreakable pact. Stronger than a pinky promise. Stronger than a blood oath.

It's a pact reserved solely for us: two daughters of con artists and best friends for life.

It was only the second time the word was ever invoked. The second time the pact rose to the surface.

The first time, I'd been the one to say the word. We were fourteen.

Hailey had been viciously bullied at our prep school. She had hoped to "tough it out" even though every school day ended in tears. I had wanted to drop out of the prep school, though it'd go against our moms' wishes.

So I'd said, "Inertia." After that, we'd never gone back. We'd changed course together.

Hailey summoning this word at the bus stop in Carlsbad swept me into the power of our friendship and the indestructible pact we wielded like a trump card.

I had used it once and she followed through, despite being afraid of the repercussions. Now, it was my turn to do the same.

I had to do it. There was no other thought in my mind then. *I had to, and I would.*

She opened her black leather handbag and pulled out a brochure. "I found this."

She passed it to me. It started sogging between my fingers, but confusion began to fade as I gazed at the picturesque New England landscape.

Vacation in One of Connecticut's Oldest & Most Vibrant Towns!

It looked beautiful and quaint. The kind of place you'd start a family and grow old. A place you'd plant roots.

Normal.

And I realized, it was her *Mystic Pizza*. The small town with only romantic troubles and college dreams. No lies.

No scams.

And she wasn't asking me to take a weekend trip up the East Coast. I didn't know how long she had carried this brochure or how much she'd thought about leaving until then. But maybe that night had lit a match, and after what happened in the beach house, her idea had detonated into a plan.

Starting over.

A chill raced across my skin.

Doing the normal thing. Was that even possible?

The wet brochure was crumbling between my fingers. "Our moms will hate us moving to Connecticut." They'd been best friends since childhood.

Thick as thieves. Quite fucking literally. Only their lives were less than glamorous, unlike our cushy and glitzy upbringing—as they so often reminded us.

The rain began to let up when I glanced back at Hailey. "We're grifters, in case you've forgotten."

I like using that word because our moms *hate* it. They think "grifting" invokes a visual of tobacco-spitting hitchhikers. Though, we have hitchhiked before, and we try not to stay in one place for too long.

"Then we don't tell them we're going," Hailey said. "We could stop running. Stop conning. We could build something for ourselves that lasts. Can you picture that?" She looked up like it was a constellation in the stars. Spelling out our real bright future.

Pain blossomed in my chest from the strange, muddled yearning. The idea of not running sounded nice. Not conning . . . I wasn't so sure. While she stared up, I looked down at our sopping wet dresses, my discarded heels, and the dirt on the bottoms of our feet.

"It's hard to imagine," I whispered. "Sounds more like a dream." *A strange fantasy.*

But seeing the desperation in Hailey's eyes again—I really did want to give it to her.

"Then let's live that dream. Let's *try*." She clutched my

hand again. "Please, Phoebe." Her round gray gaze pleaded. Begged. "I can't do it alone." A tremor shook her voice.

The pact surfaced in my heart again. "You won't be alone, Hails," I breathed.

When I was ten years old, Hailey told me to jump off a bridge into ice-cold water to save a drowning stray cat. She was too scared of heights, and I had rarely been scared of anything. I couldn't say no to her then.

I definitely couldn't say no now.

"I'll try with you," I cemented.

We hugged underneath the bus stop's pergola, still sopping wet from the storm, and we let go before an old Ford truck rode up to us.

The window rolled down. I saw her older brother in the passenger seat, and then from behind the wheel, my oldest brother careened forward into view.

They said nothing.

Their eyes said enough. *Concern. Urgency. Time to go.*

We climbed into the backseat with a secret and the start of a plan.

In the motel room, thousands of miles away from the California coast, I settle with the fact that I dived headfirst into this now well-formulated plan. Connecticut. Leaving behind our families and the paths they set for us at birth. Starting something new.

Living a normal life.

What even is normal? I grew up in hotels and one-month rentals. Every time I whimpered as a kid about staying in a city, my mom would crouch to my height with glittering hazel eyes and her blonde hair in Instagramable waves. Her charismatic, radiantly maternal face made other kids ache for her to be their mom and had older men fantasizing about a life with her on their arm.

And she'd tell me, "Why would you ever want a house in that *boring* neighborhood?" She'd teasingly gag enough that I'd laugh, and her perfect, genuine smile lit up my world. "We're doing what other people *dream of*. Never forget that, bug."

She nicknamed me *bug* since I was technically her youngest of three. *Bug* is sometimes *spider* or *sweet spider*, what she calls all of us endearingly, but all the nicknames remind me that I'm as squashable as the roaches I killed.

Maybe that's why my whole life was lived on the run. Go for the air vent and you're free to keep breathing.

Rooting myself for longer than a handful of months is foreign to me, but the idea of moving to a small town feels *epically* normal and tugs at some heartstrings.

A new town. A new name. A new, honest job. Would I really like what Hailey advertised? *Really starting over. From the beginning.*

Hailey's cellphone alarm beeps in the motel. "Mine is done." After capping her black polish, she pops up from the chair. She's bleaching her already dyed-blonde hair to a platinum shade. Nothing as drastic as me. "Want this?" She tosses a gas station bag of nail polishes.

I sift through the reds and pinks. My fingers brush the Barbie-pink bottle, about to choose that one. *This color is so pretty on you, bug.* She'd definitely love me in Barbie pink, and a knot is in my chest before I choose an off-white polish.

I shake the bottle. Unlike Hailey, my pink tee with an embroidered strawberry and my light-wash jeans aren't exactly intimidating anyone. I gravitate toward the soft, delicate look, and she gravitates toward the hard-core. Our insides do not entirely match our outsides, but do anyone's? Most people aren't what they seem to be at first sight. We know that better than most.

On Hailey's way to the bathroom, an aggressive knock pounds the door.

We flinch before going motionless and quiet.

I listen to the fist rapping outside our motel room again. Our eyes meet each other as concern builds. Did someone already find us? *No way.*

Another knock, and then a graveled male voice follows.

"It's me!"

I blink hard. It's official, our dream has become a *nightmare*. With more annoyance than fear, I climb off the bed.

"How'd he find us?" Hailey asks, sounding a lot less irritated than I feel.

"No clue." I nod toward the bathroom. "Wash out the dye. I'll deal with him."

"You sure?" She wavers. "I can deal with him if—"

"I've got it," I interject. "Really." I want to be more helpful in this whole plan of hers. She's done a lot of the preparation and legwork, and if handling *him* will take something off her plate, then I'm signing myself up.

Hailey nods and slips into the bathroom, shutting the door behind her.

I steel myself for the incoming aggravating *lecture* that I know he'll give me, and my stiff stride carries me to the motel's door.

When I swing it open, I'm met with molten gunmetal eyes, windswept dyed-black hair, and a crisp navy-blue suit more fitting for the Four Seasons than a Super 8.

Hailey's older brother.

Two

Phoebe

He's so ugly, my eyes are trying to roll into the back of my head. *Lies.* I'm supposed to be living a truthful life now, and I guess that begins with being completely honest with myself—and Brayden Tinrock has always been hot. Never even had an awkward teenage phase like me. Acne on my chin. Hair that either frizzed or fell greasy flat.

No, *his hair* teleported straight from the nineties. Full and lush with those teasing pieces always brushing his lashes. Even dyed black, his hair still carries that nineties allure right now.

Truthfully, he's good-looking in a way that can con many women and men out of their fortunes. And he knows this fact, which makes him even more of an annoying pest than he already is.

He cocks his head like I shouldn't be that surprised he caught up to me. His satisfied look begins to boil my blood.

"What are you doing here?" I snap at him. *Does he know about our plan?* Or is he just here to inform us of our next job out west? In Seattle, to be exact.

"I could ask the same thing of you," he says with equal bite. I hate his voice. How its deep, sandpaper quality sounds like the personification of sex.

He's the last man I'd ever fuck.

Just to be clear.

How his rough-around-the-edges demeanor could attract anyone is beyond my comprehension. My similar coarse grit drives more people away than entices them inside.

I clutch the edge of the door. "I'm knitting a sweater."

His eyes flit to my head, where my hair is piled up with dye. "See, if you were knitting a sweater, I wouldn't be here."

"Pretend I am, then." I go to shut the door.

He grabs the edge, keeping it open, before ramming his loafer in the doorway. And why the hell are his shoes so shiny? I glare. "You're not invited in, Rocky."

"And I'm not a fucking vampire. I don't need an invitation." He shoves closer, chest against my chest like a showdown between two apex predators in the wild. Our eyes latch.

Aggravation brews in his irises and reflects in mine. I realize he's not leaving, but I'm not about to make this easy for him.

"Say *please*," I demand.

"Fuck you," he counters.

I don't move.

His eyes flame. "Please and *fuck you*."

My nose flares, but I know when to surrender a battle in order to win a war.

Fine. I step aside.

He slides farther into the motel, enough to shut and lock the door behind him.

Hailey emerges from the bathroom, rubbing a towel against

her damp platinum-blonde hair. When she spots her brother, she plasters on a fake smile. "Hey, Rocky. How's it going?" Her casualness isn't as manufactured as that smile, and like a fire extinguisher blew at him, Rocky's anger dissipates around his little sister. She was always the calm to his storm.

Rocky and I, together, are a volcanic eruption. One that'll never end, not until the whole world is coated in magma.

"Can you give Phoebe and me a second alone?" he asks Hailey.

My whole head is searing. *Might just be the dye.* "What— you're just going to ignore her question? *How's it going, Rocky?*"

"It's going." He's staring me down.

I'm staring *him* down, and if anyone is going to win a staring contest, it's going to be me. Air suctions out of the room the longer silence stretches.

"Alone. You and me," Rocky repeats.

A conversation *alone* with Rocky means that Hailey can't be there to moderate, but maybe I can kick his ass back to wherever he came from faster without her here.

"Phoebe?" Hailey asks for confirmation.

I give her a nod.

Hesitation fills her eyes that are shadowed with heavy black liner. "Okay, but just don't kill each other. I don't need to clean up a murder today." Spike-studded backpack over her shoulder, she pauses at the door. "I'm going to grab some shit from the vending machines. Want anything, Phebs?"

"I'm good."

She sighs, then reluctantly leaves. Not gracing her brother with the same offer.

I scratch the wet, processing hair at the back of my neck.

"I have to wash this out," I mutter. His intense eyes track me to the bathroom, and he follows like a shadow attached to my heels.

Testing his resolve, I start undressing in front of him. It's a quick, thoughtless decision.

Annoy him like he annoys you, my gut always tells me. I pull my strawberry tee over my head, revealing a simple pale pink bra. He stares at my eyes, never flinching or looking down. "Seriously, Phoebe?" he asks. "What the fuck?"

"You followed *me* into the bathroom." I unbutton my jeans.

A hostile growling noise scratches his throat, but his gaze never abandons mine. Not even as I wiggle my jeans down my hips and step out of them. Mesh sky-blue panties ride high on my hips and reveal more than they hide. *I hate that undressing in front of him is easy for me. I hate that it'd be easy in front of anyone*. Thoughts intrude in a wave of bitter shame that I try to swallow down.

Use what you're given, right? Hailey has the brains. I have the body. Dissociating from my tits and ass and the rest of my physical form has become easy. *Too easy*. And in the next breath, I hate it.

Christ, I hate it.

But I don't know how to reverse time and unlearn what I was taught.

"I followed you to talk to you," he says gruffly. "I didn't sign up for the striptease."

I grimace. "I'd rather stand in front of a moving train than put on a show for you."

"Likewise," he says casually, like it's known. We would willingly jump into certain death rather than seduce one another.

Great.

And I'm seriously *not* putting on a show for him. I just want to *unnerve* him. Like a game we play. Aggravate the other before you yourself can get aggravated. I have very tragically failed right now.

I grind my teeth. "Turn around."

He does without me asking twice. *Nice*—no, he's not nice. He's an asshole. I hate that I have to remind myself of that.

He lets out a resigned breath. "Can we just have a civil conversation for five minutes?"

"Why are you here?" I counter, spinning the moldy shower handle. Letting the warm water cascade into the tub-shower combo.

"To stop you and Hailey from making a mistake."

I slow my movements as a colder chill sweeps my exposed skin. *He knows.* How? Head crawling with heat, I don't have time to ask. My brain is sufficiently frying from the outside in. Quickly, I shed my panties and bra, then step into the scalding shower.

"Fuck," I mutter before swiveling the knob to a colder temperature. *I hate you, shower. I hate you, Rocky. I hate you, hair.* Maybe if I hate everything enough, I'll find love again.

That is definitely not how that works.

Rocky takes my silence as an avenue to keep talking, even if his voice is muffled from the shower. "Moving to the East Coast without telling your parents or mine isn't going to end well."

Blue dye slips down my legs and into the drain.

"How'd you find out?!" I shout over the shower.

"Carter told me."

"What a rat." I groan.

I know Hailey has a massive crush on him, but *ughhh*. She's swept up by his forgery skills. She does that a lot. Falls headfirst for any guy that shows some extraordinary talent. I've teased her to death about the fire juggler she slept with, but to this day, she says he was her best lay.

But Carter isn't some random stranger we met in a dark alley. I first heard about him at seventeen.

"I met this guy who does great fakes," my mom said, like she made a friend at a book club who knows how to craft lawn furniture. Only instead of an Adirondack chair, my mom got a shiny new passport.

Carter is just a connection for my family. Another string in the webs we all weave. So I thought I could trust him—and maybe I still can. It's not like he blabbed to the Feds. He told Rocky. Someone that'd take a secret to his grave.

What I assume Rocky knows: Carter made Hailey and me new licenses for our fresh start. And in Hailey's attempt to *flirt*, she might have divulged the fact that we're moving (for real) to Connecticut. If Carter told Rocky all that, then red flags must have been flapping in his face.

And Rocky took the red flag, made a cape, and flew to us. Hence the check-in.

"He called me, by the way," Rocky explains outside the shower. "He knew this wasn't your next job, and he was worried."

I know this is dangerous. Those words stick to the back of my throat. Admitting to Rocky that this might be a risky plan feels like sticking my finger in an electric socket. Instead I let the silence build.

After carefully rinsing all the dye from my hair, I cut the shower off, snag a towel from the rack, pat my hair dry, and then wrap the towel around my chest. Partly, I expect Rocky to be gone. Back in his car. Left without saying goodbye.

He wouldn't.

I know he wouldn't, and I hate that I like that about him. His reliability. If I ever found myself in deep trouble, he would be there.

Hell, he's here now and we're not even *in* trouble.

Irritation bubbles again, drowning out the affection that exists. As I yank the curtain, metal rings clink against the shower rod.

Yep, Rocky is still here. Leaning against the discolored tiled wall, buff arms crossed and gray eyes fixated on me, he seems to be considering something.

Waiting, almost.

Hate sounds like a strong word, and I'm not even sure it's the right one when it comes to Rocky. He's only a year older than me. We grew up together, and we were tethered to the good and bad that happened more than anyone else in our families.

But the Job That Shall Never Be Named punt-kicked us in immeasurable ways. Whatever we were to each other, it just . . . changed us. We've been licking our wounds ever since, and aggravation and frustration simmer to the surface so much more often in his company.

He's still a Tinrock.

Our families are permanently intertwined ever since his mom dropped a snow cone and my mom gave hers to the weeping girl. They were *five*. The decades-long friendship between Addison and Elizabeth is set for life. Bound further together by their crimes, and when they had children, they taught us everything they knew.

I tighten the knot of my towel without flashing Rocky, and I step out of the shower, going to the mirror. "I know you, Rocky. You wouldn't come all the way out here just to tell me our plan is stupid. You could've done that over the phone. So what do you need to say?"

His jaw sets. "She won't go if you don't."

Hailey.

He's worried about his sister.

Concern fills his gray eyes. Why does my stomach drop? Why do I feel hollow that I'm not a part of his concern?

He doesn't care about you anymore. Not after that job.

I push aside those painful thoughts, and I rake a brush through my tangled dark blue hair. Snagging knots and yanking roughly. "She wants to do this." Pressure mounts on my chest. "She's smarter than both of us combined. She's thought all of this through."

"I get all of that," Rocky says with edge. "I know she's smart. But Hailey has always been a fucking dreamer. She's painfully idealistic. What I don't get is why *you* would want to move to some boring, pretentious college town. It sounds like hell on earth."

Maybe I want to live the Mystic Pizza *life with her.*

I'm not even sure I can be virtuous and moral, and I highly doubt I'll find my small-town romance with a do-gooder gentleman who's constantly merry and bright even after Christmas.

Hailey is hopeful, and Rocky is right. I'm full of cynicism.

Moving to Connecticut and starting over is her idea. Not telling her parents and my mom—also her idea. When we arrived at the motel, I suggested we contact them in a week or so to let them know our whereabouts. Just so they don't assume we've driven off a cliffside and plummeted into the Pacific—or worse, got caught by the Feds.

There is a bad scenario where my mom is worrying her only daughter is dead or in cuffs, and I feel awful saddling her with that panic. But Hailey was firmly against divulging our location. She's anti-conflict, and if they know our plan, it'll start the equivalent of a nuclear reactor meltdown with lectures, guilt trips, and cutting disappointment.

I think Hails is also concerned that any contact with my mom might lead me back to conning.

Maybe that's why I'm not making any calls. Hearing my mom's voice, knowing I'm hurting her by being deceptive—a person I'm used to *always* being genuine toward—it's painful for me. The only way to stay on track is to remember my best friend comes first. I'm just here to oversee the situation. A passenger on this plan. Along for Hailey's ride in case the car crashes.

I do know how to change a tire. Thanks to my oldest brother.

But I don't want *Rocky* to be right. It's making me wish I truly believed in the soggy brochure Hailey showed me. I'm fully Team Hailey. In her beautiful boat.

Not in his busted, rotted tanker.

Quickly, the stubborn side of me takes over. I rotate to him and say, "Maybe I'm tired of doing bad shit, Rocky. Maybe I want to be *good* for once."

His brows crinkle, his mouth gradually falling open. He straightens up off the wall. "What?" He looks at me like I've turned into Cruella de Vil and I admitted to murdering Dalmatians. "You're not thinking about going clean . . . ?"

Shit.

Shitshitshit.

Panicked heat bakes me. *He didn't know.* He just thought Hailey and I were settling down in some rich college town, willing to lie and cheat our way into the upper echelons of Ivy League society.

Oh fuck.

My mouth dries, and I'm more nervous about living without

the skills we were taught. Deception. Seducing. Forging. Can it even be done?

Inertia.

The pact.

For Hailey.

I need to try.

"We're doing this the right way," I say, my voice quieter. "No con. No lies. We're starting over for real."

He blinks. "You've lost your fucking mind."

Three

Phoebe

Rocky leaves the bathroom long enough for me to get dressed, and when I return to the bedroom, I catch him rifling through his sister's duffel bag. He doesn't care that I see him—or else he would've been more discreet.

What he said to me still rings in the pit of my ear. *You've lost your fucking mind.*

I rub leave-in conditioner through my damp blue hair and watch him toe the line between protective older brother and complete asshole.

I near him. "What the hell are you even looking for?"

Still focused on the bag, he doesn't glance up. "Tension wrench, bump key, burner phones, spare IDs, extra cash, all the shit she'd have on her for a job."

"Don't waste your time. Tension wrench and bump key are in the trash. IDs and burner phones have been destroyed. Extra cash is in our boots."

He solidifies. His eyes flash hot on mine. "Destroyed?"

"Yeah, they're gone. We don't need fake IDs. We just need the *one* real one."

He rises to his feet, alarm *gushing* at this point. He's the Niagara Falls of stormy concern. "You're going by your real name?"

"No, of course not." I wouldn't put my family in jeopardy like that.

A wave of relief washes over his face. "What name, then?"

The response sticks to my throat. "Phoebe." Anyway, Phoebe is a name I've used for decades. Even though it isn't the name my mom gave me at birth—it feels like mine.

Rocky intakes a tight breath, then looks away from me. I try not to understand what he's thinking or feeling—in case they're emotions I'm not in the mood to confront.

Cowardly, maybe, but our history is so deep that I'm not prepared to sink into quicksand. I'm supposed to be stepping outside of that hazard.

Starting new. "Just trust that we're doing this right," I tell him. "We want to try this out, and you know I'll look out for Hails."

He runs his fingers through his wavy black hair. For a flash, I remember those hands slipping through my hair and his rough voice against my ear in a trancelike whisper: *"I hate this."*

That is what he said to me. I. Hate. This.

Truthfully, I could never fully love when we had to pretend to be head over heels in love during cons either. But I also hate that I enjoyed the feeling of hands I knew and trusted and cared about skating through pieces of me like I was the tenderest, sweetest thing he'd ever touched.

Yeah.

I also hate that.

Rocky lets strands of his hair flop to his forehead. "I just wish you'd convince my sister this is a bad idea."

"I can't. I won't."

"I know." He glares at the ugly stained carpet and then up at me. "So you're just 'trying this out'?"

I try to ignore his use of finger quotes.

"Like an experiment?" he adds.

Tensely, I lower onto the squeaky bed. This isn't supposed to be some temporary gig where I pack my bags and bail at the first bump in the road. Hailey wants this to last, and living a normal life is *hard*. Which is probably one of the million reasons why my mom and his parents never bought into the concept. If Rocky thinks we're dead set on this new lifestyle, I fear he'll be a bigger thorn.

Let him think what he wants.

"Yeah, it's an experiment."

He rubs at his temple. "All right. Okay."

"Okay?" Surprise flits across my face.

"If my sister needs this to understand our lives are better grifting, then yeah, she can have this fucking experiment." He bends back down to her bag and zips it up. "But I'm coming with you two."

My stomach drops. "Excuse me, what?"

The door to the motel whips open. Hailey stands frozen with an armful of Doritos, glancing between us like she's witnessing a marital dispute. And *ugh*, why does my brain go there? No. I'm not married to her brother, but *yes*, we have pretended to be married.

Maybe more than once.

"Oh." With a red Twizzler between her teeth, Hailey eyes him, then me. She's cerebral, perceptive, and way too good at reading the temperature of the room. "I came back too early.

I can go raid the soda machine. Get carbonated." She throws the Doritos onto the bed and then waggles her Twizzler at us. "Don't fight—"

"Wait, don't go," I say fast and wave an angry hand to Rocky. "Your brother just said he's coming with us."

Hailey barely contemplates Rocky's involvement before brightening like a Gothic lamp. "You're coming to Connecticut? You really want to move there, too?"

"Yeah, for a bit." He stuffs his hands in his pockets. His gold Rolex watch makes him seem mega-yacht rich, but his insides are cheap.

I snort at myself. Finding humor in our lifestyle is one way to cope.

Rocky gives me a strange look.

Hailey tears off another bite of Twizzler with a flourishing grin.

Seeing her happy honestly makes me grin, too.

"Half the gang is back together," she muses, her confidence rising with Rocky here. "Just like old times. The three of us together again."

Rocky doesn't break his gaze from mine. "Just like old times."

There was a time where we'd spend months on the road together. Cramped in whatever car we found at the junkyard. I'm handy when it comes to fixing broken things, and it'd been easier driving around an old beater before we needed to "look the part" of the obscenely rich.

Rocky has a talent for making friends who'd lend him their Porsches and Range Rovers. One let him borrow his *Ferrari* for a whole weekend.

Sometimes he had some insane dirt on the mark. But in most cases, the guy just fell for Rocky's charm and bullshit.

"Old times," I say, more stilted.

Rocky and I have always had a chaotic energy around each other, but for the past two years, it's grown more tumultuous. I can pinpoint the exact day it all went haywire, so I don't have much optimism that this Connecticut town will fix things for us. My only hope is that the Rocky and Phoebe volcano doesn't explode.

Maybe I'll find someone else in Connecticut. Someone nice. Someone better.

That way I can get over Hailey's brother for good.

The three of us leave the motel room. An old faded green Honda waits in the parking lot, and Rocky veers past the car toward a motorcycle. He rode a motorcycle here in a *suit*.

Who is he?

That is a question everyone asks before he disappears out of their life like a specter. Though, I'm one of the few people Rocky sticks around for.

That should make me feel *amazing*.

Special, even. But I just want to flick him away like a spit-wad.

Hailey bumps up against my shoulder. "This'll be good. Don't you think? He's the best at convincing our parents of anything." She checks the map on her phone while she talks. "And if they call, he can sweet-talk them into believing we're on a job or something."

He's the best *liar*—I want to rephrase for her.

The best manipulator.

Yet, his true Brillo-pad personality is what he always gives me, and I should be happy that he doesn't try to manipulate me (if he does, he sucks), but I'm also too busy being annoyed right now.

"If you think he's an asset to the plan, then I guess he is one." I trust Hailey's "big picture" brain, but I have a feeling her brother is mainly here to sweep up the broken pieces of a failed experiment.

And I bet he'd prefer this experiment blow up sooner rather than later.

A new determination boils inside of me. To prove Rocky wrong. *Hailey and I can do this.*

Rocky seizes a backpack from the motorcycle's cargo area over the back wheel. Then slyly, he snaps off the license plate and shoves it inside his backpack. He's abandoning the bike.

He approaches us. "Ready?"

"Yeah, let's ditch Indiana." Hailey slips on dark circular shades and hops into the driver's seat.

Rocky and I fight for the passenger door, our hips and hands bumping.

I glare at him, and he layers one on me. "Excuse me, you're the interloper here," I tell him. "Backseat, bud." I jam my thumb toward the back door.

He cocks his head. "A Tinrock is driving, so I get the passenger seat."

I scoff. "We made that rule when we were *children*."

"And everyone has abided by it since." He keeps his hand on the door handle beside mine, our thumbs flush against each other. The warmth of his skin on mine sends a shock wave of emotion through me, my lungs reinflating—and I almost concede and draw back then and there.

He's the oldest of his two siblings.

I'm the youngest out of three. My brother, Oliver, loved the rule about drivers and passengers sharing the same last name. Whenever our eldest brother, Nova, drove, Oliver had prime-time seating.

Really, I just came up with the rule to irritate Rocky. Growing up, our families spent a lot of time caravanning one behind the other, usually on the road to the next job and distancing ourselves from the pool of white-collar crime we left in our wake.

Besides our parents, Nova was usually the one manning the wheel. Rocky was always trying to one-up him—and I loved watching Rocky's face when Oliver shoved him aside to sit up front.

And then when Hailey learned to drive, the rule backfired on me. Because she became exceedingly good at it, and now she does most of the driving.

She beeps the horn from the driver's seat.

Fine.

I remove my hand.

He takes the opportunity to hip-bump me aside.

I flip him off.

He smiles like I just gave him a royal wave.

Ugh.

I crawl into the backseat, tossing my backpack on the floor.

"Next stop, Connecticut." Hailey peels the Honda onto the road. A twelve-hour car ride ahead of us.

Rocky puts earbuds in his ears, drowning us out. Of course he's not even going to do the proper passenger-seat duties of entertaining the driver. My glare pinches my face painfully.

Hailey glances to me in the rearview and gives me a sympathetic look.

"We didn't tell the landlord there would be a *third* tenant," I whisper-hiss to Hailey. "How is this going to work?"

She shrugs. "Jake seemed chill over the phone. He probably won't mind as long as we pay rent."

I mind.

I care.

There's a lot that Hailey and I lined up before choosing this town. We're staying at an old loft apartment near the college campus. Students usually rent it dirt cheap. We have jobs at the nearby country club.

Rocky isn't in the equation. He never was.

Living honestly isn't in his DNA. Just like it's never been in mine.

Four

Rocky

There's a reason why we're called *confidence men*, Rocky," my father told me when I was ten. He stood at the bow of an eighty-foot yacht that he'd pretended to own that morning.

His guests had left only an hour before. Two oil tycoons. They each wired him a hundred thousand, an investment toward a company my father created to enhance drilling.

His creation only lived in idea, not reality. But the marks didn't know that.

Wind tousled my hair, and I pulled my blazer tighter. My father stared at me with an earnest expression, wanting me to learn. To live up to him. Back then, I only wanted to make him proud.

Now, *not so much.*

He clamped a hand on my shoulder. "Because *confidence* is the most powerful tool in this world. Having confidence and gaining confidence from others is our job. It's all you need to build a life. Never forget that." He glanced at his Patek Philippe watch and then looked back down at me. "Ready?"

"For what?"

"The next job."

His words ring in my head, and the memory sits heavier knowing I'm in a car on my way to fucking Connecticut and not on my bike heading toward Seattle.

This whole thing is such a colossally bad idea. My parents have been prepping for the Seattle gig for months and bailing on them isn't as easy as Phoebe and Hailey are making it seem.

It's unusual—the fact that my sister had *zero* plans in place to handle the fallout of ditching a job. To the point where I realize she had a plan.

Me.

She told Carter she'd be missing Seattle on purpose. She knew he'd tell me. She knew I'd show up to check on her . . . and Phoebe.

And she knew I'd be the best one to smooth things over with our parents, and I can't deny, I am.

I'm probably the only one who could get our parents off their tracks. But not forever. If I could do that, I would've cut ties from my mom and dad a long time ago.

I hate road trips.

Memories flare in the quiet and as the landscapes change shape out the window.

The night of my eighteenth birthday, my father took me into his wine cellar and gave me an expensive bottle of Bordeaux.

"You know how much this is worth?" he asked.

I nodded. The six of us had been brought up to know the price tags of brands, cars, wines, liquors. Not just so we knew which to take, but which to flaunt.

"Say it," he told me.

"Twenty-one grand."

"And that worth is still lower than your family," he reminded me. "No monetary value will ever be higher than your brother and your sister. You're the oldest, and you're eighteen now, which means you need to always protect them."

Why was he telling me this? What was the motive? The questions churned in my head back then as much as they do now.

Really, he could've just been afraid of the consequences of what we do, and he needed me to be the protector in case shit blew up on him.

The risks of pulling the rope on a mark—they were always there. Always blinking in the background like highway reflectors in the night.

Phoebe's dad was proof enough of the risks.

My father's gaze cemented on me like a cinder block. "You need to promise me, Rocky."

My stomach coiled. The older I got, the more I tried to speak less to my parents. It'd become more difficult not to spit acid and hide my curt, short tone.

"Rocky?" he implored.

I returned the wine bottle to my father.

The truth: I loved my brother and my sister. Hailey had always been smarter than me. Only a year younger. And Trevor—he could fabricate almost anything and make it look real. A month prior, he'd made a counterfeit gold coin and sold it for ten grand.

He was twelve.

"They're smarter than I am," I shot back.

"They have the brains, but you have the silver tongue." He handed the bottle back to me. "Promise me."

I stared at the bottle. Not at him. "I promise."

At eighteen, I promised him that I'd keep my sister out of

harm's way. But I promised myself I'd protect her a long time before that, and I didn't need him to drill it into my head.

And now I'm here, chaperoning this experiment under clear protest. At least, I hope it's fucking clear I think "no more conning" is a bad idea.

I glare out the window as we slow down in a town that I don't recognize. Didn't do research before coming here. Don't know who this landlord Jake guy is, but it won't be the first time I've jumped into a job on the spot. Not advised or recommended, but sometimes shit happens.

You have to adapt.

Hailey rolls the Honda to a stop at a red light, and I pull up Google Maps on my phone.

Victoria, Connecticut.

Never heard of it, but we also haven't spent a long time in Connecticut before. I can't ever remember pulling a con in this state. I click into a Wiki page on the town, and I learn some quick facts.

Sixty thousand residents.

One of the wealthiest towns in the state.

Home to Caufield University.

It feels like a place that my parents would pick for a job, but my sister wouldn't lie to me. She'd omit facts, sure, but she wouldn't fabricate some elaborate story and trick me. Maybe they're just subconsciously leaning into what's familiar. A rich-as-fuck town with a mixture of townies and visitors.

"And we're parked," my sister says, shutting off the ignition. "Best parking spot. Great weather. Looks good, right?"

She found a parking spot on the street near an overflowing trash can. The weather is cloudy. Since it's August on the East Coast, I'm predicting a swell of heat when we exit the car, and it's likely humid, being this close to the Atlantic Ocean.

She's trying too hard to make this bad idea seem perfect at the start.

My sister is a try-hard dressed like Wednesday Addams. But I can't tell if she's doing her best to convince me, Phoebe, or herself.

"Looks good to me," Phoebe says while tying her deep blue hair in a high, messy pony.

Whenever she does that, I have to look the fuck away. I don't have some ponytail kink, and I could lie (I am great at it) and say it does nothing for me seeing Phoebe lift her hands to her head—her shirt rising and her bare skin peeking—but I'll never lie to myself.

I check the view out of the window.

We're parked in front of a small bookstore called Baubles & Bookends. A coffee shop next door has the quintessential chalkboard easel outside the entrance.

"I thought you gave up collecting paperbacks last year," I tell Hailey. She's a speed-reader and reads more digital books now. We're on the move so often that lugging around physical copies isn't really practical.

"The apartment is above the bookstore, genius." That sharp, brittle voice does not belong to my sister.

I rotate in my seat so I can stare into Phoebe's brown eyes. "Convenient. Maybe you can finally learn to read."

Her nose flares, but it's her lips forming an annoyed pucker that draws my gaze.

Phoebe Graves has been my best friend, my sister, my girl-friend, my lover, my wife. For all that we've pretended to be, and all the roles we've taken, I'm one hundred percent sure that I have *zero* idea what she really is to me. No fucking clue.

I'm not sure a word exists for it.

But I know what we aren't.

We're not together, and it's good. I need that in indelible ink as a reminder of what can't happen, and two years ago, we figuratively signed the agreement.

I was twenty-three.

She was twenty-two.

Most cons are well thought through. Planned in advance. Some take weeks. Some months. All are agreed upon by our parents.

One led us to the worst night of our lives.

Phoebe calls it the Job That Shall Never Be Named. I won't ever name it, but I do have two words for it. Fucked up.

Things have been explosive between us since.

Still in the car, she flips me off.

My brows rise. "That's it?" I expected a verbal retort.

She flips me off with her other hand.

I roll my eyes and unsnap my buckle.

"Wait," Phoebe says hurriedly. "You're not coming inside like that."

I frown, glancing down at my navy blue slacks and white button-down. Suit jacket is on the middle console. There is an art to flaunting wealth, but nothing about my wardrobe is too showy to where it'd be tacky.

"What's wrong with this?" I ask, hearing the grit in my voice. It comes out more with Phebs, and it's probably because she's annoying as fuck.

Trust me (everyone eventually does), she'd say the same about me.

Phoebe unclips her seat buckle. "You look rich, and we're supposed to be middle class."

I try my best to keep my jaw set and not on the floor. "Middle class?"

We rarely pretend to be middle class. Usually, it's only for social proof. Like, when someone in the family needs a shill to vouch for their con. At times, that shill can be less wealthy and desperate, a role that typically doesn't last long.

The principals (what we call the main runners of the con) most always need to appear wealthy in order to gain trust.

Phoebe tilts her head. "Looks like you're the one who'd benefit from reading more."

A rough groan dies in my throat. "I know what middle class is. I just don't see how it's a good idea for both of you to pretend to be something you have *very* little experience pretending to be."

Hailey is rechecking info on her phone while she tells me, "We're not pretending. That's the point, Rocky."

They're not pretending?

As shitty as it is, I prefer deceiving people. Being openly myself is not only a risk but it's too fucking *personal*. I've spent more years lying to strangers than I have being truthful, and Victoria, Connecticut, isn't changing that.

"You be whoever you want to be, Hails," I tell her. "But I'm not a middle-class bitch." I leave the car to Phoebe's loud retort.

"Be a rich bitch, then! *Asshole*."

My lip twitches into a partial smile, then I shake my head a few times and rewire my mouth. When Phoebe exits the backseat in a huff, I ask her, "Am I a bitch or an asshole? Make up your mind."

"You're a bitchy asshole and an assholey bitch. Happy?"

"To be two things at once in your eyes, I'm over the fucking moon." I check a buzzing text message on my phone. *Nova.* Phoebe's "oldest" brother. He's asking how far away I am from Seattle. Not responding, I slip my cellphone in my pocket.

Phoebe eyes my phone with slight skepticism, then gives me a strange once-over, and she's stalling on my gold watch. Worth more than ten grand. She knows that I have more power if I appear rich. And without power, I can't really help her or Hailey when all of this goes south.

I slide past Phoebe, staring her down while she tries to stare up at me. I ignore the flex of my muscles and the heat in my blood. Quietly, I manage to whisper, "Move out of this rich bitch's way."

Her shoulders thrust backward, but she doesn't say a thing in response. Just watches me walk past to the trunk. Hailey pops it from the key fob, and I grab my sister's duffel.

Phoebe sidles next to me.

I take a short glance at her. "Can't stay away from me?"

She's glaring ahead, and she reaches for her luggage. "I've got mine."

"I wasn't going to touch yours," I tell her casually. "I know how you are."

"Independent, capable, wonderful." She hikes the strap of her bag over her shoulder. Eyes set on me in defiance.

"Stubborn, snide, quite the opposite of wonderful."

"Sounds like you."

We are similar. I can't even deny that. It's partly why I was fucking confused she didn't pump the brakes on Hailey's plan. To want to live a moral cookie-cutter life—that's not Phoebe.

That's not me.

We stare one another down. Neither of us even blinks as we refuse to break our petty contest.

Hailey taps the hood of the car. "Hey, we're already five minutes late." She skirts around us, the chains on her belt loops rattling while she walks briskly onto the path. "There's no time for you two to argue right now."

Phoebe mutters under her breath, "We can make time."

I don't know if she intended for me to hear, but I just act like I don't. Hailey texts while Phoebe and I trail slowly behind her.

A deep blue apartment door is next to the entrance of the bookshop, but there isn't a buzzer or keypad. We let Hailey outpace us, and we fall further back. This is something we do. Phoebe and me.

We consciously put ourselves side by side during jobs. And outside of jobs.

A piece of her blue hair has escaped her pony. It splays against her white strawberry-printed tee. She liked Strawberry Shortcake the way that kids like unicorns and ponies and wholesome shit when they're younger.

She's grown out of the cartoon, but if she ever sees anything with a strawberry, she'll be tempted to buy it. Usually only things she can pack. Baseball hats, T-shirts, the occasional key chain and magnet. Sometimes I think about the soup-bowl strawberry mug she left on the bed's end table in a Four Seasons.

I called once we were long gone, but housekeeping couldn't find it.

I scrape a coarse hand through my hair the more this nostalgia barrels through me. Reminiscing about the *good times* is dangerous because the *bad times* are hot on its heels. Then I'll find myself cradling a fistful of gnarled memories, trying to squeeze them to death. And never succeeding.

Strawberries.

Phoebe catches me staring at her. "What?"

"Nothing." I focus ahead.

"You're being weird," she snaps back.

"I could say the same about you. Ever since the last job—"

"Leave it *alone*, Rocky," she whisper-hisses. "Seriously."

I shake my head a few times, grinding my teeth, and it's fucking impossible to drop Carlsbad. How can I? What happened during that job? I have no clue, and yeah, it's grating on me like I'm *eating* sandpaper. Because I know something bad went down, but neither Hailey nor Phoebe will explain it to me or to Nova. Not even when we picked them up from the bus stop that night.

They just say the same things:

We're fine.

The job is over.

Just leave it alone.

And now all of a sudden they've decided to stop grifting? I catch her blistering gaze. "You both chose to stop doing what we do after the fallout of the last job. One plus one equals—"

"Two, yeah, great—you can do math. Bravo." She's prickly.

I'm rougher, and the heat of her glare isn't smoothing my grating edges or the glare I send back. So she lets out a long-winded sigh and spins toward me while we're on the sidewalk.

Hailey is busy phoning the landlord outside the apartment door.

As a jogger passes us, we both politely wave. He nods back, and then a thirtysomething woman pushes a baby in a stroller along the cobbled sidewalk.

I nod. "Good afternoon, ma'am."

She smiles. "Afternoon. Ugly weather, huh? Looks like rain."

I look at the graying clouds with interest, even though I couldn't give a flying shit about a storm. "Hopefully it'll pass. You stay dry out here."

"You, too." She slows just a little to ask, "Are you two new in town?"

"Yes," we say in unison. It annoys both of us.

The woman doesn't notice. "Well, welcome to Victoria." Her smile brightens. "I hope you like it here."

I already hate it. "I'm sure we will." I wave her goodbye.

Phoebe forces a tight smile at her, and after the woman is farther away, she stakes her glare back on me. "If you're going to be here with us, you *can't* bring up Carlsbad every two seconds." She takes a tense breath. "I'm serious. It's over. In the past. Leave it there."

"I don't even know what I'm leaving behind." That's what scares me.

Her brown eyes look dead. Nothing is in them. No emotion. It tears and stabs at my insides, and my jaw aches I'm clenching it so hard. I hate that dissociative look. I've seen Phoebe check out too many times before, but rarely ever with me.

"You don't have to know, Rocky."

I want to know.

I force down the rebuttal. Seeing that I'm not getting what I want—and no way would I ever manipulate Phoebe—I just change the subject altogether. "How much do you know about your landlord?"

"Jake?" She studies my sister at the door. "I know enough." Her defenses slowly lower while we continue to hang back. "Hailey handled most of the details."

So my sister got the loft, and Phoebe is just along for the ride. I'm not that surprised. Phoebe's role in the family isn't to plan cons or gather intel. Hailey does more of the logistics.

I just wish Phoebe was behind the reins on whatever they're doing. I lean closer to whisper, "Don't you ever get exhausted of being my sister's lackey?"

"See, this is why you need a best friend, Rocky. So you can

understand that best friends aren't puppets or pawns or *lackeys*."

"You left out *doormats*."

"Fuck you." She gets in my face.

My blood heats the longer we lock eyes. I have a strange urge to grip the back of her hair—but not hatefully. "Fuck you, too—"

"He's coming down to let us in," Hailey tells us with eyes that say *Stop fighting*.

We cool off, but on the way to the door, Phoebe sticks her tongue out at me. I shake my head and holster a slanted smile. An emotion tosses inside me that I'm purposefully ignoring.

I stand behind both girls, my backpack hooked on one shoulder and the strap to my sister's duffel on the other. Hailey keeps tapping the sole of her combat boot while we wait for Jake.

It's a nervous tell that our parents would hound her for, and I make a conscious effort not to lecture my sister.

We're not on a job.

I don't know what this is. Not really. And that puts me on edge more than a three-month preplanned con.

The door opens.

Jake emerges with the towering confidence of a man who always gets what he wants. He's well-dressed in a navy polo with the Hackett logo on the breast, Sperry shoes, and the latest model of an Apple Watch on his wrist. Light brown hair, crystal blue eyes, white skin tanned from the sun, and a strong jaw—he has the posture of a high school quarterback who still shows off his letterman jacket.

And he's younger than I thought their landlord would be. Mid-to-late twenties. Maybe older than me.

Definitely not better looking.

He's not ugly, though. That's unfortunate.

Hailey and Phoebe exchange smiles, and I resist rolling my eyes again. Inwardly, the eye roll is fucking strong.

Jake *leans* on the doorframe like he's modeling for a fashion ad. Jesus Christ.

His attention is on my sister first, taking in her goth makeup and the ripped fishnets and chains. "You must be Hailey?"

"Yeah, that's me." She's too nervous to smile. "You must be Jake?"

He's still assessing the fuck out of her. *Who is this guy?* "I am." He nods, running his gaze over her spike-studded backpack. "Jake Waterford. Welcome to Victoria." He extends a hand.

His intentions aren't clear. Either he's guarded or I'm losing my touch here and can't read him that well.

Phoebe reaches back and curls a hand around my wrist, and I realize I'm about to take a step forward. She's keeping me from pushing out in front of Hailey.

My sister shakes his hand. "Hailey Thornhall." She lies with ease and motions over to Phoebe. "This is my best friend, Phoebe."

She immediately detaches from me. Cold, biting air replaces the warmth of where her skin touched.

"That's me," Phoebe says, "the best friend."

His gaze swings to her, and I recognize the look in his eyes. It's one I've seen a thousand times. One I've given to Phoebe. It's want, desire, curiosity. It's everything I fucking hate. My body goes rigid. *Don't react.*

Don't react.

Do not fucking react.

It's a mantra I've repeated over and over throughout the years and hammered into my skull. Just so I wouldn't fuck up a job. But this isn't a job, and it makes it so much harder not to cut forward and shove him back.

But I don't own her.

I don't want to.

I just hate the way men look at her. Like they can take her and use her and discard her when they're done.

"I like the hair." Jake gestures to her head, then sucks in a breath. "But you *might* have some trouble with that if you're still planning on working for the country club. Servers have a strict dress code around here."

My sister already told the landlord their job plans? Before even meeting him?

Phoebe looks just as surprised.

Jake glances back at Hailey's face. "No nose piercings either. Or the thing in your eyebrow."

Phoebe focuses on him and asks, "Nipple piercings are big, bad, and ugly, too?"

It draws Jake's gaze down to her tits.

And like a reflex, Phoebe hooks her fingers on her shirt and begins to lift.

Without thinking, I catch her around her hips and press her to my side. "Coming through," I tell Jake and "accidentally" shove my sister's duffel into his gut on my way inside.

He grunts and shuffles farther backward while I bulldoze through the door. Phoebe stays tucked against me as we enter the stairwell together.

A lone bike rests against a rickety, steep staircase that I'm guessing leads to the loft. After almost flashing her landlord, Phoebe still hasn't pulled away from me. She turns toward my chest, her eyes distant and her arms wrapped around my waist.

I drop my lips against her ear. "Phoebe?" I rest a hand on the back of her neck, my thumb stroking her skin.

She breathes slowly and winces at herself. "I'm fine." Her thick brows bunch, and when she realizes she's hugging me, she immediately lets go and steps away.

Yeah, I definitely already hate it here.

"She's a free spirit," Hailey tries to cover casually. "You know, free the nips." She mimes lifting her shirt but doesn't go as far as Phoebe almost did.

"Right," Jake says with a slow nod. "Just another warning, nipple-freeing is also frowned upon here."

"Shucks." Hailey produces a half-hearted smile and points at the stairs. "Is that the apartment?"

"Yeah." Jake is busy studying me, keys in his hand. "Who are you, exactly?"

I watch Hailey squeeze past Jake in the cramped stairwell, just to reach Phoebe. The two girls speak quietly while I stare down their landlord.

"I'm Rocky."

"Rocky?" He sounds skeptical.

"Problem?" I ask too roughly.

"I've only ever heard of dogs and cats being named *Rocky*."

"It's a nickname," I try to say amicably, but I'm dying to add, *Numbnuts*.

"What's your real name?" He's staring me down now. "Are you staying here?" He looks like he's preparing to say, *you can't*. "I was only told there'd be *two* tenants, and I don't have your ID."

You're not getting it.

I have five in my wallet, and none of them are names he needs to see.

Jake seems like the type of person who remembers to cross their *t*'s and dot their *i*'s. His suspicion of me isn't overt paranoia. Not when he's about to invite three con artists into his home and his town.

There's just nothing he can do to stop it from happening.

Before I can respond, he's turning to Hailey. "It's only a two-bedroom."

"I'm not staying, man," I say, like we're friends. "I'm just passing through for a week or two. I'm Hailey's brother."

Hailey smiles, and I see it's a genuine one. I could've easily lied and said we were just friends, but this is a sincere piece to her new life. I'm not actively trying to implode this for her. She'll realize on her own that it won't last.

Jake studies my features, then hers in a quick second. With her mountain of dark makeup and platinum-blonde hair, it's hard to see we look anything alike.

I'm pegging him as *uptight*. A stick-in-the-mud. The kind of person who has a daily routine and can't fathom breaking it. I am a wrench who appears like a *fixer* to all your problems, but I will purposefully break shit without you realizing.

For someone like him, I'm a nightmare.

Doubt still pinches his brows.

"I work in Manhattan, but I'm remote for a few weeks," I explain further. "I wanted to spend some time with my little sister. Help her get settled in a new town. Make sure she's not staying at a serial killer's apartment."

Hailey's smile vanishes. *"Rocky."*

Jake eases a fraction. "No, it's okay. I get it." His brows rise. "I'd do the same for my little sister." He looks everywhere but at us—a tell that he's either lying or he's containing emotion.

"You have a little sister?" I ask. Common ground is good. I can work with that.

"She's not around anymore." *Don't say it*. "She passed away last year."

I'm the asshole.

Phoebe is trying to smother a smirk. Her eyes ping to me, and I swear they say, *Assholey bitch*. And honestly, I'm just glad they're saying something other than nothing.

I relax my shoulders and motion to him. "Sorry about your sister. I can't imagine . . ." I shake my head. "That'd kill me."

"It's okay. You didn't know." His eyes linger on my clothes. "Manhattan?"

"You've been?" I ask before he can question who I work for.

"Yeah, plenty. For family things."

Family *things*? That's too vague, but I don't press because A) not here to make a fake fucking friend, and B) don't need him pressing my backstory that I'm creating on the fly.

"I have a cousin who lives in Brooklyn, too," Jake adds. "He's kind of an asshole."

"Most of us are." I force a smile.

Jake forces one back, and it's as though we both know we're full of shit right now. That we don't really appreciate or like one another. If he were a mark, it'd be an uphill climb to gain his trust. But I don't need him to like me or even really to trust me.

I just need him not to fuck with Hailey or Phoebe.

"You're not going to tell me your real name, are you?" Jake realizes.

"Not unless you end up in bed with me. And sorry, man, you're not really my type. Too tall."

He lets out a short laugh that sounds more like an irritated sigh. "Okay, fair enough. As long as you're not living here—because if you are, I need your ID."

"Fair enough." I use his words.

He's not easing, but he drops the issue. "Apartment is directly above the bookshop." He points to the staircase. "Always lock the stairwell door on your way in and out. Homeless people will try to crash in here when it gets colder." He puts a foot on the first stair, about to lead us to the other locked door. "One more thing."

"Yeah?" Hailey frowns, wanting badly to just get inside the loft.

Jake swings around, but he's not looking at her. His attention is back on me. "If Hailey is your sister, what's Phoebe to you?"

Everything.

Nothing.

None of your fucking business.

I open my mouth to decree us as *just friends*.

"We're divorced," Phoebe suddenly announces.

What?

A record scratches in my brain, but I force my expression to remain blank. Not letting Mr. Uptight see anything on my face.

"Newly. It was mutual," Phoebe adds like word vomit, her face flushing.

The lies keep coming, and I add nothing.

Phoebe is glaring at me to say something, but now I'm trying not to laugh.

"I hate him," she concludes. "With a *passion*."

"Oh-kaaay," Hailey draws out with wide eyes and tries to extinguish this burning ship. "This way?" She moves ahead of Jake and guides him up the stairs away from us.

Like always, we linger behind.

"Divorced?" I whisper to Phoebe. "What happened to wanting to live honestly?"

"I *honestly* feel like you're my ex-husband."

"I'm honestly not your ex-anything," I tell Phoebe under my breath, carefully watching Jake ascend the stairs with my sister. He's not looking back at us. Not as I add, "I've always been dishonestly yours. And it looks like that's not changing."

"I guess not." She takes a preparing breath.

I can't tell if she's pissed there is one glaring lie in the start of her truthful life, but maybe she realizes being fully honest is impossible anyway.

We can't tell anyone about our pasts without incriminating ourselves and our families.

I can't hate what I do. It's who I am. And I am and I've been many fucking things in this world, but self-loathing is not even in the same universe as me.

Five

Phoebe

Things are off to a spectacular start. Should I pop the champagne to my newly divorced self? Bring out the charcuterie?

Clearly, I need to toast to my stupid quick thinking. I had an opportunity to be truthful, and I didn't take it. Maybe Rocky is right, I can't do this.

No, the stubborn part of me is screeching.

I'm not throwing in the towel yet, not when we scope out the loft and Hailey keeps casting anxious glances and smiles at me. She wants to be here, and I'm not screwing this up for her more than I almost already did.

Flashing my landlord that I just met? Why? Why was that my *gut* instinct?

I hated myself in that smallest, most jagged second, and that hate swelled up like an unpoppable balloon inside of me. If Rocky hadn't been there . . .

I would've gone through with it. I would've showed Jake my pierced nipples like I was at Burning Man or a *strip club*.

We were in public. It wasn't smart. It had D-U-M-B written all over it. Just so, so *dumb*.

And I should feel grateful that Rocky stopped me, but I just feel like *I* should've had the power to do that myself. I should be more in control of my actions and my body, and I shouldn't need to rely on another person to stop me from making a bad decision.

Instead of dunk-tanking in a vat of humiliation, I remind myself that Jake just thinks I'm a free-spirited hippie who prefers being in the nude. *Thanks, Hails*. It helps shake off what happened.

Jake shows off one of the bedrooms, and Rocky is standing closer to me. I sense the familiar, comforting heat of his muscled body, and I force myself not to turn and look directly at him.

Divorced.

We're divorced.

I could've chosen any relation under the sun. Brother-sister. Stepsiblings. Coworkers who just mildly hate one another. But I chose something *intimate*. I'm never living this down. Because this is supposed to be the final backstory to my new, permanent life.

There's no way to avoid the tension as we all inspect the loft in near silence. If I could open a window and parkour away from here, I would.

Jake ends the tour of the small two-bedroom loft with *another* side-eye at Rocky. I swear if there were an Olympic competition in side-eyeing, Jake Waterford would take gold.

I'm only slightly jealous.

With a deep breath, I try to focus on our new home. *The positives*. The little kitchen has seafoam-green cupboards and an opal backsplash. It comes fully furnished with a beige sofa, barstools, and a two-person glass kitchen table. We didn't even need to buy bedding. It's all provided.

I do another eye sweep, noticing the rattan lights above the kitchen counter and the cozy brick fireplace.

Quaint and dainty. The kind of place my mom would rarely choose for a one-month stay, let alone *forever*. It's not exactly the Ritz or a multimillion-dollar mansion, but it's cute and ten times better than any motel.

Thinking about my mom makes me want to call her. For a second. Just to hear her voice and the comfort inside her kind words. She always knows what to tell me when we start over. "This city has our names written all over it, bug," she'd say into a wide, charismatic grin. "It's perfect." Her belief was genuine—so genuine and real that I'd remind myself in doubt or fear, *it's perfect; this city is ours*.

I could call her.

I could go against Hailey's desire and just dial my mom, and as tempting as that sounds, I know her. There is absolutely *no way* she'd approve of what we're doing. Stop grifting? Ditch the next job? It's like quitting the family business and setting the fam on a course for bankruptcy. There won't be jubilation and pats on the back.

Also, we're not running a steak restaurant where they'll need to find a new chef and hostess. You can't just hire con artists off LinkedIn. We're irreplaceable, and I know by leaving the "family business" so abruptly we're making the Seattle job harder and riskier.

I'm used to being a team player, and so this sucks. It'd suck seeing anyone leave, if positions were reversed. We help each other. We keep one another safe, and with even one missing link, the threat of being caught grows.

Though, I know my mom would want me to be happy first and foremost, even if that means saying goodbye. But I really believe that *she* believes I'd be unhappy without conning—and maybe there is a . . . semi-large part of me that *also* believes this, too.

So I can't call her. She'll say exactly what's already zipped through my brain. *This new life isn't for me. I'm hurting my brothers by leaving the family in the dust. I'm only thinking about Hailey and our pact, and I can't put her first forever, can I? How will we survive? I love what I do too much to really let it go.*

The temptation to return to my old ways will be too strong if she's here. So I pop the fantasy of a phone call and turn my attention back to the kitchen.

The stainless-steel appliances all seem new, too, and if I had to guess, I'd say it's been recently renovated. The pictures Hailey showed me made this place look more worn. She told me the rent was twelve hundred a month, and I'm starting to wonder if it's increased.

"Can I speak to you?" Rocky asks his sister under his breath, but he's close enough that I hear. "Just for a sec, Hails."

She excuses herself with her brother, and they talk hushed near the windows, one of the panes lifted. Sheer white curtains billow in the gusting breeze, a storm brewing outside.

I stay in the tiny hallway. Just hanging out, twiddling my thumbs and trying to avoid my phone. I've had a few texts from my brothers, and I'm not jumping at the opportunity to tell them, *Hey, I'm not going to make Seattle.*

I already hear Oliver's bemused, *"What the fuck."* I smile thinking of him. He has a sort of spirit that shouldn't fit inside one body, a spirit that's always bursting to come out. "Reel it in" is a phrase that seems made *just* for Oliver. No one else gets told that on jobs but him.

"That's really it," Jake says to me.

I lift my gaze. "Thanks for the tour. It's a really nice place."

"Yeah, it's not too bad." His voice sounds stilted. He's coming from a bedroom, and to reach the living room and kitchen, he needs to pass me in this narrow hallway. When Jake begins sliding past, I stop slouching to let him by, but his knees still brush against my body.

Heat flushes my neck.

And then when we're in line with one another, his gaze plummets to my boobs. His face twitches, maybe knowing that was uncouth or whatever, and before he apologizes, I blurt out, "I'm really sorry about . . . um, almost flashing you earlier. My bad."

My bad?

Ugh, I want to crawl in a hole.

His lips rise in a soft smile. "It was . . ." He tilts his head and finds a word. "Unexpected."

I'm still cringing at myself. "I must be your first—*first* girl who tried to flash you, I mean." What the fuck is wrong with me today?

His smile widens into a laugh. "You're definitely not the first, Phoebe Smith." *My fake surname.* It blows past me while amusement glitters his blue eyes.

What is he—the playboy of Victoria? Every girl wants to go wild and topless in front of him? Still, the way he says it, it doesn't sound exactly like *boasting.* Just something commonplace to him. He's so used to seeing tits or having girls bend over backward for him?

I don't know.

Maybe he's just trying to make me feel better.

"I'm not the first?" I process out loud. He's loitering in the cramped hallway with me, and his height is more apparent as I crane my neck. It's hard not to place his beauty in a high percentile, and instead of seducing him for a job, I'm supposed to just . . . be myself?

"Not the first." He nods.

"I prefer being seventh in life, anyway." I shrug. "Bottom tier. Solid placement. *Unassuming*." I smile at him, but I feel the uncertainty in it.

Maybe my real self is a bumbling fool. That's . . . scary. I already want to exchange her for the confident, cool version.

"Unassuming is a good place to be here," Jake says softly. "You don't want to stand out or race to the top."

If he's advising that I stay away from the upper echelons of Victoria's social structure, then I must appear like easy prey already. Freeing my nipples isn't exactly a first-class ticket into charity galas and country clubs. But I'm done trying to appear like the social elite.

We're middle-class bitches. And I'm hoping my mom and Hailey's mom have been wrong. I hope we're both going to like it here.

"So lock the front door," I note his warnings. "Re-dye my hair. Take out any piercings, and don't try to mingle with the top dogs. Is that all?"

"Barely. I could write a four-hundred-page textbook on What Not to Do in Victoria."

"And I'd let Hailey read it."

His attention veers to my best friend, who's still talking with her brother in the living room.

"She'd probably even devour your rule book in a couple minutes," I tell him. "But I appreciate the warnings, even if we might not take all of them."

His smile is gone. "I hope you're serious about loving seventh place."

I frown. "Why?"

He straightens off the wall, his entire body brushing my body now, and I don't shrink back as he says, "Because in this town, everyone else is busy chasing after *first*. And no offense, you're not equipped to be there."

Okay, Judgy McJudgy. He can act like he has me figured out, but he has no idea. *If only he knew . . .*

Before he begins to pass by, I ask, "You don't want first place?"

His eyes grip mine in a hotter beat. "I didn't say that."

I hold my breath like if my lungs expand, he won't be able to slide past me. A silly thought. He easily walks beyond the hallway and enters the kitchen.

I'm following behind him, aware that he's the typical man that my mom chooses to date. Clean-cut, good-looking, wealthy. At least, I'm assuming he's rich from his bravado and if he owns this loft himself. Then again, maybe it belongs to his parents?

He must be twenty-seven, twenty-eight?

Too young for my mom. She usually dates men twice her age.

She'd love him for me, though.

He's a good one, bug.

It irks me, and I wonder if there are any guys in this town she'd disapprove of. My eyes flit to Rocky, and my stomach overturns. His approval rating is astronomical with my mother. He's polling a grand one hundred percent.

Jake wouldn't be that high. But it'd be close.

I turn back to my landlord.

He has a nice butt. Perky in his slacks. I watch him flip open a binder on the butcher board counter.

Rocky clears his throat behind me. I look over my shoulder, and his brows rise. *Okaaay*, he caught me checking out my landlord's ass. It's not a crime.

"And?" I whisper.

He crosses his arms over his chest and his expression

flatlines. "Nothing." He says it in a way that abandons the actual meaning of that word.

And he keeps saying that: *Nothing.*

Whatever's going on with him, I can't worry too much about it right now. He's not even supposed to be here.

"Emergency contacts are in here with some helpful information in case I missed something." Jake flips a page. "Right, so we only have off-street parking. Street sweepers come Wednesday mornings, so you'll have to move your car somewhere else tomorrow."

"No worries," Hailey says, reading his binder upside down. She reaches over and flips a page for him and keeps reading. "We're just happy we could find a place in Victoria. Options were really limited."

I look around again. *Twelve hundred a month?*

I start disbelieving.

"Everything rents out quick because of Caufield," Jake explains and watches Hailey flip another page. "Fall semester starts next week."

"Then why is your place still available?" Rocky asks skeptically. He leans casually beside a bookshelf with classic hardcovers.

Jake motions to Hailey. "Like I told your sister over the phone, we just finished renovations on this place. It was only online for about an hour before she called about it."

So it is new?

I try to catch Hailey's eyes, but she avoids my gaze.

"Your credit turned out great, and we prefer working professionals. Students tend to trash the place. So it was a plus that you're twenty-four and already graduated college."

"We actually . . . didn't graduate," Hailey admits slowly. "We're high school graduates, basically." She gives him a slight smile and does this weird breathy laugh that I fucking *mimic*. I kid you not.

Rocky is trying so hard to smother a smirk that he rotates to inspect the stupid fireplace.

I blame the fact that nine times out of ten, we've been Ivy League grads. I know way too much about Yale, Harvard, Princeton, Penn, etc.—from their mottos, their common hangouts, their best dining halls, anything that I can use to strengthen the lie that I went there.

Jake gives us a sympathetic look.

Like we're embarrassed to only wield high school diplomas.

"I shouldn't have assumed," he mentions.

"Oh, you should have," Rocky butts in, his arm on the fireplace mantel. "Except assumed *the other way around*."

I shoot him a glare.

"They could've gone to a community college," Jake tells him.

"Oh, thanks," Hailey mutters.

Jake regroups fast, holding out a hand. "Not that there is anything wrong with community college. I'm sure it's a great form of education."

Rocky is laughing.

"Can you stop?" Jake retorts.

"I don't know, can you?" Rocky questions. "The hole you're digging is big enough for a body—"

"So you'll be leaving by Friday?" Jake cuts him off with heat.

Humor fades from Rocky's face. "Not by Friday."

It's only Tuesday.

Jake closes the binder and slowly looks to me. "If your ex-husband stays for longer than a week, this isn't going to work out. This place isn't big enough for three tenants."

My gut drops. "He's *not* living with us." I swing my head to Rocky. "You'll be out by Friday."

He narrows his gunmetal eyes at me. "I'm not letting my sister get murdered by Patrick Bateman."

Jake glowers back. "Really? Patrick Bateman? Clever."

Rocky stands off the fireplace. "I don't know you, so I can't trust you, and I'm assuming that feeling is mutual."

Jake doesn't deny.

The fact that Jake hasn't kicked us out is truly a miracle at this point. He could rent this place to anyone else, and it'd be less trouble than dealing with Rocky.

"You don't have to trust him," I tell Rocky. "He's not your landlord." Normally, Rocky is easy to get along with. (Unless you're me.) To strangers, he's charming, even. I'm not sure why he's showing Jake his actual Brillo-pad personality. I turn back to my landlord. "Thank you for everything, seriously. We're really happy to be here."

Hailey puts a hand on the binder. "Appreciate the notes."

"I'm glad they could help." Jake eases for half a second. "But seriously, guests shouldn't be here more than a week. If he's not out by next Tuesday, you'll breach the lease, and I'll have to kick you out."

Fuck.

"Understood," Hailey says.

He looks to Rocky. "I'll be back to check."

"Counting on it," Rocky says dryly.

Jake glares, then slides over some papers on the counter. "Sign here. I'll also need the first two months' rent up front. Check or Venmo work."

Hailey skims through the paperwork, speed-reading.

I ask Jake, "What was rent again?" My chest constricts like I'm waiting for a rubber band to snap.

"Three thousand a month."

I restrain a wince. Train, meet my face. The impact hurts.

Hailey slides me a subtle look that says, *We've got this*. Her silent optimism does nothing to quench the unease in my stomach. Especially since I'm now a hundred percent positive that she lied to me. What were the photos she showed me?

Were they even of this loft?

I hate that I can't remember.

How are we going to afford this with our country club jobs? Sure, our cut from the Carlsbad job *might* cover two months' rent, but after that we're going to have to figure something out.

I'm starting to wish we did a long con with a multimillion-dollar payout before we came to Victoria. They're more dangerous, but the money doesn't run out as fast.

I pull out my phone. "I can Venmo."

Jake gives me his number, and I send him the payment.

He checks his cell. "We're good to go after you sign." His eyes lift to me, and he slips his cell in his pocket.

When it's my turn to sign, I see all the apologies from Hailey. Those gray irises are pleading, *Don't be mad at me, Phebs, please.*

I barely read over the contract, trusting her still. Quickly, I sign my new fake name on the line.

Phoebe Smith.

Jake nods in thanks and gathers the papers together. "One more thing. There's a charity clambake next month. It's an annual event, so it'll be crowded and noisy around here. Just giving you a heads-up."

Charity clambakes.

Country clubs.

It feels like the life I pretended to be a part of, except

I'm not a patron of the club or invited to the clambake. I'm someone on the outside looking in. If I should be excited for something new, then why am I just a tumbleweed of stress?

Jake is gone. Door shut, footsteps echoing away.

Hailey whirls to me in an instant. "I'm really sorry, Phoebe—"

"Three thousand a month?" I interject in shock.

"Wait, you didn't know?" Rocky frowns.

"No. I thought we were living in a shitty loft that we could actually afford."

"We can afford this," Hailey defends. "Look, you know how country clubs work. If we serve the right people, we could earn enough on tips to cover the rent."

Could being the key word.

It's a gamble.

"Why did you lie to me?" I ask, trying to bury the hurt in my voice. "You never lie to me. And were those pictures even real?"

Her breath shortens. "Some of them were, yeah. The others . . . I found on Google Photos."

I got conned.

By my best friend.

Ouch.

"But listen." Hailey talks quickly, while I stare at my feet. "You wouldn't have come here if you knew this was the price. And it was the only thing available in town."

I want to tell her we could've lived anywhere else. But it's not totally true. There are cities and towns I'd never return to just in case certain people remember my face.

And it's always been hard to stay mad at Hailey. Her intentions weren't evil, and she's being up front now. My anger starts to wane, even if being out of the loop feels like spoiled milk in my stomach.

"Loop me in next time," I tell Hailey. "I promise I'm on Team Hails."

She smiles softly. "Deal."

We do our secret handshake that involves two pinky hooks and a fist bump explosion combo. Rocky is flipping through one of the books on the shelves, pretending to ignore us.

My phone rings, the sound shrill in the sudden quiet. I unearth it from my pocket. Both Hailey and Rocky zero in on the cell.

Caller ID: Unknown.

Muscles tighten in my stomach, and I hesitate to hit the big red button. *Hang up on them.* If someone is calling from a burner phone, it's likely one of my brothers.

Should I answer? Lie to them?

I can't lie to Nova or Oliver. Hell, even shutting them out of this new life feels weird. Wrong. Love isn't sand in an hourglass, able to be flipped and drained the minute it's turned in a new direction. If anything, the love between my brothers and me is made of steel so thick you'd need wrecking balls and jackhammers to make a dent.

They're eventually going to realize we're not going to Seattle. They're eventually going to panic and come find me like Rocky found his sister.

I'm almost banking on it. Because a big part of me is hoping they do come and play this honest game with me. The other part knows that quitting a life of deceit, for them, is about as likely as Rocky becoming Jesus Christ.

It rings and rings, and my pulse speeds; I'm terrified of being torn in two directions. I've already made my decision. *Stick by Hailey's side.* So I let the call ring out and bide my time.

Hailey looks a little guilty. "You're positive you don't want to talk to them?"

"They'll call back later."

And I'll reject the call again like the worst sister ever. Yay me.

"They will," Rocky says, too assured. "No one can do the Seattle job without you, Phoebe."

He doesn't need to remind me of the next con. The new clip joint scheme has been in the works for a while. I'm numb to the idea. It's one we've pulled before.

"Oliver will do it," Hailey contends, and my stomach curdles again, not loving the fact that my brother might be taking my role in clip joints.

"Maybe I should go back, just for this one," I mutter.

I expect Rocky to take this response like a tanker of gasoline and ride off to our parents at superspeed. Instead, a darkness shadows his brooding gaze. "There's no time."

"I could drive—"

"You're already here." Gravel in his voice roughens the words. "Just leave it to them to figure out. And when your brothers call, you let me talk to them."

Hailey turns to me. "I like this plan."

I do and then I don't. Rocky isn't exactly *besties* with my brothers, and if he tries to manipulate them, they will lose their shit.

I'd pay to see those fireworks.

And I don't know what that says about me. I like watching explosives blow up in Rocky's face? Or I'm just way too used to the big Double Ds called Drama and Danger, and no matter where I go, I can't live without them.

Six

Phoebe

Harsh lights expose an empty nightclub at three p.m. before opening. Barren of most employees, this naked shell is the realest part of tonight. Truthfully, it's my favorite part—the *before.*

"Flip the bottle. Twirl around," Oliver narrates behind a swanky bar. He flips a bottle of Belvedere with the grace of a master juggler, the sleeves of his white button-down rolled to his elbows. He whirls in a circle, winks at Hailey beside me—who doesn't notice him (her nose is in a book)—and then passes the bottle from hand to hand. "Make them look at your face, not your hands. *Smolder.*" He tries to catch Hailey's attention with winks. He mouths, *Hey there, sexy.*

I laugh hard. "Your smolder is no match for . . ." I lift the back of her book. *"Ariadne."*

"Who is she? I'll smolder her, too."

Without looking up, Hailey eats from a bowl of bar nuts. "She's the wife of Dionysus."

"She married the God of Wine," Oliver realizes. "So she has taste, then."

Hailey flips a page. "Leave her alone. Her life is tragic."

"Aren't they all." Oliver slides over a purplish cocktail to me. I didn't even see him pour the drink, let alone add cranberry juice.

"What do you call this?"

"Vodka cranberry. Nothing complicated." He splays his hands on the bar, waiting for me to drink it.

I take a sip. "Mmm." I smack my lips and cringe at the sharpness. "This isn't Belvedere."

"It's painfully cheap vodka."

I set the glass down. "What happened to watering down the Belvedere?" That's what Oliver has been doing the past few weeks. He found similarly shaped bottles, poured a quarter of Belvedere in each, and then diluted them. Saves us money on the inventory, and we can still hike the prices and charge obscene amounts for a single glass or a whole bottle. Doesn't matter which.

"They're not getting wasted enough."

He means the marks. The people we're trying to con.

"I've relabeled all the bottles already," he adds, swishing the fake Belvedere.

Smart. "Did the godfather approve?" I joke about the Tinrocks' dad.

"No, but the godmothers did." He means our mom, Elizabeth Graves, and her best friend, Addison Tinrock. Oliver reminds me, "They're the ones who run this place."

One month ago, Elizabeth and Addison took over this

struggling establishment. New management made Vanity Nightclub more exclusive. High rollers only. At least that's according to word in the town. Spread by my brothers and the Tinrocks through other VIP circles in Vegas.

It's made pulling in high-end clientele easier. Gaining trust is an art form.

And we're all artists.

"Everett Tinrock is the one who enforces the rules, though," I remind Oliver.

Everett could've easily been the one to purchase the failing club alongside his actual wife, instead of my mom buying it with her. Just because he didn't, it doesn't mean that he's beneath them in some con artist hierarchy.

"He's a stickler for rules only because he's paranoid of ending up like Dad." Oliver mimes slamming jail bars shut. *"Burghm."*

I snort. "Is that the sound of metal hitting cinder block?"

"Yes, it is, Phoebe Graves. You win at charades."

I pat myself on the back.

He smiles and tries to take away the shitty vodka cranberry.

I cup my hands over the glass. "Hey, I'm drinking that. It's Belvedere, incredibly smooth." I take a sip, and this time, I don't grimace. "And that's what I'm going with when someone asks me why this tastes like asshole."

He gasps. "You've tasted asshole before?"

Hailey laughs at her book, but she's definitely laughing at him. His grin widens over at Hailey, then his deep laughter cascades when I flip him off.

I lift my glass. "Bartender, you never carded me."

"You're twenty-one, aren't you? You just had a birthday recently," he teases.

I'm smiling, and I reach across the bar and shove his shoulder.

"Happy birthday," Hailey says from her book.

"Thank you," Oliver and I say in unison.

I shake my head at him. "She was talking to *me*, dummy."

"Hey, don't you dare call your big brother a dummy. We share the same genes, so that makes you—"

"Also a dummy," I say unabashedly. I wear my lack of smarts as *fact*. Not necessarily with pride.

Oliver leans over the bar. "You're not dumb, Phoebe."

"You have to say that. You're related to me."

He purses his lips in such an Oliver way that says he disagrees.

"What's the markup on a bottle of Macallan?" Nova asks while checking his phone and walking toward the bar. Stern lines crease his forehead. "Ten grand?" He's asking all of us.

"I thought it was more," Hailey mentions.

"I thought it was less?" I chime in.

"It's more." Oliver procures a notepad to check.

I glance between Nova and Oliver.

The three of us look too much alike. Natural dark brown hair. Same cocoa brown eyes. Olive skin tones and heart-shaped faces. We had to make conscious choices to appear different.

Nova buzzes his hair.

Oliver dyes his strands a lighter shade of brown.

I keep mine dark and use makeup to plump my lips and widen my eyes. Honestly, I do the bare minimum, and I should one hundred percent thank my brothers more. Anytime Mom has pressured me to dye my *eyebrows* and cut my hair, they remind her that wigs exist and they're already doing shit to look less like me.

I guess the irony is the less we look like one another, the closer we've become.

"Markups aren't supposed to matter that much, right?" I ask my brothers. "We're still going to slap on an insane service charge."

"And hostess fee," Hailey pipes in. "And the fees for the broken bottles that they don't remember breaking. Overtime fees, for sitting in the VIP section for longer than allowed."

"Fees for breathing," I add, which is a fake fee that makes Oliver grin and Hailey smile.

"Numbers matter," Nova says seriously. He's the cleanup guy. The getaway driver. The one who ensures *none* of us ever get caught. I see Nova as the fail-safe. The last rope that'll break our fall, and I can't imagine what it's like being that person.

I can't reply to Nova—not when another voice booms throughout the empty nightclub. "Has anyone talked to the bouncers?"

Everett Tinrock.

The godfather.

And in actuality, *Hailey's* father.

Air suctions from the bar. We're all sitting stiffer and breathing less. Pissing him off just comes with lectures that I've already memorized, and I'm not in the mood to be talked down to. We're not twelve anymore.

As Everett approaches, he instantly shuts Hailey's book. "Go get ready. The other servers should be here soon."

Hailey obeys without much protest.

"The bouncers will be here on time," Nova tells Everett. "They know if no one can pay the bill, they'll need to escort them to an ATM."

"Good." He eyes Oliver, who's busying himself behind the bar, basically removing himself from the godfather's long to-do list.

Everett side-eyes Nova. "What are you wearing?" he asks.

My brother is in a cargo jacket. "I'm changing later."

"Change *now*. I wouldn't believe you're the general manager of this place unless I was blackout drunk."

Nova just nods and pockets his phone.

"Phoebe, you need to change, too," Everett decrees. "It's time."

It's time.

Nova gives me a long look, but I don't want to see the emotion he's battling. I don't want to know what's tumbling inside his head. I just want to do my damn job like he's about to do.

I have a purpose—a thing I'm good at. And tonight, we're supposed to bank three times as much as all the nights before. I won't screw this up.

Neon lights blink frenziedly inside the club. Music thumps harsher against my temples—a sensory overload I'd like to unplug from with a shot of whiskey. Or even Oliver's shitty vodka. But I know it's better if I stay sober and in control.

So I've been pretending to sip tequila shots, cocktails, *anything* that men keep buying for me. As a bottle girl, I'm hired to socialize with different VIP sections and coax them to order more alcohol. But my mom specifically told me, "You're something between a bottle girl, a stripper, and an escort, bug. You'll be the girl all the men want in their section."

I think she severely overestimated my sex appeal.

Even though I'm scantily dressed, the pole dancers are

drawing more attention and tempting more men. They actually have talent, and even if I would grade my lap dance skills as a solid B minus, I'm not the second coming of Marylin Monroe.

I could use a strong drink, and the sheer amount of will-power to not down bourbon right now is impressive on my part. I'm giving myself some kudos in case this all goes hay-wire. Might as well be self-congratulatory now.

I won't screw up. The reoccurring thought is a banging gavel in my head.

I'm not channeling a deep confidence. I'm just so afraid of being the one to mess up an entire con. It's as if every cell in my body resists the idea of failing. Like failing equals death, and self-preservation will kick in before that happens.

"We're not selling by glass tonight!" Hailey shouts over the music to a VIP table, a pen and pad in her hand. "Just by bottle!"

I try to concentrate on familiar voices, not the hands roam-ing up and down my hips. Meaty hands. *I hope he washed them.* I intake a tense breath and force a sultry smile, leaning only a little closer. The mark is named Henry Something-or-Other.

It's not that important for me to remember. He's mid-forties and here for "business" as a consultant to tech firms.

"Like Google," he's said five times already. Must be some *amazing* company, considering all of his business buddies are already sloshed in our VIP section of leather couches. They're salivating over the cute redhead shimmying against a pole on a circular platform. One businessman mimes grabbing her boobs, and I restrain the urge to glare and simultaneously eye roll.

I grind lightly against Henry's lap.

"Bottle girl!" his friend shouts loudly at me, the one who

just squeezed the air. Basically a breath away from biting his knuckles and coming in his pants. "Come here, baby!"

I flash a flirty smile. "I'm with your boss."

He laughs. "He's not my boss!" This prick is a little younger. Thirties, maybe. Henry Something-or-Other is supposed to be my mark. He's the one I'm positive has loaded pockets. All the VIP tables have a ten-thousand-dollar bottle service minimum. And that's before the markup.

Two days ago, Trevor Tinrock swiped Henry's ID when he exited a high rollers lounge at a nearby casino. Trevor even placed the wallet *back* into Henry's pocket, all without Henry knowing. He's been cleared. Background checked. No connections to anyone too powerful. No one that could come after us. And it didn't take much influence from Everett to persuade Henry to come to the club.

Most of tonight's revenue is coming from *him*. And he has no idea yet.

"I'm not his boss," Henry confirms with a grin. "We're coworkers. Why don't you show him a good time, too, yeah?"

Shit.

While straddling Henry, I slowly run a finger down the nape of his neck and drink in the trail I draw. "Shouldn't he find his own bottle girl?" I lean closer and murmur against his ear, "I want to be yours."

I feel his dick harden against my thigh.

I'm nothing, really. Weightless. Floating. *Hoping* he wants me, even if that kind of yearning for him is gone inside of me. Faded into oblivion. Impossible to reach.

He's grinning. "You'll have to find another girl, Reece."

"Hey, hey!" Reece waves toward a male server, but Hailey is quick to answer and beelines for my section. Her slim-fitting black dress is much classier than the red lace panties and bra

I'm wearing. My getup is considered "an outfit" but let's be clear: it's lingerie.

"Can I help you with something?" Hailey asks him. "Another—"

"A bottle girl. The best you have." He snickers with his friends and downs a flute of champagne.

She jots down on the pad. "Right away." The way she says it, I know she's never going to bring anyone out to him. They'll wait and wait and still be charged.

Henry's warm breath heats my ear now. "You available for a private show, sweetheart?" His drunken, half-lidded eyes meet mine.

"One more bottle?" I coax.

He waves quickly at Hailey. "Another one of these." He points to the ice bucket before she turns away. It's a thirty grand three-liter bottle of Dom Pérignon. Triple the price of its retail value. But it's not a particularly unique year. He was sold earlier on how this case of Dom we just got imported is one of the most *exclusive* champagnes in the world, and that is true. About the rosé.

This'll be his third bottle of overpriced Dom.

After another scribble on her notepad, Hailey dashes away.

Henry's hand traverses down my thigh, inching closer and closer to the lace of my panties. I slide backward, off him, but playfully smile while showing off my ass. I do the *Legally Blonde* thing—bend and snap.

"You like that?" I tease.

"*Love* it, sweetheart." He winks a drunken, oozing wink.

I'm floating into nothingness. And as I turn my back to Henry, I see another couch that faces ours.

I see him.

My pulse hitches.

Paddles jolt my lifeless insides.

Rocky has an arm over the black leather couch, a cigar burning between his fingers, and glass of iced bourbon in his hand. In his demeanor alone, he looks born from rare champagnes of the world and worth more than the oxygen everyone is breathing.

And he's staring right at me.

Seven

Phoebe

THE CLIP JOINT (CONTINUED)

Men are clustered around Rocky, laughing and drinking and drunkenly flirting with another bottle girl. She's halfway splayed over a buff guy who's likely a pro athlete, chitchatting with her breasts in his face.

This is her actual job.

She's likely better at it than me, and I can't even be impressed or envious. Not when Rocky is fixated on me. His powerful gaze descends my body in a languid, hot stroke, like he's making rough, sensual love to me from afar.

I'm lassoed and fastened to his captivating aura. To the way he wants me and covets me in one glance. I can't break away, and a pounding feeling is reaching inside of me, pumping my blood, quickening my pulse. *More.* Something in me is screaming and ripping and pleading for more of this feeling. More of him?

I don't like it.

I'm scared I'll miss it when it's gone.

"Baby," Henry coos, his hands slinking down my hips.

Rocky passes his cigar to the athlete, no longer focused solely on me. My heart nose-dives. Rocky's dazzling grin lights up his photogenic features.

His spirited laugh is infectious, the bright noise commanding the entire group of men. They share in the sound. He pats another guy on the back and motions to a server. He holds up three fingers.

She nods.

"Another round." Rocky celebrates loudly enough for me and most of the VIP sections to hear.

They hoot and holler.

"You're the man, Cooper!" another mark yells to Rocky.

Cooper isn't footing that bill.

Cooper will disappear and leave them to pay.

But right now, he's the man of their dreams. He'll be their nightmare later.

Henry yanks me back onto his lap. My shoulders thump against his chest, and as his hand dives between my legs, I grip his wrist and flip around to face him, my playful smile in check. "That's not part of the show."

He grins. "It could be. Couldn't it?"

I mull this over with a teasing smirk.

"Come on," he breathes, fingering the strap of my bra. "What about for the right price?"

"The right price?"

"Everyone has a price, sweetheart. Even your pussy." He laughs like it's a sexy joke, but he's not joking.

"For you, sir . . ." Hailey interjects, placing the new champagne bottle in the ice bucket. Her eyes flit to me for half a second, but I pretend not to notice.

Henry gives Hailey a seedy, slithering once-over. It's now that I stiffen, that my stomach unsettles. *Don't look at her like that* blares in my head like a blowhorn.

He must feel me go rigid because he laughs and turns his attention on me. "Jealous, aren't you?"

I sense Hailey leaving.

"You're *mine*, remember?" I tease. "I like attention."

"Oh, I can give you all the attention you want, Angel."

I hate my alias. *Angel*. Whatever. Oliver chose it. He thought it'd be funny.

As Henry gropes me again, I don't know how I feel other than unbothered. It's me. Not Hailey. I can live with that.

A groan rumbles from his throat. He grabs my hair in a tight fist. "You have a back room here?"

I slide my hand against his jaw in a caress. "This way." With my other hand, I take his palm off my ass. His grip on my hair loosens.

Quickly, I begin to lead him to the back, and within a minute of trekking through the club-goers and servers, Rocky suddenly cuts off our path.

He's blocking me and the mark.

"Excuse me," I say, but I don't try to pass.

"You're leaving already?" His covetous gaze caresses against me, and my breath jettisons, my body blazes, and I couldn't name this feeling for a million dollars.

Lust is too ruthless, and *love* is too tender. What I feel for Rocky is something crafted solely for him and me.

"She's leaving with me." Henry suddenly pushes out front. "Who are you?"

Rocky grins a shit-eating *fuck you* grin. "No one to you. I'm just interested in her." He looks down at me. "What's your name?"

"Angel." I cross my arms, more standoffish toward him than to Henry.

"Angel, that's pretty—"

"She's with *me*," Henry forces. "Move."

"At what price?" Rocky asks me. "I'll double what he's paying."

"I . . . I don't know what he's paying." I play confused.

Henry goes red in the face the longer I stare at him, waiting for an answer. "Two thousand."

"Five grand," Rocky announces. "You and me, Angel."

I look to Henry like he's my knight in shining armor. I don't want to be bought by the wrong man. *Please, save me.* "Do you have more?" I whisper, trying not to wish for Rocky.

"Seven."

Rocky grimaces, a little ticked off. "Ten."

"Fifteen." Henry sees that Rocky has a limit somewhere.

"Thirty," Rocky says like it's a sledgehammer. The knockout punch.

I squeeze the life out of Henry's hand. Before he hesitates, I whisper, "You can do anything to me. Anything you want."

Lust is more potent than a drug. His gaze is on my tits and ass. He bites his lip, and I'm outside of my body, watching his leering eyes from a distance.

Rocky's jaw muscle tics. His gaze darkens and knifes into Henry. He's silently seething, maybe partly for show. I see him curl his fingers into fists at his sides, but I'm surprised when he pockets them.

For the shortest, rawest second, I look deeper at Rocky.

Fight harder for me, I want.

I intake a sharp breath. *I want. I want. I want.* I'm swallowed inside the tornadic desire. The screaming and clawing and yearning inside of me that circulates at a vicious rate.

I want him.

Don't I? Isn't that what this feeling means?

His whole body is strained. Maybe because he knows he has to give me up. He isn't supposed to outbid the mark.

He isn't supposed to have me.

"Fifty thousand," Henry suddenly announces, his hand on my ass.

"*Fuck,*" Rocky grits out, venom in his eyes. How much is real—I couldn't even say. He needs to look angry about losing, but he's not storming away.

"Let's go," I tug Henry toward the back room, a knot lodging in my throat.

I try to swallow it.

And just like that, Rocky is gone. Lost in the throngs of VIPs, bottle girls, and more servers. I approach a red velvet door. The back room is rigged with a silent alarm, and as soon as I open it, an alert will ping Nova.

We go inside.

The room itself is empty except for another leather couch and bucket of ice with Dom.

I drop his hand. "Thanks for that back there. Want a drink to start?"

"No, I want you." His meaty hands grip my waist, pulling me closer.

I laugh. "Hold on, cowboy." I shimmy away from his hands. "It has to be up front first."

"Later."

"My boss will be pissed. It has to be now." *Come on, Nova.*

His face is flushed, eyes still glazed from the alcohol. I take a playful step backward, but Henry stalks forward as if it's a game.

"I'm serious," I tell him with the tilt of my head, my pulse in my ears. "Up front."

He's out of breath. "Later." He reaches to grab me. I try to shove my instincts down—to let him touch me and not break character.

Drop your arms, Phoebe.

Don't push him.

Don't push him.

He clutches my hips, and the door swings open.

I step out of his hold faster than a bolt of lightning, and relief washes over me when Nova enters the room, his suit crisp and tailor-made for his six-one build.

"Fifty for the room with her," Nova tells the mark. He has the face of a no-bullshitter. He means business, and I can only assume he crossed paths with Rocky, who told my brother the price of the deal.

"Who the fuck are you?" Henry wobbles on his feet.

"The *manager* of the fucking club you're in," Nova curses. "Fifty *thousand*, what you promised if you're actually good for it. If you can't pay, someone else will, and you can get the fuck out of my club."

With all the alcohol and service charges, his bill is going to be higher than that.

"I'm good for it." Henry sways but takes out his wallet. He hands Nova a credit card.

"Go grab some protection," Nova tells me.

God. What every sister dreams of hearing from her older brother.

Bury me tomorrow when I burn up replaying this *mortifying* moment. I say nothing and go into the bathroom, where a silk robe is hanging on a hook. Quickly, I tie the black robe around my body.

Nova slips inside.

With buzzed dark hair, designer suit, and skin tanned from the sun, Nova carries himself like every morning is a battle. Every night is a war. And there's no rest when in combat. But the only person I think he's battling is himself.

Oliver says he's neurotic.

I think he's just trying hard. Really hard. To not fuck up like our dad did. To prove to the godfather that he's more capable and dependable.

He has the portable credit card reader in his right hand. "You're done for the night."

I'm not surprised. This was probably the biggest payout of the day, and I shouldn't screw someone else. It'd draw more suspicion. There are people here who won't feel scammed in the morning. Those people are the ones who keep returning and urging their friends to come along, too.

"Cool," is all I say.

He has Henry's credit card hostage, but he can't dillydally. He studies my eyes. "Platypus?"

I smile. We came up with that code when we were kids— me, Oliver, and Nova. Platypus means we feel like we've fallen flat on our stomachs. *Splat,* Oliver would say and fall belly down on a mattress. It's funny that we didn't choose armadillo.

Actual roadkill.

We just chose a duck-billed mammal that floats on its stomach. I guess losing yourself inside a con doesn't make you feel run over.

It's something else.

"No." I shake my head. "Polar bear."

The king of the arctic, Nova said at twelve. *Polar bears think humans are easy prey.*

Nova relaxes a fraction. "Okay, good. I'll text you when you can leave."

"Perfect." I lean on the bathroom sink. "See you later, *big brother*."

He shoots me a look like I'm insane. Henry could've heard me, but I wasn't even that loud. "Be careful," he whisper-growls, and then he's gone.

I'm stuck in the bathroom.

Sitting on the toilet lid, I scroll on my phone and try not to picture Nova and Henry. Or worse, Rocky.

What I know is happening: Nova will return with another bill after already charging the fifty thousand. He'll ask for a wire transfer or more credit cards. The bill will be *heavily* inflated for bottle service, gratuity, and every service charge under the sun.

Henry will balk and ask where I went. Nova will tell him that I'm coming back and to wait for me. After some coaxing, Henry will pay the extra bill and he'll wait in the room until his suspicion grows. Then he'll return to the club to try and track down Nova or me. He won't find either of us. If he tries to ask where we went, everyone will say we already left.

What I know won't happen: he won't report us—not when he paid for sex. He won't tell his friends because that would mean facing the embarrassment of being duped. And no one likes to be made a fool of.

In the end, he'll slump on home and convince himself that this night was just one of misfortune. A wave of bad luck.

Once Nova's text pings my phone, I leave for the club's private dressing room. I try to keep my head down, but like a cosmic slap in the face, I lift my gaze and I see Rocky in a darkened corner. He's lip-locked with the redhead who'd been dancing on the pole.

Muscles twitch around my mouth. Am I trying to smile or not vomit? I let out the longest sigh of my life, and I work my jaw to force out these feelings. But they still tumble strangely in my stomach. My eyes burn, even after I've reached the dressing room, pulled on a sweatshirt and jeans, and left the club.

I take a cab to the heart of the Vegas strip. I'm lost among the lights, street performers, and bachelor parties.

Yet, he still finds me, even without modern novelties like sharing my location on a phone or a text to say I'm right *here*.

I'm standing on the sidewalk in front of the Bellagio fountains, but my back is to the water that arches and dives in mesmeric patterns. I'm just staring out at a fake Eiffel Tower. It glitters in the night.

Rocky slides beside me, close enough that we could either be friends or sudden acquaintances. I wonder if other people constantly analyze their body language and question how others are perceiving them. I wonder if this is just something con artists have to be paranoid about.

"Am I that predictable?" I ask him under my breath.

"To me. Yeah." He still wears the same expensive suit, but his commanding smile and eyes are gone. "I didn't think you'd be anywhere else."

This isn't our first time in Vegas. Or my first time viewing the Eiffel Tower light show. It's my favorite part of Sin City, and not because I've never been to Paris and it's the closest I'll ever come. But because it's Fake Paris.

A replica of the real thing. I guess I appreciate the façade.

Rocky loves the Masquerade Hotel & Casino more, but I can't help but get stuck here.

"You all right?" he suddenly asks in a deep, husky breath. It sounds like a whisper only meant for my ears.

"Are you all right?" I volley back, finally looking into his eyes. "Your tongue disappeared back there. Thought maybe we opened a magic club instead of a nightclub."

His lips twitch into a smile. "Funny."

"Funny like *ha-ha* or funny like *go fuck yourself*?" I ask.

"Definitely like *go fuck yourself*."

I laugh under my breath, and it feels like a truly genuine emotion tonight. Except it wheezes out like a dying hyena as I remember his lips and her lips. I'm cringing. "Did you get her number? Going on a fun date tomorrow?" I try not to appear desperate for the answer, but I'm standing on the very edge of the question, prepared to free-fall.

"No and no." He checks over his shoulder. "You know I don't date anyone I meet on jobs. Not for real, anyway."

Dating is a hot-button topic among the Tinrocks and Graves. Unless it's a relationship for a con, most of us rarely get past the third-date stage.

After the third date, everything gets more serious. More personal and risky. And there's only so much of our true selves we're allowed to share.

Sex is easier for all of us. Sex barely has any strings. Sex can even have no names. I wonder if our moms ever considered that they'd end up raising promiscuous, relationship-phobic kids.

Rocky glances back at me. "She was just trying to dodge some fucking jackass at the club."

"So you stuck your tongue down her throat?"

He lifts his brows. "After I pulled her away from him and said she was with me, yeah—she kissed me."

This hurts. It shouldn't hurt, but being in a fake relationship is something he does often *with me*. "How chivalrous."

"I probably enjoyed it as much as you enjoyed that *fucking . . .*" He trails off as malice seeps from his voice, unable to find a suitable term for Henry. "That *fuck* all over you."

"It was fine," I mutter, a numbness swirling. I roll up my sweatshirt sleeves.

Rocky takes a deep breath. "But seriously, Phebs."

"Seriously what?"

"Are you all right?" he asks again.

His concern knocks into me. "Yeah. I am." I shrug. "It was easy." Something gnaws at me. Guilt, maybe? I just hate that it was so easy. "Was it supposed to be hard?"

He stares back out at the sparkling, fake Eiffel Tower. "I don't know."

Me either.

After the light show ends, we walk a few blocks down the strip, passing club promoters who try to entice us with our names on guests lists and free VIP tables. One guy is one hundred percent a scammer. He's asking a couple girls for twenty bucks up front through PayPal. It doesn't always take one to know one, but the girls are falling for his act.

As we pass the promoter, Rocky sends him an intrusive, intense look that causes him to stumble over his words.

"And . . . uh, yeah, you know what," the scammer says to the girls. "It's on me. Don't worry about PayPal."

We never slow our stride, and I tell Rocky, "Keep that up and people are going to think your heart is moral."

His lip nearly twitches into a smile. "That's the point. Make everyone believe I'm an upstanding citizen. *Wholesome.*" He thinks for a second. "People like him just hate looking into their reflections and seeing what's staring back. I know what I really am."

"You like looking at yourself?"

He raises his brows at me like I'm a breath from calling him Narcissus. "I don't have a problem with it. Do you?"

With looking internally at myself? With contemplating my immoral deeds? Henry was a fucking slimeball, and I block out how his hands slid over my ass and the smell of his bad breath. And I just revel in the fact that he's out of pocket a large, embarrassing sum.

I don't regret it.

"I can look at myself," I tell Rocky. "The mirror isn't really my enemy." I'm happy that I contributed to tonight's victory and payout.

I'm useful.

He says little in reply. We continue our casual pace along the strip. Enough space between us that we could be strangers, but not when our gazes catch for longer than a second.

We could be friends.

The distance begins to shrink with each step. His fingers brush against my fingers, and a tingling sensation accelerates my pulse.

We could be secret lovers.

Reaching a hot dog stand, we break apart, and I know we are none of those things and something else entirely.

We grab some street food before taking a cab back to the penthouse.

Rocky and I share the quiet with each other, and it's a comfortable silence until we hit the glitzy elevator.

He turns to me. "I've been thinking about what you said," he breathes. "About it being easy."

"Yeah?" Goosebumps line my skin.

"Yeah." He nods, his gunmetal eyes on mine. "And I think if it were hard for us, we'd be bad at our jobs. It's supposed to be easy. We're supposed to enjoy it."

"I thought you said you didn't enjoy it?" *Didn't he insinuate that?*

"Not kissing a stranger," he tells me. "Gaining their trust. That's power. It felt fucking good." A frown knots his brows. "Didn't it for you?"

Yes. I like power.

It makes me feel safe.

I'm also afraid of it. We don't watch the numbers tick higher as we ascend. Our gazes are on each other. An understanding breathes between us like pure oxygen.

"Yeah," I murmur. "It did feel good."

A string of yearning pitches my pulse. *Step closer, Rocky. Touch me, Rocky. I want you all over me, Rocky.* I imagine him thrusting me against the elevator buttons. I imagine him gripping my face with the fierce affection of a lover, of a come-hell-or-high-water companion.

I imagine his heart hammering against my heart. A carnal ache winds through me in a torturous, torrid beat.

His gaze flits to my lips.

My breathing shallows, and yet, we're the same side of a magnet. Unwilling and unable to unite. I've never kissed him outside of a job. His lips have only touched mine with stipulations attached. *This is just for our roles.*

I already hear my mom. "Look how attractive he is, bug. Look at how he's looking at you. He adores you."

The men she chooses are . . . not good men, and yet, she wants me with Rocky *so badly.*

The obstinate pieces of me resist her advice to go after him.

She once told me, "He's so cute, bug. Look at him. I think he likes you, too."

"I don't like him," I lied.

I trust my mom completely, but when it comes to which men I should be with, it's about the only advice I dump in the garbage can.

I feel myself resisting the draw toward him, but Rocky turns his head away first.

He hasn't made a move on me outside of a con, and I doubt he ever will.

I'm numb as I exit the elevator, floating into a great, endless nothingness.

Eight

Phoebe

Step One: Find a place to live
  Step Two: *Get a real job*

With step one complete, I focus on the next part of our plan to live honestly. This isn't a temporary life that I can ditch tomorrow and erase for good. This is supposed to be a permanent thing—a part of my career résumé that I can build upon. *Permanence.* It's definitely new for me.

I've never had a normal paycheck.

Don't have a social security number.

Never passed a driver's test to get a license.

If I even have a real birth certificate, my mom hasn't showed me. I understood, even at a young age, that having paperwork means being tied to something—to someone.

We can do this.

I breathe in the encouragement as Hailey and I walk into a five-story, white brick mansion near the New England coast. Thanks to being spritzed by the sprinklers outside, my heeled boots squeak on the marble floors. The manicured green lawns and freshly planted peonies all scream, *Country club!*

The squeaking I'm making screams, *Outsider!*

"Fuck," I mutter under my breath, trying to tiptoe like an idiot. I feel like the Grinch coming to steal Christmas from the residents of Victoria—which *shouldn't* be the case. I'm not here to steal.

So why do I feel like I'm up to no good?

"You're fine," Hailey consoles, her fair face seeming bare without the heavy dark eye shadow and black lipstick. Though, she's still wearing eyeliner. "You're not supposed to be prim and proper."

"I'm just supposed to be me." I try to scrape wet grass off my boot and onto the marble. Under my breath, I add, "The only problem is being me means being a liar." I *am* a liar. I *am* a deceiver. These things have been ingrained deep inside me, and they don't just go away with the snap of a finger.

Hailey sends me an encouraging look. "We're working on that part."

I'm supposed to learn how to be better. Be good and truthful. Not sure how to do that without ripping parts of my personality away.

For Hailey, I remind myself.

The two words might as well be branded on my heart.

I'm trying to make this work for Hailey.

I won't screw up.

She scours the empty rotunda for an employee, and I twirl around and take in the glamorous surroundings. Through big, spotless windows, I see the wraparound porch with cushioned rocking chairs and an impressive golf course. Victoria Country Club also has an Olympic-sized pool. It kinda sucks we can't go sunbathe and drink piña coladas all afternoon.

Hailey glances at her Betty Boop watch face. "I swear the orientation was supposed to be at nine." Her natural-brown brows furrow like she's struggling with getting a fact wrong.

"Katherine is probably late." I help myself to a beverage from a refreshment cart. Cucumbers float in a water jug, and I fill up a polished glass.

Hailey browses a table of magazines.

I squeeze at her side. "Oooh, *Celebrity Crush*." I grab the gossip rag and sip my cucumber water.

"I don't know how you can read that." She's already flipping through a *National Geographic History* magazine titled, "Hellraiser: The Hideous History of Satan." "Maybe two percent is actually true."

She's not wrong. "But even though people know ninety-eight percent is likely garbage, they can't help themselves and want to believe it's true," I tell her, flipping the page. "I'm one of those people when it comes to celebrities, Hails. I want to *believe* my favorite boy bander is dating my favorite actress. Aren't they cute?" I flash a photo of the alleged couple shopping at the Grove in L.A.

Hailey has the best deadpan expression. "It's staged."

I examine the photo. "Even if it's pretend love, it's way more of an exciting love story than the boring girl-meets-boy, girl-dates-boy, girl-marries-boy. I like twists. Girl-realizes-boy-sucks, girl-dates-girl. Or girl-hates-boy, girl-sleeps-with-boy."

"Girl-pretend-loves-boy?" Hailey questions. "Boy-pretend-loves-girl?"

"Exactly."

She looks up from her magazine. "Sounds more like you and my brother."

I try not to tense. "No, what I have with Rocky is diabolical love." I turn a page. "Two stubborn hotheads imploding at the same time."

"A proven bad combo," Hailey concludes while skimming the *National Geographic* with interest.

It shouldn't hurt hearing her say that, but my stomach clenches.

Even though Hailey and I are best friends, she's not the one I confided in about liking Rocky when I was younger. Rocky is her brother. It just seemed messy and complicated, and I was afraid she'd want us together as much as my mom did. I needed Hailey to reinforce the idea that we are truly a bad combo. And maybe she's right.

Rocky and I are combative. That isn't a healthy ingredient in a relationship. Not that I've ever been in a real one.

"Totally," I agree with a page flip. "You're the smartest person I know, so your wisdom is my road map."

"I'm only book smart, Phebs," Hailey says casually.

I scrunch my brows. "Now, that's a big, ugly lie."

She's still reading, but her cheeks redden, her skin a pinker and fairer tint than mine. "I know useless facts about useless things. I don't know how to fix a toilet or hot-wire a car. You have tools. I have paper."

"Paper is useful."

"Sparingly. Only at specific times for specific needs." She shuts the magazine, resigned to these facts about herself.

And I wonder how we arrived at this place. Where it's just easier to see how amazing the other person is—and it's harder to see those same amazing qualities in ourselves.

"I love paper," I tell my best friend.

She smiles over at me. "I love tools."

We're both grinning when heels suddenly *tap tap tap* against the marbled floors. We turn around at the same time a fortysomething woman approaches in a stiff but quickened strut. Reddish hair slicked into a perfectly neat bun; nothing about this woman is out of place. Her black wrinkle-free pencil skirt hugs her curves, and a gold nameplate is fastened to her silk blouse: KATHERINE RHODES, MANAGER OF GUEST RELATIONS.

She's slightly out of breath and ten minutes late. Her tardiness is the only scratch in her polished armor. It's unseemly. How could she?

The horror.

The dry wit inside my brain almost makes me smile, but I smooth my lips together so I don't come off as a smart-ass.

Her finger juts out toward the entryway. "Was that you?"

I realize she's pointing at the grass I smeared on the marble. No hello, no greeting, just an accusation. *Awesome.* I open my mouth to lie, but I stop myself short.

"We're here for the job," Hailey says quickly. "I'm Hailey Thornhall. We talked over email."

Katherine appraises Hailey's attire: black slacks and white button-down. It's the dress code in Katherine's email that I'm also following. Hailey no longer has an eyebrow piercing or a lip ring. We're both making efforts to fit in . . . except, I didn't dye my hair back to brown.

I like the blue, and the email said nothing about hair color.

Katherine has two small tote bags hooked on her arm with the country club's logo: a budding pink mountain laurel. "You're both new and I'm too busy to repeat myself, so one mistake is fine—two is fireable." She rips the glass out of my hand. Water sloshes back at me. *What the* . . . "This is for guests. You're not a guest here."

I pat the wet spot on my blouse. "Noted."

She glares at my dry tone.

I want to bristle and act like I belong the more she tries to make me feel small. But I'm in no power position here, and I end up feeling like a wet poodle, tail between my legs.

"Sorry," I mutter.

Her sharp gaze cuts to Hailey. "Magazines are also for guests." She takes the *Celebrity Crush* from me, and when she collects the history on Satan mag from Hailey, she stiffens at the title and the thick streak of eyeliner that shades Hailey's gray eyes. Katherine is probably thinking Hailey cracks out a Ouija board every night and communes with the devil.

I smooth my lips to holster a smile.

That couldn't be the furthest thing from reality, but she's not asking us about ourselves—she's just telling us to do as she says.

More quickly, she hands us the totes. "An orientation pamphlet is inside as well as a map of the country club. Whichever one of you made the mess on the floor, clean it up ASAP, and fix your hair." She's staring at me.

My face is on fire. "What's wrong with my hair?"

"It's a mess."

It's in a pony, but at least she didn't comment on the color.

"Get those pieces out of your face."

I agree to this with a sheepish, "Okay." I'm so glad Rocky isn't here to see me wilt like a dying petunia.

"I can't give you the tour today." She takes a hurried glance at her watch. "We're dealing with a situation at the pool." After a glimpse of her phone, she lets out an annoyed breath. "Okay, well it looks like one of the Koning boys is walking you through the orientation today. I need to handle this."

Before I can ask what the hell a *Koning boy* is—Katherine zips off and exits out the double doors to the wraparound porch and patio.

Hailey and I exchange a *what the fuck* look.

"Koning?" Hailey frowns. "Like the beer?"

Skepticism pinches me, and my best friend follows me into the bathroom. I collect a bundle of paper towels. "Is Koning a family?"

I know the brand. Koning is just about everywhere in America. It's the drink of mind when I think of football and beer. Their Super Bowl commercials are also pretty legendary. All of them incorporate sperm whales and the classic Koning gold crown.

Hailey searches the internet on her cellphone. "And your suspicions are . . . correct. The company was founded by a family in 1826."

"I didn't want that to be true." I fix my hair into a neater pony, a little more nervous at the idea that we might've found ourselves among beer aristocracy. This isn't a tiny independent brewery. Koning is the biggest rival to Anheuser-Busch, the company that makes Budweiser.

The Konings likely have money and prestige, two qualities that are like catnip for my family. It has the smell of a long con, and I'm not supposed to be sniffing out a new job for the Tinrocks and Graves.

"It'll be fine," Hailey says with nonchalance, but she's gathering more paper towels at a rapid speed. She seems a little anxious.

It does sound . . . unbelievable that the Konings have roots in this little Connecticut town, and we just so happened to have picked this place to establish a new life.

Returning to the entryway, I'm on my knees and scrubbing at the grass stain on the white marble. Hailey kneels with me and helps clean the most stubborn green streak.

"I doubt anyone related to that family is here," I tell Hailey while we scrub. "Maybe some infamous beer-drinking frat boys are running around the country club and they pound six-packs of Koning Lite."

Hailey takes a good look at the glittering chandelier in the main rotunda. "More like bourbon-drinking boys."

"I'm more of a beer drinker these days."

I startle at the familiar voice behind us. He rounds our knelt bodies, and we look up.

"You." Hailey gapes.

Jake in his fancy sport coat and leather boat shoes has his arms crossed like a disappointed dad. "Me," he says while Hailey and I pick ourselves off the floor. I wad up all the dirtied paper towels, and Jake is practically pouting at my hair.

I feel like he's channeling most of his disappointment into the fact that I ditched his advice. But in this new normal life that I can have, I *want* blue hair.

"Koning boy?" Hailey asks the important question. "What does that even mean?"

His arms drop with a heavy exhale. "*Katherine.*" He groans. "She's known my brothers and me since we were small." He says this like it'll answer the question.

"You're heavy beer drinkers—the Koning boys?" I ask, though my voice sounds tight. Stilted. I'm questioning every-thing now. *He can't be that rich.*

"My mother's maiden name is Koning," he explains.

Okay, he is that *rich.*

Hailey maintains a stoic face. "So your family owns the beer company?"

Jake nods.

I go rigid. "Do they own this country club, too?" Why else would he be Katherine's choice to give us the orientation?

"Yeah." Jake sighs heavily like he didn't want to have this conversation today. "We do."

"Why didn't you say something?" I cross my arms like a disappointed mother. He had every opportunity to tell us who he was back at the loft. He knew we would be working here.

"I didn't feel like talking about my family." The way he says it, there's a subtle note of bitterness there that I'm sure few would catch.

"That's fair," Hailey says, like she totally gets being cagey when it comes to family.

But this is different. We're hiding crimes.

What's he hiding?

"It feels a bit disingenuous," I tell Jake. "You knew we would be working here, and you were giving us tips so we wouldn't be eaten by the upper elite, but in reality, it was just so we fit into your country club's standards."

"It was both," Jake says. "We have a dress code. One that your best friend seems to respect more than you." He's staring at my hair again.

"It's dark blue. Not cotton candy I-went-to-Disney-World blue, which I understand would distract people from their mai tais and pickleball lessons."

He shakes his head. "That's not the point—" He cuts himself off as his phone rings, and not with the automated ringtone. "Highway to Hell" by AC/DC blares in the echoing rotunda. He stares me down while fishing it from his pocket, as if waiting for a smart-ass comment.

I have none.

I'm just shocked he'd do a contrarian thing. Most people set their phones on vibrate.

Turning his back to us, he takes the call. "I can't help right now, Trent. I'm giving an orientation to the two new servers."

Hailey isn't a lover of major confrontation, and this whole thing with our landlord is becoming messier by the second.

She leans closer to me. "We don't have to work here. There's still that job opening at the bookstore."

We vetoed that job when only one position became available. We want to work together, and maybe it's asking too much to have the perfect job *and* be able to work with my best friend. If I have to sacrifice one over the other, I'm ditching perfection.

"No, we can do this," I tell her.

She stares harder at me. "You sure?"

"Positive." With my finger, I draw an X over my heart, promising her.

Hailey tries to relax.

Jake's voice pitches louder. "Seriously? Fine." He growls, "I said *fine*, Trent. I'll handle it." He hangs up the call and turns around.

"Talking with the devil?" I joke. "There's a magazine for that."

He's confused.

I flush. "Because the song . . . 'Highway to Hell' . . . and a history magazine—you know what, never mind." *Fuck my new life.*

"Is everything okay?" Hailey asks him.

"Yeah, it's fine," he says more gently this time, pocketing his phone. "Let's just get on with this so you both can start your shifts." He treks down the long corridor with zero pause. Hailey and I nearly jog to keep his lengthy pace. "There are five dining rooms at the club, including the patio dining. Katherine will email the shift schedule at the start of the week, but things change hour by hour. Guests choose where they'd like to dine, and if extra hands are needed in another area, you'll be shifted there."

He barely slows at a set of double doors. "Guest locker

rooms, library, and anywhere that isn't a dining room is off-limits. Sometimes we need more servers at the pool and for snack service; again, you fill in where needed. Banquets and events are frequent, and as full-time staff, you'll be expected to work those."

He pushes open the doors. Circular tables, burgundy leather chairs, and glitzy chandeliers fashion this elegant, warm atmosphere. Light streams through the tall windows, so it can't be a smoking parlor. It's likely the main dining room.

"This is the main dining hall," he announces.

I smile. Okay, my deduction skills aren't too rusty yet.

"Anything you hear in VCC stays here. These guests pay for privacy, and they do pay a lot of money. Which reminds me . . ." He turns to me. "Don't expect tips. We're a no-tipping club since it's rolled into the dues."

No tips.

We were banking on *tips* to afford rent.

And why did he look at me when he said that? Do I appear desperate for cash? Is it because I almost flashed him at the loft? Most people I can read somewhat well, but he's more like fogged glass. I hate that.

He flags down a petite girl around our age. With inky black hair in a cute, sleek pony, she's dressed in the same black slacks and white button-down as us. "Chelsea," he says. "This is Phoebe and Hailey. They'll be your trainees."

Chelsea plasters on a smile that seems artificial. "Great. Follow me."

After Jake passes us over to Chelsea, my phone buzzes. Three times. He notices, side-eyeing me with too much interest, and I wait for him to disappear before checking the incoming texts.

206-555-1983: It's Oliver. Now I'm seriously worried. Where are you??

206-555-1983: Just give me your coordinates. Nova & I will come to you wherever you are, no questions asked.

206-555-1983: If someone stole this phone and fucked with the girl who owns it, you've messed with the wrong person.

I type out three different responses and delete them just as fast.

I'm okay.

I'm fine.

Don't worry.

I decide to do the worst sisterly thing and say nothing. A pit is in my heart and stomach. Rocky said he'd handle my brothers. I just hope I'm not making a mistake by letting him take the wheel.

Nine

Rocky

I was thirteen the first time my parents left me alone with Hailey and Trevor for longer than a week. My mom zipped up five designer dresses, packed away heels; her reading glasses were slipping down her nose, chestnut hair already blown out from the salon.

I was sitting on a plush ottoman at the foot of her bed, pretending to be interested in a stack of baseball cards she'd bought me.

"The Graves need our help in Dallas," she told me. "We'll be back in a few weeks."

I licked my lips, picturing Nova, Oliver, and Phoebe alone somewhere. Abandoned while Elizabeth Graves got herself in a mess she couldn't escape. "Shouldn't I go with you?" I questioned.

"Not this time, Brayden." She stood and kissed the top of my head. "Be good." The advice usually came with a smirk, one she'd share with Elizabeth. But without her best friend at her side, she seemed more somber. She tossed her favorite hardbacks in a carry-on Loro Piana bag. Moving faster.

I asked four different questions.

Did a job go bad?

Is Nova involved?

Why will it take almost a month?

Is Phoebe all right?

My father tightened his black tie. He gave me a sterner look. "It's not your concern. You're going to watch out for your brother and sister. You're in charge while we're gone."

I sighed out roughly. "Just let us go with you."

"It's safer for you here," my mom consoled.

"I can look out for them there!"

"You're *not* coming," my dad finalized. "And that's the end of it."

I glared down at the baseball cards. I hated being in the dark more than I hated playing babysitter, and they weren't explaining shit to me.

At thirteen, I felt entitled to answers.

To the big picture.

In hindsight, I was too young to be trusted with *everything*. If I knew less, then I'd have less chance of incriminating myself if we were caught. But what my parents did, it was just as much to protect themselves as it was to protect us.

Selfish. The older I became, the more I realized they were all fucking selfish. At the end of the day, we were their little pawns, and I was in no position to outmaneuver them.

I stopped arguing about Dallas.

It was odd for us to be separated from the Graves for this long.

I wanted them back.

I wanted her back.

My parents left. We were staying on the sunny coast of Savannah. Warm, sticky heat bathed me on a freshly painted wraparound porch. My seven-year-old brother ran around the lush front yard, trying to catch crickets in his palms.

I was about to call him back to finish his homework. Until I noticed the textbook on the rocking chair—all the math had been completed, penned directly on the page.

"He only has a few more years left in him," Hailey said from a hammock.

I frowned. "What?"

At first, I thought she was reciting something from the paperback in her clutch. But she glanced over to the yard. To Trevor. "I overheard Mom and Dad talking. They said he only has a few more years before his 'cuteness' wears off."

My stomach gnarled. "Before he gets older," I rephrased.

She nodded. Trevor was the youngest, and we'd all pretended to be the innocent, bright-eyed, and bushy-tailed kid before. Anything to make our parents seem more trustworthy. But Trevor would be the last. Then he'd have to figure out where he actually fit into the family.

His purpose.

His role.

But I didn't think he'd have a hard time figuring it out. Like our sister, he was brilliant. I was glad he was nothing like me.

Slowly—or quickly, depending on your vantage—I was becoming *bitter*, cynical, and protective. I'd lost faith in most of humanity. It'd become easy to fuck everyone over, knowing that most people would just as easily screw me.

Trevor wasn't jaded by people yet. He didn't have rough edges. No bone to pick with anyone. No venom in his veins.

I liked that for my little brother.

Nearing Hailey, I rested my shoulder on the column her hammock was tied to. She began reading again. Artwork of a moth decorated the cover. Maybe a science book? She read so much that it'd been hard to keep track.

Before I could ask, she said, "Have you ever heard of a *Phengaris rebeli*?"

I shook my head.

"Commonly known as the mountain Alcon blue butterfly." Her eyes left the book and planted on me. "No?"

"Alcon blue . . ." I took a seat beside her on the hammock, and Hailey tucked her legs to make room for me. I eyed the page. "I don't think that was in my biology textbook, Hails. What's so special about it?"

"As a caterpillar, it tricks worker ants into bringing it into the colony. They'll dote on the caterpillar. Bring it food and give it protection. All because the caterpillar makes the ant believe it's also an ant. The queen ant to be exact."

Damn. I raised my brows. "How?"

She smiled at my interest. "Worker ants and queen ants emit different sounds. This species of caterpillar learned how to tell the difference and mimic the queen. Then they evolved so that their progeny knew how to do it, too." Our gazes drew back to the yard where Trevor gently cupped a grasshopper between his palms.

The weight of this comparison compressed against my chest.

"The caterpillar has it all figured out, then. Mimic the queen. Get what you want without breaking a sweat."

She blinked. "The caterpillar is the parasite."

I let that sink in. "Would anyone want to be the ant?"

The naïve fools.

The desperate, trusting marks.

That would never be me.

"No one would choose to be deceived," she rationalized.

"But there will always be ants and caterpillars. And the caterpillar will always win in the end."

She nodded, thoughtful about this. She'd always been thoughtful. Her eyes fell back to her book. "It's comforting in a way," she told me. "Knowing that we're not unique. So many other beings in the animal kingdom adopted this lifestyle first." She smiled at me. "Who doesn't want to be queen, right?"

Ever since Hailey taught me about the mountain Alcon blue butterfly, I remind myself to *mimic the queen.*

It's what I do when I arrive at the country club. I barely lift a finger while the unsuspecting ants let an imposter inside their colony.

My new identity in Victoria, Connecticut, has more truth than I'd like, but I've already established I'm Hailey's brother, so I'm obligated to play within that parameter.

Name: *Grey Thornhall*

Occupation: *Investor (of what, to be determined)*

Why I'm Here: *Considering moving to Victoria*

Relationship Status: *Divorced*

I contacted Carter to forge a marriage certificate and divorce papers. Phoebe's lie cost me four grand to make indisputable. Just another day at the office.

A cobbled patio frames a wide pool, but most of the outside area is grass. My lounge chair even rests on the lawn like I stepped onto the English countryside. Dark sunglasses shade my eyes, and I watch a manager corner a couple college-aged guys on the other side of the pool.

She gesticulates angrily with her hands.

Before she arrived, the guys were doing cannonballs in the water. A toddler could piece together why she's upset.

I *hate* rich pricks. Ironic enough, since I spend most of my life pretending to be one.

With a tightness in my face that I'm trying to relax, I glance at my phone in my fist.

Trevor: They said they needed me here. I can't desert Mom & Dad.

I keep rereading the text, and my jaw aches the longer I grind my teeth. Why he cares about them is a question for a therapist that none of us go to. But regardless of our mommy and daddy issues—that only *I* seem to be harboring, out of everyone—I hate that I left him in Seattle to do their bidding without me. I hate that we're not all together.

That does include Phoebe's brothers, even if I'd enjoy stranding Nova on a remote island for forty-eight hours. She gave me the reins to talk to them on her behalf, and I know her. She'd never lie to them. Never manipulate them. *I don't want to either.* But I haven't fully decided what I'm going to tell them.

I did make a decision about my own brother. I told Trevor: **We're in Connecticut. I'll give you the coordinates to come out here. This stays between us.**

Will Hailey and Phoebe be happy I outed their location? Probably not, but I trust Trevor won't say anything to our parents. Having him here will also be good if things go sideways. And really . . . I need him out here and *away* from our mom and dad. It's enough reason for him to have the truth.

I send another text to my brother: **I want you here. If you ever** change your mind, I'll come get you myself. Our parents will be fine on their own.

"It's that time of year." A girl steals my attention. She's in the chair beside mine, watching the manager lecture the douche-bags. Sunglasses are perched on the top of her head, and her brown eyes flit to mine. "The Caufield undergrads are back."

I pocket my phone in my swim trunks. "They can afford this?"

The dues are a hundred thousand a year.

A bill I paid this morning on the contingency I'll be pro-rated what I don't use if I decide not to move to Victoria. But I had enough money from my last job to swing the cost.

"Their parents can. And believe me, this place is important for networking if you want to secure interviews and internships with the best companies after college. Their parents will front the bill, no problem." She swings her legs to the side of the lounge chair to face me. Her white bikini contrasts with her warm brown skin. "I'm Valentina." She holds out her hand. "I don't love my name, so I usually just go by Val."

I lean forward to shake it. "Rocky."

Her eyes light up. "Please tell me that's your actual name. We can commiserate together."

"Nickname," I tell her in a husky breath. "And your name is beautiful, Val."

She blushes, then smiles. I can tell it's genuine. The zygo-maticus major muscles on either side of our cheeks are some of the hardest muscles to control consciously.

Hailey reads books.

I read people.

All I want from Val is information about this town. And I'm forcing myself not to do a sweep of the patio. I haven't seen Hailey or Phoebe, and that's primarily why I'm here.

To spy on my sister and her best friend on their first day being "normal"—whatever the fuck that means.

"You'd be the second to like it," Val tells me. "Right behind my mother."

"We have good taste, then." I smile over at her. "Your mother and I."

She laughs brightly.

No ring on her finger, but she's reading a business text-book. The way she referred to the students as *undergrads* means she's already earned her undergrad degree.

"Please tell me you'll be around the club often," she says. "You can tell her yourself." *She's prying.*

I take a sip from my vodka soda. "I'm considering." My phone buzzes in my pocket.

"If you're in business, there are a lot of connections to be made here," Val says. "I'm getting my MBA at Caufield, and I already have three guaranteed positions after I graduate."

I pull out my phone, half paying attention to her now like I'm important shit. This wouldn't be a good ploy to use on everyone, but she's giving off "desperate to be liked," which makes establishing my credibility and roping her in easier.

"I already have a job," I tell her.

Heat radiates off her face. "Of course you do. I mean, you're here." She clears her throat and bows toward me. "What do you do, anyway?"

"I'm an investor," I say, more disinterested as I glance at the texts on my phone.

206-555-1983: This is Oliver. I can't get a hold of P. Are you with her?

Nova: Where the fuck is my sister?

Looks like I can't keep delaying "the talk" I need to have with her brothers. They'll just keep blowing up my phone. And I can't blame them. I'd do the same thing trying to find Hailey.

"There's a party this weekend," Val tells me. I break away from my phone to give her my attention again. She lights up. "All the locals and some caufers—that's what we call Caufield students—will be there. You should come."

"I'll check it out."

She gives me the info, and I plug it into my phone.

I sit up, resting my feet on the ground. "So what do you call the people who aren't locals or caufers?"

"Skunks."

Again, I already hate it here. But honestly, I hate it everywhere.

I lift my brows and grin in the sunlight. "Creative."

She laughs. "If you do move here, you'll be a local before you know it. No need to worry."

"I'm not worried. You can call me a skunk, Val." I slip my phone in my pocket again. "It doesn't mean I am one." I finish off my vodka soda and stand. "I'm going to have lunch in the dining room. Join me?"

I could pick her brain more about who's who here.

She smiles. "I'd like that, actually. Let me change out of my suit first, and I'll meet you there."

Collecting people wasn't this easy when I was younger. Teenage Rocky would work twice as hard to reach the same outcome. It had less to do with my skills and everything to do with my age. The older I am, the more people believe the bullshit I sell.

Twenty-five is still young enough to elicit doubt that can ruin a job, but with a five-o'clock shadow and routine trips to the gym, I do whatever I can to be nondescript in age. Passing for thirtysomething without question or hesitation.

Valentina doesn't question my age.

She doesn't question my status.

I've pocketed her for the future. I can't tell what use she'll be, but within a matter of minutes, she's bought into the version of myself I'm selling in Victoria. And that alone is priceless.

I leave the pool area with a natural, self-important gait that Phoebe would mock outside of a con. And to be clear, this is how I always fucking walk. Like I've been where my feet are landing a hundred times already, even if it's the first time they've touched this part of the earth.

When I head to the locker rooms, I hate that I'm thinking about her.

I should be thinking about Val and the social hierarchy in this town. Things that'll protect my sister and Phoebe if shit blows up.

As I shrug on my sports jacket, a familiar voice suddenly catches my ear.

"You're not selling her horse," Jake whispers hurriedly. "She's only been gone a year, Mom. You can't just erase everything she loved."

Desperation.

It's an emotion easily preyed upon.

A row of mahogany lockers blocks Jake Waterford from view. Or rather—Jake *Koning* Waterford. A "fun" fact I discovered this morning on a thorough search into the club. Jake is wealthy and emotionally unhinged from his sister's death.

He's a great mark.

But he's also my sister's landlord, and that muddies the so-called well enough for me.

For our parents, it wouldn't matter. They'd swim, drink, and frolic in polluted waters, and they'd convince you it's a natural, healthy spring. That it's what's best for you.

And you'd believe them.

Shit, if they were here, Jakey-poo would already be strung up on a dartboard. He's lucky they're too invested in Seattle and he won't become the target.

Smooth things over with Jake.

It's on my to-do list. At the bottom, but it's on there.

I gently close the locker and slip into view.

Jake's eyes flash with shock, then annoyance. "I have to go, Mom. *Please* don't do anything until I get there." He ends the call and shakes his head in disbelief. "What the hell are you doing here?"

Ten

Rocky

I'm a member here." I rest my shoulder on a locker. He stays impossibly stiff. Guy needs a back rub and a laxative. I try to stay casual. "I'd ask you what you're doing here, but you own the place."

"My family owns it," he corrects me, like there's a distinction. He looks me over, and lines crease the spot between his brows as confusion builds. "What do you mean you're a member? You said you were *just visiting*."

"I am," I say and survey the hall of lockers. "But I'm considering moving here. I'm in a transitionary period in my life so I thought . . . Why not?"

Jake's confusion persists. "You can afford this place."

It's not a question. He knows I can. I'm here. I wait. He just stares. My brows rise. "Was there a question in there, champ?" *Shouldn't have said it like that.*

He rolls his eyes. "Your sister is a server here and you're a member. Make it make sense, *Rocky*."

"Grey Thornhall." I reintroduce myself using my new alias.

The ID is already in my wallet. I think it's a white flag of amnesty. A *let's start over, Jake* declaration.

His eyes tighten. "And you don't go by Grey? Why?" He sounds accusatory.

Jesus Christ. Why wasn't I nicer to him when I met him? *Because I didn't think I had anything to gain. Because Phoebe and Hailey aren't here on a job.*

Because I'm not a nice person.

I could've been "fake nice"—easy enough.

Yet, I wasn't with him. I don't know why I couldn't pretend for a hot second, and that honestly is disturbing me.

He might be wealthy, but he's still like a little baby deer. As far as I can tell, he's not oozing all the nefarious traits that typically come with being the heir of a billion-dollar corporation, and he's not rude or entitled or showboating.

Is that why it's more difficult to be fake nice with him?

Because he might not be an asshole?

That's dumb. I also hate that it might be the answer.

"You can call me Grey if you want," I tell him. "I'm just more used to Rocky."

He digests this in silence.

Okay.

I stand straighter. "My sister is stubborn. She wouldn't take a handout if I force-fed it to her, and I'm not into forcing anyone into anything. She wants to make it her way. On her own." That's not a complete lie, and I'm surprised I'm still not slathering on the bullshit.

Maybe somewhere, deep down, I know he'd sniff it out. Because I didn't sign up to "be honest in Victoria" like Hailey and Phoebe did.

"And I don't come from money like you," I add. "Some of us had to build what we have."

Jake doesn't take this as an insult. He just nods like he gets it. *Interesting*.

We're both quiet for a second.

And then he asks, "Your ex-wife didn't get anything in the divorce?"

"That's what prenups are for." I hesitate to deepen the lie. To imply she's the kind of girl you'd make sure to file a prenup with before marrying. It turns my stomach.

Jake might not be the kind of person who'd chuckle and grin and say, *I get that, man*.

He might not get it.

Just like I don't.

There isn't a type of woman who's "made" for a prenup, but I feed off the type of men who believe there is. And I sure as hell don't want to put Phoebe down, so I keep that thought to myself.

"That's what prenups are for?" Jake repeats with heat. "So you took everything and left her nothing?" He says it like I'm a piece of shit.

"She took the car."

Jake glares.

"It was a *Porsche*." I purposefully use the incorrect pronunciation to put us on better footing. It's the common pronunciation. *Common ground*.

"Por-*shuh*," he corrects.

I blink. "Por-*shuh*," I repeat how he says it, trying not to roll my eyes.

He's already rolling his.

God, this guy might be *my* worst nightmare.

He looks me over again. "Now I really don't feel bad about kicking you out by Tuesday."

"I'm still friends with my ex," I remind him. "I'm not some

abusive fuckhole, and you're not saving the day by housing her and my sister."

He stares at me like he's Luke fucking Skywalker, and I'm Darth Vader. *I do have dad problems.* I blame Nova for the comic book references circling my head.

Fuck him.

Fuck Jake.

I'm about to self-eject from this conversation, but Jake beats me to it. "You have money to go somewhere, make sure it's not my loft." He leaves the locker room, irritation springing off him like a musky cologne.

I exhale a heavy breath, and my phone buzzes again. This time with a call. I check caller ID, then I let it ring out before slipping into the bathroom.

It's a single stall.

Private.

I scan for cameras.

None.

I'm quick to call back.

He answers on the second ring.

"Nova," I greet.

"Why isn't Phoebe answering our calls?" He's whispering.

"Hi to you, too."

"I'm not bullshitting today, Rocky."

I knew this was coming. With my back to the mirror, I lean on the sink, and I scratch an old scar at my neck. "She's done with clip joints."

A long pause. "Why didn't she just say that?"

The truth is, Phoebe would've done anything to ensure Oliver wouldn't end up in her role during clip joints. She'd do the same thing for Hailey and Trevor and even *Nova*, if given the chance. Maybe partly because she believes that's all she's good for.

"She's embarrassed," I lie.

"I'll talk to your dad—"

"And say what?" I step away from the sink.

"I'll think of something."

I tense. "Don't *Dean Winchester* this."

He mutters something that sounds like *fuck you.* "You know I hate when you call me that."

"You're named after a comic book character who flies in space with a dorky gold helmet, and you have a problem being called the guy on *Supernatural* who goes to Hell in exchange for his brother's life?"

"Nova is a part of an intergalactic police force with hundreds of comics—you call me *Winchester* not because you think Dean is cool but because you think Dean kisses his dad's ass and doesn't protect his brother in the right way."

I exhale again.

He's not wrong.

I lift my brows. "Dean is the cool one, though. I could call you *Sam*."

Nova bypasses that comment and says, "If I was up your dad's ass right now, I wouldn't be whispering in a fucking coat closet. I would've told him who I've been calling when he asked. I would've *lied* and said Phoebe is on her way, even though I have no goddamn clue where my sister is."

Connecticut.

I want to be on the same page as Nova. I could even use his help. I trust him more than I'll ever trust our parents.

Turning around, I face the mirror and rake a hand through my hair. "She's safe."

"Is this just about the clip joint?"

I pause. "Phoebe should tell you herself."

"Clearly she doesn't want to." His hurt constricts his voice. "So give me something. Is she coming back?"

"Probably not anytime soon."

"Not before the job starts?"

"Doubtful." I take another beat. "She might not come back at all. She's taking a break. Her and Hailey."

"A break?" His worry cascades over the line. "Is this because of Carlsbad?" He was in the car with me that night. He knows something happened, and like me, he's in the dark.

"I think so."

"But you don't know?" He's on edge.

"It hasn't been confirmed. Look, I'd tell you and Oliver to come out here, but you're going to need to cover for the girls. Don't let our parents know where they are."

"You never gave me a location."

"Do you need one?"

"If Oliver and I can get out there after the job, yeah, I do."

I shouldn't.

Should I?

I want us all together. It might be the fucking death of us. "Victoria, Connecticut. And, hey, I'm being serious, Winchester. Don't tell them where we are. If you come out here, it better be without a tail—or I'll never call you *Nova* again," I whisper with heat.

"Understood. I'll cover for the girls. Any suggestions?"

I stare up at the ceiling. "Tell the godmothers the girls are caught up in another job in Indiana. It started as Phoebe being a catfish online. I swung around to help. We'll be late to the clip joint."

"What happens when it starts and you're all not here?"

"Tell them we're held up, and I'm only communicating with you. It's easier."

"Got it." I hear scribbling.

For fuck's sake. "Are you actually taking notes?"

"No one will see it. It's in a journal."

"If you think my dad doesn't go through your diary, you need to have a new four-letter name. Starting with *F*. Ending with *L*."

"*Fool*? Thought that one was your middle name."

"No, that's *fuck you*."

"That one belongs to my sister."

I almost smile.

"Yeah" is all I say.

"The journal won't leave my pocket, Rocky. You have nothing to worry about. Just . . . fucking trust me." He lowers his voice again, and I wonder if he hears people outside the closet.

"You're not the one I don't trust," I mutter, and I'm not sure if he hears me. I don't care if he does or doesn't. I appreciate that he's helping keep Phoebe and Hailey safe in Connecticut, but if any of this leaks to our parents, they could so easily manipulate him and I doubt he'd see it.

"I have to go," Nova whispers.

When we hang up, I stare at the phone, my muscles coiled in taut bands. Why am I trying to help Hailey and Phoebe succeed here?

It's not so they can live without deception. I still don't believe in that.

But there has never been a point where it felt possible to truly ditch our parents. Let alone leave them in the dark across the country. Hailey and Phoebe have done it, and with Nova's help, maybe this will actually work for longer than a couple weeks.

I feel inflated with an optimism more suited for my sister. But still, this might be the way out from *them*.

Our parents.

I've wanted to knock over the queens and king since I was a teenager. Since I felt the insidious grip they have on me.

It's seemed too impossible to escape out from under them.

It might still be. Because if they find out where we are, they're going to see what I see when I look around Victoria.

The perfect marks.

Eleven

Phoebe

Three hours into my shift and Chelsea has released me alone in the wild. Mostly because the widowers have grown an interest in me—or rather my assets.

"It's what we call Mr. Burke, Mr. Ortiz, and Mr. Cunningham," Chelsea told me after she referred to three well-groomed, middle-aged men as "the widowers." They've been huddled near the main dining's stately fireplace, drinks in hand and the latest tech gadgets on their wrists.

I caught Mr. Burke staring at my ass after I replenished his liquor, and Chelsea slipped me a sympathetic look. "You're new, and they like shiny new things. Once another girl comes in, it'll pass."

Yeah, it'll pass on to her. Like some sort of new-girl parasite.

I'd rather just take one for the team, I guess. Let the parasite die with me. So when Chelsea tells me they've requested me as their server, I'm not as disgruntled as maybe I should be. It's not like there's a perk to serving Lusty Eyes over there.

They can't tip me.

And no tips mean no extra cash for being ogled like a rare prime rib. The attention might feel better if I was suntanning on the bow of a fifty-foot yacht while sipping a strawberry daiquiri, not waiting hand and foot on the rich elite.

Hailey is busy taking drink orders from a cluster of older ladies, all in pickleball skirts and visors. Chelsea has been hovering over her like a momma bird worried about the weakest baby in the nest, but Hails is holding her own.

"Where are you from, sweetheart?" Mr. Burke asks me before I can make a quick escape.

"Nowhere really," I answer vaguely with a sheepish smile. "I moved around a lot growing up. Can I get you anything else, Mr. Ortiz?"

"A new business partner," he jokes with a chuckle.

We all laugh.

So funny. What a comedian. I smile through my grimace. "I wish I could help you there. I don't have a mind for business."

"That's too bad."

Mr. Burke downs his liquor in one swallow. "I'll take another Cognac." He switched from bourbon to Cognac thirty minutes ago.

I take his empty glass. "Delamain again? Or would you like to try something better?"

"Better?" He laughs, his brows slowly elevating in intrigue. "You know your Cognacs, Phoebe?"

"I love a smooth Cognac."

"What do you have in mind?"

"Rémy Martin XO. It's not as sweet as what you've been drinking, but you might enjoy the flavor. It's nutty." The word rolls off my tongue like a red-hot suggestion, and the smarmy smile he produces makes my skin crawl.

Ugh, I hate myself for somewhat flirting with Mr. Lusty Eyes, and for what? I'm Miss Zero Tips McFool.

"That, then." He stares right at my boobs, not even hiding anymore. "Let's try it." Now back to my eyes.

"I'll be a minute." I turn to leave.

"I'll be here."

I'm sure you will be. As I walk far away from the widowers, an uneasiness tosses my stomach. Not from being ogled. Not from me subconsciously flirting.

But because I *lied* to him.

For one, I can't stand Cognac, and I didn't recommend him another brand because I thought he'd enjoy it more. I just sold him one of the highest-priced Cognacs in the club's stock. Just to empty his wallet. At least, from what I've seen so far, it's one of the most expensive liquors. (I didn't take a thorough inventory of every bottle.)

Those are just white lies, though.

It's not like this was a pig in a poke.

Avoiding the widowers, I check on other guests for a few minutes. Refilling waters and asking if they'd like anything else. It's not so bad. Some tables are fun to visit. Two posh, gorgeous women, who are newly married, smell like Chanel and lilies, and they give me an insider tip.

"You have to go to Victoria Arts Cinema." Jasmine hangs on to my wrist with earnestness; a beautiful sapphire bracelet sparkles on her dark brown skin. "You'll *love* the classics."

"They just played *Silence of the Lambs* last week," her wife, Traci, says. "Isn't *The Shining* all next month, Jas?"

"Oh, it is!"

I might've mentioned that I'm a horror movie nut. I smile, a genuine one this time. "Maybe I will like it here."

"This town has its downsides, trust me," Jasmine says, letting go of my wrist. "But there is good in Victoria."

I'm not good.

My smile teeters. "I should let you two get back to it. Anything else in the meantime?" I wish they'd give me a laundry list of drinks, but they're easy and let me go without any new requests.

Maybe I really can do this.

The newfound confidence lifts me as I slip behind the mahogany bar and fill a pitcher of water.

"Please tell me you haven't been giving them that water." Katherine's brittle tone stiffens me, and her horrified face comes into view.

Shit . . .

I frown. "It's purified." There's a purifier *on* the faucet.

"Fiji water only," she whispers under her breath, careful not to cause a scene, but luckily, the bar is situated farther away from the guests. "Chelsea should have told you this. Did she tell you?" Katherine is already whipping her head left and right, searching for Chelsea like a predator seeking its next meal.

I see Chelsea first. She's dealing with a crotchety woman who keeps sending back her coffee. *Too weak. Too hot. Not the right milk.* I've heard it all in passing.

Katherine catches Chelsea's attention, and while she beelines for us, I say quickly, "She did tell me."

"She did?"

No.

"Yeah, I just must've forgotten. Sorry."

Katherine glares at me like I'm a complete idiot. And I stifle the glower I'd love to send in return. It dies inside my burning lungs as I breathe.

"Tell her what?" Chelsea asks our boss, coming in late to the conversation.

"Fiji water stuff," I mention. "I forgot you already told me."

Chelsea's lips part, and her fearful side-glance to Katherine is thankfully only noticed by me. I try to enlarge my eyes to tell her not to say the truth.

Lies can be good.

Lies can be helpful.

Right?

"You are *exceedingly* slow," Katherine says to me.

Well, fuck you, too.

I drop my head like a battered employee and stare at my boots.

"She's learning," Chelsea interjects hastily. "I promise she has what it takes, Katherine. Just give her a week."

Katherine purses her lips, taking the longest second to ponder my fate. She wants me roasting over a bonfire, and it is slightly uncomfortable knowing Katherine could eat me for dinner like a cooked hog.

Being on the bottom of the food chain sucks. People like Katherine thrive off making others feel inferior and small. And that sort of power is gross to me. It deserves *some* push-back or a big ugly consequence. Like being swindled out of a grand or two.

But no, I will never mention this to Rocky. I don't need to hear him say, *Told you so*, like a kindergartener. Over my dead and charred body.

I'm quiet behind the mahogany bar. Submissive. Shrinking into myself, and Katherine seems satisfied enough.

Finally, she opens the fridge beneath the bar, revealing the middle shelves filled to the brim with Fiji bottles. "Do better," she snaps at me.

I just nod.

With one last glare, she struts away.

"So no pitcher?" I ask Chelsea.

"I'm *so* sorry," she apologizes in a whisper.

"It's fine. I probably would've forgotten even if you told me." *I wouldn't have.* But I don't want her to feel worse.

She's already clutching her chest like her heart skipped several beats back there. "Thank you for covering for me with Katherine. She can be such a B-I-T-C-H." She hands me water bottles out of the fridge.

"Is there a no-cursing policy, too? Because I'm going to fuck that rule in the asshole." It's a joke, but Chelsea lets out a wheezy laugh.

My face falls.

Okay, she's anti-cursing.

"I just . . . don't really like it, is all. It sounds . . ." She crinkles her nose.

"Right . . ." *Unladylike.* "I have brothers, so . . . habit."

Oliver doesn't even swear that much. It's dumb that I'm blaming this on my brothers. It's also dumb that Nova barely gets told to stop cursing like a drunken sailor, and yet, when I say *fuck* there might as well be fireworks and air horns alerting the world that PHOEBE GRAVES CURSED!

Truth about my adolescent-turned-adulthood foulmouthed behavior: Nova, Rocky, and I all rubbed off on each other.

Really, that's what I like to believe. Some truths aren't truths at all, but just what we let ourselves believe is real.

Chelsea motions to the water bottles in my clutch. "You fill the pitcher with the Fiji. The water purifier is used to wash produce."

Good to know. I prepare Mr. Burke's Cognac and then finish refilling the pitcher with only the *best* Fiji water.

"I need you to take table 6," Chelsea says quietly.

"Okay," I agree without looking up.

Chelsea zips away as the old lady flags her down for more coffee. I already know table 6 is in the sunroom. Details like that are easy to remember.

Cognac and pitcher on my tray, I push through a set of French doors and into a bright, marbled sunroom with chess sets, rattan couches, and bistro seating for couples. The air smells like lemongrass and honeysuckle.

When I see who's seated at table 6, my feet glue to the floor.

Twelve

Phoebe

Rocky . . . with a girl.

The iron bistro table is intimate and tiny. Her long legs are crossed, ankle brushing against Rocky's knee. Her yellow floral sundress is provocative yet classy, and I'd think it's cute if I didn't have this involuntary desire to burn it.

Great.

I work my jaw so I'm not scowling. *You knew he'd be at the club today.* Keeping each other in the loop is generally how we all operate so that no one trips up. But I don't like that he's positioning himself in a role that requires more lies. And why is he sitting with a beautiful girl? Sure, I haven't seen her face yet, but from the back, she's already a twelve out of ten.

I capsule my feelings as I approach the table.

The pretty girl is reading over a menu, her back facing me, and Rocky easily shifts his gray eyes to mine.

"Phoebe," he greets. "How's your first day going?"

Before the girl can peer over her shoulder, I come directly to their table like the amazing, dutiful server I am.

She lowers the menu to study me. "Wait, you know *her*?"

He didn't even mention me to this girl? It would've been so easy for him to just say: oh hey, so I have this ex-wife that's working at the country club.

Nothing, though. I didn't even get a freaking honorable mention. It shouldn't hurt.

It doesn't hurt.

It doesn't.

Is it because I'm the pleb here? The service.

My stomach twists, and I answer her first. "I've never seen his ugly face before."

Rocky's eyes darken and nearly roll, but he hasn't shifted off my gaze. Not once. "She's my ex-wife."

The girl tries to be polite and stifle a cringe, but I can read the muscles in her face. "Was it recent?" she asks him and me.

Rocky is quick to answer, like maybe he's worried I'll dig us further into a hole. "Not really," he says. "But we've remained friendly since she's my little sister's best friend."

I'm not sure why that unnerves me. That that's all I am to him. Hailey's best friend.

He's not on a job, so there's nothing to ruin here.

Rocky sits straighter from his relaxed position. "Val, this is Phoebe," he introduces us more formally.

Val extends her hand to me. "Valentina de la Vega."

I shake and balance the tray with one hand. "Nice to meet you, Valentina." And when I drop her hand, I blurt out, "He's a jerk—just FYI in case this is a date situation."

Valentina is caught off guard. "It's . . . it's not." She lifts the menu to hide a flash of discomfort or awkwardness. *I've* made this awkward, if that wasn't clear.

The heat of Rocky's glare intensifies on me. I genuinely just pissed him off. Maybe I should add a third *D* to Drama and Danger.

Destruction.

"Water?" I ask them.

"Can you excuse me, Val?" Rocky asks her. He's already pushing out of his chair, the iron scraping against marble.

"Yeah, no problem."

She seems nice.

Sweet, even.

She's the kind of girl I'd never pull a con on. Or I'd try not to. It's not always up to me who the mark is.

Rocky stands up and hisses in my ear. "Follow me."

I do as I'm told, hating that I'll take orders from him. But there's something exhilarating about the fact that I'm drawing his attention away from Valentina.

Rocky leads me through the French doors. Back in the main dining room, we're abruptly stopped by Mr. Burke.

"Phoebe." He grins. "I've been looking forward to that Cognac." His desire drips down me with zero subtlety.

Rocky has gone rigid. While he's assessing *my* situation, I do what any good server would do and smile brightly. "I have it right here, Mr. Burke."

I'm about to pick up the Cognac.

"Come back over, will you? I want you to have a taste, too." He turns to lead me.

"Oh, I couldn't—"

"The club won't mind. Trust me." He's about to catch my hand, but Rocky steps into *my* situation like a territorial grizzly.

"She's actually preoccupied at the moment." The dangerous look crossing his face is enough to cause Mr. Burke to tilt his head and become flustered.

"And you are?" he questions.

"Grey Thornhall." His gaze only darkens. "Her husband."

"Ex-husband," I cut in. And make no mistake, Rocky purposefully made me clarify this, so the widower knows where my *ex* stands.

Rocky keeps staring Mr. Burke down. "And you are?"

"Weston Burke." They don't shake. Instead, Mr. Burke takes the Cognac off the tray I'm holding. "Your ex-wife was telling me about the best Cognacs. She loves a smooth one." His attention flits to me. "Nutty, didn't you say this was, Phoebe?" The corner of his lip rises as if we share a dirty secret.

He's trying to embarrass Rocky.

"Notes of almonds," I lie. I have no clue what nut it tastes like.

Rocky could unspool the lie I've woven. He knows my disgust toward Cognacs, but he doesn't insult me or criticize me. It'd open a door for Mr. Burke to think less of me and possibly do the same.

Instead, he rests a protective hand on the small of my back.

Mr. Burke notices, then eyes Rocky more keenly while sipping the Cognac. "You're new here, Grey?"

"Visiting," Rocky says curtly. "At the moment." He appraises the ceiling and walls with a short glance. "Who knows? Maybe I'll make this place my home like Phoebe has."

"Well, advice from someone who has been here for *four* generations," Mr. Burke says, lifting his glass toward his lips. "You don't fuck with another man's Cognac."

Is he seriously trying to correlate me with his stupid liquor? I'm biting my tongue so hard to keep from speaking. I feel myself instinctively tucking closer to Rocky.

"Wise words," Rocky slingshots back.

Instead of waiting out the cockfight, I spin around Rocky.

"Excuse me," I say to them. Katherine could be hawk-eyeing me from across the dining room for all I know. And getting canned on day one is not the goal here.

I veer toward the bar to continue my actual job, but Rocky is hot on my heels. I'm about to tell him off until I detect the raw urgency in his eyes.

Fine.

Setting the tray on the bar, I follow him out of the dining room, through the rotunda. Down another hall, and we bypass the state-of-the-art gym with more Fiji water at guests' disposal, I'm sure, and suddenly, Rocky has found a nice, totally cute *storage closet*.

Tennis balls, baskets of rackets, croquet sets, and a volleyball net are surprisingly crammed in disorder on shelves and the floor.

He shuts the door behind us, and as soon as he faces me, he whisper-sneers, "What the fuck is wrong with you?"

"What the fuck is wrong with *you*?" I sneer back. "This is my *job*. Mr. Burke could get me fired for what you pulled back there."

"He won't."

"You don't know that for sure, Rocky," I nearly shout, but I try my best to keep whispering.

"Firing you does nothing to hurt me, and that rich prick would rather *use you* to fuck me over. I made the enemy."

I flame. "And I'm just the pawn between you two? Just the *thing* you can tug back and forth with no say?"

"You think I wanted to piss all over you like you're a fucking fire hydrant?"

I breathe hotly, a strange hurt crossing over me. I shouldn't be upset that Rocky is saying he hates possessing me. I should want to maintain my own agency. I'm not a *thing*. But still, I wish he would answer with, *I'm yours as much as you're mine.*

Rocky reads me quickly.

I stiffen and thread my arms defiantly.

"You liked it?" he questions.

My cheeks burn, and I don't deny it. "There was no reason for you to mark your territory. I was *fine.*"

He steps forward. "There was no reason for you to piss all over me in front of Valentina," he retorts, like it's the same.

Is it?

Were we both just claiming each other?

Tension stretches taut the closer Rocky stands. He grips the shelf beside my head, and the musky scent of his cologne is familiar and dizzying.

I refuse to step back. Our gazes bolt together with smoldering heat, and very quietly, I say, "I didn't enjoy pissing on you either."

He doesn't ask why I did.

It's obvious enough that jealousy played a factor.

Rocky slips a scathing glare over his shoulder. At the door. And I have to assume that was reserved for Mr. Burke. Especially as he says, "Those men aren't changing, Phoebe. You could start your new life anywhere, but you chose the upper echelons of society with misogyny ingrained in its ether. How Mr. Burke spoke to you is what these bastards do."

"And what'd you do?" I shove back, wounded. "I loved the part where you told him to *fuck off* and go eat shit for treating me like a naked mannequin."

Hurt flashes through his eyes. "I'm playing with the deck of cards on their table."

True meaning: *He has to be a rich prick, too.* "That's bullshit," I say. "You're not here to *con* anyone, Rocky. You don't need to be one of them!" I step closer at the same time that his hand encases my mouth to catch my near shout.

My body is welded up against Rocky's muscled chest, and my pulse is pounding in my veins, his heat swathing me in familiarity and comfort.

His chest rises and falls with heavy breaths against me. Like I'm chasing him around the tiny storage closet.

He pushes forward until I have no option but to shuffle back. My spine crashes into the shelves. Our latched eyes scream untouched notes of padlocked desire, and the tempo accelerates between us—his hand sheathing my cheekbone, my nails clawing at his back.

Rocky grips my hair, his forehead bowing toward mine. Heat surges, and a whimper scratches my throat. *Holy shit*.

The noise in his throat is husky, deeper with coarser frustrations and cravings. *"Phoebe."*

My name is a warning. A *we can't*.

Neither of us moves away. He's pressed to me, his thick hardness bearing against me. My pussy throbs like a tortured drumbeat, aching for the feeling of him inside me. Desire swirls like the hottest perfume, and yet, there's the greatest *pull back* to this push forward. An invisible barrier prevents Rocky from completely reaching me.

He eyes my lips like maybe he wishes he could kiss me.

I stare at his lips, wondering if he ever will. *We agreed we never would.* But I can't deny how good his body feels against mine. This shouldn't feel like home. This shouldn't feel right.

We know what we are together.

My mom's greatest dream. Which is my worst nightmare.

It scares me. I flinch against him.

"Phoebe?" He releases his clutch on me and inches back. The distance is uncomfortable and stinging.

I avoid his gaze. "That was . . ."

"Appalling?" he offers roughly, a huskiness in this throat that he clears with a deep guttural sound. It's sexy, honestly. His arousal.

"The worst," I say dryly and risk a glance.

He's scraping a rough hand through his perfectly disheveled hair, his face twisting in thought. "How can I walk in there and be honest, Phebs?" He gestures to the door. "You think anyone will respect me if I tell them what I'm really *honest-to-God* thinking? I've already imagined setting this place on fucking fire. You think that'll help you?"

No.

I can picture the dark depths of Rocky's bitterness and contempt for most people. It's not a recipe for a welcoming cocktail. It's poisonous. Worthy of being exiled from the town.

And how he responded to Mr. Burke is what he knows how to do. He's used to being another apex predator.

It'd be more difficult to change.

Hell, it's hard for me. I stayed quiet while Rocky tried to protect me. It's what we usually do in these situations. So I shouldn't be shocked that we naturally fell into the roles again.

"I don't think it would help me in the long run, no," I whisper more softly. "And I get you're looking at the big picture here, which I appreciate." It's strange that he's trying to preserve the longevity of my stay in this town instead of imploding it. "I just wish I could've told Mr. Burke to fuck off without risking my job." I shrug. "And I wish you could've done that for me in the meantime, too."

Rocky contemplates this for a tense beat, a pain in his eyes that he tries to shift away from me. After another rough hand through his hair, he tells me, "I talked to your brother."

My heart lifts. "Which one?"

"Nova. I let him in on your plan here."

Surprise jumps my brows. "Everything?"

"Vaguely, yeah. If you want to reach out to them, it should be safe. They know to keep this quiet from our parents."

Relief washes over me. I didn't have to be the one to risk jeopardizing Hailey's plan. "Thanks, Rocky." I see the glint of the time on his watch face. "Shit. I need to get back to work." We've been in the storage closet for fifteen minutes. "I really am trying to keep this job."

"Obviously." He sounds unenthused.

I try to fix my limp ponytail, and I panic at the lack of mirror. "Is it straight?" I ask Rocky. "Are there messy pieces?"

"Come here." He motions to me with two fingers.

I hate him for making me visualize those fingers inside me. "You come here."

He rolls his eyes, then rounds my body. His chest brushes against my back, and his height is a shield protecting every single inch of me.

"Don't bite my hand off," he says roughly.

"I'll try not to."

Rocky unties the pony and collects my deep blue hair in one hand. With the other, he smooths the baby hairs away from my forehead. I shut my eyes and sink into the melodic motion of his hand sliding against me. His fingers slip around my ear, and the sensation zips a tingle down my arms.

I sense him tying the pony once and then twice. Until it's tight and a little higher than the middle of my skull.

"And there you go," he says, his voice a husky gruffness. "The best ponytail of your life."

"Let's not go that far." I spin back around. "It's average."

His smile peeks, a shadow of one while he examines more

of my face than my hair. "It was above average before I was here."

My lips part at the unusual compliment. "Thanks?"

Rocky forces a wry smile. "You're late."

"Oh shit." I bolt for the door and power walk down the hall. If Katherine noticed my absence, she doesn't let on when I return to the dining room. The widowers have left, and Chelsea sends me to the pool for snack service.

Everything is falling into place.

I peek over my shoulder, expecting to see Rocky watching over me. Less like a guardian angel. More like a two-horned demon.

Hailey passes me with a tray of mojitos.

"Hey, Hails." I catch up to her side and keep her brisk pace. "Did you see your brother?"

"Yeah. He just left the club. Why, do you need something?" She halts midway to the sunbathing guests.

I try to ignore my disappointment. "Uh, no. Just curious how long he'd spy."

"Longer than I thought," she admits. "Hey, maybe we should ask him to pick up Italian for dinner?"

Can't escape Rocky. It's always been a comforting idea, hasn't it? "Yeah, go ahead."

Thirteen

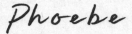

Phoebe

FOUR YEARS AGO
THE BADGER GAME
Princeton, New Jersey

I hate secret societies. They're dramatic for no reason. Highly pretentious. The whole cloak-and-dagger bit would be cool on Halloween, but not on an average day in a musty old basement of an Ivy League. That's what crossed my mind last month when my mom told me I'd be joining a secret society at Princeton.

I *begged* her to let me be recruited into a sorority. I could go through rush, pledge, and make "fake" everlasting friends. "Girls are just as loaded in Kappa Phi Delta, *please*," I pleaded, like the rest of my life was at stake, even if I knew the job would only last a semester.

While applying a sheen of pink lipstick, she slipped me one of her *this has already been decided* looks and then shook her head. "Who's going to be your second in a sorority? Rocky can't do that job with you."

Rocky. Rocky. *Rocky*.

It was always about Rocky. I could feel her silent push of him toward me and me toward him. And she wasn't wrong— I loved doing jobs with Rocky. I just hated that she saw how much I loved having him around.

"He could start dating a friend that I make," I said, forcing down a cringe at the suggestion. "It'd put us in the same social circle."

"No—"

"I could bump into him—"

"No." She capped her lipstick. "You focus on what you're good at, bug. Okay? Leave the logistics and placing the roles to Addison and me. We've pored over these plans for weeks and thought of every scenario, I know what'll work and what won't."

I wasn't ready to let go. "What about Hailey? She could be in the sorority with—"

"Phoebe, please." Her eyes sank consolingly onto me. "You need to do this *with* Rocky. You both work well together. What do I always say?"

I took a sharp breath. "Stick to the plan."

She smiled. "Sweet spider." She brushed her fingers through my hair like I was still a child, and for some reason, her sugary nature melted the scowl that began to form. The soft parts of my mom were warm and inviting. Maybe they were even reminders of how much she loves me and cares. "We're only doing what's best for you, you know that?"

I nodded.

"You're going to college." She smiled, like it's the biggest adventure. "It'll be fun. Just give it a chance?"

I wanted to. Not just for myself, but a little bit for her. I still hated the idea that I could be the screwup. The one to foil Addison and Elizabeth's painstakingly constructed plans.

That wouldn't be me.

And the scary part—college has been fun. The past three months, I've enjoyed the Ivy League experience with Hailey, Rocky, and my brothers. I'm twenty, and in another life, maybe I'd be here for real. But there's no mistake in my role.

Everything here has been devised. Each lecture I sit in has been expertly selected by Hailey. She made sure I'm in all the classes with our marks. Add in some charisma and "chance" encounters, and it only took a few weeks for Rocky and me to be selected for initiation into the Firefly Club.

But the plan my mom wants me to stick to—it hasn't wavered, up until tonight.

"What do you mean this is it?" I whisper to Nova. Why is he walking so fast? I rush to reach his side and power walk just to keep up with his strong gait.

Oliver is more lackadaisical behind me. With his easy stroll, black preppy peacoat, and light-brown stylish hair, he looks like he's in a Burberry ad and not in a house on fire.

"Mom called and says it needs to happen tonight," Nova whispers back. "We've gotta be out of New Jersey by tomorrow morning."

What? "That's . . . insanity."

This changes the con we've already set up, but Nova just points to the dorm room at the end of the hall. "That's Rocky's room?" He has to ask since he hasn't been in this dormitory before.

In fact, I haven't seen Nova face-to-face in three whole months. We weren't supposed to cross paths until after winter break. Sometime in January. It's still December, and the unspooling threads of this tapestry we've carefully woven are putting me on edge.

"Yeah, it's his dorm," I tell my brother.

Once we approach the door, I hear an audible, high-pitched sound of pleasure. "OhmyGod, OhmyGod, ahhh!"

I freeze, all thoughts exploding out of my brain.

"*Right there*. Oh my . . . *fuck*. YES!"

Nova pounds a hard, angry fist on the door. "I can't fucking believe this."

I can believe it. Rocky hasn't been, and will never be, a Virgin Mary. And at college, Rocky—sorry, I mean *Cole Miller*—has quickly earned a reputation in our coed dorm hall for being a sex god.

Which is the nice way of calling him a player and a whore.

What isn't nice are the girls on my hall giggling about the guys I've brought over. One of them wrote *slut* on my door's whiteboard. Hailey has had five times more sex than me, but yet I'm called the slut?

If it's not about quantity of sex, then what makes me sluttier than anyone else? I just want answers to these human questions—why people look at me and see someone worthy to sleep with and not someone worthy to be with. That's all.

Nova's knock goes unanswered and largely ignored.

Rocky must only be listening to his cock.

With the *thump, thump, thump* of a headboard against the wall, this is sounding more like raunchy sex, and power-drilling my eardrums would feel better than listening to him rock another girl's world.

"I can call?" Oliver waves his phone behind me. He's already phoning Rocky, but evil images invade my head now. Of destroying Rocky's chance at finishing.

"I vote we just walk in," I tell them. "Is it locked?"

Oliver must hear the strain in my voice because he passes his phone to Nova over my head, just so he frees his hands to cover my ears.

The moaning and heavy grunts are muffled against Oliver's palms, but my stomach won't unknot. "I'm fine," I mutter and reach for the knob.

Nova beats me to it, and surprisingly, it's unlocked. He barrels into the dorm to expletives and shrieks. Within a solid second, the brunette girl darts out of the room with her dress inside out, and as a muddled concoction of guilt and jealousy stirs inside of me, I try not to make eye contact with Heather.

Yeah, I recognize her deep blue doe eyes and thimble nose. She lives in the dorm room beside mine, and she knows me as Rocky's *sister*.

She side-eyes me on her way out.

Cool.

While Oliver slips into the room to join the guys, I loiter in the hall with crossed arms and a boatload of nerves over this mess.

"Was that necessary?" Rocky growls, and I peer through the cracked door. Catching a glimpse of Rocky's bare ass, I watch him hold his boxer briefs to his crotch. The trail of hair below his belly button teases my gaze toward his dick, and I wonder when Rocky became a man.

It wasn't a flick of a switch. God didn't suddenly anoint him with manhood one day and sprout hair on his chest. The planes of his body have been carved and chiseled with muscle for years, and I've felt those boyish arms at eleven and twelve become firmer and fiercer at thirteen, fourteen, seventeen, twenty-one as they've wrapped around me.

"We don't have fucking time to waste," Nova tells him.

"*You* shouldn't be here," Rocky sneers in a whisper. "You're early."

"It's been moved to tonight."

Rocky fumes in place, stunned to silence until he snaps,

"You're kidding me? It's too *soon*. We haven't laid the proper groundwork."

"My mom had to tie things up early with her fiancé."

"Ex-fiancé," Oliver clarifies.

"We need to leave tomorrow," Nova finishes.

It's about Mom's safety—why this is being rushed.

Rocky lets out an incensed laugh. "So Elizabeth screws up with her rich boy toy and puts us at risk—?"

"Hey." Nova glares. "She didn't have a fucking choice."

"I'm trying to protect *us*," Rocky nearly shouts. "Shit, do you even know how much harder this is going to—?"

"Your mom and my mom think we're ready," Nova cuts him off.

"They're not fucking *here*," Rocky refutes with a deep-seated, almost guttural plea to his voice.

I slide into the dorm room quietly and shut the door, but my presence might as well be a Formula 1 crash. Metal ripping through the air. Fire and explosion setting flame to the tension.

With one hand and his balled-up underwear still covering his cock, Rocky glares at me and then points at the doorway I just came through. "You can walk your ass right out of this room if you're just going to blindly take your brother's side."

Oliver makes a noise that's a cross between a laugh and a snort. "I thought we were all on the same side?" He bends a hip against the window, relaxed inside this four-car pileup.

Nova and Rocky ignore him, their gazes fixed to me, waiting for my response. Nova's gaze weighs heavier on me, practically telling me—*you're my sister*. It's hard to just brush that aside, but I'd like more facts about how this is supposed to play out.

"Maybe tell me what their new plan is for tonight," I say to Nova. "Then I can decide which one of you is being an asshole."

"Both," Oliver chimes in.

Nova shoots him a disapproving, brotherly look. "No one asked you."

"No one ever does," Oliver says. "Middle-child syndrome and all." He lights a cigarette casually and sticks his hand out of the cracked window.

Rocky drops his voice. "What'd they say?" He's asking Nova, too.

"It's our responsibility to figure out how to wrap it up. We're to contact Everett if we still need a fifth man."

I try to let go of the uneasiness. As we've gotten older, they have given us more responsibilities and jobs of our own. Being treated like an adult with more decision-making feels good. Maybe after rejecting my idea of pledging to a sorority, this is my mom's way of saying, *I trust you, bug. You're capable and ready.*

But is that just a façade? Is that what they want us to believe? Rocky's faith in our parents has waned over the years. Maybe if I was the child of Addison and Everett, I'd start doubting, too. But my mother has a gentleness and love for me that has never felt fabricated, and I refuse to let Rocky's own issues with his parents shade my view of mine.

Rocky angrily steps into his boxer briefs. His back facing me, he pulls a collegiate tee over his head. "They're not here," he says with heat. "If this blows back, we're all done. *Us.* Not them. You all know what happens if we get caught." A heaviness weighs the room, and I'm sure we're all picturing prison bars. Rocky adds, "We should be deciding when it's time to pull the rope." *Pull the rope.* It's what we call it when we're ready to persuade the mark after the principal has gained their confidence. Roped them in.

For this job, we're supposed to pull the rope after an intense bout of hazing.

The Original Plan: Rocky and I are initiated in round 1. Oliver is initiated in round 2. Rocky, already a member of the society, is set in a power position where he controls the hazing doled out to Oliver.

The Problem: Rocky and I haven't been initiated yet. So no one will be standing beside the president of the Firefly Club, Matthew Wentworth, during this secretive ceremony.

The New (Worse) Plan: The three of us will all be initiated at the same time in round 1, and we'll *all* be hazed by Matthew. In this scenario, we have way less control. It's definitely not ideal.

"They've done this longer than us," Nova counters. "If they think it's time, then it's time, and they understand nuances that we don't—that we *can't*."

"You know, I see your lips moving, Winchester, but all I hear is my dad," Rocky growls. "He feeds you so much bullshit these days and you can't even see it, man."

Nova scowls. "Or maybe you're just blinded by your own oversized ego. You wanna prove *so* badly that you're better than them—"

"Because *we* are!" Rocky shouts. He takes a step closer, and quickly, Oliver slams the window shut as Rocky's voice escalates. He snuffs the cigarette out on the windowsill and shares a silent look with me. We know where this is headed.

Nova glowers. "Don't make this about *us*. This petty bullshit with your dad has always been about *you*. You wanna cry and act like a petulant child with daddy problems. Boo *fucking* hoo."

Something dark flashes across Rocky's eyes, something unreadable. Nova takes a threatening step forward, and this is where I rush in. Oliver darts between them in a snap. Faster than me.

"All right, all right." Oliver pushes their chests. "This stopped being fun, like, ten minutes ago."

"Agreed," I say and instantly regret opening my mouth. Nova and Rocky stare down at me again like I'm the judge about to determine which one caused the murder.

My stomach roils. It's not a fair choice.

I trust Rocky with my life. Christ, I would trust Rocky with my *nine* lives if I were a cat and had extras to lose. Of the four of us in this room, he's the one who can rework the con and salvage what we've done here.

I take a short breath. "Are we really going to walk away with nothing? The past three months will have been a waste, and honestly, Matthew Wentworth is a prick. He sent his buddies *nudes* of his girlfriend."

He even sent them to *Rocky*, who's his new "cool" friend. Partly, Matt has warmed up to Rocky's Cole Miller persona so quickly because Cole paid for Matt's two-grand dinner bill like it was nothing.

Matt realized Cole Miller was loaded and born from an affluent family who owns textile factories. He realized he's a friend worth having in his circle.

I continue, "But maybe you three don't care as much about what he's done."

"I care," Rocky says sharply, hotly.

"*We* care," Nova tells me.

"So why can't we still do this?" I ask Rocky.

Nova scrapes a hand across his tensed jaw a few times. He eyes Rocky, knowing he's the one who can reconstruct this mess.

There'll always be a part of Rocky that seeks to prove he doesn't need our parents. If they say *do this now*, a little voice inside his head might be screaming, *Do it later!* Yet, for all his pushback against the godmothers, Rocky hasn't ever abandoned us to carve his own path.

He's always stuck with his family and mine.

Rocky scratches at the tag of his shirt's collar. Frustrated, he tugs his collegiate tee off, his abs flashing into view, and he rips out the tag. Fitting his arms through his sleeves again, he says, "We'll do it tonight. At the initiation. I'm going to have to bring you in early, Nova. You're switching spots with Oliver."

"Why?" Oliver frowns.

"You do too much," Rocky says with heat. "I need this person to say almost nothing."

Oliver sighs heavily, not excited. "Whatever's best." He points in a circle to all of us. "I'd like this documented that I'm a *team player*, merci beaucoup, mes amis." His French accent rolls off the tongue naturally and sounds authentic.

Nova looks grateful. "Thanks, Ol."

I mentally scratch out Oliver's name and rewrite *Nova*.

"Nova hasn't been selected," I tell Rocky. The two of us were given a wax-sealed envelope a week ago that only detailed the time and place of the initiation. Nothing else. Nova has no invite. "Matthew doesn't even know who he is."

"Just leave that for me. I'll vouch for Nova." He turns to him. "You're Jay Thompson. We'll keep it as J.T., and you"—he slips his dark gaze to Oliver—"keep your phone close. Be in the car with the luggage."

Oliver is now the getaway man.

"How do we do this if you're not doling out the initiation with Matthew?" I ask Rocky.

He wears a haunted expression. "This might get bad." His grim eyes flit to me. "Walk out if it's too much to handle."

"I'll be fine." I glare. *I'm not the weak link.*

His penetrating gaze is unflinching on me.

I hate that I like it. I hate that I don't want him to *ever* look away.

I cross my arms. "What if it's too much for you? Will you walk out?"

"I don't have that fucking luxury, *Abby*." He uses my fake name.

"Then let me help you," I snap back and step toward him, our bodies barely an inch apart. The movement strikes the air with a hot rod. Breath is caged between him and me, and neither of us unfastens our gazes that dive deeper and grip and claw like lifelines to one another. "This isn't all on you, *Cole*. Don't push me out of this because you're afraid of what'll happen. I can take it."

Just barely audible to me, he breathes, "You shouldn't have to take it."

It pools into me, but I don't let it overflow. I hold my ground as brutally as he's seizing his, and I say, "I'm. Fine."

And like he knows I could tell him the same thing—that he shouldn't have to take it, but he will because there is a part of him that enjoys the con, too—Rocky just breaks the standoff. "Let's do this."

"Great," I say tensely, avoiding Oliver's and Nova's intrusive stares. My face roasts knowing they just witnessed the intensity between Rocky and me.

It wouldn't be the first time.

Rocky is stewing in his own thoughts while he puts on pants and grabs a beanie. He covers his black hair that's dyed the same exact shade as mine. "See you tonight, *sis*."

I've been ready for our sibling relationship to die.

And thankfully, it ends tonight.

Fourteen

Phoebe

THE BADGER GAME (CONTINUED)

At this abandoned lot with a boarded-up gas station, I wait with Rocky, Nova, and two other potential initiates: Claire and Kendra. Snow crunches under my feet near the broken gas pumps, and I hug my pink puffer jacket around my body.

Nova pushes the bridge of his horn-rimmed glasses. They're actually prescription since his vision is awful, but with the style of glasses Rocky picked for him and the trench coat, he resembles a buff nerdy TA. Someone of importance, yet meek.

"It's so cold," Claire says with chattering teeth, rubbing her mittens together. I notice how she tries to grab Rocky's attention, but he purposefully ignores her.

He's playing Candy Crush on his phone.

"You want my scarf?" I ask, already taking off the classic taupe Burberry scarf.

"Really?" Her eyes light up.

"Yeah, it's kinda warm for me." I like the bite of the cold. My mind is alert and less at ease, and sometimes it's better to be on edge. I'm not all altruistic. Partly, this also helps me have an ally going into initiation.

"Thank you *so much*." Claire wraps the fabric around her pale neck that's patchy red from the cold.

Kendra slips me a tiny smile, and I send one back. Her fiery red hair cascades out of a purple pom beanie, and her parka seems warm.

Not even five minutes later, a van rolls up to the gas station, exhaust pumping from the pipes. I glance warily to Rocky (aka my fake brother).

He straightens up and slides his phone in a long black peacoat.

No one exits the van.

Shit.

I breathe hard out of my nose, my breath smoking the air.

"What's taking so long?" Claire asks.

They know Nova shouldn't be here. Whoever is in the driver's seat has to be counting five heads when there should only be four.

Taking matters into his own hands, Rocky strides to the passenger door. He knocks on the window. It slides midway down. He speaks for maybe a minute. No more than two. He's being handed a phone, and all I hear is Rocky's end.

"I know. He's cool. Childhood friend." Rocky laughs into the phone. "I know, I know. It is like that, isn't it?" Pause. "Don't go easy, man. Do your worst. I wouldn't want anything less."

Do your worst.

I'm antsy, and I retie my hair into a messy pony.

Once Rocky returns the phone to whoever is in the van, the window ascends, and my fake brother takes a few steps away from the vehicle.

Cloaked in a dark green robe, a person emerges from the passenger side. A hood is shrouding their hair, and a smooth gold mask conceals their face. I notice a firefly broach on the robe and silk cloths in their hand.

"Line up," the masculine voice says. "Turn around."

Yep, melodramatic.

I want to say that I hate every minute of this, but I'm forcing down the urge to full-on beam.

We do as we're told, and the cloaked figure comes behind each of us, tying the cloths around our heads.

I'm blindfolded.

Erotic? The anticipation races my pulse, and the thrill of the mystery and tonight's con is a heady, exhilarating mixture I'm guzzling. Without word, we're whisked into the van and off to the next location.

Once we're all piled out and directed in total darkness, my heeled boots clank on what sounds like cement or marble. The temperature lowers as we descend at least ten stairs. Colder . . . until we reach some type of opening, and a sudden heat bathes my cheeks.

Hands rest on my shoulders, halting me. A second passes, or two. *Scary.* I smile a little. Okay, I can admit that secret societies can be cool in their drama and clandestine spookiness. *The Skulls* might have been panned by critics, but I've always loved that movie. And I'm starting to feel like I'm on a set.

I wonder if my mom knew I'd enjoy this more than a sorority.

"I'm Number One." That smooth bravado belongs to Matthew Wentworth. I recognize his prickish voice already. "The five of you have been granted a gift. Only the brightest and worthiest ever reach this stage, and if you succeed here tonight, you will wield and protect all the secrets of the Firefly Club, as every member has done before you since 1786."

"Seventeen eighty-six," people chant.

I smooth my lips to withhold a grin.

The Firefly Club isn't as secretive as they'd like to believe. I've already done my homework and learned that there are ten active members—two of which were *elated* to spill the beans to me about Matthew and company—so I imagine Number One goes to Number Ten.

"This is your final test. You may remove your blindfolds."

After untying the silk cloth, I scope out the candlelit cellar. *A wine cellar.* Behind the ten robed Firefly members, wine barrels disappear into the dark depths of the cavernous space. The circle of candles they've lit around us flame against the dank walls and crated bottles. Waxy residue drips onto the stone floor, and I notice the other initiates inspecting our new surroundings, too.

Rocky is beside me on my left, hanging at a protective distance that a brother would, and Nova is right next to him like a close childhood friend. On my right, Claire is still shivering, and Kendra keeps to herself on the end.

Number One (aka Matthew *Prick*) is the only Firefly member wearing *red*. The scarlet cloak makes his ashy white neck and hands look pallid in the light. With all their hoods drawn and gold masks on their faces, I can't really distinguish who the others are.

I stifle asking them which one is the unfortunate Number Two.

One thing I know—every Firefly Club initiation is different. It's designed to push boundaries. I'm hoping this is mostly *Fear Factor* style, and they bring out plates of worms for us to eat. But I know it'd be better for the con if it's something worse.

Do your worst.

Rocky has already started provoking him, but I still don't totally understand how this will play out. Because Rocky *needs* to maintain a trusting friendship with Matthew. Even by the very end. He can't feel slighted.

He can't be pissed.

Scarlet-cloaked Matthew parades himself in front of the other members. He walks the short line of initiates. "And so we begin." His blue eyes flash through the holes of his mask, skimming the five of us, but when he lands on me, he lingers with a gleam.

He's going to test Rocky through me. He knows we're brother and sister.

I can already feel this switching into not-so-fun territory.

"All of you," Matthew says, thankfully referring to every initiate and not singling me out yet. "Take off your jackets. Set them behind you."

I shed my pink puffer.

Rocky strips off his black peacoat with a grin. He eyes the space like this is cool shit. There is absolutely no way he's truly entertained by Matthew's display of dominance. It would naturally irk Rocky. But I wonder what he's really thinking, and sometimes I wish I had a front row seat inside his brain during our jobs.

"Shirts and pants next," Matthew decrees.

Claire balks. "Seriously?"

"Do as he says, roach," a green-robed figure pipes in.

Roach? I guess we're cockroaches until we become fireflies.

Rocky avoids eye contact with me. And I sheepishly look away from him while I shed my pink top. Though I can't see Matt's mouth through the mask, his blue eyes are grinning at me.

Fuck you, I want to shout.

With pissed off haste, I start unbuttoning my jeans.

I'm happy that Rocky is blocking my view of Nova and my brother's view of me. Both guys quickly strip down, and I try to squash the desire to peek at Rocky's ass and how the boxer briefs mold his package.

Do not look.

Kendra follows my pace and sheds her long-sleeved shirt.

Claire is gaping at me like this is unbelievable, but I shrug, trying to be encouraging. A pit forms in my stomach, knowing she's sort of caught in the cross fire tonight. *I'm sorry.* This initiation can't be easy, but Rocky was the one supposed to be in the driver's seat as a Firefly member dictating what Oliver does. I was just supposed to advocate for Rocky.

This isn't how we wanted it to be.

Claire more reluctantly pulls off her blouse.

Matthew walks the line of initiates again, but this time, he makes an elaborate show of stopping in front of me.

Rocky is starting to feign confusion.

I narrow a glare on Matthew. His pompous eyes hover over my breasts, pushed up in a lacy white bra that leaves little to the imagination. My matching panties ride high on my hips, and I pretend to be virginal and shy and hide my bare stomach.

Claire takes a tense breath beside me.

And I'm glad she's okay.

At least he's only looking at me.

A tracker is stitched in the lining of my bra, and the only thing I need to ensure is that he doesn't grab my boob. Which I sincerely thought would be unlikely.

Yet, here we are. With this sleazebag pretending to be Mr. Hotshot. The difference between him and us—we don't believe in these delusions.

"Abigail Miller," Matthew says my fake name. "Take off your bra."

"Come on, man," Rocky tells him lightly with raised brows. "That's my sister." A threat lingers in his deep voice, but then he laughs into his next words. "Be a little more creative."

He's not just my fake brother tonight, but a *vile* asshole of a fake brother.

Matthew laughs, skin stretching at his eyes. He must be smirking. "You have my word, roach." I keep my bra on.

He snaps his fingers. Firefly members come forward with trays of shots.

A fear of mine is now unlocked. I've maintained a massive fear of being drugged since I was a little kid and my mom drilled into me the horrors of roofies.

The clear liquid resembles vodka, but it could be laced with GHB.

"Oh, I'm allergic," Claire poorly lies, her breath hitched.

"Take the damn shot, roach!"

I put the shot between my lips. Pretending to down the shot, I cough hard and roughly, and while they're watching me hack, I buckle over and pour the vodka onto my coat behind me.

Rocky and Nova have other sleight-of-hand tricks, but I can't watch them fake the shot.

"Swallow, roach," Matthew tells me.

I swallow and grimace.

"On your knees!"

All five of us obey, and another Firefly member emerges with a wooden paddle.

Okay, this *is* kinky.

While our asses are paddled one by one, Matthew crouches

down to me and reaches toward my face. I flinch a little, but that hardly dissuades him from going in. He tugs my hair tie.

And the long tendrils of my hair spill out around my cheeks. He twirls a dyed-black strand around his finger. I bite my tongue to keep from spitting in his face.

"All fours," Matthew tells me as the Firefly member finishes Claire's spanking and reaches me.

Placing my palms on the cold stone, I remain on all fours and try to focus on the ground, but Matthew pinches my chin and forces me to look at him.

The paddle strikes my ass with a light *smack*.

I try not to smile. It's not terrible. Could be a lot worse.

"Harder," Matthew instructs.

The next whack jostles my body forward, and the sting burns my skin.

"Again," Matthew says.

As I'm spanked once, twice, *three* times, arousal builds from the stinging pressure, and I imagine Rocky watching. He shouldn't be—he's my fake brother tonight. But the idea that he *could be* pulses a need, and my pussy throbs.

On the fourth spank, when I begin to refocus on the mark, my head floats away from my body. And then Matthew—with his ugly little hand gripping my chin—he tries to rotate my head toward my fake brother.

I fight against him. "You're *sick*," I sneer.

"Look at him."

Rocky can't protest too much, and reluctantly, I set my scorching gaze on him. He's looking away while the paddle strikes my ass with force. I jolt forward, breathing hard. *That's leaving a welt.*

"Look at her," Matthew says to a kneeling Rocky.

I see the tic of his jaw muscle. I see his nose nearly flare. He tries to maintain composure, and like a lever is flipped, he lets out a dazzling laugh, one that glimmers his gunmetal eyes. "You think I care about her? This is nothing," Rocky says.

The next *smack* is more painful than the others. Like the paddle shot-putted my heart a million feet out of my body, I feel hollowed hearing him say that out loud.

Until Rocky looks at me.

His eyes aren't his eyes. They belong to Cole Miller, but he's in there. With his tensed jaw and the slight dark crinkle of his brow, Rocky is in there, and my pulse beats again, at a fast rhythm I like and need.

Matthew is watching Rocky watch me get spanked. The power play is disgusting. I hope we're the first this secret society has done this to, but it's hard to believe we could be. After what happens tonight, maybe we will be the last.

And thank God Rocky isn't my actual brother. I'm banking on the idea that Nova is tuning this out on the other side of him.

"Harder," Matt orders.

Rocky's lip twitches in rage, just barely.

With a hard *whack*, the paddle pushes me forward again, and I curse under my breath. Matthew holds my face upright, so I won't look away from Rocky. *Jesus.*

I'm smacked. Jostled. Incredibly aroused each time Rocky and I lock eyes. My heat pulsates like a heartbeat between my legs. Each low thump just reminds me that I would rather be turned on than feel the nothingness crawl into me. But I'm thankful no one can see my arousal. My wet panties are the only evidence.

Rocky clenches his jaw. He has to rub his mouth and pretend to slightly smile like it's hilarious, but I see past that. I see him gripping onto his willpower and struggling not to end this here.

Whack. That one hurt, and not in a good way. I lurch forward, and Rocky almost reaches out to me. *No.* We have this in the bag. We've come this far. We're okay.

"Harder," Matthew orders again.

I'm smacked so hard, my arms buckle beneath me, and I fall on my chest.

"Stop," Claire cries out. "You're hurting her."

"I'm okay." I breathe sharply, not wanting her to capture any heat. "Really, I'm fine." Now my elbows throb and my ass burns.

"Satisfied?" Rocky asks with a slanted, cocky grin.

Matthew finally distances himself from me. "Next."

After the paddles, I'm no longer the center of Matthew's obsession, and more tasks are doled out in a frenzy. Firefly members pour freezing buckets of water over our heads. Animal blood is smeared on our faces. Run-of-the-mill hazing that has Kendra vomiting after being told to down a cement-mixer shot and has Claire silently weeping and shivering.

Any minute now, our fifth should be barreling through the wine cellar so we can *finally* pull the rope. My wet hair sticks to my cheeks, and the biting chill from the ice water and the dank cellar is pounding my temples.

I hug my arms around my shaking body.

"Stop," Nova snaps and spits out a cement-mixer shot someone tries to force in his mouth.

I swing my head in his direction. He wipes his lips roughly with the back of his hand. The curdling mixture of milky Baileys and acidic lime would make anyone puke.

"Take the shot, roach!" Matthew shouts.

Rocky is on his feet and laughing, animal blood streaked

on his cheeks and abs. "It's not that big of a deal, man. It's a *shot*." He says it like it's child's play. "Give it to me." He motions with his fingers, biding time for our fifth to show.

"Another, *roach*," a Firefly member orders, busy funneling shots to Kendra, even after she puked. Her eyes look glassy.

"She's already drunk," I snap at him.

Matthew hears us. "No more shots." He raises a hand to the Firefly members, and they fall back behind him. "On your feet, roaches—you two only." He addresses Rocky and me.

Rocky is already standing, but I pick myself up, cold puddles beneath my bare feet.

Matthew laughs while eyeing my body, and I'm not the fucking dummy here. After being drenched with water, my white panties and bra have become see-through. He tips his head to Rocky. "Your sister has nice tits."

Nova is a brick wall. He's scowling at his feet. Unmoving.

It takes Rocky the longest second to answer Matthew. With a level tone, he asks, "What do you want, Matt?"

"Number One," he corrects.

Rocky just forces a smile.

"You like your sister, roach?" Matthew wonders.

"She's my sister."

I breathe harder like I'm being hunted, and most of the nauseous anticipation is real. I have no idea what Matthew is doing, and our fifth is late. *He should be here*.

With a cock of his head toward me, Matthew suddenly says, "Kiss her."

Fifteen

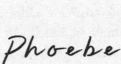

Phoebe

THE BADGER GAME (CONTINUED)

Rocky laughs. "You're joking."

"Kiss your sister, *roach*."

Rocky lets out a weaker laugh, then shrugs like, *whatever*. He faces me, and the raw, provocative desire to sink into his protective arms and never leave just *tunnels* into me. It's a freight train. A bulldozer. A semitruck that slams against me, and I let myself get run over. Until I swallow back every ounce of this feeling. This yearning.

For a flicker of a moment, his gaze switches into something not even close to brotherly.

I refuse to uncross my arms.

He gently runs his fingers against my cheek and lightly kisses the other one.

"On the lips!"

Rocky laughs harder, but the strain in his throat reverberates the sound into a deep cackle. He gestures with his head to Matthew and asks me, "Can you believe this guy?"

"Just get it over with," I mutter.

He rolls his eyes, and his hand begins to encase my cheek with strength and possession, fingers slipping into my hair. His head tilts, and as I shut my eyes, as my heart slams out of my rib cage, Rocky presses his lips to mine. Warmth explodes in my body, and what should be a peck shatters in the way his fingers tighten through my hair—in the way he draws me against his firm, bare chest. The kiss is pinning me to him, and selfishly, I cling and clutch, and when he teases my lips open, there is desperation on his tongue and a longing that tornadoes between us.

The wine cellar is silent.

Once Rocky breaks away, our breath comes shallow and a little wanting, but he changes his into a laugh and a radiant grin. "How's that, *Number One?*"

Matthew is in shock until he shares in Rocky's laughter. "You sick motherfucker." Matthew grins, and they literally fist bump, bro-hug.

So gross. I uncross my arms. To keep from physically embracing Rocky, I dug my nails so hard into my arms that half-moon indents mar my skin and sting.

"Do you hear that?" Claire squeaks from the stone.

The door bangs open, and a flashlight beams down into the stairwell.

A cop appears. He intakes the clandestine shit show. Blood-stained faces, wet bodies, reddened asses, and robed figures lording over us.

"Oh shit," a Firefly member swears.

I hold my hands up, as do Nova and Rocky. It causes everyone else to follow suit.

Once the cop sees Kendra nearly passed out next to her vomit, he touches his radio. "I'm gonna need backup." To all of us, he says, "All right, you have the right to remain—"

"Whoa, whoa, what's the problem, Officer?" Matthew asks, tearing off his mask. His prickish face and curly blonde hair come into view.

"Hazing—"

"I'm suing," Nova cuts in before the officer can list all the crimes. He stands up from the stone. "What you did is fucking heinous. Do you see *her*?" He's pointing to Claire.

She nods repeatedly, sniffling, but the waterworks ignite the longer everyone focuses on her. I bend down and splay her jacket over her shoulders, and I check on Kendra. Her pulse is weak.

"She needs the ER—"

"She's *fine*," Matthew says. "Everyone is fine." He speaks to the Firefly Club members who whisper amongst themselves, stiffening in doubt and fear. "My father—"

"I don't care who your father is," the officer snaps, but in the same breath, he zeroes in on Rocky and me. "Cole. Abby?"

Hope strikes Matthew's eyes. *Oh, you're not getting out of this that easily.* "Cole." Matthew smiles over at him like, *Fix this.*

Cole nods, then rushes over to the officer. With the officer's hand on Cole's shoulder, it's clear they're friendly. Because they're literally father and son.

Everett is wearing an actual police uniform. Not a cheap Party City costume.

"You're *not* suing," Matthew sneers quietly to Nova.

"I could go to the public," Nova says, more emboldened. "I could *bury* all of you."

"Lighten up, bro!" another guy shouts at Nova.

"This could ruin their lives, their *futures*, J.T.," I tell Nova, my fake brother's childhood friend. "We knew what we were signing up for."

"I'm so dead," some dude mutters, his hands on his head and his mask already trampled on the stone. "I'm so fucked."

"My dad is going to kill me," a girl cries.

Cole pats the officer's chest in thanks, and Matt intakes a breath and nods to my fake brother. "What'd he say, Cole?"

Everyone notices the officer lingering in the narrow stairwell. Barricading the exit.

"He says we can make this go away, but we have to go through my lawyer. He doesn't take on new clients, so you have to do this quick." Rocky is dialing a number. "His name is Pierre."

"Claire," I whisper, since I need to leave soon. "*Claire.*"

She sniffs. "Mmmh?"

"Can you call a friend to come pick you up?"

She nods over and over.

Nova has bent down to Kendra. He's helping her sit up. "Are you okay? Can you hear me?"

She moans. "I . . . yeah?" Gently, Nova rests her back against a wine crate. He collects her clothes.

"Take Kendra to the hospital," I tell Claire.

"Okay," she blurts into a squeak. "Okayokay. Kendra?"

I move out of the way and let Claire crawl to Kendra's side. Nova hands her Kendra's clothes, and she covers Kendra with the warm parka. After I fumble putting on my shirt and jeans quickly, I back into the shadows fully clothed. I watch as Matthew speaks to Pierre.

Also known as Oliver Graves.

"Okay . . . yeah . . . I can do that right now," Matthew says, then focuses on the other Firefly members. "Get your phones out. You each need to wire thirty grand to this number. It's the lawyer's retainer fee."

If anyone bats an eye at the high price, they don't question

Matthew, not at the risk of looking cheap, and a few friends cover for those who can't pay in full.

Not long after all the wire transfers go through, the sighs of relief follow, and Matthew hugs Rocky like he's his archangel and not a devil in disguise.

The officer doesn't press charges. He leaves before the desperate students realize there was never a cop car parked outside.

Nova is pissed and pretends to have a fight with his "childhood friend" on their way out. Rocky calms him down for show.

Tomorrow morning, we'll all be gone like a fever dream. And the Firefly Club will remain what it is. A secret.

Snow flurries are salting the night sky, and I pretend to call our personal car service. While we wait, we use Nova's T-shirt to clean the blood off our bodies and faces.

Oliver arrives in five minutes, and I climb into the backseat of the black Rolls-Royce. I'm squished between Nova and Rocky since Hailey is in the passenger seat; heat blows through the vents and instantly warms my frigid skin.

No one says anything for a hundred miles.

The clock blinks 4:32 a.m.

Sitting on my sore ass is painful, and I slide further down the middle seat. Sort of angling into Rocky is the comfiest position, and he curves his bicep around me to tuck me against his chest. The *thump* of his heartbeat could soothe me to sleep.

He rests a calming hand on my head, and he watches me as I canvass the tensed lines of his jaw and the darkness shadowing his gaze. *He's not all right.* I try to sit up, but he keeps me there and I ease back against him, concern flaring inside of me.

The silence is eating at Oliver. "Okay, is anyone going to tell me what happened?" he asks, his eyes flickering to me in the rearview mirror while he drives. "Phoebe?"

Hailey rotates in her seat. "Phebs?" She studies my slowly drying hair and the way I'm leaning into her older brother.

"I'm good." *I really am okay.*

"Platypus?" Oliver questions.

I shake my head. "Polar bear." We walked away with three hundred grand. Matthew will wake up to the realization that he's not the big man on campus. He's a fool who was so obviously tricked, and he opened the door for it to happen to his peers, too.

It's not enough, a nagging thought grates at me.

I wish I could call him a piece of shit to his face. I wish I damaged more than his pride. I wish he would hurt as badly as he hurt those girls. He's wealthy enough that thirty grand probably means nothing.

Embarrassment is the punishment, and sometimes, it just feels weak.

I hear my mom in my head. "You have his money. That's the point, bug." The payout might be everything to my mom and Addison, but the fancy lifestyle we're living isn't the reason I relish tricking people out of a tiny fortune.

Craning my neck to the other side, I touch Nova's arm. "Platypus?"

He's quiet. Gazing out the window, the snowy landscape thickens in white as we drive north.

"Nova?" My pulse skips. "Platypus?"

"Platypus," he says in the quietest, deepest breath.

I take my hand off him. Unsure if this is about me or seeing Kendra nearly pass out and hearing Claire cry and doing nothing to help. He's not regularly in those positions. Usually, he'd be behind the wheel keeping the car warm.

We're in the middle of nowhere when Oliver drives onto a snow-blanketed dirt road. He parks near a skeletal tree and a small, iced-over pond. Most of us get out. Nova pops the trunk.

And while my brothers begin removing the license plate, Rocky strides angrily over to the pond's rickety dock. His fury could melt the snow with each maddened step.

Rage. It boils at a higher temperature inside Rocky, but it's quietly simmering in me, too. There is no vindication great enough to satisfy the cruelty of tonight. We can't stick around long enough to even revel in someone's misfortune.

I see him ache to rip the world to pieces, and it's comforting to know I'm not alone.

Hot tears prick my eyes, and I chase after him.

Rocky screams out into the nothingness of the icy dark, and the guttural noise ricochets inside me like a stray bullet. Pain punctures the shield I think I've been wearing all night.

Carefully, I climb on the squeaking dock, my pulse racing. My blood on fire. "Rocky?"

He twists around, and swiftly, he cups my cheeks with two warm hands, looking deeply into me. My chest lifts with a strong breath. My heart pumps, and I wanted that prick to pay as much as Rocky did.

Really *pay.* To bleed more than just cash. If we had it our way, I wonder if he would've. I hang on to Rocky, holding his hands that encase my cheeks.

"Fuck. Him," Rocky grits out, his eyes reddening and glassing.

"Fuck him," I breathe into the frosty air, my voice breaking painfully.

Rocky slides his arm around me as I hug him. He's bringing me closer in a tighter, fiercer embrace. He puts a hand on the back of my skull, like he's afraid someone will come behind me and yank me away.

"I swear to God, Phoebe . . ." His voice sounds choked on my name, and he can't finish what I think is a promise or a threat. "I swear to fucking God." It comes out hot under his breath.

All I know is that I couldn't do this without Rocky. We're all the children of confidence men and women, living inside a train that hurtles forward with busted brakes and no signs of stoppage, but Rocky and I are in the same passenger car. We always have been. Sitting there together, peeking out of the opened door as the landscape whizzes past us, wondering where the hell we're going.

And I could tell him.

Right here, I could tell him how I need him. I could tell him how tonight is better because of him. And tomorrow will be brighter because he's there. But I can't . . .

The words are balled in my throat. I'm afraid of being someone's burden. I don't want to saddle him with another bag of weight. It's better if he knows I can do this on my own.

I can do this without him.

And maybe I can.

But maybe I'd hate every second of it.

His firm chest melds against my soft body while he's holding me against him. And the speeding tempo of our pulses never slows, never dies down. We're set on overdrive, me and him.

Destined for the thrill of a hunt. But also for the pain at the end.

When we slowly draw back, his gaze drops to my lips, and I remember the feeling of his lips against my lips—the desperation and longing. It swirls around us like a cyclone dipping from the sky. Snow kisses his hair as more flurries descend, but Rocky doesn't kiss me again.

I don't kiss him.

The job is over.

It's strange to feel so bound to someone but to have never kissed outside of a con. Yet, the way his fingers hook mine is intimate and loving.

"What are you to me now?" I whisper.

He shakes his head, uncertain, but he grips my gaze. "I'm just your Rocky."

My Rocky.

It overwhelms me for a long moment. "Quoting ancient history?"

"Not that ancient."

"I was four." I let out a pained laugh.

His name back then was Reed Donahue, an alias that had likely changed a handful of times since his birth.

The Tinrocks hadn't even chosen the "Tinrock" family name until later—not until after I nicknamed Rocky. On a summer morning, we were playing in a garden, and I told him, "You're Rocky."

He said, "You're Phoebe."

My name was Natalia Abruzzo. The Graves weren't the Graves yet either. But Rocky chose my first name—the one I've kept close all these years. Just like I chose his.

"No," my four-year-old self told him with stubbornness. "You're *my* Rocky."

He was five, and he held my little four-year-old hand. "You're *my* Phoebe." He kissed my cheek.

I giggled.

Life was simple then. Four and five, playing in a fairy garden outside a multimillion-dollar mansion.

Back at the icy pond, as snow falls heavier, I whisper strongly, "You're my Rocky."

He's hanging on to every word like we've flown to the past and brought the good, happy bits to the present, and his fingers curl around mine. Before I can also add that I'm his Phoebe, my brother calls us over.

"You two!" Nova shouts. "We need to head out!"

Rocky releases my hand. "Our chariot awaits." He forces a dry smile.

I try to ignore the flip of my stomach. Neither of us rushes back to the car. We linger. We're always loitering around each other, stealing seconds. Minutes.

"Are you the princess or the fairy godmother?" I ask.

"Always the princess," he says with more bitterness. Most would be okay with being royalty and not the actual pumpkin or a mouse, but Rocky wants to wave the wand and not be at its mercy.

Fairy godmothers aren't evil.

I'm perfectly fine in the role I've been granted. It's what I'm good at. What I excel in. *Stick to the plan.*

Sixteen

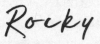

Rocky

At the two-person glass kitchen table, Hailey scribbles on a notepad. Tucking blonde hair behind each ear, she scratches out numbers and writes new ones in a frenzy.

I play a puzzle game on my cell from the beige couch. Keeping an eye on my sister and an eye on connecting three cherries isn't too hard. Should I be looking for another place to stay? Sure. Jake's weak threat about making sure I'm moved out of here by the end of the week hangs over my head like a limp piñata.

I'll deal with that later. Right now, it's hard to ignore the large exhales and huffs coming from my sister.

When I focus back on my phone, the timer has run out on the game. FAILED flashes across the screen. *Great.* Just what I love to see.

Pocketing my cell in my black leather jacket, I head to the kitchen. "Hails . . ."

She pins an elbow on the notepad, trying to be casual about hiding it from me. "Yeah?" She tilts her head, an attempt to appear all innocent and shit. She's wearing a black baseball hat with red embroidery that says, SATAN'S LIL HELPER.

"What's wrong?" I eye the notepad.

She quickly unburies it from her elbow and flips it over. "Nothing."

"You should be thankful Mom and Dad aren't here to see how *bad* you are at lying." I tsk dramatically. "They'd be so disappointed."

Hailey studies me and my unpleasant tone. "One would think you'd be better at hiding your hatred toward them."

"Do I need to hide it from you?" I question.

She shakes her head, and I sink into the vacant seat across from her. Stuffing my hands in my leather jacket, I slouch against the chair.

Hailey keeps her arms folded over the notepad. Her nose piercing glints in the light. "You should be happy that we're here, away from them, and that I don't *need* to be good at lying anymore."

Happy?

My face twitches into a grimace. *"Happy."* I try to remember real happiness. Not something fabricated, not anything warped.

The word is thick and heavy in my mind. Infused with tar and toxins. I've had happy childhood memories, but so many are twisted into stark reality now. Ones where I played soccer at a Manhattan prep school. I made a friend and laughed at his house over chicken parm and ice cream. Just to realize later in life that I was a tool used to screw over his father. A stepping-stone for my parents.

I was stepped on.

Repeatedly.

I was so happy.

Pain flares inside my chest, and I look at Hailey. "I'm fucking thrilled they're not around. I'd be happier if they were dead—"

"*Rocky*," she hisses.

"They can't hear us."

Her cheeks redden. "I wasn't scared they would." Her eyes fall to her notepad. "You shouldn't talk about Mom and Dad like that. They taught us everything we know."

God, I wish my sister could see what I see. Why am I stuck here alone? Is my vantage that fucking distorted from everyone else's?

I stare at her black chipped nail polish. In most cases, she would've always needed a fresh manicure in the past. "You just said you don't need to lie anymore, Hails. So what use do *you* have for what they taught us?"

Hailey is quiet again. "I don't want to con anyone anymore." The conviction in her voice startles me. "They taught us we have the power to do anything and be anyone, and we can make *anything* work, Rocky. I have to make this work."

"Why?"

Why is she so adamant?

Hailey says nothing.

I roll my eyes, frustrated, and I end up asking, "What about our parents? You think you'll be okay with never seeing them again? Because I don't think they'll ever let you go."

"I don't either," Hailey agrees. "But they'll have to get used to Phoebe and me living two very normal and moral lives."

I'd say she's dreaming, but fear tightens her collarbone and elongates her neck.

My jaw clenches. "You are scared."

"I know it might be . . . hard for them to accept this if they find us." She chooses her words carefully but doesn't mask her anxiety. "And that *if* might be more probable as a *when*."

"I can't argue with that logic," I mutter quietly, ire bubbling beneath my blood. Should I be happy that my sister isn't best friends with the devils beneath our floorboards? Sure—maybe there's a teeny-tiny fucking chance she'll see our parents for what they are.

Maybe she won't.

It doesn't change the fact that she's sitting across from me *afraid* of the people we're supposed to trust with our entire lives. Hell, they have our entire lives in a *vise*.

Hailey catches my raging glare, and she intakes a deeper breath. "I am really glad you're here, Rocky."

"In case they find you?"

"Yeah, and because I love you more than I could ever love them. I hope you know that."

I've never distrusted my sister, but she's saying exactly what I want to hear instead of proving that in an action. *She's not our mother*, I remind myself. Hailey wouldn't toy with my emotions to get what she wants.

The longer I'm silent, the more Hailey frowns. "I love you, Rocky."

I push aside any gnawing doubt. "I love you, too." I stand from the chair. "I wouldn't be here if I didn't love you."

"And Phoebe," she adds.

I force a smile. "And *Phoebe*." Saying her name pumps a heat through my veins and twists my insides. Did I forget her?

Never.

I could never.

I walk to the humming fridge and scour the barren shelves for leftovers. "The difference is that she doesn't want me here." I take the aluminum container of fettucine, and I find a fork, then return to my chair.

"I think she'll come around," Hailey says.

She thinks. "So she hasn't secretly told you that she loves me hanging around town?"

"If she's thinking it, she hasn't told me."

It stings. I don't know why I pictured Phoebe gushing about me to my sister. It doesn't sound like a Phoebe Graves thing to do. These days, she's more likely to stake my picture with a knife.

I stab the pasta.

Hailey peers down at the notepad again. Her gaze flits nervously to the bathroom, where a shower runs. Phoebe currently occupies it. I make a habit to try not to pick apart my sister's friendship with Phoebe. They feed off each other in a way that seems toxic to me, but I don't have a fucking best friend. So what do I know?

I fixate on Hailey's caginess. "Is this about Phoebe?"

"Is what about her?"

"Your anxiety." I point my fork at the notepad. "And that." I eat the cold fettucine.

"I'm just crunching numbers . . ."

After I swallow a bite of pasta, I stab at a piece of chicken. "Let me guess." I look up. "You can't survive off your meager savings and hourly work at the country club?"

Hailey lets out a soft, resigned sigh.

"That's a *yes, you're right, Rocky.* And I'd say I'm shocked but that'd be a lie, and apparently, you've outlawed my favorite thing to do." I flash a dry smile that vanishes as soon as her eyes grow wide.

She glances nervously at the bathroom again. "Just be quiet. *Please.*"

What the hell?

I frown deeply. I'd ask her when she started keeping secrets from Phoebe, but it wasn't long ago that my sister blindsided Phoebe about the price of this loft. I'd rub in the fact that living honestly for Hailey has meant being more deceptive toward one of the few people she'd never deceive.

But I love my sister, and I won't rub salt into a clearly infected, open wound.

"I don't get it," I say. "You didn't crunch these numbers before coming here?"

She rereads her notes. "I did the math correctly. But every other country club I've been to didn't have a *no-tipping policy*. We were going to rely on tips."

Seeing Hailey's plan foiled before my eyes is expected. It's what I thought would happen, but dread slowly churns my stomach. I want this to work for them. Or else they might pack their bags and head to Seattle, returning to the world where our parents dictate their every move.

"And now what?" I ask her.

She opens her mouth to speak, but the shower cuts off. Her eyes flit to the bathroom again.

I lower my voice to ask, "Is there a reason you're keeping this from Phoebe?"

Her lips flatline. "I just don't want to worry her."

"Because *you're* worried." I look her up and down. "Are you throwing in the towel already?"

"*No,*" she says strongly. "I can't give up this fast. We're staying here."

Relief washes over me in a wave.

She continues in a whisper, "At the rate we're working, we'll only be able to afford the loft for three more months. Then . . . we'll have to either get different jobs or a different place to stay. Chelsea Noknoi at the country club—a *friend*, not a mark," Hailey cuts herself off quickly. "Add that to your mental Rolodex, please. I know she's in it."

Of course Chelsea is logged in my fucking head.

Server at VCC.

Father is Thai and British. Mother is American. Brother is a family doctor in town. Both of her parents are divorce attorneys, and Chelsea is dating a local rowing coach. Her entire family would be considered upper class or at least upper middle class almost anywhere, but in Victoria, doctors and lawyers are lumped in with the "working class" of society.

If you work too hard to earn your money, you're not rich enough.

Old money runs Victoria.

"She's not a mark," I confirm to Hailey. "What about her?"

"Chelsea told me some people rent out their sailboats to live on. Maybe we could find an affordable one?"

I twirl fettucine on my fork. "Or you accept my generosity."

"Your generosity comes from conning."

"And your savings don't?" I eat another dry, chewy bite.

She lets out a long breath. "You're not a solution, Rocky. You're a temporary Band-Aid to the problem, and this has to last. It *has* to." Her desperation heightens to a new level.

I swallow, and the pasta sticks like a rock in my throat. Once I steal my sister's glass of water, I wash down the lodged food.

"Everything okay?" Phoebe's voice pulls Hailey and me from our conversation.

I take one look at her. *"Phoebe,"* I groan. "Put some clothes on."

She grips the towel loosely around her hips. Topless. And

I'm doing everything not to stare at her tits. But the fabric at her thighs hypnotizes me, the hem of the towel slipping against the soft flesh between her legs. I watch a bead of water roll down to her knee before I find the willpower to avert my entire fucking gaze.

"I'm in a towel," Phoebe combats. "And this is *my* loft, and it's not like . . ." She trails off with a frustrated growl.

I stake another noodle, knowing what she was about to say. *It's not like you haven't seen me naked.*

But she won't speak it out loud. Those words are tucked close to a memory, a night, that both of us agreed to forget.

But it's hard forgetting. In the back of my head, I can still *feel* the warmth of her body in my hands, and I hear the quickening of her heartbeat and I taste the strawberry off her lips. Being close to Phoebe is like being drowned in ice water.

It wakes every nerve ending. It makes me feel out of control. And so, so alive.

That night two years ago was the worst con we've ever agreed to, and surfacing that baggage is uncomfortable—for both of us.

I chew on a gristly piece of chicken.

"Are you seriously eating my leftovers?" Phoebe accuses, coming to the table. Thankfully she's tightened the towel *above* her tits.

"This takeout is from *Wednesday*," I retort. "It's Saturday. If you weren't eating it tonight, it belongs in the trash." I make a point of eating another noodle. "I'm saving you from a trip to the bathroom."

"Hope you have fun taking one there."

I flip her off.

She ignores me. "You okay, Hailey?" She carries real worry for my sister.

Hailey tries to hide her notepad again. "Yeah. Everything's fine."

"Actually, it's not," I interrupt. "Hailey crunched some numbers, and you two won't survive three months."

Hailey's jaw drops like I just took her ball of trust and free-throwed it into the trash.

I'm helping you, Hails.

She throws her pen at me.

I catch it midair.

Hailey groans and buries her face in her hands.

Phoebe's brows knot. "Hailey?"

"Okay, it's kind of true." Hailey cringes as she comes up from her palms. "I just don't want to worry you."

I stand, and I slip the pen behind my ear and pick up the aluminum container. "This is a good time to remind you both of the skills you've been taught." I dump it in the trash. "We can do a short con tonight at the party—"

"What party?" Phoebe and Hailey ask in unison.

"I was invited to a boathouse party by a girl at the club."

"Valentina," Phoebe realizes.

"You both can come along with me—"

"I'd rather eat sawdust than go to a party tonight," Phoebe cuts me off and shoulder-shoves me to reach the fridge, still in nothing but that damn towel.

"We're not conning anyone, Rocky," Hailey reinforces. "We're done for good."

I know she wants to be, so I look to Phoebe. "A little three-card monte, Phebs?" I ask with raised brows. She swerves around with a bottle of Yoo-hoo, considering.

I lean on the kitchen counter. "You need the money, and it'll be fun."

After she takes a long swig from the chocolate drink, she

wipes her mouth with her wrist, and I can tell she's really thinking about it.

"No." Hailey looks between us. "She's not doing it. *Phoebe?*"

Phoebe winces. "We need the money, though." And there it is . . . Phoebe's weakness will always be protecting my sister.

It's likely mine, too.

"There are other options," Hailey says. "We can still do this the right way." She slips a tiny scowl at me. "And you need to find your own place *soon*. Before you get us in trouble with Jake."

They've let me crash on the couch every night since we arrived in town, and if I want this to pan out for them, I do need to abide by Jakey-poo's rules and help them make rent.

"I won't get you two in trouble," I assure them. "That's the *antithesis* of what I've ever fucking done."

They relax.

Phoebe caps her Yoo-hoo. "Hailey is right. We're done conning. But I changed my mind about the party. I'll go."

I'm about to ask why when she adds, "I'll be a sec. I have to get dressed." I watch her exit the kitchen with a quick, lengthy stride.

"I'm not going," Hailey says from the table. "I want to plug this into Excel."

"You're leaving me with Phoebe?"

"As if you two aren't always alone together." She stands up from the table, nose in her notepad.

I aim a faraway stare at the brick fireplace, letting those words sink in.

Seventeen

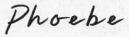

Phoebe

For a moment, I was about to actually agree to three-card monte tonight. A quick con to get a couple hundred. Just to keep us afloat longer. It feels like the easier route to just fall into my old ways, and for Hailey, I'd jump into that slimy pool of deception again.

I'm starting to think that I can't actually be *good*. That my only tether to what's right is Hailey's moral compass. Maybe I don't have much of one myself.

A seagull flies at my face, disrupting my thoughts and siphoning air from my lungs. "Jesus!" I duck while Rocky cackles next to me like a wicked witch.

I glare. "It's not funny."

"You break a mirror this morning?" he asks as we walk along the cobbled street together. He's superstitious in a way that's utterly ridiculous. He hates black cats, avoids walking under ladders, and despises anyone who opens an umbrella indoors.

I call him out on it. "You can't be superstitious when you've pretended to be a psychic. There's some sort of contradiction there."

He opens his arms like he's asking for hugs from the world. "I'm full of contradictions." He looks to me with a twinkle in his eyes. "Feels good not to give a fuck, Phoebe. Maybe you should try it tonight."

He's trying to push me to work a con tonight. *He won't succeed.* I have to think about Hailey and how upset she'd be if I tarnished the *one* thing she's hoping for. This fresh start.

Rocky and I are headed to the party, and this town is small enough that it's only a twenty-minute walk to the boathouse. My mom may have scoffed at a lot of rules and laws, but drinking and driving was never one of them.

And *hopefully* there will be booze at this place. Though, alcohol isn't the reason I changed my mind about the party.

"You're like an ugly little devil on my shoulder," I tell Rocky. I mime flicking imaginary him off my left shoulder.

He doesn't volley back an insult. Instead, his gaze sobers on me. "Want to make a deal with the devil?"

I'm about to reject him on principle, but his earnestness gives me pause. "What kind of deal?" I wonder.

"I'll stop trying to coerce you into your old ways if you just tell me what happened in Carlsbad."

My face sours, and mention of Carlsbad somersaults my stomach. "No." My pace carries me faster and harder down the cobblestone.

Rocky easily keeps up. "Phoebe—"

"We've been over this," I cut him off and then stop dead in my tracks. His chest bumps up against me, and he towers a good several inches above me. I'm five-eight in these heels, not short, and he hasn't moved a millimeter back. Ugh! With heated words and heavier breath, I snap, "I've left that night in the past, and I need you to do the same."

He stares down at me, his eyes sinking into a darkness. "It was something bad—"

"I'll make you a deal," I interrupt him again. "First one who gets laid tonight gets one wish granted. Your wish is that you'll get a very detailed *amazing* explanation of that night."

"And your wish?"

"Is for you to drop it forever."

He looks me over, and his gaze is a hot wave stoking my skin. At first, I think he might reject the deal, but instead, he says, "How do we even prove it?"

"Send a picture of your postcoital self."

He gives me a harder look. "We don't take pictures."

A very big rule among the godmothers. Selfies aren't taken on a whim. They're meticulously planned and given a ton of forethought. A social media presence can be a crucial part of a fake persona. But it's not like we're posting these pics.

The threat of anyone scrolling through our phones and suspecting our bad deeds is low, but not nonexistent, which is partly why the rule exists.

"I'm living honestly now," I tell him as the wind grows angrier. I hug my arms to my chest, just dressed in jeans and a short-sleeve white tee. "I can take pictures, and if you want to win, you'll risk it."

His jaw sets, and he glares up at the night sky.

Rocky has his hands stuffed in his leather jacket, a white button-down beneath. *Business* and *bad boy* rolled into one mildly attractive look.

Okay, *mildly* might be too tame. He's Carolina Reaper hot. Pieces of his black hair skim his forehead as the wind roars.

This has always been his style outside of long cons, but it's more than Rocky's clothes and good hair and sculpted muscles that draw flames around him. The dangerous flicker in his eyes allures me like Gretel drifting toward a gingerbread house, and even seeing the perils, I still want inside.

I always have.

It's easy to visualize men and women drooling over him as soon as he slips into the party. He'll have no trouble finding a one-night stand.

Why did I suggest this stupid thing? My stomach is in knots, and I wait at the precipice of a cliff for his answer.

A huge part of me hopes he'll go back on this deal. Reject it. Be so *unable* to even think about hooking up with someone else when I'm in a hundred-foot vicinity. The same way my insides flip and flop at the idea of fucking another person when Rocky is so near.

It feels like betrayal.

But we're not together.

I know. I know.

Maybe I need a physical reminder that Rocky and I aren't together. Won't ever be together. Something to push me *away* from him when everything else pushes me closer.

I'm supposed to move on in Victoria. Not backtrack to what's familiar.

Rocky lets out a low, deep breath, and he unburies his hands from his jacket. Unmistakable is the gold ring on his wedding finger.

My lips part, stunned and baffled. "We're supposed to be *divorced*," I whisper.

He's already tugging the ring off. "We are."

My mind reels. "But you're playing the part of what . . . ? Bereft husband who wishes he could be back with his wife?"

"Not anymore," Rocky says quietly, his eyes sinking on mine.

It hurts. I wish I could rewind.

He pockets the ring. "I wore it so the widowers would stop hitting on you." He says it like the ring was nothing. A ploy. He was just trying to protect me from unwanted attention.

Okay.

Scratch the rewind. Press play.

Except, with the way we stare into each other, the emotion pooling between us is deeper than his words. I'm sixteen in the backseat of a Lamborghini with the son of a plastic surgeon. Parked at sunset with ocean views. This guy was twenty-one. Too old to be with me, but he didn't know my age.

He didn't ask. When he kissed me, I felt nothing.

I wasn't even there.

Until a fist banged on the window, and I jolted.

Rocky appeared, needing a hand with his car's dead battery. He took over the con, but he wasn't supposed to key the Lambo at the end.

To think there is *zero* feeling in what we've done and what we do—that'd be the greatest lie we tell ourselves. And even though we're in the business of lying to others, we're usually truthful with ourselves, so I'm positive Rocky has acknowledged the messy, unwieldly emotion inside our jobs.

Inside us.

The wind settles down, and I uncross my arms, making the first movement in what feels like an eon.

It wakes him from a similar stupor. "You want to do this. Fine." Rocky extends his hand. "First one to get laid wins."

Everything is tilted. *Wrong.*

I shake his hand anyway.

Eighteen

Rocky

This was a fucking mistake. And I don't cop to making them that easily, but as I weave through the half-drunken party that's already body-to-body in the boathouse, I realize how quickly I've lost Phoebe.

"Can't we take this up to the house?" someone whines. "It's so hot in here."

The house is the mansion at the top of the grassy hill. The boathouse is detached and basically serves as an in-laws' suite: two bed, one bath, wine cellar, high-tech kitchen, and wood-paneled living room that's accommodating a hundred people at minimum right now. Last I checked, the rooftop is holding half as many, and Phoebe wasn't there.

Where the fuck is she?

I shouldn't be searching for her. I should be *seducing* and *flirting*. Two words that dump a heap of salt in my brain. To flirt and seduce are cheap tricks everyone uses to get what they want.

Even me.

"No, *no one* is leaving the boathouse," a girl says loudly and clearly over the thumping bass of today's Top Hits. "My dad doesn't care about this place, but if you trash the main house, I'll be written out of the will."

A guy laughs.

"I'm not kidding, Karl!"

Reaching a sliding glass door, I stick my head outside. *Is she here?* The upper deck faces the bay, and a gust of salty air and cigar smoke hits me. A couple men up-nod. The one wearing a Ralph Lauren polo and loafers gives me a suggestive once-over. "Do we know you?"

You wish.

"Not today." I slip back into the masses and check my watch.

It's been ten minutes.

What the fucking *fuck.*

Why can't I find her?

Why am I still looking for her?

She's probably in some back room getting dicked down. I comb a rough hand through my hair. *No.* I'm not letting those unwanted, puke-inducing thoughts raid my brain.

I pass more bodies, the age range about twenties to early thirties. A mixture of locals, college students (haven't warmed up to calling them *caufers* yet), and *skunks.*

Then there's me. I'm something else. A snake that's found a crack in the foundation, slithering my way inside.

No one hired a bartender, but the booze is flowing. It's an informal party, held by the girl with blonde waves and a perpetual wince. "Really, Karl?" she keeps saying. "Were you raised in a barn?"

Her friend oinks, and laughter follows.

Hilarious.

I shift further through the house and overhear a couple girls chatting by a large Murano glass vase. "Jake was *supposed* to be here tonight, but he got a call from his mom."

His name sends obnoxious smoke signals to my head. He's the last person I want to think about right now, and I'm about to walk away when I hear, "I'm surprised he doesn't loathe her. She treats him like her errand boy compared to his other brothers—"

The host of the party suddenly rounds this way with extreme worry. "Get away from the vase." Her eyes pinpoint to the fragile Murano glass near the girls.

I take my cue to leave this area.

As I make my way around the house, I gather her father loves Italy. He's either traveled there frequently, is Italian, or just has an admiration for the country. Or maybe it's all three. Most of the artworks on the walls are Italian painters. I recognize Caravaggio's realism and dramatic contrast of light and dark. And instead of hanging family pictures, the boathouse owner framed landscapes of Venice. I walk past photos of the canals and the Bridge of Sighs.

Houses say a lot about people.

Yet, the more information I'm collecting, the more a grating sensation rubs me raw. *She's fucking someone right now.*

Yeah, I am a thousand percent distracted. Not only from learning more about the people in this town but from getting laid, too. Can't even be shocked that Phoebe is a mental disruption. She's been a jackhammer carving out a chunk inside me since we were kids, and I couldn't excise her.

Mostly because I never wanted to.

Why would I evict the one person who I trust more than anyone else in this dog-eat-dog world? I never need to put on a false pretense with Phoebe, and where most people probably couldn't stomach who I really am, she always could.

I weave and slip around college students. One drunker guy in a Caufield Lacrosse tee tries to fill his glass with an empty bottle of Absolut. He rattles the bottle like more will magically appear.

The liquor cabinet is nearby, and I pluck a full bottle of Grey Goose from the half-empty shelf. I hand it over. "Here."

He sees and immediately grins. "Thanks, man." He pats my shoulder and pours the liquor.

"Hey, we're about to run out of beer," I tell him. "I'm collecting some funds to grab some more."

"Yeahyeah. No problem." He sets down his glass and takes out his wallet. I watch him fish out a couple hundreds and absentmindedly give them to me.

"Thanks, bro." I pat his arm like he did me and slip back into the crowd. It feels as easy as breathing. Asking for money. Having people give it to me.

Sliding the cash into my back pocket, I decide to return to the rooftop. *To look for Phoebe.* I'm not deluding myself. I know that's what I'm fucking doing.

Chatter disturbs any semblance of quiet up here, and then a high-pitched scream pierces the night: "Collin!"

Collin Falcone backflips off the rooftop and splashes into the bay. His friends strip buck naked and join him. Others start goading women to do the same. Bras fly, then panties.

Under the moonlight, more people begin skinny-dipping.

A blonde girl slinks into my line of sight. She tries to steal my attention as her fingers toy with the strap of her deep red bra.

Sidney Burke.

Nineteen-year-old Caufield student majoring in Economics.

Daughter of Weston Burke, a widower and prominent member of Victoria Country Club. Also known as the fucking prick who acts like Phoebe is his on-call escort.

And oh yeah, we hate each other. Publicly.

Gossip is currency in small towns, and my stock shot down after pissing off Weston. Not that I care. As long as I'm not banned from the club and these social circles, I'd rather make an enemy out of him. I've walked more dangerous lines.

"I heard about you," Sidney says, trying to draw me back. "I'm Sidney."

I know.

Being a pawn between a father and a daughter—that's not my idea of a good time. So if she's looking for me to fuck her to stick it to her rich daddy, she'll have to use someone else.

And I know better than to stoke a war with someone who already recognizes my trigger is Phoebe.

"You're Grey, right?" Sidney asks and drops her bra at her feet.

My head is leveled and unmoving, and my gaze is trained in precision on her face. Her lips form an uncertain *O* as I let her see malice cross me.

She's trying to seduce me when I'm supposed to be seducing any living, breathing body. People make this shit too easy, and I've bypassed multiple chances to win the deal I made with Phoebe.

I'm actively losing at this point.

"I'm not good for you," I tell her darkly.

I'm immoral, unethical, and deceitful.

Sidney teases the hem of her panties, not deterred yet. "Maybe I'm not good for you."

Not only is my dick limp, but my brain is so far out to sea. Irritation pinches my brows, and I harden my gaze so I don't roll my eyes halfway across the ocean.

"You're single?" she wonders.

"Divorced." I cut my eyes to the water and try to see if Phoebe joined the other skinny-dippers. She could be on the dock already, below the house where the boats are stored.

I haven't checked there yet.

"I heard about that, too," Sidney says.

"You came," someone says behind me. The new voice pulls me away from my search and from Sidney.

"Val," I greet, grateful for the easy escape. "Thanks for the invite." I sense Sidney picking up her bra and laughing at a comment her friend makes, brushing off our exchange as she joins a huddle of girls.

"Anytime." Val cups a mixed drink. Her face lights up more, glad to be remembered. "How are you liking it so far?"

I could play it up with the cliché, *Better now that you're here*. Flirt.

Seduce.

Things that'll take me a step closer to learning about Carlsbad, but I'm already half-assing this by scowling.

I stare out at the water. "Skinny-dipping, expensive liquor, and shitty music. My favorite." I don't conceal my normal dry tone.

She frowns but then plays it off. "Yeah, the music sucks. Alexa can't pick songs for shit."

Where's Phoebe? A sadness weighs on me, and I stuff my fists in my leather jacket.

Val notices my empty hands. "Want a drink?"

"I could use a whiskey." I find myself back at the liquor cabinet and wet bar. This time with Val, and while I pour amber liquid in a glass, she's trying to convince me to attend the town's clambake.

"It's hit or miss on who attends, but the food is always amazing. You really should come, and I . . . uh," Val begins to stammer.

I look up from the whiskey, capping the bottle. *Phoebe*. My pulse skips, and I steel my jaw.

She's stuck in the short hallway, trying to push through the crowds to reach either the bathroom or the bedrooms. *She's not alone.*

A taller, lean-built man has his hands on her shoulders. Directing her forward, even in the traffic jam. Glasses frame his angular face, and a bad taste fills my mouth.

Archer Fitzpatrick.

Twenty-eight-year-old English professor at Caufield.

Son of Stella Fitzpatrick, who's the best friend of Claudia Koning Waterford (owner of the Victoria Country Club).

I'm short-circuiting—caught between pushing toward Phoebe and cementing in place. But before I decide which route to take, Phoebe sees me.

With Valentina.

We're staring one another down. Blood courses through my veins, and my feelings aren't jumbled. They aren't confusing or enlightening.

Jealousy is ripe inside me. It's aged into a heady richness over so many twisted years.

Seeing as how she's en route to a bedroom and she hasn't sent a post-fuck text, I'm catching her before the final act.

"I think that's your ex," Val says, as if Phoebe and I aren't currently glaring at one another across the living room. "Oh, I think she's coming over here."

Phoebe leaves Archer after a few quick words, and she

beelines for us at the wet bar. Her dark blue hair is tied in a messy pony, and her thick brows are crinkled with hot purpose.

She's not sleeping with him. She's coming toward me. The alleviating thought is squashed fast. Because Archer is waiting for her in the hallway. His arms cross with slight impatience.

"Hey. Valentina, right?" Phoebe asks, trying to be polite, but her lips are pinched in an angry pout. A smile is lost inside of me. Getting under Phoebe's skin is an enjoyment, but her hot-blooded entrance and that fucking ponytail are burying a need in me.

Why her?

I'm pissed that I can't get rid of her. I'm pissed that being around her makes me want to hold her and do bad things to her, and I'm pissed that when she's gone I only want to find her.

"Yeah, Valentina," Val answers hesitantly, still not offering her nickname to Phoebe. She studies me, then my ex.

I take a swig of sharp whiskey. It burns going down. "Can I help you, Phoebe?" I hear the coarse grit in my voice.

"No." She glares. "I'm not talking to you. I'm talking to Valentina. Just want to give you some advice about this one." She jabs a thumb at me.

Val looks more curious. "Ohhkay. What about Grey?"

Phoebe steals the whiskey out of my hand. "He has a *massive* penis."

Val nearly chokes on her mixed drink. "Oh my God." Her eyes widen up to me.

I stare unblinkingly at Phoebe. She has seen my dick before (not an unfortunate fact, but one I should regret), and if this is her attempt at cockblocking me, she's swerving into a wall.

"Classy as fuck," I tell Phoebe.

"Again, *not* talking to you." Phoebe is on a mission.

I shake my head, and I try to shadow a smile that twitches. I steal my whiskey back before she takes a sip, and I swallow more.

"Massive penis," Phoebe repeats, "but—"

"Always a *but*," I jump in.

Phoebe is annoyed, and I'm loving pissing her off as much as she's been aggravating me. *"But,"* she emphasizes, "you know what they say. Size doesn't always matter. Not when you don't know how to use it."

I lift my whiskey to my mouth. "Sounds like a *you* problem."

"It was a *you* problem," she lies.

We've never had sex.

She wants to fabricate a sex life we've never had? Fine. I can play this game better. "See, that's not what you told our marriage counselor. You said, and I quote, 'The sex was *never* the problem.'"

Her cheeks turn rosy, but she continues to acknowledge Val. "I just want you to be aware of what you're getting yourself into."

"You never could handle me in bed," I tell Phoebe, and instantly, I regret the lie.

Her gaze snaps to me in hurt. Real hurt. "You never gave me the chance." Her voice is stinging.

I couldn't.

We can't.

I push a hot hand through my hair.

Val shifts her weight, noticeably uncomfortable and confused. What Phoebe said to me makes no sense in our fake marriage. "I should let you two talk this out." She waits for me to say, *No, stay.*

But I don't.

I let Val go, and once she's out of earshot, I swallow more whiskey. "Putting on a master class in bitchery?"

"Bitchery. Assholery." She steals the whiskey out of my hand again. "I've learned from the best." She downs the last drop.

"Thanks for the compliment," I say dryly.

"Phoebe!" Archer calls out to her, and as she whirls around to follow the voice, I leave the bar and match her stride.

Nineteen

Rocky

Phoebe tries to cold-shoulder me. "Sorry, Archer. You still want to go somewhere quiet?"

He assesses me—Grey Thornhall, territorial ex-husband with zero fucks to give. Being this openly destructive in a new town is almost cathartic.

I stare right through him with the darkest, most scathing glare.

"*Rocky,*" Phoebe whispers between her teeth.

I haven't said a word to him.

Archer wavers with an uneasy smile. "Actually, I have somewhere to be. Maybe another time, Phoebe." With that, he makes a quick exit.

Phoebe spins on me. "Are you serious? Why do you have to be the living embodiment of 'fuck around and find out' right now?"

"I'm being myself," I tell her, scoping out the drunken college students. People are watching us. "Isn't that what you want me to do?"

She growls, huffs, and storms into a pit of dancing students. For the next forty-five minutes, we keep the closest tabs on each other. We splice conversations and rip through any unfamiliar hands. When a dripping wet, half-naked Collin tries to grind on Phoebe, I intervene.

When Sidney leers close, Phoebe is the natural disaster no one wants to be around except me. I'm swept inside her chaotic sphere that matches my own.

We both aren't stagnant, still people. We're fueled by tankers of gasoline. Made to endure and keep going beyond exhaustion, and we don't stop.

We never fucking stop.

Not in the living room. Not on the roof. Not down below where the boats are stored. She chats with Rachel Rawlings inside the wooden Venetian boat tied to the dock. It ends as soon as I appear. Just like Damian Bennett's short-lived proposition to blow me ends with Phoebe's demonic glare.

We're some of the most sober at this party, and too many people are singing and slurring Justin Timberlake's "Cry Me a River" at the top of their lungs to notice our cockblocking war.

We aren't doing this to stop the other from winning the deal. I've never been in the market to fool myself.

I'm doing this because I don't want Phoebe to fuck someone else.

Plain, simple, and petty.

Her reasoning is the exact same. Trust me. (You should by now.)

The drunker the party, the more time it's taking to cut through sloppy hands—and I can't take it for much longer. Since I'm older than her, I try to take the high, mature road and find the brake pedal first.

Seizing Phoebe's hand, I pull her swiftly into the bathroom and lock the door.

"Deal is off," I declare.

Phoebe frowns. "Why?"

"You know why." I switch on the sink faucet and then slide open the glass shower. I turn it on. Warm water gushes out. The sound will muffle our voices well enough.

Phoebe pretends to be interested in a jar of potpourri *made in Italy*. "I want you to say it," she breathes.

"You want me to say it?" I say with control, but I'm on the verge of combusting. Phoebe sets the potpourri down, her hands gripping the sink behind her, and I face this girl in a pseudo standoff we've had for years.

Our hate isn't real. It's the armor we carry to shield us from the truth.

But our frustrations—those are real.

It goes *far* beyond sex, but while Phoebe stands there with her nipples hardened through her white shirt and her breath shallowed, sexual frustrations attempt to take precedent. Carnal thoughts ignite.

Me, pushing her up against the wall beside the towel rack. Whispering in the pit of her ear how I'd *devour* her. Tearing off her jeans and panties with rough speed. Spreading her open for me. Spurring a moan out of her—being inside of her for the first time in my life.

I've jerked off to the mental image of ramming so deep into Phoebe and watching her come on repeat and holding her beneath me. It's a fucking classic in my head, and I never *ever* dreamed it'd be a reality.

I still don't dream that impossible dream.

Because I know it can't come true.

I inch closer, stretching tension.

Her neck lengthens and shoulders draw back with anticipation.

"I can say it," I tell her, an aching foot away. "I. Can't. Have. You." My words are cold and dark between us. "As long as we're working for our parents, I will *never* be able to have you. I will *never* be able to give myself to you. But it physically pains me to see you with anyone else—and if I can't have you, then no one else can."

She's breathing heavy, empathy blistering her gaze. "Same."

Same. "There we go," I say heatedly. "We said it. Now what, Phoebe?"

She lifts her shoulders. "I don't know, Rocky. Maybe we just get it over with and don't make a big deal out of sleeping with each other."

I'm shaking my head, my jaw tightening.

"Rocky—"

"No." I hold her gaze. "If I fuck you, it won't be for power or for money or for *them*. It'll be because *I love you* and every ounce of my being couldn't contain the love I have for you, no matter how much I should've."

She blows backward, lips parted. It takes a solid minute for her to speak. "Don't do that."

"Do what?"

"Don't say those words." Her eyes glass and grow angrier. "We don't say *I love you* to each other off jobs."

Funny how the words always felt too intimate to say to one another, but I've been swimming inside the emotion for years.

Dirty, destructive *love.*

I've been in love with Phoebe since I was a teenager.

"You don't want to be loved by me?" I put that out there, trying not to feel my stomach churn saying it.

"It's not that." Her voice cracks. "Fuck, Rocky. What kind

of happy ending is there? What's the point of loving someone if you can't have them?" Her gaze bleeds into mine. "Hearing it, feeling it—it's suffering and anguish."

No shit.

That's what we're doing here. That's what we've been doing. Tormenting ourselves.

I comb another hand through my hair. Steam begins caking the mirror behind Phoebe, and the vapor thickens the heat already stirring in me.

"I hate your mother," I say in a murmuring sneer.

Phoebe isn't surprised. "I'm the one who's rebelled against her desire to hook us up, so maybe you should hate me instead."

"Yeah, that's not happening," I growl out. "The depth of how much I hate your mother is nontransferable. And you don't need to protect her from my hatred, Phoebe."

She frowns, possibly not realizing that's what she was doing. Phoebe would sacrifice herself to protect her mom. One who'd likely redirect a gun at her daughter if it meant saving herself.

My mother is just as selfish.

They're trained manipulators, and Elizabeth and Addison have made their daughters believe that whenever anything good happens and goes to plan, it's their doing. Elizabeth is why Phoebe succeeded.

Elizabeth is why Phoebe is happy.

Elizabeth knows best.

"I'm not trying to protect . . ." Phoebe trails off, frustrated. "You act like she's walked all over me. I've *resisted* her wishes when it comes to you and me, Rocky. I've told her I don't like you just so she wouldn't be obsessed with us."

"And manipulate us," I clarify. "We're afraid of the same thing."

"No." Phoebe shakes her head. "I'm afraid of my mother being too involved if we ever get together. You're afraid they'll manipulate us if we even have sex and they find out. I mean, you might even be paranoid about *kissing* me outside of a job for that reason."

I say nothing.

Her breath hitches and eyes widen. "I'm right? That's why you've never made even a single move on me when we're not working. What are they going to do?"

I look into her like she's trying to repaint a dark history in pastel colors. I just remember that night two years ago. The night we rarely talk about. The one that changed everything. "We're not even together, and they wanted us to *fuck* on a job."

"Maybe we should've!" she almost shouts, her frustrations boiling over. She releases the sink to push out against my chest.

My muscles flex as she bumps up against me, but I don't move. I stare down and meet Phoebe's challenge.

"Maybe I should've crawled on top of you," she continues hotly. "Maybe I should've sunk down on you. Buried *you* inside me. Rode you until you couldn't see straight. Given you the night of your fucking life."

I grit down on my teeth, reading her quickened breath. "Maybe you should've." My voice is sandpaper. "Maybe you should've done all the things you've never wanted to do, you natural-born *liar*." I watch her neck flush. "You've never wanted to make the first move. You're waiting for me—"

"No," she protests, but the truth is all over her face.

"—to take you in my arms. To hold you."

She shakes her head, pain deepening her gaze.

"To kiss you. To fuck you." I dip my head down, consuming her in a never-ending glare that tears at my insides. Her arousal parts her lips as we both imagine me overtaking her, and my whisper hits her ear. "I will make you come and *come*. Again and again and again. Until you're quivering underneath me, long before I fucking come inside you."

A tiny, wanting moan escapes from Phoebe. *"Rocky."*

It's a *fuck you, Rocky*, for turning her on. But I might as well have fisted my cock the way my body reacted to her saying my name. She shoves my chest, and I'm already taking many steps back. Spinning away from Phoebe, I pace the short length of the bathroom, pushing angered hands through my hair.

"And still," she says tightly. "You don't want to risk sleeping with me."

Jesus Christ.

I hate even being on a different line that's on the same page as Phoebe, let alone a completely different chapter, and I'd like to think we've been reading the same book.

"You know why," I shoot back, and as fun in theory as it might be to do a whole friends-with-benefits thing with Phoebe, it won't work.

We have too much baggage and history and *feelings* to fuck with no strings attached. And I can't promise that if I start sleeping with her, I'll be able to easily stop.

"Rocky, they're not *that* evil. If anything, we're the ones making our lives a living hell."

I let out a strained laugh. She's not wholly wrong—we have made a home in hell for ourselves, and sometimes I believe that's where we like to reside.

"Not that evil," I repeat, staring at the gathering steam on the mirror behind her. "Your mother is manipulative."

"We're all manipulative," she contends.

"She's manipulative toward *you*," I rephrase. "Our parents have been manipulating *you* and *me* and *all of us*."

She shakes her head. An apology nearly softens her brown eyes because she can't see what I see, and it's uncomfortable being so far removed from the perspective of the person you care about.

An acidic taste slips down my throat.

I should've protected her from them. I should've protected *everyone* from them. The single most important task my father ever gave me—to always protect my brother, my sister, and the Graves—I failed the instant I was given it.

"HEY!" a guy shouts outside the bathroom. "I need to piss!" The doorknob jiggles.

"Who the fuck is in there?! Are you taking a shower?"

"Oh my God, is this really the only bathroom?" someone whines. "The line is so long."

Phoebe glances warily to the door.

"We're not done," I tell her as I go to the door. Carefully, I crack it wide enough that they can see Phoebe inside with me. A staggered line weaves from the bathroom down the short hallway, and the complaining nails my eardrums. "Hey, hey, hey!" I shout over them.

They shut up to listen.

To which I say, "Fuck you. Fuck you. Fuck off. I'm fighting with my ex-wife. If you have a fucking problem with that, go piss in the ocean." I slam the door on them and lock it.

"Come on, bro!"

Phoebe scrolls on her phone and plays a heavy metal song on high volume. She tosses her cell on a fuzzy mat near the door.

To hear her in privacy, I move closer again, and I grip the edge of the sink on either side of her hips.

"They're not evil," she repeats in a murmur.

"They've made all of you believe we're their sweet little spiders." I breathe. "But we're not spiders to them. We're the *moths* they've cocooned in their webs, and they've kept us trapped for years."

Fear flickers in and out of her eyes. "That's an exaggeration."

"How?"

"When we were young, of course we weren't given the same amount of responsibility, but they *have* given us more. And when you're putting together a team, it makes sense that you look at each person's strengths and weaknesses and compatibility. They're always just doing what's best for us."

"What's best for the job," I correct.

"What's best for us is best for the job. It's always been that way, and they're just giving us the fancy lifestyles they wished they had at our age."

Her mother is speaking.

"You know the minute I started hating them?"

"The exact minute?" She looks me over. "No. You remember it?"

"Yeah." I narrow my gaze on her. "I was *fifteen*. I confessed to my father something I shouldn't have. I trusted him with something priceless." I cock my head. "I told him how I felt about you."

Her face slowly falls. "You actually said the words to him?"

"I told him I had a fucking crush on you. How much blunter could I be?" The pain of this mistake flares like a new sore and not something a decade old. "And you know what they did?"

She's in slight shock.

"Over the next ten years, they chose what I was to you.

They made me your brother. They made me watch you get groped by rich shitbags. They made me your boyfriend. They made me stand ten feet away and do nothing while you were defenseless with men who could've crushed you. They made me save you on a turntable, over and over again. They made me your husband. They took my feelings for you and they put them in a motherfucking *blender*."

She's unblinking, haunted.

The cords of my muscles burn as they're stretched in tense bands. "Does that really sound like something a loving, caring parent would do to a child?"

"Rocky . . ." My name is gentle from her lips.

"The minute I started hating them," I say, "was the minute I realized they would try to take my one vulnerability and use it against me. The cold hard truth: I'd rather *die* a thousand fucking times than be conned once."

She nods, understanding.

I'll never stop lying and influencing others for my gain.

I can't.

It's inside me like roots tethered to my veins. I love how it feels when I ask for something and I'm given it. The power is a drug. But more than that, I'm made for this, and deserting it leaves me weak . . . vulnerable to manipulation.

"We're all bad people, Phoebe. But they take the cake."

Phoebe drops her gaze to her feet. "I didn't know Everett knew . . . I mean, they likely all suspected we liked each other. Do you think he told our moms?"

"Yeah."

"But you're not sure?"

"There it is," I say dryly, "the doubt."

She glares. "Skepticism isn't a bad thing."

"But you can't be skeptical *of* our mothers? Just the other way around."

She's letting them off the hook and prepared to fry my father for misusing my trust in him. So I'm a little shocked when Phoebe admits, "Okay, maybe they're partly to blame. I don't know yet."

I haven't let go of the sink beside her hips.

Her gaze brushes over my chest and flexed biceps. I study the beautiful planes of her heart-shaped face, a quiet second breathing between us despite the running shower and the heavy metal music.

There is fond history with Phoebe that pulls me into a trance. All the roles we've played. All the lies we've lived together. It's twenty-plus years at the other's trusting, loving, devoted side. It circles us in moments and minutes and silent hours.

"Being with you gives them power over me," I whisper to Phoebe. "It always has. I've felt weak and vulnerable and used. And I don't trust what they'd do if we really got together. You say your mom would be too involved. I think that's an understatement."

Phoebe weaves her arms over her chest and cups her elbows.

The strain between our bodies prods me to push up against her. To hold her face again and pin her to the sink—but I keep the desire chained and barricaded in my head.

"We're back where we started," Phoebe says under her breath. "You know it *hurt* being close to you on a job, knowing that's where it lived and died. I need to move on from you—that's the only way this works."

I let go of the sink like a knife sliced through my gut. But what did I expect?

We'll never be together. Move on.

"I'm going home," Phoebe says, slipping past me. She collects her phone off the fuzzy mat. "It's better if you don't follow me."

I breathe hot breaths through my nose, my eyes burning. The door whips open and Phoebe storms out into the drunken party with the rage of an abused ex, while college students gawk from her to me.

"Duuude," one guy says. "You fucked up."

"Thanks for the commentary." I leave with a similar wrath burning my feet across the ground.

Twenty

Phoebe

It's been a week in Victoria and a few days since the boat-house party, and I try to dump my energy in anything other than Rocky. But his words from the bathroom that night are a wrecking ball in my head.

He told his father he had a crush on me.

It'd been different just theorizing our parents saw a "spark" between us. Knowing they had legit knowledge that Rocky liked me and they just disregarded his emotions . . . and even toyed with them—it makes bile rise in my throat. I feel sick and furious, and I'd like to have strong, *nasty* words with Everett.

Trust is invaluable to us. I can't wrap my head around how he could betray his son. Above all, that's his *child*, but I always thought our parents cared more for us than the average parent.

Because they brought us into their fabricated worlds and didn't leave us out.

They've been genuine about who they are and what they do, and they could've so easily lied. Hell, normal parents keep their kids in the dark all the time. They hide their youthful stints with drugs. They hide affairs.

Once we were a good age where we'd understand the gravity of what our parents do, they told us *everything*. They even taught us their trade.

We've been their accomplices. Their partners in crime.

Everett had no reason to be that cruel. I can only assume that he sidelined Rocky's feelings for the supposed betterment of the con.

Now I understand why Rocky wouldn't trust him most of all. Our moms . . . I don't know. I'd like to ask them directly what Everett shared, but asking them means talking to them—and they apparently believe Hailey and I are in Indiana dealing with a catfish gone wrong. Despite the urge, I still won't call my mom and make things messier.

At least things are going *amazingly* on the normalcy front. *More lies.*

Everything is a struggle. Money, work, trying not to lie my way through life. But each time I think about *why* I'm here and *why* I'm putting myself through unnecessary torture, my resolve returns tenfold.

Hailey wants this. And I'd do just about anything for her.

Which included punt-kicking Rocky out of the loft this morning. It's been a week. His time here has expired, and he told me he found another place in town anyway.

He's not leaving *yet*. I partially expected him to be long gone after the boathouse party. *Move on, Rocky.* But then I remembered he's not here to ignite a small-town romance with me.

He's here to watch out for his little sister.

So he's staying. For how long? He might not even know.

Today and tomorrow and forever is about my life *sans* that asshole. So I employ three strong words every time he invades my brain.

No more Rocky.

I bump my hip against the bookshop door, hands filled with two disposable coffee cups. I'm not a big coffee snob, but Hailey will be able to tell this is drip. I looked over her Excel sheet this morning, and we have to cut out some of our usual luxuries. Including our morning cinnamon latte macchiatos, something that our moms got us into when we were teens.

Winding around a couple of bookcases, I spot Hailey standing in the back flipping through a paperback. I'm about to head to her when a store clerk intercepts me.

I take quick note of his well-groomed beard, black-rimmed glasses, blue-green plaid shirt, and tan Sperry boots. Twenties or thirties, I guess. It's hard to tell with the beard. His name tag reads MASON.

"Excuse me," he says earnestly. He glances sheepishly toward the back of the store at Hailey. "Do you know her?"

I try to contain a smile. He must like Hailey.

But he's obviously intimidated to approach her. Chains are linked on the belt loops of her black cargo pants, and her combat boots are studded with spikes. Her black lipstick matches the smoky shadow that shades her gray eyes, which are pinched in concentration.

She's giving off resting bitch face.

As her best friend, I can confidently say she's out of *everyone's* league. I have yet to meet someone good enough for her. It definitely won't be Mason here, but he's not bad looking and I can play the part of wingwoman. He just has to have some sort of talent to catch Hailey's eye.

"I know her," I tell him. "She's my *best* friend." I don't know why I emphasize *best* like I'm a toddler who just made her first friend.

He lets out a breath of relief. "Great. Can you tell her she needs to stop reading the books? This isn't a library."

What?

Okay, now I'm mad.

"It's not a crime to flip through some books before buying them," I defend her instantly. "How else will she know if she wants to buy it?"

"She's not *flipping* through the books." He lowers his voice to an angry whisper. "People who flip through books don't go page by page, front cover to back. I've stood here and watched her read *three* books in the span of twenty minutes." His eyes flit to her, but Hailey is absorbed in her paperback, not even breaking her gaze from the pages.

Sure enough, she is flipping each page. Very quickly.

"You've been watching her for twenty consecutive minutes?" I ask with the raise of my brows.

He eats air, chasing after words in his head. "I . . . that's not the point. She can't read the *entire* book."

"Don't be silly," I say more casually, trying to play it off. "No one can read that fast."

"Obviously, she can," he refutes. "And as her *best* friend, I'd like you to tell her to either stop reading the books front to back or better yet—buy a book."

I narrow my eyes. "And why can't you tell her yourself, Mason?" He's been watching her for *twenty* minutes after all.

Flush ascends his neck. "She looks . . . you know . . ."

"Like she'd dick punch you?"

He rolls his eyes but doesn't deny it.

Truth is, I'm the one who's seconds away from dick punching. But I'm not leaving this town tomorrow. I have a reputation and all. So I take a steadying breath and say, "I'll let her know."

I leave his side.

"Wait—which part?" Worry clings to his voice, but I don't give him the satisfaction of a reply.

Hailey still doesn't glance up from her book when I step to her side. I clear my throat.

"Hold on," she says. "He's about to confess his love—oh wait, he killed her."

My eyes widen. "Really?"

She frowns. "Yeah . . ." She shuts the book and looks at the cover. "Oh, I thought I was reading a romance. I think this might be a thriller."

"Maybe it's both," I tell her, handing her the extra cup. "Villains have to fall in love, too."

She places the book back on the shelf and takes the coffee. Her gaze swings past me. "That guy has been staring at me for twenty minutes."

She's more perceptive than I give her credit for.

"Yeah, he wanted me to tell you that this isn't a library. You can't read the books without buying them. But he's an asshole and was too chickenshit to come tell you himself, so until he does, you can do what you want." I hold my cup up to her and she cheers with me.

As soon as we both take sips, she winces. I wince off her wince.

Okay, maybe I *am* a coffee snob.

"This is . . ." Hailey peers into her cup like she can find the problem.

"Awful," I agree. "Who knew our mothers would ruin our coffee palates?"

Like I summoned her from the ether, my phone pings with a *beep beep* that sounds like a Minion from *Despicable Me*.

Hailey's face falls. "Don't look at it."

"It'll eat at me all day," I refute, and maybe I'm more nihilistic after what Rocky confessed. A bristling anger has trumped some fear. I set the coffee cup on a side table beside a decorative ceramic bear holding a sign that says HELLO MY NAME IS: WILLIAM SHAKESBEARE.

Clicking into my cell, I see the caller ID: LAURIE STRODE. My favorite horror movie mom.

I've never seen my mom wield a knife like Jamie Lee Curtis's character in the *Halloween* franchise, but I've always thought she's just as resilient.

My stomach does a nosedive at the text.

Laurie Strode: It isn't like you to want to miss out on a job, bug. Call me. Worried about you.

She still cares about me. She always has. And I'm not lumping her in with Everett. Innocent until proven guilty, right? I should give her the benefit of the doubt.

Hailey reads the text over my shoulder. Then her phone beeps with the normal preset tone. She swings off her black studded mini-backpack and fishes out her cell. "They're probably at brunch texting us at the same time," she theorizes. As soon as she clicks into her messages, she sighs and hands me the phone.

Mother: The Belle is missing at the ball. Clock has struck twelve. Where's Alice?

Hailey and Addison love talking in riddles together. I never understood it, but Hailey said it's fun word games.

"Why couldn't she just say you're late?" I ask, returning her cell.

"She did." Hailey's about to chuck her phone into her backpack when it beeps again. I read over her shoulder.

Little Brother: Did you find a new job?

"What do I say?" Hailey asks. Like me, it's a lot harder for her to ghost her siblings.

"Just tell him to talk to Rocky." Shirking the responsibility on Rocky doesn't feel great, but his whole purpose for being out here is to make sure we don't get into trouble.

No more Rocky.

How's that going for me?

Superbly. Just . . . so wonderful. I'm doing backflips down the aisles.

She starts composing a text, and the chimes to the bookshop door jingle.

Jake Waterford has entered the chat. He catches my eyes, and I figure I'll just get a friendly wave, but he surprisingly approaches.

"Is he gone?" Jake asks.

I jerk back. "That doesn't feel like a country club welcome. Didn't you take cotillion?"

He side-eyes me. "I'm not really in the mood for perfunctory politeness." He glances over at Hailey for a quick second. "Is your brother out of the loft?"

Hailey texts on her phone and says, "Oh yeah, he left this morning."

"Can you show me?" he asks.

Her phone beeps, and her lips downturn at a new text from her brother. "I'm kind of busy . . ."

I turn to our landlord. "I'll show you, since you seem to have a hard-on for evidence."

Jake blinks slowly, like this is not the outcome he'd hoped for. Hailey was his first choice. Noted. He takes a readying breath before he just nods. He follows me out of the bookshop and then up the flight of stairs to the loft.

I push the door open, and Jake asks, "Mind if I just check all the rooms?"

He hates him *that* much? I can't remember the last time Rocky has rubbed someone this raw. "Sure," I say. "Don't forget to check under the beds. I hear that's where the monsters live."

Before Jake can move toward my bedroom, two guys emerge from the room. The leaner of the two has a crooked grin as he says, "Don't know of any monsters under any beds. But I can point you in the direction of a few."

I ignore the confusion wafting from Jake's body. I can't help it. I grin. "Oliver."

"Little sister."

Elation surges as I rush toward him and go in for a hug, barely registering the truth he spoke out loud. His arms swoop around me in brotherly affection. At six-foot-three, he's much taller than me. Wavy pieces of his light brown hair fall into his eyes, and his long trench coat looks like something from a Banana Republic catalog. He pulls off the preppy style with pure ease.

Oliver was helping Mom with a job in Minneapolis while we were in Carlsbad. I haven't seen him in person in a good four months.

"Phoebe." That voice comes from deeper in the hallway.

I break from Oliver to see Nova propped against the wall, his muscles flexed, hair shaved short. He has light facial scruff, and he wears his usual *we need to talk about business* expression along with his staple utility jacket that he mostly wears *off* jobs.

I want to hug him, too, but I hesitate since he hasn't called me his sister.

His eyes flit to Jake. "You are?"

"Landlord," Jake says, crossing his arms. "I'm not sure if Phoebe told you, but guests aren't allowed to stay longer than a week and Rocky has already capped that perk out."

Pretty sure that's not how the rental contract phrased it, but I don't want to ruffle Jake's precious peacock feathers more than Rocky has.

"We won't be staying here," Nova confirms. "I take it you're not a Rocky fan." Oh, my brother is definitely prying. He must know it's strange for Rocky to have already made an enemy in town.

"To put it mildly," Jake says. "How do you know Phoebe?"

"We're both her brothers," Oliver clarifies first, and I can't remember that truth feeling this good. A brightness swells in my chest, and I breathe in the filling sentiment.

"The three of us," Nova chimes in, "we're not just brothers and sister."

I go still. *He's not going to . . . ?*

He won't say the whole truth.

Is he really . . . ? My head is spinning.

Twenty-One

Phoebe

Nova never shifts his intense gaze off Jake. Not even as he says, "We're triplets."

The truth bomb explodes at my feet.

I'm stunned for a long, *long* second. When's the last time we've told someone the depth of our relationship? Uh, almost *never*.

Most of the time they refer to themselves as my older brothers—because they technically *are*. Just older by minutes instead of years.

I want to be just as excited about living inside the *whole* truth, but nerves are swarming me.

Jake's brows rise in surprise. "Triplets?" He swerves his head to me. "You didn't mention that."

I shrug. "It's not something I bring up."

"Seems like a big fact about yourself."

Oliver grins. "We treat her like a little sister, so she likes to distance herself from our triplet status."

I roll my eyes. "They *try* to treat me like a little sister."

"How much older are you guys?" Jake wonders.

"Fourteen minutes," Nova says.

Oliver holds up ten fingers. "Double digits for us both."

Still lording that over my head. The excitement of Oliver's and Nova's presence starts to recede. Why are they even here? Does this mean our mom is on her way? What about Addison and Everett?

Before I can try and ditch Jake, Oliver heads to the kitchen. "I brought donuts. Why don't you join us, Landlord?"

"I wish I could," Jake starts.

I look up at Oliver. "He's actually on a one-man search party for Rocky."

"I wouldn't phrase it like that." Jake side-eyes me again.

"How would you phrase it?" Nova asks curiously.

"I'm making sure her ex-husband isn't crashing here. That's it."

Neither of my brothers bat an eye at the ex-husband title. Probably since Rocky has been too many things to me, not because Rocky gave them a heads-up about it.

"I don't know how well you know her ex . . ." Jake trails off. Okay, now *he's* prying for info.

"Too well, unfortunately," Nova grumbles.

Jake stiffens in what I can only register as a protective stance. Great, Nova just validated Jake's bad feelings about Rocky.

Oliver is only staring at me. His lip lifts in a sympathetic, knowing look.

When I was younger, instead of confiding in Hailey about liking her older brother, I told my brothers instead. Both of them.

Oliver has always had a knack for compassion. He's like a heating blanket, able to dial up the temperature and even suffocate if he wants, but Nova is more like steel.

"Did he do something?" Nova wonders, reading Jake's posture.

Jake just looks to me to verify or deny.

I'm not unearthing anything. "No, as much as I love this Rocky crusade," I say with a prickly tone.

"There's no crusade," Jake interjects with an outstretched hand—as though he's worried I'm going to fling myself into Edward Scissorhands' arms if the Hate-on-Rocky parade continues.

Jake is a good guy.

And he's been sniffing out Rocky's bad-guy behavior since day one. After the boathouse party, it's likely shot to astronomical levels. The rampant gossip has turned into a broken game of Telephone, all of which I've overheard at the country club.

Did you know Grey and his ex-wife fought for five hours?

Did you hear that Grey punched a wall?

Phoebe couldn't stop crying. She was sobbing on her way out the door.

I heard she's the problem. Couldn't please him in bed. He deserves better.

Add in the fact that most everyone there was *drunk* and probably didn't remember shit, it's mostly all exaggerations and lies.

Jake could very well believe all of it for all I know.

A string of tension is cut when Jake sees the lilac donut box on the kitchen counter. "Those are from Seaside Griddle?"

Oliver nods. "I'm told only the best in town."

Jake hesitates for a second, considering staying. Oliver and Nova must want more intel from my landlord. There's no other reason to want him here. We all migrate into the kitchen, and I gather a couple beers from the fridge for my brothers.

Koning Lite.

I wish I was kidding.

Jake side-eyes the beer bottles, and I flush, wanting to tell him I bought a twelve-pack *before* I knew his whole name. But his phone suddenly rings with a chime that sounds a whole lot like an instrumental tune of "Bad to the Bone" by George Thorogood & the Destroyers.

He audibly groans while fishing for his cell, and instead of answering, he presses the button to silence the call.

"Who was that?" I wonder. Okay, now it's my turn to pry.

Jake gives me a look like I broke a cotillion rule. "Did anyone teach you manners?"

Four different cotillion classes in four different states. Though, I did only finish one. We had to leave before I completed any of the others.

"Manners are a choice," I tell him, sliding the beer and bottle opener to Nova. "And sue me for wondering who you hate enough to give that ringtone to."

He blinks. "My mom."

"Joke?" I wonder.

"No joke. Unfortunately."

Oliver laughs, taking his uncapped beer from Nova. "That's great. I like this one." He tips his bottle toward Jake.

Jake looks between the three of us. "And what do your parents do for a living?"

The energy in the room shifts, but I'm not sure Jake can pick up on it. *Dad is in prison.* Has been since I was a kid.

Mom . . . well, that's going to be a tough one to explain.

"Boring corporate shit," Nova says in a swig.

"Phoebe pissed them off enough that she got her trust fund taken away," Oliver adds. "We're just in town to make sure she's doing okay."

I guess it's a decent cover story. At least I won't have to pretend not to know some upper society ways if I came from it at one time. And maybe . . . maybe that is the truth? A piece of it at least.

Jake glances at me with more and more curiosity like he's gathering pieces of my history. He won't ever have the full picture, though. I can't let him have it.

"You're not on good terms with your parents?" He asks the question that he knows the answer to.

I shrug. "Not really."

"You're the kind of guy our mom would set Phoebe up with," Oliver mentions. "If she met you, I'm sure she'd already have wedding invitations made."

Oh God. I almost go for a donut so I can throw it at him.

Nova cringes at the idea of me dating.

"Thank God she's not here, right?" I say to Jake. "I mean, in another life maybe I'd fake date you to get her off my back. But . . . that's another life." *Why am I still talking?*

"And thank God that's another life," Jake says bluntly.

Oh, ouch.

Does the idea of fake dating me really turn him off?

I'm roasting alive. Turning on my heels, I hide my face from him and then look up.

Oliver slips me a sweet smile into a sip of beer, like we're in on a joke and Jake is the outsider. It relaxes me, and I already realize how much I really love having my brothers here.

"Well, I hope your stay in Victoria goes smoothly," Jake tells my brothers. "If you need any advice about spots in town, Phoebe has my number."

He spins around for the door.

"Wait," I say, confused. "You haven't checked the rooms for Rocky yet. You don't want to look?"

His eyes flit to Nova and Oliver for a second then back to me. "I trust you."

No, he doesn't. I just think he's not in the mood to go through my brothers.

"Thanks," I say, accepting that fake little trust like a precious trinket.

He nods once and leaves.

Nova and Oliver are quiet for a standard five minutes. The three of us unspeaking as we settle more around the kitchen. Nova starts the microwave, and Oliver switches on the fan, creating more ambient noise.

I take one of the chocolate donuts with pink sprinkles.

It's interesting how the three of us can be apart and come together again like no time has passed. It's that way with the Tinrocks, too, but for me and my brothers there's something deeper here.

We shared a womb together, after all. But it's even more than that. We have that scarlet *A* from our dad's missteps that sent him to prison. His absence left our mom with three kids to raise, and it was never easy. When I was six, we lived in a glittering penthouse in Chicago, and she'd been cooking nonstop since her new husband called and told her he was returning home early from his work trip in New York.

She was always a loving, dutiful wife to each and every husband she married.

And we were never her triplets. Usually, one of us was from a different marriage. Sometimes we were half-siblings. Other times, Nova was the eldest, and Oliver and I were twins.

Our relationships always varied but our truth remained close to our hearts.

Each of her husbands was different. Some worse than others.

Sheamus couldn't stand Nova, and when he laid a hand on him, our mom packed our bags and left in the middle of the night. She gripped the steering wheel of her white Corvette. "I promise that won't ever happen again." Steely-eyed and remorseful, she braved a glance to Nova. He didn't cry. He was glaring out the window, pain in his eyes.

"You hear me, spider?" She touched his shoulder. "It won't happen again."

But it did.

It happened in different ways to each of us because the men she married were never *good* men. The saving grace was knowing every house we lived in, every city we moved to, and every despicable man she married was always temporary. The moment our mom would find out what happened, she'd empty out their bank account and pack our bags once more.

We'd leave.

But she never made that promise again. Not after the first time. I think, maybe, she knew it hadn't been a lie, but if she said it again, it would be.

Through it all, Nova, Oliver, and I grew closer. We were shelter, familiarity, and permanence.

Now they're here in Victoria when they should be in Seattle, and their presence should bring the usual comfort, but my stomach is unsettled. They were helping keep my cover. Now what does Mom think?

I've never bailed on a job before. Not like this.

Before I can ask, Oliver tilts his head to me. "Ex-husband has you down?"

God.

"With Rocky, it's an eternal hell—he never has me up," I mutter, avoiding Nova's intense gaze. They might know about my young crush and how Rocky never made a move on me, but I didn't open up about the agreement Rocky and I made two years ago after *that* job. The Job That Shall Never Be Named. It felt too . . . raw.

Most of the time, it's easier to be openly disgruntled than lovelorn.

Nova grips his beer in a fist. "Your landlord thinks something bad happened between you two."

"Just small-town gossip. It's been the same old, same old with me and him, and I'd much rather hear about you two."

"Same old, same old," Oliver says lightly. "I fuck around and tell. Nova fucks around and shares absolutely nothing."

"There's nothing to tell," Nova retorts.

"Liar, liar, pants on fire," Oliver says with a rising smile, then swings his head to me. "A blonde girl left his room last night."

Oliver and I exchange a big grin while Nova takes the heartiest swig. Then tersely, Nova says, "Okay. Let's talk about important shit."

"You don't think you're important?" I tease.

"You *are* important, big brother," Oliver says, coming over to him just to skate a hand over Nova's shaved head.

Nova pushes Oliver's chest with little force.

Oliver laughs, but when the bright sound fades, Nova's "back to business" face returns.

I tear off a piece of frosted donut. "Does Mom still think I'm in Indiana?" I finally ask.

"No," Nova says. "She thinks you, Hailey, and Rocky got sidetracked, and you're all doing a job in this state."

"She knows I'm in Connecticut?" *Great.*

"Rocky said it was the best route," Oliver clarifies while he goes to start a pot of coffee. "Or else we'd all get caught in a lie and they'd be here tomorrow."

Nova adds, "We told her your new job is more lucrative than the Seattle clip joint."

"And she just . . . let you guys come?" I frown deeply. "They'd been planning the Seattle job for months . . ."

"It's handled," Nova says. "To tell you the truth, Mom started dating someone new, and I don't think she wants you out there with him around."

Oliver stares far away at the coffeepot. "I can't wait until she bleeds him for all he's worth."

My stomach sours. "He's that bad?"

Nova tips the beer to his mouth. "She could tell I was getting pissed."

Oliver loosely threads his arms, leaning in the corner where the counters meet, his ankles crossed. "And I was on my way."

"To getting pissed?" I ask.

He nods. "About there."

"You were already pissed, Oliver," Nova clarifies, eyeing our brother. "You threw a drink at him. With the fucking glass."

"It slipped out of my hand."

Guilt bites at me. For not being with them.

Nova turns back to me. "She actually asked us if you need help with your job, and that was the least subtle hint she could give."

She prompted them to come out here.

I look to Oliver for more details since Nova tends to skirt around them. "What was he like? The boyfriend?" I wonder.

"Handsy," Oliver says. "He gropes her in public. He'd probably do the same to you, if you were available."

Available. Like I'm a hotel with a vacancy sign.

My mom, for as much as she taught me about seduction

and influence, has always shielded me from her marks. Not in a competitive way. It's more protective. Like she knows there is a seedy, rough part of our job, and it's usually designated to the one who has to "encourage" the mark.

Sometimes . . . I do wonder if I do the same thing with Hailey. If maybe I learned that bit of being a shield for others from my mom.

I chew slowly on the donut, processing, and then I swallow. "You two do know that I'm not out here on a job, right?" Last time I asked Rocky, he said he told them everything but vaguely. Whatever that means.

"Rocky caught us up on all of it this morning," Nova says. "You're out here for real, and we didn't want to mess that up for you."

"No offense, sis," Oliver adds. "But this plan of yours seems like it was fueled by crack cocaine. You and Hailey didn't smoke up on your last job, did you? Or were there some magic mushrooms involved? A little peyote to cleanse the soul." He mimes taking a drag.

Nova looks right into me at the mention of *the last job*. Carlsbad.

I swallow a rising lump. "No magic mushrooms," I tell Oliver. "This is just a new thing. We're seeing it through." *For as long as we can.*

"Hmm." Nova makes a gruff noise under his breath.

Oliver pushes away from the counter. "Well, it's lovely that you want to be all Goody Two-shoes. But not all of us were built that way." He holds up three fingers. "Scout's honor I won't wreck anything up for you and Hails."

Oh no . . .

Oh *no*.

My eyes go wide. "You two aren't doing a job here."

"We won't," Nova says, downing the last of his beer. "Rocky already made us promise."

Rocky.

A gross sentiment fills my body. I can't describe it other than attraction toward that silver-tongued jackass, and I want the antidote. STAT.

"But," Oliver says with a wry smile, "we're not subscribing to your new-wave hipster style of living."

I roll my eyes. "You mean being a good person."

Oliver makes a gagging sound.

Nova cracks a smile. "He's right. We're sticking around, but we're here on our terms."

"And we promise not to fuck up yours," Oliver says, resting a hand on my shoulder as he comes around me to pluck a donut.

He keeps his arm across my shoulders, and I find myself leaning a bit of my weight into my brother.

Their support means a lot, even if they're drawing the same line in the sand as Rocky. I want to say that it'll be easier with them here. But that's not true.

Watching them mold a life for themselves that will be better than mine . . . easier than mine . . . is going to be hard to witness. I'm not sure I'm strong enough to stay on this path.

But I want to be.

I have to be.

I won't screw up.

Twenty-Two

Rocky

Waves slap against rock. Phoebe kicked me out of the loft a month ago, and the melodic sound of the sea has woken me up every morning since. I try not to get used to small things like that. The tranquil splashes and the calming mist. Try not to *like* them.

People romanticize places and create nostalgia out of it. But places are nothing more than spots on a map. Locations your feet stand on.

I can't have sentimental fucking feelings for a place.

That's for the dreamers. The fools.

I'm living in reality, even if it's a reality of my own creation.

A thirty-foot sailboat is tied to the end of a dock. It's a piece of shit. Engine busted. The mast bent. Paint chipped off. No one would be shocked if I said I hauled it in from the junkyard. This morning, I swing a hammer at the cracked sink. Gutting the bathroom has been cathartic. Demo isn't something I do in my normal day-to-day.

Maybe I need this.

Shirtless, sweat trickling down my neck and chest, I swing again. Bits of sink hit my goggles. An indie rock song blares out of my phone. On paper, this should have been the best month of my life. No parents around to force me to do their bidding. *Swing.*

But it feels weird to only have received a couple general "checking in" texts. *Swing.*

The truth: I've never even tried to get out from under our parents. I couldn't do it unless someone else agreed to it first.

Because I don't want to be alone. *Swing.*

My breathing heavies. Their shortage of communication unsettles me like the overworked cliché—the calm before the storm. I can't let my guard down, and the more I live on edge, the more I want to explode.

Swing.

The sink cracks completely off the wall.

"ROCKY!" Nova's voice comes from the top of the boat.

I set the hammer against the wall and reach for my cell, turning the volume down. "Yeah?!" I call out and walk into the galley. Lifting my goggles to my head, I see Nova from the hatch.

"Can you come up here?" he asks. "We need to talk."

"Come down here."

He glares. "I'm not going down there."

Last time he was in a hull, he vomited all over Oliver.

"We're docked, dumbass," I say. "How else are you going to learn to get your sea legs?"

"I have land legs, asshole. Get up here."

I pull my goggles back down over my eyes. "I don't take orders from you." *I don't want to take them from anyone.* I go for my hammer again.

"*Rocky*," Nova says with an intensity that stops me cold. "It's about my sister."

My grip tightens on the hammer. Muscles flexed at mention of Phoebe. *Is she okay?* I could ask. But I don't need her brothers giving me updates when I have two fingers and used them to text her this morning. It went something like this:

Me: Awake?

Phoebe: Yeah, thanks for the wake up text. *sarcasm*

Me: Just want to make sure you're okay with serving five hundred elitist assholes at the clambake today.

Phoebe: I'm okay with serving the four hundred and ninety nine of them.

Me: Knew you hated Jake

Phoebe: I was talking about you 🖕

Me: 🖕

She seemed her normal peachy self. And we're still hitting the same fiery notes with each other. Yet, I'm hesitating to blow off Nova.

I take another second before throwing the hammer down and ripping off my goggles. In an agitated stride, I leave the only good therapy session I've had all year.

As I make the short climb to the top of the boat, wind hits me all at once. Nova has already left the sailboat entirely.

He's standing on the wooden dock.

The same dock of that boathouse party a month ago. The same boathouse I've been renting since Jake banned me from the loft. It was easy to convince the Reynolds' to rent it out to me.

The narrow, wooden Venetian boat sways in the dock beneath the house. Sailboat's mast wouldn't fit under there, obviously, so it's tied on the dock that extends further into the bay.

I walk to the edge of the boat and stare down at Nova. "You know it's safer to have a conversation on the boat." It's why I got the piece of shit—other than to take out my pent-up feelings on it, that is.

Nova crosses his arms over his chest. "Not happening."

I squint in the sun. "What's on your face?"

"It's called a mustache."

"Gross, man."

He flips me off. "Are you coming down here?"

I let out another annoyed breath and make my way down to the dock. "Your fear of water really needs to be looked at."

"I'm not scared of the water, and you know that." He glares at me. "God, sometimes it's impossible to talk to you."

My feet hit the dock, and I smile dryly. "Could it be because I don't want you to talk to me?"

He opens his mouth to reply but an obtrusively loud noise comes from the neighbor's dock.

A seal.

Hercules (Hailey named him) flaps his flippers at us and continues that honking sound. He's out there every morning. Same time.

Every day.

But all he really does is make funny noises like he's trying to cheer me up. Hercules would be a better roommate than

Nova, who constantly has to "get on the same page" as me as if we're in a perpetual group project that I never signed up for.

Nova waits for the seal to quiet down before turning back to me. "Phoebe and Jake."

My body stiffens like those three words are literally repellent. "Is there a question there or are you just trying to make me punch something?"

Nova eyes me up and down. "You don't like them together?"

"They're not *together*," I say, like he's insane. Unless I've been sleeping under a rock for the last month—oh wait, no. I've been at the country club almost every day keeping tabs on the main players in town.

One of whom is Jake Waterford.

"I didn't say they were." Nova looks at me like I'm the one jumping to conclusions when he opened this whole conversation with just their names. "He's been stopping by the museum and asking about her."

Great. Just great.

I glare at the sky. Nova came into town with Oliver—wait, scratch that—he was *manipulated* into coming here by Elizabeth Graves. They see it differently, fine. But it doesn't change the fact that their mom bumped them off the clip joint job, and that's sketchy as hell.

When Nova got here, he inserted himself in the museum as an art curator. He's not the best at talking his way out of a hole, but he can tell a forgery from the real deal in a heartbeat.

"Asking about her?" I frown. "Like what?"

"Casual shit, but I know he's prying. I can't tell if it's because he likes her or because he doesn't trust her."

I want to say it's the latter, but that'd be because I hope it's not the former. And Jake liking Phoebe . . . Phoebe and Jake . . .

I don't like the scenario.

I *hate* the scenario.

I don't much like him.

I *hate* him. But he's not special. Right now, in this moment, I hate every fucking one. I'm grinding my teeth and glaring at the bay.

Nova watches me too keenly. "I thought you'd have some insight."

My only insight is a deep-seated jealousy that has gnarled around my veins and arteries. Every pump of blood is more toxic fuel in my soul. "It doesn't matter." I rake a rough hand through my hair. "He's not her type. She wouldn't go after him."

"I don't know about that," Nova says. "Now that my sister is on this new honest-life kick, she has more options in the love department."

More options.

Other than me—but he won't say it.

I shift my weight tensely. The past month has been rage piled upon rage.

I can't move on from Phoebe.

I just can't. I never could. And if she's unwilling to break away from our parents for good and I'm unwilling to be with her until we do—then we're at a standstill that I can't fucking stand.

With this new lack of communication with our moms, there are nights where I've just wanted to throw in the towel. Where I've imagined they're gone forever and they'll never find us. Where I've fantasized about showing up at the loft and shoving her against the wall and kissing her like she's the only love of my *entire* life.

I almost hate the sheer strength of my willpower and control that constantly prevents me from doing reckless fucking things. Like leading with my heart.

More options for Phoebe?

Her love life has been cradled in my hands like mine has been in hers.

On so many jobs, we've pretended to be spouses. Pretended to be lovers. I've had my tongue inside her more times than I can count. Kissed my way down her neck and trailed my lips between her breasts. I've grinded up against her body, feeling the softness of her limbs against the hardness of mine. Felt the smooth curves of her hips and the warm heat of her breath. I can smell her sweet floral scent without Phoebe even being around. I've been in wealthy, toxic circles where I had to keep both of us in one piece. Where her body was mine to shield and protect.

Talk about *options* makes me want to break everything inside that boat.

We were *never* given options. Not for anything. And he wants to stand there and tell me that things have changed? Everything in me is dying inside. A slow, aching decay. I don't know how to keep my shit together.

I don't know if I want to anymore.

"Is that what you think is going to happen?" I ask heatedly. "Phoebe is going to make a clean break and fall in love with the golden boy of the town. Have some babies and live happily ever after."

Nova has a soft smile, like I painted a happy, blissful future for his sister. "Beats the alternative."

"Which is?" *Say it, you bastard.*

He stares at me. "You."

I shove him. I can't help it. I just push. He stumbles back, but he doesn't fall. I'm burning alive.

Nova is kerosene. "You *know* you wouldn't be good for her," he growls. "Don't get mad at me for saying it out loud!"

I know he's right.

I hate that he is.

But I just can't stand to hear it. I shove him even harder, and this time his boots teeter on the edge of the wooden dock. He grips onto my shoulder before he plunges into the water, taking me with him.

All my anger that I was fueling into the boat, I just channel into Nova. We're wrestling, dunking each other. Drowning one another. Briny water scalds my esophagus. Shoots up my nose. Pierces my seething eyes. Until I feel hands pushing me and him apart.

"Hey, hey! Get the fuck off each other!" Oliver screams. He's wading in the water with us and trying his best to separate us.

He's shoving me more than Nova.

I settle down enough to seize the dock and cough up some seawater. Nova's equally gassed, choking on air.

"Jesus, are you two *trying* to kill each other?" Oliver asks, swimming to the dock in his suit. He climbs out quickly, white button-down suctioned to his chest.

I don't say anything, still catching my breath. I spit the salty taste out and push a hand through my wet hair.

Nova pulls himself easily onto the dock and lies on his back. His chest heaves in and out.

Oliver looks between us. "You know, I'll give you both a free session with me. Therapy would serve you well."

"I'll pass," Nova says gruffly.

Oliver joined a private practice when he arrived in Victoria, and his growing list of regular clients looks like a CVS receipt. The ladies love the sexy new therapist in town. He has no credentials other than watching *The Sopranos* and our damaged, fucked-up lives for twenty-plus years.

But this isn't his first time pretending to be a therapist. Probably won't be the last. And yeah—ethics are bent and warped in every direction, but sometimes we just don't care about those.

"Rocky?" Oliver asks me.

"I'd rather beat up my boat."

"Looks like you were beating up my brother." Oliver isn't as carefree as he'd have most believe, and I see the thinly veiled threat in his eyes.

"He got caught in the cross fire," I say tightly while pulling my body onto the dock. Standing and dripping water, I reach out a hand to Nova.

Going head-to-head with Phoebe's brothers is a tale as old as time. So is the part where we dust off the dirt under our feet and keep trekking along.

Nova rubs at one of his reddened eyes. "Is that your hand?"

And I realize, he lost a contact in the water. Goddammit. I bend down and clasp his forearm, helping him to his feet.

"Thanks." He plucks the other contact out and blinks repeatedly.

"Does Jake asking about Phoebe even matter, Nova? The moment our parents come to town, everything will change."

"That's why I'm asking." He pinches his eyes and then blinks again. "They're going to want to know if he'd be a good mark. I'm just figuring out what to tell them."

I nod. "We tell them Victoria is off-limits. No long cons, for any of us while we're here. If we all agree, they won't have enough shills or principals to pull shit off."

"No long cons?" Oliver thinks, the corners of his eyes creasing in the start of a wince.

"We do that for our sisters," I tell him. "Phoebe. Hailey."

His eyes flit sharply to me when I say my sister's name.

Ignore that, Rocky. I'm trying. "They don't want to be roped into a job, so we need to make sure they aren't. Yeah?"

He immediately folds. "Okay. I'm in." He turns to his brother.

Nova takes a deep breath, dropping his hand from his eyes. "All right." With another heavy breath, he tells me, "Your dad isn't the Big Bad Wolf, Rocky. There are no sides here."

There will always be sides. And I hate the scenario he painted. Because in that situation, we're the three little pigs in straw houses, trying to protect our fragile, vulnerable lives.

Twenty-Three

Phoebe

The old, *old*-money folks won't even talk to you other than to request things," Chelsea told me on my second day. "They'll just treat you like wallpaper. Sometimes that's even better."

Her words are felt full force today during snack service at the pool. Lounge Chair 15 has not even bothered to learn my name (it's on the fancy little golden name badge). No, he just calls me *skunk*. A fact that Katherine said is town tradition.

I return to the outdoor pool bar with a scowl, which grows even fiercer when I see who's behind the bar. Jake Waterford has his sleeves rolled up like a pleb. And he's adding ice into the cooler. I'd say I was hallucinating, but after a month, I've learned that Jake isn't just a Koning.

He's his family's gopher boy. The third son.

Not in line to take over the billion-dollar business.

Not the spare heir in case the first son bites it.

He's the one they call on for all their secondary priorities.

The country club. The real estate. If he had any aspirations, they were squashed early on.

And now he's here, filling up a cooler.

"Where's Erik?" I ask, looking around for the usual bartender and clutching the serving tray under my armpit.

"On the patio getting the bars ready for tonight," Jake says. "We need all hands on deck for the clambake."

"Interesting," I say. "I don't see your brothers here. Did they lose their hands?"

He shoots me a look. I haven't met Trent or Jordan yet. They've never stopped by the country club. At least, not while I've been serving. Even his parents have been MIA, but it'd be impossible not to notice their phone calls. Jake has ruthless ringtones for each of his family members.

"And your brothers?" Jake asks me. "Are they coming?"

"Two mai tais for lounge fifteen," I say, avoiding. I figure Jake will phone a mixologist friend to help, but he pulls out a glass from beneath the bar.

My brows rise. "You sure we don't need Erik?"

"I can make a drink," he says, like I'm being silly. He procures the rum next, and I hear the squawk of a seagull flying overhead. Once the noise dies and the sun drifts behind a fluffy cloud, Jake turns his head to me. "I assume your ex-husband will be in attendance."

"I don't keep tabs on Rocky." *Lie.* My stomach sours. It's hard to know what's a normal white lie versus a bad one constructed for personal gain. They're all the same in my head. Every lie is a building block to the next.

Changing topics quickly, I say, "When will they stop calling me a skunk?"

Jake laughs. "You?" He looks up at my blue hair tied in a *slightly* unkempt pony. "Never, most likely."

I grimace. "Well, what about Hailey?"

Jake's face sobers. "They're still calling her a skunk?"

"Yeah," I say, like it's mean. Because it *is*.

He shakes his head, skin pleating between his brows. "I don't know. Maybe a year? When it looks like she's a local. The ladies who attend Tuesday book club seem to be warming up to her already."

My brows shoot up again. "Are you keeping tabs on Hailey?"

He glares at me while plopping tiny umbrellas in the drinks. "No."

Okay, fine. He slides over the drinks, but before I take them, I ask, "Your brothers really aren't coming?" I'm serious this time. I can't imagine my brothers bailing on something super important to me, and this clambake charity auction has been a big deal to Jake.

It's the *annual event,* Katherine has reminded me twenty times. It's supposed to mark the end of summer as the warm days of September begin to turn cool.

Maybe Jake doesn't run Koning, but he's in charge here, and I can see there is a part of him that wants to prove he's capable to his parents. That feeling—I know it so well.

"I don't know." His voice is tight, and he wipes off the bar with a rag. "They might show up. They might not. I don't have brothers like yours."

"Like mine?" *What is that supposed to mean?*

He chucks the dirty rag under the bar. "They seem to have your best interest at heart, and they're cool."

He's been making friends with Nova and bonding over their mutual dislike of Rocky.

It's unsettling.

Jake sets his blue eyes on me. "Maybe it's a triplet thing."

"Maybe," I mutter, then I straighten up from a slight slouch. "Well . . . if I ever do meet Trent or Jordan, I'm going to have words with them."

Jake gives me his usual *no you're not* look. "I will make sure that meet and greet never happens."

"You'll have to shadow me around for eternity, then." I place the drinks on my tray. "Which might be your own personal hell."

"You're not that bad."

I glance up at him, a little shocked by the compliment. "Joke?" I ask.

He winces. "Why do you always think I'm joking?"

"I didn't think you liked me." I shrug. "And you're Jake *Koning* Waterford. People treat you like you're flesh-and-blood aristocracy around here. I'm not bowing at your feet, so why would you like me?"

His jaw sets for a second, then his eyes dart to my hair. "I envy you. How's that?"

My stomach tosses for a second. "Now that *is* a joke."

He groans. "Just accept the compliment, Phoebe."

"Explain the compliment, Jake."

He takes a deeper breath, like this isn't easy for him to say. "I don't know exactly what you did to lose your trust fund, but you had the nerve to risk it." He stares past me like he's thinking of something else. "Some days I wish I could . . ." His voice trails off, his gaze darkening with an invasive thought.

"You wish you could piss off your family?" I finish for him.

He lifts a shoulder in a shrug, then he shakes his head. His eyes flit around me again. "I can't."

"You could," I urge, and I don't know why I'm tempting him toward the dirty pools of rebellion. *Drama. Destruction. Danger.* Am I Jake's little devil on his shoulder?

His uncertain gaze meets mine. Possibly he sees I'm bad for him because he says, "I have more to lose than you probably did."

Ouch.

Burn?

But valid.

Even with my new backstory, I don't hail from a generations-old family legacy. That's all him.

Before I can reply, he's distracted by a guest in a red bikini, coming over to place some drink orders.

I'm about to take the drinks to lounge fifteen when a darker storm cloud shields the sun. A clap of aggressive thunder follows.

Red Bikini lets out a gasp of surprise. She reroutes her attention to the sky. "You don't think it'll rain, do you?"

As soon as she says it, a raindrop plops on my nose.

"Shit," Jake curses and takes out his phone. "It wasn't supposed to rain until tomorrow . . ." He groans at his screen. Not good news.

The clambake is supposed to happen on the patio and lawn. Fairy lights are strung between the pop-up tents, and circular high-top tables have already been carried and placed systematically on the grass. "Isn't it partially covered?" I ask, referring to the tents.

Lightning cracks the sky.

"Koning!" Katherine's shrill voice is worse than the thunder. She stampedes over in her usual pencil skirt getup. I'd be impressed by the speed at which she can move in that thing, but I can't summon that feeling when it comes to her. "Did you see the lightning?"

"Hard to miss," Jake says into a deep sigh. "We're going to have to move everything inside."

Her lips purse. "We don't have time. The event starts in less than an hour."

The wind grows wilder, and one of the umbrellas to the lounges starts flapping madly. Jake and I move in unison, running over to grab the umbrella before the fabric breaks from the pole.

I grip the base. He seizes the top.

And just like that, the skies tear open, and it starts absolutely *pouring*.

"I have it!" Jake yells over the thundering wind and rain. My wet hair sticks to my chin, and I'm squinting through the sheets of rain that assault us. I let go of the pole so he can tug it out of its base.

"Get the others!" he shouts.

I scan the patio and spot four more umbrellas, plus cushions on *every* lounge chair that look ready to take flight like we're in Tornado Alley. Everyone else has vacated the pool area, even Katherine.

Kicking into gear, I hustle around the pool, my heeled boots sinking in soggy grass, and I take care of another umbrella and start collecting cushions under my armpits. I throw everything inside the sunroom that's closed to guests during pre-clambake prep, and staff help stack my heap neatly against the wall.

Chelsea slips me a worrisome look, eyeing my drenched hair.

I don't blame anyone for choosing not to brave the elements. I mean—we have to work tonight, and I now look like a drowned cat. Maybe Katherine even told them not to go outside.

At least I'm not alone.

Jake's clothes are soaked, his button-down suctioning to

the ridges of his *eight*-pack. Yep, I can clearly count each defined muscle that would likely rival Rocky's Adonis physique.

No more Rocky.

My brain has been slow to process the memo.

Jake Waterford surprisingly doesn't resemble a stray caught in a squall like me. No . . . he might as well have returned from a sailboat photo shoot with a sexy stormy theme.

Sexy stormy—I didn't even think that could be a thing until now.

On my fourth trip inside, I notice how the staff that organizes the cushions and umbrellas are all women, and they're glued to the big windows. I don't think they're storm watching.

I follow their rabid attention and see Jake has peeled off his button-down. Rainwater drips along the sculpted tracks of his chest. I wonder if he knows he's in a one-man Magic Mike show right now.

Veering back around, I drop the cushions on the floor and catch Chelsea's eyes. "Where's Hailey?" I haven't seen her.

"Katherine has her plating hors d'oeuvres."

I return to the pool. It takes two more trips before all the flyaway items are safely secured. Jake braces the door open for me, his hand above my head, and I could cheer at *finally* being inside for good. But my waterlogged clothes feel like fifty pounds, and the air-conditioning is on full force.

Goosebumps immediately form on my arms, and I can't stop trembling. The staff are all gone now. Katherine must have corralled them into the dining room.

Jake's leather shoes sound squishy as he turns to me. His eyes flit from my head to my feet, his concern apparent as I keep shivering. "Do you have a change of clothes?"

"No, I didn't pencil in *getting soaked* on my to-do list today."

He nods slowly. "All right. I think there might be a spare uniform in the locker room. Follow me." He walks briskly, and with his long, tall legs, I have to almost jog to keep up.

My phone buzzes, and I see it's Hailey. I answer quickly. "Hey." I'm almost out of breath from Jake's pace.

"Hey," she says. "Katherine wants to know where you are. She's freaking out." *Of course she is.*

"I'm changing in the locker room," I say. "I'll be there when I don't look like I swam across the Atlantic Ocean."

"Got it," Hailey replies. Then adds under her breath, "She's on a tear. Take your time. I'll stall."

I smile and calm my shaking limbs. "Thanks, Hails."

She says a quick goodbye and hangs up.

In the locker room, Jake opens a cardboard box. "There are some standard blouses and pants in here. You can see if any of them are your size."

I touch the edge of the box, but my eyes are on him. I try not to stare too hard at the firm valleys and planes of his body. Or the way his slacks sit perfectly low on his masculine waist. *He's gorgeous.* I can very clearly see that, and maybe I should kindle little embers of lust that must be lying dormant in me.

He's not Rocky.

That should be a good thing—the best thing. I push down the strange flip of my stomach.

"What about you?" I ask him. "What are you wearing?"

He leans past my body to unlock a locker. I see a tux inside. "I was going to change anyway," he tells me.

"That's lucky."

He hangs the soaked button-down on the rod. "Preparation isn't luck."

"I'll remember that next time I need to whip out a boarding school motto." I break my eyes away from his toned biceps to peruse the box. "Let me guess, you were on the row team in college?"

"Polo team."

Horses. Mallets. Oliver once had to play polo on a job. I'm not as good around animals. I've always had a strange feeling that they can sense deception better than humans. And I'm not alone in that theory.

"Thanks for helping with outside, by the way," Jake says. "I know it wasn't ideal."

"Shouldn't I be thanking you?" I ask, rummaging through the box. "It's my job. You could have left me out there alone."

"I wouldn't do that."

Again, he's a good guy. And clearly, the opposite of my type.

"Doesn't it get frustrating doing the right thing all the time?" I ask because I'm genuinely curious. If I'm the devil on his shoulder, then maybe he can be the angel on mine.

"What do you mean?"

"I mean, we could have said *Fuck this clambake* and just left all the cushions outside. Forced Katherine to risk her perfect coiled hair."

"You know, for a split second, it did cross my mind."

My brows jump. "Jake?"

He laughs. "Settle your excitement, Rebel Without a Cause."

Okay, I'm smiling. I'm just glad he's not perfect—the bar to be a good person has lowered in my eyes. It seems more feasible to reach. "I'm just shocked that your polished armor has a chip in it."

"If you knew me," Jake says, "you wouldn't be so surprised."

If I knew him. Here I thought I had gotten to know him decently well. My mood punctures like a popped balloon.

Then his gaze lingers on me for an extended beat. Tender, almost, and I sense him canvassing the length of me. I can't tell if he's checking me out from the outside or the inside, and it puzzles me in a new way.

My cheeks burn while I find a dry blouse in my size, and we both work on undressing. I peek back at him. He slips another glance at me. The silence is weighted and unclear, as if we're partially shrouded in steam.

Once I fish the buttons of my damp blouse through the fabric slits and Jake begins unzipping his wet slacks, we turn our backs to one another. I can hear him stepping out of his pants, and I toss the blouse on the bench.

Shimmying pants down my hips and thighs, I'm tempted to take another tiny peek at him. Fall into the pool of lust, right? Maybe it'll heat me up.

I twist my head over my shoulder and see his round ass perfectly molded against damp blue boxer briefs. Rocky has more muscle definition around his waist with a V-line that dives toward his cock, but they're both classically attractive like one of Michelangelo's sculptures.

I imagine they'd be competing in the same museum, vying for the most attention. And oh my fucking God, why am I thinking of Rocky *again*? Especially when I'm looking at Jake.

Ughhhh. It's like he's attached himself to my frontal cortex.

Jake casts another glance back at me, and our eyes catch. A warm flush ascends my neck. Instead of breaking the gaze, we allow each other to ogle. To check one another out. It's a good distraction, one I plummet into with wide open arms.

"Nice ass," I tell him.

"Likewise."

I laugh. "So polite."

He spins around completely to face me and steps closer.

"You want me to be rude?" He reaches past my arm to the locker next to me. His skin brushes mine, and I go still.

His eyes fall to me as I cage my breath. He adds, "Pretty sure that's your ex-husband's gig."

Mention of Rocky prolongs my exhale.

"But maybe that's what turns you on," Jake says, sliding an arm through his fresh button-down.

In only a bra and panties, my near nakedness doesn't make me feel exposed. It's his words that send me through a whirlpool of emotions.

"I have many turn-ons, Koning," I say sharply. "Politeness is just bottom rung."

"That says a lot," he replies, eyes flashing up and down my body like he has me all figured out.

Hardly.

Still, I'm frowning and feeling as if he's stripped me even more bare. "Why?"

"Just didn't know why you would have married a guy like him," Jake says. "He's the kind of person I would have warned my sister against. Red flag city. But maybe he's a god in bed—who knows?"

I wouldn't know.

My throat swells, unable to say that truth.

The entrance to the locker room creaks open. *Shitshitshit.* Crouching behind the cardboard box, I scramble with my new blouse.

Where are the armholes? *Come on.*

It's probably some middle-aged club member, like one of the widowers. Oh God, please don't let it be Mr. Burke.

Jake, in a half-buttoned shirt and boxer briefs, inches out of our row. "I'm changing in here, man." *That's what locker rooms are for.* To change.

He could've chosen a million other lies or a Koning "this is my locker room" power play to deter the person.

Instead, he goes with the truth. Noble, yes. Helpful, I don't see how. Where's the bad guy when you need him? It hurts, how much I actually miss being around Rocky.

I don't hear the door shut.

I only hear footsteps coming closer to this row of lockers.

"Yeah, sorry," Rocky says, not sounding sorry at all.

Rocky is here?

Did I just manifest him? Relief that it's not Mr. Burke washes over me. And then I remember I'm in lacy pink panties and a white bra while Jake is half dressed. This is bad.

Very, very bad. I hasten my search for this stupid fucking armhole. I've literally turned the blouse inside out.

"I'm just looking for Phoebe," Rocky says, his gravelly voice speeding up my pulse. "Hailey said she was in the locker rooms."

I internally groan. It's not Hailey's fault. But I also can't hide from her older brother. This isn't a secret I want to keep—especially since it's innocent. So I'm not exactly scampering into the dark depths of the room.

Not that I'd have time anyway.

Just as I straighten up out of a squat, Rocky comes into view. He stops short, his muscles flexed.

I speak fast. "I know how this looks—"

His tightened gaze pings from Jake to me. "Yeah. Like you two fucked in a locker room."

Jake groans. "Jesus."

"We were just changing," I say. "We got soaked in the rain."

Rocky is at a low simmer. His jaw sets, thinking it over. Would I be just as upset if I caught him with a girl? Highly likely.

It's hard not to feel possessive. But maybe this is good for us. Maybe we need reasons to just . . . move on? *Then why does it hurt?* I blink back a stronger emotion and hurriedly pull on the dry blouse, a knot constricting in my lungs. My panties are still wet, but I can't do anything about that. Tension amasses in the room the longer the silence extends, but I don't know how to break it. I don't know what to do.

I glance at Rocky like *Help*.

He takes a steadying breath, and his eyes go dark. Blank. I don't like it. Then he turns to Jake. "She's all yours, man."

Jake glowers. "She's not an object you can gift me. So, no thanks."

Rocky winces. "That's not what I meant." He curses under his breath and casts an apology my way through his eyes. "I meant I'm not interested in her."

Ow. He's burying a knife in my chest. But I know we've stabbed each other before. We have thousands of blades dug into our sternums. Our backs. We've lived our lives walking around, invisibly impaled, and slowly bleeding out.

Jake doesn't take his eyes off Rocky. "I figured that's what a divorce means."

Rocky tries hard to keep his face impassive. He just nods a couple times and leaves.

"Jackass," Jake breathes out.

My instant reaction is to go comfort Rocky. Protect him. Side with him. But I know what he did was *for* me. Pushing me away for a moment. Reminding each other *this is what has to happen*.

My phone buzzes, and I check a text.

Hailey: Can't stall any longer. Katherine is looking for you.

I take a calming breath, finish getting dressed, and tie my wet hair into a tight ponytail. When I arrive in the kitchen,

Katherine beelines for me. An aroma of hairspray immediately invades my senses. I blame that on my queasy stomach.

"Phoebe, where have you been?" She doesn't give me enough time to answer, pushing me to the nearest counter. "You will serve champagne all night. That's your *only* job." She's placing the flutes gingerly and perfectly on my tray. "Walk around and when your tray is empty, get it refilled and go back out there." She inhales a tight breath and drills a warning look on me. "A toddler could do this. *Don't* mess it up."

Low chatter echoes from the main dining hall, and the savory aroma of clams permeates around the bustling kitchen. How long had I been in the locker room?

My head feels like it's filled with helium, ready to soar off my shoulders. I stumble into the crowded dining hall, squinting through the candlelight.

Hands fly toward my tray, grabbing and taking without a single glance in my direction. I try to be effortless and weave between bodies.

But I'm not all here.

I collide with a fortysomething woman, likely around my mom's age, who's in a velvety emerald dress. The five champagne flutes teeter on my tray, and I attempt to right them up, but champagne tips back and spills on my blouse. The next second, every flute just tumbles to the floor with a loud *crash*.

The room goes eerily quiet, all eyes on me. The heat of the attention combined with my own overturned feelings sends me into a tailspin. The woman casts me a withering glare. "Name?"

My head cycles through a list of aliases:

Piper
Paige
Petunia

Penelope
Patty
Parker
Paisley
Palmer

Hundreds of eyes on me, I can't breathe. I want to run. I'm about to when I catch Rocky out of the corner of my eye. He takes a step toward me, but he stops suddenly like he's walked into an invisible barrier.

And then I feel a hand on my shoulder.

Twenty-Four

Rocky

Jake made it to her first, and for the first time in my life, I feel second best. A step behind. It gnaws at me as I watch him put his hand on her shoulder and dip his head to her ear. She nods, her panicked face calming at whatever he says.

I slide in closer, slipping behind a couple of ladies.

"She's going to get fired," Mrs. Kelsey muses.

"No doubt," Ms. Davenport agrees.

I step in front of them, having a better view. Phoebe edges closer to Jake's side, and when he wraps his arm around her waist—I freeze. I'm thrust backward in time.

At eighteen, nineteen, twenty . . . all the years I had to stand and watch her entertain other men. My muscles sear and pull taut.

"Mom," Jake says to the woman in an emerald gown, who I know to be Claudia Koning Waterford. "I'd like you to meet my girlfriend, Phoebe."

My world shatters in one single instant. I can't . . .

I can't watch this.

With quicker, angrier strides, I push past bodies to leave the dining hall. Whispers surround me. Eyes follow me. She's my ex-wife in this town, and gossip is thriving about our tumultuous, caustic marriage, so my feelings right now are justified. I don't hide them. I fucking can't.

I just can't.

The rain has let up, but the sun has already set. Lamps illuminate a series of paths, and I leave the country club, my feet carrying me down the lit boardwalk to the club's private beach, farther from the light and onto the darkness of the sand. Did I cause this?

I told him he could have her. Did she choose him?

Was there a choice?

Fuckfuckfuck.

I pace the beach, hands laced on my head. *Keep your shit together.* I can't breathe. I squat down like I've run a marathon, like I've been gut-punched, and my scalding eyes pierce the raging ocean.

She's gone.

You lost her.

She's gone.

You won't ever have her.

Maddened, furious tears prick my eyes. Pain swelling up inside me, I do everything in my power to contain the scream that wants released. *You're in public. You're in public.* I slide my hands to the back of my neck. I want this to stop—please make it stop.

I hyper-focus on my shortened breath. On the pieces of hair that brush my forehead as a gust blows across the beach. I itch at the fucking tag that scratches at my neck. Biting down so hard on my teeth, my jaw is aching. My bad knee begins to throb in the squat, and I touch the sand, sensing the grit slipping through my fingers.

My gold watch sits heavy on my wrist, and I unclasp it, holding the watch in the pit of my palm. My sleeves feel rough against my wrists now.

Nausea builds, and I spit out onto the sand and then stand up. Breathing, breathing.

Fuck these sleeves.

Fuck this tag.

"So what do we do now?" Phoebe's voice whirls my attention to the boardwalk, and I almost want to laugh in agony. Dear *God*, you won't let me escape her, will you?

I rotate slowly around and see Phoebe and Jake approaching. They haven't noticed me yet, too dark down on the beach, but I make myself known.

"Hey!" I scream at them.

Jake stops in his tracks. Phoebe doesn't, and as she sinks into the sand and comes toward me, Jake decides to follow behind her.

When they're closer, I say dryly, "There's a million other beaches. Go find another one. Better yet, the ocean's right there. Have at it." I wave a hand toward the sea.

Phoebe doesn't shoot a normal snide retort back, but her arms thread over her chest. I'd say more from the cold as temperatures dropped, but what do I know? I've only been around her my entire fucking life.

She holds my gaze for a long beat before saying in a hushed breath, "Jake just asked me to fake date him."

Fake date.

I don't think I heard that right. "Excuse me?" I look to Jake, who approaches at a slower pace.

He side-eyes Phoebe. "I thought we weren't going to tell people the truth?"

"Rocky doesn't count as *people*," she says.

Jake sighs out. "Yeah, it's *fake*." He speaks quietly, too. "She needed help keeping her job."

"And he finally found the nerve to piss off his mom," she says.

"It felt good," he adds, and they share a look like that means something to them.

My ribs constrict against my lungs.

She's hugging her arms tighter around herself. *She's definitely cold.* I'm only wearing a button-down. I have nothing to offer her.

Jake starts taking off his suit jacket.

Just dump another shovel of dirt on top of me. I'm already choking on it.

Phoebe continues in a whisper, "It's a mutual arrangement."

She says *arrangement* but I hear *con.*

She's pulling a con *with* Jake Waterford. Not for money but for another gain.

He's in *my* role as her fake boyfriend.

And now she's putting on his suit jacket. Well, isn't this a fairy tale.

"Great," I say, hushed. "Cool. You two are fake great for one another." I make a *perfect* gesture with my fingers.

Jake glares, then twists his head to the gathering audience on the boardwalk. Women wield champagne flutes like popcorn. He expels a tense breath. "What did I get myself into?"

Man, you have no idea.

I look to Phoebe, her frame cocooned in his suit jacket. I rub my mouth, my lungs on fire with every sharp breath, and the worst part: I want to hug her right now.

I would bring her into my chest and warm her with my body—but I can't anymore. I'm just her *fake* ex-husband.

Her fake boyfriend has a leg up on me.

Whatever standstill Phoebe and I were at—it's shifted dramatically. It needed to, but this direction is flipping me upside down.

"You two are really doing this?" I ask in a quiet breath, staring at Phebs. This goes against Phoebe's whole goal of being a moral citizen of Victoria, but I know this is a good thing for her. This pivot will help her gain a better reputation in town. She'd be using him a hell of a lot more than he's using her. It's the right move, even if I hate it.

"Just for a little while," Phoebe says, avoiding my gaze.

I turn to Jake. He's scowling out at the ocean now like it personally affronted him. I got him all wrong—thinking he was some straitlaced prep. And I usually don't screw up when I read people. That annoys me.

I move closer to them to avoid being overheard, and I ask Jake, "You hate your mom that much?"

His gaze flits to me, and the look in his eyes is one I know well. It's what I see when I stare into the mirror. And he says, "I don't trust her."

Twenty-Five

Phoebe

W ho proposes to someone in two months?" The rhetorical question leaves my lips as rose petals flutter from my palm. I scatter them across the floor of a penthouse suite in a snazzy five-star hotel.

Rocky stages the bar, popping a champagne bottle and dumping the contents down the drain. His gaze swings to me. "In this case, someone disgusting who gets off on deflowering women."

I am a virgin.

At least that's what my fiancé believes. Patrick Alistair. The twenty-five-year-old senator's son swiped right on my profile sixty days ago.

All kinds of dating apps exist online, but people only ever really hear about the mainstream ones. But there are dating apps for every kind of flavor, and it just so happens that the My Valentine app is for virgins. Its business model states how it helps unite two heterosexual individuals who are abstaining until marriage.

It took me an hour on the app to recognize that it's a hot-bed for wealthy men to find girls, offering them money and trips. Some called themselves *sugar daddies*. I didn't mind the ones that were up front about being sugar daddies. It was the Patrick Alistairs that left a sour taste in my mouth.

He claimed to be a virgin.

I knew he wasn't.

He made me visit a doctor to have her confirm my hymen was intact. We had to rent an office space, convert it into a women's clinic. Addison Tinrock pretended to be a doctor, and she kicked out Patrick when he tried to stay in the room *during* the procedure. Once he was gone, Addison rolled her eyes like he disgusted her, too, and we shared a look like we were glad he was going to be fleeced.

It's been an eventful two months. I've dodged most kisses and physical forms of affection, which Patrick has accepted as a sign of my purity and demure demeanor. It's only reeled him in more.

He's gross in a different way than handsy dirtbags at bars. His face writhes in revulsion when he sees a girl wearing a sundress in public. If he catches sight of even the slightest PDA, he calls her a whore. His judgment toward women has made me burn up and seethe, and I'm elated this job is cycling to an end. So he can finally get a nice kick to the balls.

Rocky finishes staging the bar with emptied glasses and spilled liquor. I toss the last of the petals on the king-sized bed.

There is one final task before completing the job, and it's staring me in the face.

Rocky crosses the room, seizing my gaze. We haven't talked

about the last thing our parents told us before we left for the hotel.

Everett, Addison, and my mom gathered us together at a safe location in Brooklyn. The fancy brownstone they were renting was a part of their lavish New York lives, and my mom was playing the role of my sweet-hearted, fashionable aunt this time.

I wished Hailey was doing this job with us. I hadn't seen her in a couple weeks since she was in Staten Island getting new passports from Carter for the next job.

"They *have* to be convincing," Everett said to my mom and Addison, tension high in the living room. A fireplace crackled, and no one was seated. We were all on our feet, and Rocky gripped the mantel like he was forcing himself not to implode.

"We will be," I assured, not totally understanding why they thought we'd fail to pull the rope.

My mom slipped me a kind smile. "I have no doubt, bug. We're just trying to figure out what the mark will believe."

Everett shifted his weight with slight ire. "This is called Your Lover *Is* Cheating—not Your Lover *Might* Be Cheating. If he walks in on his fiancée kissing another man, you think he's the type to be sold that easily?" Everett looked between his wife and my mom. "Because I don't think he'll accept it."

"They'll be under bedsheets," my mom volleyed, her arms weaving over her baby-blue chiffon Vera Wang dress, complete with an elegant halter neckline. "His imagination will fill in the blanks."

Addison looked vexed and upset as she pushed her cat-eye Balmain frames up the bridge of her celestial nose. "He's right, Bethy." She spoke to my mom. "He wanted *in* the room to see her hymen."

I touched my burning temple, roasting as they discussed my freaking *hymen* in front of Rocky and his dad. I cast a quick glance to Rocky, and his tightened jaw could've cut glass. He wasn't staring at me, though.

"He's a pig," Addison snipped. "A pig who wanted *proof* of her virginity. He'll want the clearest proof that it's been taken."

"I could go back to the fake doctor," I offered. "You could tell him my . . ." I was on fire. ". . . that I'm no longer a virgin."

My mom shook her head quickly. "No, we have to pull the rope earlier."

Addison nodded. "Once he catches you, his fiancée, in the act with another man, we need this to wrap up immediately. He can't have time to make good choices. Good choices for him are—"

"Bad things for us," I finished what Hailey's mom always said.

"Exactly."

Everett expelled a rough, troubled breath. "So there's supposed to be no room for doubt, and the mark has to believe his fiancée is cheating on him *instantly*. And he won't believe that if he catches them just kissing in a hotel room because . . ." He waved his hand to my mom to finish.

She stared off in thought, twiddling her diamond stud earring. "Because he might convince himself it's nothing." Concern softened her voice. "He could delude himself into believing what he wants to see. That his fiancée is still *pure*."

Addison drummed her lips. "The other principal is supposed to come in and verify what the mark sees."

Oliver was the other principal. He'd grown a two-month friendship with Patrick, and recently, he warned him against marrying me.

Patrick wanted to live with his head in the sand and pretend like I was his perfect picture of purity. And then Oliver had suckered him in by saying, "If this blows up in the future, it could destroy your father's political career. Better to nip it now, man, and not make the biggest mistake of your life by marrying a cheating whore."

Patrick had listened.

"Look," Oliver had said, "maybe I'm wrong, and if I am, I'll be happy to be and see you marry the girl of your dreams. But I'll make you a bet. If you're right and she's not cheating, I'll give you the money for the Lambo we both love." For weeks, they'd bonded over being car aficionados and Formula 1 hobbyists, and they had their eyes on a limited-edition Lamborghini.

Worth half a million dollars.

"If I'm right," Oliver had told him, "you give me the money for it."

It wasn't chump change to Patrick, but his family could definitely afford a high-risk bet if he lost. His mom came from football royalty, and not because there was a quarterback in his family. His grandparents owned an entire NFL team.

Patrick had agreed to the bet, thinking I was still perfectly his, but he'd wanted clear, definitive proof of me cheating. Not a text message string that could be fabricated or a Photoshopped picture. He needed to know one hundred percent that I was every whorish thing Oliver painted me as.

Everett grimaced. "This'll be an uphill climb for Oliver if he has to convince the mark. He'll think he's just trying to get the damn car. The indisputable proof has to come from *them*." He pointed toward Rocky and me.

How much Patrick needed to *actually* see—that was the argument.

Everett spoke to Addison. "This shouldn't be hard for them, hun. They've kissed plenty of times. None of us would be surprised if they've already had sex—"

"We haven't," Rocky growled through his teeth. "Not that it's any of your fucking business."

Everett made a concerted effort not to glare back at his son.

"There are feelings there, Bethy," Addison reasoned with my mom.

I interjected. "I wouldn't go that far." I whirled to my mom. "*Mom.*"

"You have kissed him during jobs, bug," my mom said. "Would it be that bad to go just a little further?"

I froze. Would it be? Was I just making this unreasonably harder on everyone?

Rocky was grinding his jaw, a rough, angered hand scraping through his hair. Until he pushed away from the mantel. "What do you want us to do? Fuck each other on the job?"

No one said anything.

Addison and my mom exchanged a glance that I couldn't decipher. They'd shared many of those over the years. Glimpses reserved for very best friends. For those who know the depth of you from the inside out.

"We want no room for doubt, Brayden. That's it," Addison told her son.

"It's half a million dollars," Everett said slowly, like the money would matter. "Your mother and I would do more for less. Hell, we've all *done* more for less."

I felt like a toddler throwing a stupid tantrum. I knew my mom had been in her fair share of uncomfortable positions, and they weren't asking me to be with a stranger. This was Rocky.

"I'll do it," I suddenly said. My stomach clenched, knowing

I was agreeing to leapfrog over a line that Rocky and I never crossed.

He stared straight at me, breathing harder and harder.

"Brayden, please," Addison whispered.

And finally, he said, "Okay."

At the brownstone, I wasn't as nervous. Back there, it felt like a blueprint. Less real and more imagined.

Here, seeing Rocky come toward the rose-petal-strewn bed where I stand—this is very real.

I almost wish he didn't dump expensive champagne down the drain and on the bar counter. Could've used a tiny buzz to quiet the nerves, but we're pretty good about keeping clear heads during jobs.

"Ready to pop my cherry?" I quip with less flirt and more bite. It's the realest me, and the realest him stalks closer with a dark look in his eye.

I watch him pursue me with zero hesitance. Whatever disturbed him at the brownstone has been silenced, and he drinks in more than the softness of my thigh, which peeks from the sultry slit of my glittery silver dress. He consumes more than the diamond necklace dripping down my plunging neckline, more than my teasing breasts.

I intake shorter, quicker breaths. My heart accelerates at an adrenaline-charged rate.

I'm not bait to Rocky. I'm not a lifeless mannequin. I'm not cattle needing to be appraised and bartered. I'm not the hundreds of different faces I've worn.

I'm just Phoebe.

His black bow tie is already unraveled around the collar of his white button-down. Dark hair devilishly disheveled and his gaze fixed unwaveringly on me, he looks ready to devour the entire world with me inside it.

"Forget your cherry was popped years ago?" he retorts in a deep, husky breath. Nearing me with quiet footfalls. Closer, *closer.* "And not by me."

Oxygen thins, and my collarbone juts out as I chase after breath. "Disappointed?" I sling back.

He's only inches away, his cologne an intoxicating sandalwood and pine scent, and his gaze drops to my lips. "*Devastated,*" he says dryly, but despite his tone, the truth of that single word bleeds through his pinpointed eyes, driving a dagger straight through me.

I twist the blade. "You cry yourself to sleep every night?"

"Every. Single. Night." His voice is a serrated breath in the quiet. He towers over me, staring down, our gazes practically nail-gunned to one another. "I *wept* over you. Over what I'd never do to you." His fingers skate along the curve of my hip with a tortured slowness. No zipper to my dress; he reaches around to my lower back, where a few knotted strings cinch fabric and accentuate my shape. "How I'd never bend you over."

My pulse quickens. I never break his molten gaze that verges on a glare. How a glare can be laced with sensual, desirous things is beyond my comprehension right now, but I feel myself searing an identical one into him.

"How I'd never slide my hard"—he loosens one string, his fingers brushing the bare flesh of my lower back—"long *cock* between your legs and fuck you senseless. How I'd never make you writhe and cry and moan." His other hand nestles against my flushed neck. "And you. You would've loved every. Single. Second. Of me."

Arousal gathers like an active volcano inside my body, and I sway against his grazing hands like toxic fumes cloud the room.

"Thrusting," he says, untying a knot with one last pull, "so deep inside your wet . . . virgin pussy. You would've seen stars for endless fucking days."

The cocktail dress slackens at my hips like a pillow sack. Once he glides the thin straps off my shoulders, the entire dress cascades in a silver pool at my heels.

My expression wields a strange amount of power over Rocky, possessing him more than my perked nipples and the bareness of my body. Even as his fingers slip in the lacy band of my white thong, he's glued to my eyes and my lips.

My pulse hurries in a lovesick pace, but I tilt my chin up to meet the depth of his gaze. "You wanted to be the first inside me so badly," I taunt, a headiness still swirling between us.

"*So badly,*" he parrots, his fingers climbing up my neck. "Tell me, Phoebe. When I wasn't the first to fuck you, how long did you cry over me?"

I'm barely breathing. "Every. Single. Night." I try to deadpan, but the words are caught in a tangled moan.

Rocky clasps the back of my skull, and he kisses the everloving fuck out of me—a desperate, raw kiss that explodes me to his chest with force.

I gasp as smoldering pleasure surges, as the blistering seconds burn into timeless moments. I rip through the buttons of his white shirt, and he tears it off his arms, tossing it aside. Bare chested, he unbuckles his belt, and I kick off my heels.

He presses his forehead to mine and breathes huskily, "You want this tonight?"

I want you.

"I want it." This is the greatest confirmation. He wastes no time cupping the backs of my thighs and hoisting me around his waist. My heart is beating out of my rib cage. I claw at his hair, our kisses ravenous and edged with poison. Being with

Rocky feels lethal—like it could end me at any moment—and yet, I loathe the very idea of stopping.

He hurls me on the bed, and I bounce on top of the fluffy hotel comforter, rose petals smashed under my back. Our gazes are fucking before our bodies even touch. We forgo slipping beneath the cover and sheets, and as he crawls over my body, he tears my lacy thong down my thighs and legs.

This is happening.

I hate how good he makes me feel. I hate how much I truly love every. Single. Second. *Of him.*

Because this will end soon. *Don't look at the clock.* It's dumb not to check the time. We're on a job, but I find myself avoiding the digital clock on the nightstand like it's a bomb ticking down.

Rocky places a kiss on my kneecap before rising back to my lips. We're tangled in each other, and sweat already glistens on his chest and beads up on my thighs. He takes a second to peel off his black boxer briefs, and when he falls back down—hands rooted on either side of me—the sheer heat of his hardness rubbing against me is enough to prick all my nerves.

I pulsate, aching for him, and I reach up the same time he bows down—kissing again. The kissing part is safe. It's what we've always done. Toy and tease and eke out an unbearable tension, and that tension stretches tenfold tonight.

He clutches my thigh and spreads me wider around his waist. *Oh God.* A shaky cry scrapes against my throat. "*Rocky.*" It sounds like a warning.

He pauses, his chest inflating and deflating with rapid, hot breath. I feel him searching me. "You want this?" he asks again.

Yes. I hang on to the back of his neck, panting. "I . . ." *Don't look at the clock.*

It'll all end tonight.

It'll end soon.

"*Phoebe.*" He clasps my cheek with equal parts care and urgency. "Do you want to have sex with me?"

Every artery and blood cell in me is screaming, *Yes!* "Keep going," I breathe out.

"That's not an answer."

"Yes," I snap back and arch up to kiss him.

Rocky resists at first, but he descends back into the deadly vapors of our arousal. Lip-locked. His tongue slides against mine, dizzying me again, and I could lose myself to this moment. To him and time. So terribly, I want to.

We're on a job.

It beats painfully at my heart and mind.

His muscles flex as he grinds forward and cups the back of my head. Not entering me yet, but the pleasure of being this close to Rocky comes with an anguished strain that won't release.

He knocks his knee against my other leg, stretching me even wider, and I'm opened for him.

It'll be disrupted. Patrick will come in midway. It'll all fucking end.

That's what's supposed to happen. What has to happen. What I agreed to.

An emotional ball of pain wells, and I try to ignore the pit in my ribs. Most everything in my life has been temporary, but Rocky never has been. Tonight, he will be.

It hurts.

It hurts.

Why does it hurt?

I clench his hair with both hands, my knees locking and other joints rusting beneath him.

He goes eerily still, likely sensing the rigidity in my body. His brows are knitted together, face twisting through tormented, labored sentiments while he sweeps me. "I can't," he says in a rough, choked breath.

Our gazes latch, and there is so much untouched brewing under the surface.

I want this. But not like this.

I know that, too.

My eyes sear, hurt and relief jumbled together. "This was too far," I murmur. Sex might just ruin everything between us. Hooking up on jobs is already messing with me. "I don't want to keep doing this." I shove his chest, but Rocky is already leaning off me.

With a racing pulse, I grab a soft feather-and-down pillow and hug it upright against my naked frame. Rocky is kneeling, and I avert my eyes from his erection. He checks the time on the digital clock near the bed.

Less than ten minutes and Patrick will be here. We don't have the luxury of cracking open a bottle of wine like we're jilted lovers stuck in a room together—where we can "talk it out" for an hour and dig through the mess we just created.

My "fiancé" is still supposed to catch us in the act.

Yay us.

But Rocky isn't hustling to reconstruct our decaying plan. He climbs unhurriedly off the bed, his muscles constricted in harsher bands. "Our parents will keep using us, Phoebe." He pushes his fingers through his hair and grabs his boxer briefs off the floor. "If we ever have sex, they'll use *that* as a reason to put us in more positions we don't want to be in. You know that, right?"

I'm not sure how much of that is true, but I do know how

much I hate this feeling. "We should never have sex," I realize. "Maybe we should never even date."

Rocky is rigid, motionless. "We have to date for jobs."

My cheeks roast, and I bristle. "Okay, so when we're not on a job." *Not that we've ever dated off a job before.* "I just meant that dating or being in a real relationship shouldn't be a future possibility. It should be . . . banned. Off-limits."

He lets that sink in, looking deeper into me. "You want to agree to it?" he asks, like he needs these three commandments written in stone:

Phoebe and Rocky Shall Never, Ever Have Sex.

Phoebe and Rocky Shall Never, Ever Date Outside of Cons.

Phoebe and Rocky Shall Never, Ever Honestly Be Together.

I don't want to *pine* after him. I don't want to think about him when I'm with other men. I just want to know that the door is closed for good.

"Yeah," I say firmly. "I do." I extend my hand, and Rocky steps over to the bed, covering himself with his balled-up underwear, and he shakes on it. He holds on to my palm for too long, and the worst part, this isn't over.

We have to pull the rope.

Everything is worse, when I thought it'd be better with the declaration, the agreement, and our admission. The tension doesn't dissolve—it wrings painfully tight.

I'm bare underneath the sheets, lying as stiff as a prickly cactus, and Rocky has left for the bathroom.

"You're cutting it close!" I shout at him. We have *three* minutes. How the hell am I supposed to make fake sweet love with him now?

A knife slices through my lungs with each inhale.

Rocky returns to the room as naked as he left. He chucks

his crumpled boxer briefs near the bed, and then he throws a filled condom on the ground. Oh fuck. I widen my eyes at him, but he's not looking at me. A towel is in his hand, a green silk robe . . . and a knife.

What's he doing? I try to be polite and avoid glimpses of his cock. It feels wrong to even peek now.

Rocky tosses me the robe, and I slip my arms mechanically through the silky fabric. He wrenches the comforter and sheets off me. Cold bites my exposed flesh, and he piles the bedding in a twisted heap on the floor.

We're barely looking at each other at this point. And when we do, his jaw tightens and my body flexes strangely. And it hits me.

I think we just broke up in the middle of a con. Not that we were ever *together* in any traditional sense, but we were something. The possibility of what we could be always quietly simmered between us, and now it's festering painfully.

He's back to kneeling on the bed. With the knife, he pricks his finger.

"What are you doing?" I ask him.

"We're giving that bastard what he's afraid of." Blood bubbles on his fingertip, and he stains the hand towel with crimson droplets. "A deflowered virgin."

"Smart." I actually like this plan, but I'm unsure if it'll work.

He sucks his finger and shuts the knife into the end table drawer. "What position are you thinking?"

Another pit forms in my stomach. We never talked about missionary or doggy style or any single position beforehand because we planned on the sex being natural.

Now we're switching from an exhilarating manual transmission to dull automatic, and I just want this over with.

"Probably a position where he can see my face," I say.

"Lie on your back with your head at the foot of the bed."

This is a good option. I can still wear the robe and just have the fabric be a tantalizing tease, slipping slightly off my breasts. But I won't be flashing the mark, and I wonder if Rocky thought about this, too.

Instead of Patrick catching us in the act, we talk it through quickly and agree for him to catch us right as we finish.

With my head careening over the edge of the bed, Rocky grips my hips, but he wads the bloodied hand towel near my center. His cock isn't touching me, and I'm not inspecting how hard he is. If we just finished coming together, then it wouldn't matter anyway.

Once our phone pings, we know Oliver is in the hallway. He had his "friend" from concierge (aka Everett) give him the keycard to our hotel suite.

I act like I'm coming *loudly*, and Rocky fakes a heavy grunt.

"Yes, baby!" I cry out. "*Oh my God,* baby, that was so good. Fuck, *yes*."

"Yeah, you like that, Dalilah?" Rocky pants but stares at the entryway. "I knew you would, honey."

The door flies open. My head upside down, I see Patrick roll to a horrified stop. "Dalilah?" He's sheet white.

"Oh my God." I tighten the robe around my naked frame, the strand of diamonds like a cold drip of water between my breasts.

"Get the fuck out of our room!" Rocky shouts at Patrick. "How the hell did you even get in here?!"

The mark is slack-jawed, suffocating on his own shock. His wide eyes ping to the cum-filled condom, the rumpled bedding on the ground, the romantic rose petals, my discarded lacy thong, and then back to me, where my legs are still spread around Rocky.

I hide my face, feigning shame.

Rocky takes a heavy, fake post-sex breath and skates a hand through his damp hair, acting as though he's piecing together this mystery, too. "Honey?" He speaks gently to me. "Do you know this dweeb?"

I drop my hands. "I, uh . . ."

Rocky pulls the bloodied rag out from between my legs, and Patrick loses it. "No, no, nonono," he repeats with a frantic shake of his head. "This isn't happening."

I spring off the bed. "Patrick, *Patrick.*" I go to him, robe secured with three knots around my body. "I'm so sorry." I try to sound distraught.

Rocky is leisurely collecting his boxer briefs and putting them on, the elastic at his hips, but when I risk another glance, I see so much strictness straining his muscles.

Patrick threads his fingers on his head, pacing back and forth near a black-and-white framed photograph of Times Square.

As I come closer, I see Oliver skulk farther into the entryway, observing his fake friend closely. *Thank you for not coming all the way inside this room, Oliver.*

Patrick restarts his hysterical headshake. "No, *no.*"

"Patrick." I reach out to him. "I'm so—"

He slaps me right across the face, so hard that I stumble backward, and the sting is instant.

"HEY!" Rocky yells and shoots forward the same time Oliver does.

I blink, and Rocky already has Patrick by the collar. There is no pause in him. He slams a brutal fist into the mark's cheekbone. The anguished cry that ejects out of Patrick is of a man who has never been physically harmed before. Yet he was so fucking quick to slap me.

I holster a glare. *I'm supposed to be sad, upset.* I blink a few more times, my emotions cycling through a washing machine.

"*You motherfucker,*" Rocky sneers through his teeth, about to lay another fist in him.

"Stop!" Patrick cries and crumples against the wall with his hands raised. "Stop! BRIAN!" He's calling for Oliver, and my brother is forced to squat down to this asshole and be his saving grace.

"Back off, man," Oliver says to Rocky in a voice that sounds unnaturally tight for my brother.

I taste the iron of blood in my mouth. My lip throbs.

Rocky's fury bleeds into the hotel suite. He could so easily beat Patrick to a pulp, but if the mark feels justified in going to the cops and trying to press assault charges, it could jeopardize all of our lives.

A punch for a slap needs to be the cutoff.

Rocky knows this, and he wields more restraint than even I understand. It's as though he can rewind a volcanic eruption, gathering magma and withstanding the burn just to force the destruction down.

Slowly, Rocky begins to release his grip off the mark, and he retrieves his slacks, belt, and white button-down from the floor. "Come here, honey." He gestures to me, and I find it hard to move.

Why . . . ?

I blink a few more times, vaulting between nausea and an emptiness. Rocky approaches me fast, and he holds my face with tenderness and inspects my lip. It must be split.

"You okay?" he whispers so quietly.

I try to nod.

I just want this awful job to finally end.

"Go get dressed," he murmurs.

Right. I power through the night. While I get clothed in record time in the bathroom, I tune out the verbal lashing between Rocky and Patrick.

I come out and Rocky clasps my hand. I can't tell who's gripping tighter, me or him.

"You're good, Patrick. I have you," Oliver says and tries to calm him down.

Patrick watches in horror and revulsion as I choose to leave with my lover who "deflowered" me over him.

The rope has been pulled, and Oliver is tasked with closing off the final bits of the con.

Rocky and I are out of there. We don't talk. A silent subway ride later where we remain holding hands, we climb into a parked Chevy in the Bronx, and we let go.

Nova is behind the wheel. He's driving us to Staten Island, where we'll meet up with Hailey. *Finally.* While I lie across the backseat, Patrick eventually texts me horrifying messages about how I'm meant for eternal damnation, and he calls off the wedding.

Oliver relays via phone call that a grateful Patrick agreed to make good on losing the bet. According to Patrick, Oliver just saved him from a lifetime of misery and deceit. He'll wire his friend the money. He's sending half tonight, half tomorrow.

I fall into a light sleep and only wake to Rocky and Nova yelling.

"You have no idea what you're talking about," Rocky nearly shouts. "No idea."

"It's always the same with you," Nova retorts with a

similar heat. "You act like he's Satan, when he's nothing even close."

Rocky growls, "Oh, he's got you fucking fooled, man. You're playing right into his bullshit."

Nova grits through his teeth, "God, I *wish* I had your father. Don't you get it?! He treats your mom with nothing but respect. He *adores* her. Like she's not someone to abuse at the end of a fucking night. He's never laid a hand on you or your brother or your sister. He'd drop anything to be there for his kids, and you don't even see it. You don't even know the *good* that you have when it's right in front of you."

The car goes silent.

I think they'll leave the fight there.

Until Rocky speaks.

"Take him, Winchester. He's all yours."

Twenty-Six

Phoebe

Halfway between dreaming and awake, my fluffy white comforter is ripped off my head. I groan through the sunlight of the Saturday morning, only in a cropped pink tee and panties. Hailey crawls onto the mattress beside me, her phone to her ear. "Yeah, Dad, we've been doing well."

Wait, what?!

I shoot up like Hailey zapped me with electricity. Her worried eyes meet mine. Why is she talking with her dad? Why did she answer that call?

She taps the speaker button, and I hear Everett's voice. "I could use some more ideas for the next job. When do you think you'll be done with yours?"

Hailey and I share a cautious look. It's October first, and we've sufficiently been evading our parents for a month and a half. But in that time, they've become aware we're somewhere in Connecticut, and they believe we're working on a new job of our own. Lies usually don't weigh on me. But I've never lied to my mom like this. I'm drowning in a vat of guilt for keeping this one alive, and I hope that when my mom learns the truth, she doesn't hate me for it.

"We're unsure when it'll be finished," Hailey says casually enough. "We're just playing it by ear right now."

Everett goes quiet for a second. Hailey tucks her legs to her chest on the bed and bites at her thumbnail.

Sensing her major anxiety, I wrap an arm over her shoulders and mouth, *We're good.*

She drops her thumb and rubs at a bruise on her kneecap.

After another strained moment, Everett says, "Plans are necessary. They can be malleable, but you shouldn't be playing anything by ear."

Hailey winces, and she puts the end of her phone to her forehead in distress. I can't say anything—I'm not supposed to be on this call.

After a deep sigh, Hailey says, "Yeah, I know." Her eyes shift to me, and I see the guilt in them, too. She mouths, *Should I tell them?*

I shake my head hurriedly. *No, no.* We do not tell Everett the truth about how we're done conning. After what Rocky told me, I trust Everett the absolute least of all our parents.

Hailey wavers, then mouths, *He could be cool.*

I make an X with my arms. Do Not Pass Go. Hell fucking no. He won't be *cool* about us ditching everything we were taught.

"I have to go," Everett says before Hailey can decide. "I'll call back in a couple weeks about your proposals. Brainstorm in the meantime."

He hangs up.

Proposals.

One of Hailey's tasks is to formulate new cons in new towns—a task that my mom and Addison usually handled until Hailey got older. Nowadays, they all share in passing the pen that draws the blueprints. I've joked before how Hailey is the secret mastermind behind all the jobs—but that joke lands with less humor now that we're trying to make a clean break.

Hailey groans and falls back against my pillow, just wearing checkered pajama shorts and a black cotton tank top. "That went *soooo* bad."

"Why did you answer his call?"

"It was an unknown number," she replies. "I thought it was Trevor."

"Shit," I breathe out. As I lie down next to her, our shoulders bump up against one another. We stare up at the ceiling, nothing special but a fan spinning slowly.

But it's not yellowed or moldy.

It's been a nice ceiling. A nice home.

Her voice goes soft. "I want this to work so badly, Phebs." Her head lolls to the side, and our eyes meet, hers carrying a heavy weight. "But my dad is right—plans are necessary. And this entire thing was half-baked from the beginning. I thought Rocky could stall for us and buy me time to figure out a way to tell our parents . . . but time is running out. And whenever I imagine telling them we're done, I picture my mom's *crushing* disappointment and the worst kind of guilt-fest from all three." Her voice teeters. "I-I've never wanted to confront them with these types of feelings, and I-I-I don't know how . . ." She stammers. "Even when we dropped out of that prep school back in the day . . . it wa-wasn't this big. Our moms knew we wouldn't be there . . . in that city f-for long anyway."

She means back when we were fourteen and I invoked *inertia*. The pact. When she had to muster the courage to rebel against their wishes with me.

This time is different. More permanent. A more drastic change in course.

I pop up on my elbows quickly, my heart clenching. "Hey, Hails. There's still time. We can figure it out, and I'll be right there with you when we tell them we're done grifting. You're not alone in this." *And hopefully they'll understand.*

My words pierce whatever's going on inside of her. Silent tears leak out of the corners of her eyes. "I'm failing you—"

"What? *No.*" I angle toward her. "If anything, *I'm* failing *you.* If I remember correctly, I'm the one fake dating our landlord. This was our new beginning as honest people, and I royally fucked it."

"You did not." She rubs her nose with the bottom of her tank. "You had a minor blip. A relapse. And anyway, I could see you and Jake hooking up for real."

My stomach twists at that idea. "Yeah, right. I think Jake tolerates me." I splat back down on the mattress.

"I think he likes you," Hailey says thoughtfully.

"We're just using each other," I mutter and then nudge my knee against hers. "What's with the bruised kneecaps?"

She sits up on her elbows now and glances at the black-and-blue marks. "Country club storage closet, the floor there wasn't soft."

Storage closet. The memory of Rocky pushing me up against the shelves of tennis balls and croquet mallets suddenly surfaces and bathes heat against my cheeks. I can almost feel his fingers clenching around my hair.

I smooth my lips to keep my breath steady. "Were you digging around for pickleball rackets?"

"No," she says, "I was just blowing Erik."

I sit all the way up and face her. "Erik? As in Bartender Erik?"

Hailey shrugs. "He's hot and sort of has a Brad Pitt circa *Fight Club* edginess. He has a ton of tattoos."

Now that I think about it, Erik always wears long sleeves. "Did not know that . . ."

"One is on his thigh."

"Definitely did not know *that*."

She smiles, then shrugs. "I like giving head. It's fun."

I crinkle my nose. "I still *loathe* blow jobs, and I know you said the more I do it, the more I might like it, but it's always been work. The only part I do enjoy is when, or if, they grab my hair."

Again, all I can do is picture Rocky's commanding hand sliding up the base of my neck. His fingers weaving through my hair and scrunching tightly. Pulling. The hot breath of his teasing lips creeping up my collar.

I try to act very interested in my fluffy comforter while heat ramps up across my body. I should confess my sins to a higher power for having these stupid dirty thoughts about my best friend's assholish older brother while I'm right in front of her.

Hailey sits up fully now and crosses her legs. "I like watching their face. It turns me on seeing them lose their shit over something I'm doing."

I still can't subscribe. I mostly know what I like (I'm sure I haven't discovered *everything*), and blow jobs are firmly off my list of turn-ons. "It hurts my jaw when I do it," I tell her, "and it looks like it busted your knees." I'm smiling.

She smiles back. "Sex bruises are my favorite bruises."

I lean back on my hands. "Print it, frame it, make a T-shirt out of it."

"Sell it for five hundred bucks and say it's award-winning art—rare, one of a kind."

"It was hung up in the Met. Didn't you hear?"

We laugh, and when our smiles soften, Hailey says, "Speaking of Erik and Jake . . ." She reaches for the end table and turns the digital clock. "We have an hour before our double date starts."

I rock back. "Double date?"

"Yeah, I called Jake to set it up." She scoots to the edge of the bed. "If you want to fake date the most eligible bachelor in Victoria, you're going to need to make it look real."

Hailey and logistics. A match made in heaven. Or hell. Depending on how you look at it.

I shouldn't be surprised that she's fallen into her usual routine much like I have. But is this it for us? Is this what we're made for? As she climbs off the bed with a staggered breath, I see how she tries so hard not to break down and cry again.

"I'm going to make it work here, Hails," I tell her. "I promise. And if your dad calls back, just tell him we're between jobs and building connections right now."

She thinks this over and nods. "Yeah, okay. That might work."

"Sooo . . ." I draw out the word. "Is this thing with Erik serious?"

"What? No." Her lips downturn. "It's just casual sex."

"It's a double *date*."

"Okay, but we're not dating." She looks flustered. "You know I have a three-date max, *and* you know how I've always imagined I'd be with someone in our field."

"Carter." I clarify where her heart lies.

She sends me a deadpan look. "Shut up."

I'm grinning. "You loooove him."

"You're awful." She throws a pillow at me, smiling. "His forgeries are literal masterpieces, and he undercharges me for fakes, so . . ."

She's blushing.

Dating a guy in our field.

No application necessary. High risk. And almost impossible to quit.

She wants a romance like her parents. Solid. Committed. Everlasting.

Addison and Everett's love story is one for the storybooks. She was pretending to be a graduate student at an Ivy League. He was pretending to be a professor, and they both tried to con each other out of a sizeable chunk of money. Addison pulled it off. She boarded a train with my mom that was heading to the West Coast, and when the train started clunking along, Everett strolled down the aisle and sat right across from Addison.

He smiled and congratulated her on the win.

They've been together ever since.

This is the first time I've heard Hailey talk about things she'll miss in her old life. Her dreams of dating a con artist. A future she painted for herself.

I've never shared in that future. Because I never looked that far ahead. I tried not to romanticize what could be.

I slide off the bed. "Maybe Erik has some hidden talent that'll make you go wild."

She bites the inside of her lip. "Yeah." She seems sad, giving up the idea of Carter. When she sees me staring, she says, "This is better. I know it is."

I frown, wondering why she's trying to convince herself. She'd been so ready to die on her sword for this new life after Carlsbad. I thought I was the only one having a hard time with it.

"You take the first shower," I tell her.

"You sure?"

"Yeah, I'm going to figure out what to wear on my fake date with my fake boyfriend." *Who's strangely not Rocky.*

She smiles, but it wavers in and out before she leaves my room.

Twenty-Seven

Phoebe

Hailey never told me where we'd be having our "double date." I figured we'd be meeting up at a coffee shop or something, but the closer we get to Victoria Arts Cinema, the more my heart races.

"*Hailey,*" I whisper-hiss. "A movie date?"

Her pace is brisk while she applies black lipstick without a mirror (the realest talent). "I told Jake you're a horror genre junkie, and this was his idea." She elbows my side. "Isn't he thoughtful?"

That's not my immediate reaction. My brows knot into what I hope isn't a permanent frown. "Where have you been having all these solo chats with Jake?"

"Baubles & Bookends." She caps the lipstick and dumps it in her backpack. "He's a big J. D. Robb fan." The chains attached to her cargo pants jingle as we walk in town, passing a bicycle shop and breakfast diner.

"A movie date might be too much." I gather my hair into a

pony, hot all of a sudden, but after tying the lumpiest pony, I just let the blue strands fall against my white dress.

We're almost late due to my massive indecision on what to wear. I'm basically in a little white dress—the sidekick of the little black dress—and is it too sexy? The neckline is borderline modest, and the fabric flows more than hugs my frame—but it's still *white*.

White is pure. Virginal. Which my mom would say attracts men more than repels them. And typically, you'd want to be attractive toward a date.

Even a fake date.

But do I want to attract *Jake*?

I should. He's a portal away from Rocky, and in theory, it should be easy to jump through. But it's like the wardrobe takes me to family-friendly Narnia when I'd rather go to depraved Westeros.

Honestly, these confusing doubts never cropped up this high when I was fake dating Rocky. Picking an outfit shouldn't be this complicated—for anyone!

Hailey senses my nerves. "Are you freaked out about kissing him in a dark theater?"

"I honestly didn't imagine kissing Jake at all, but now that you bring it up, you can erase Nervous Nelly off my ID." She hears my sarcasm.

"First-date jitters," she teases me now, and I elbow her side. We break into smiles together, and then I blow out a breath.

"Okay, fine." I lower my voice. "The guy I have the most experience *fake* kissing is your brother."

"So this is even more perfect. You gain more experience fake kissing . . . or not kissing, maybe just fake-being-with-Jake, who's not Rocky—"

"Which is a good thing," I interject, trying to pump myself up.

"Yes, it is."

"And you gain more experience in real dating."

She nods, now looking a little nervous. "Yeah . . . it's a win-win all around."

"Yep."

We don't relax.

By the time we reach the eight-screen theater—the bulbed marquee advertising mostly classic horror movies now that it's October—we're ten minutes late. So neither of us are surprised that Jake and Erik are already inside, waiting beside the concession line.

Erik *does* have tattoos. A knife and skull are inked across his arm, and his black shirt says SINK PISSER in the top corner, a demon on the back.

Hailey really found her edgy match.

She goes in for a hug with Erik immediately, while Jake and I stop about a foot away from one another.

Why is faking it so hard with him?

Pretending to be in a relationship has been my job so many times . . .

"You look . . ." He scans the length of my body, and I check out his crisp blue button-down and khakis, returning to his eyes to see what lies behind them. I can't really tell, but I do see a smidge of lust bobbing his throat. ". . . beautiful."

"White is my color?" I joke more than flirt.

He lets out a throaty vacillating noise, unsure how to answer. *At least I'm not the only indecisive one.* "You've looked beautiful in everything you've worn, Phoebe." It's a soft compliment with a tender smile.

"Thanks," I breathe. "You look great, too." And I mean that.

A group of twentysomethings in Caufield University sweat-shirts are noticeably gawking at us from the self-checkout ticket machines.

How did I become the center of town gossip?

Jake slides an arm casually over my shoulders and leads me into the concession line. While we wait behind a few other groups, I spot Hailey's platinum-blonde hair as she disappears into Theater 4. *Come back*, I want to tell her like I'm a newly fledged con artist.

I can do this.

I'm not *that* rusty.

I loosen my joints and sink into Jake's embrace. He gazes down at me with more curiosity than desire. He asks if I've seen this movie before, and I go off on a tangent about the greatness of horror films.

"There's a lot to choose from," I explain. "Horror has *so* many subgenres." I count off on my fingers. "You have slasher, psychological, comedy, paranormal, monster, found footage, splatter films, body horror. There's a type for whatever mood you're in." And am I excited the theater is reshowing *Friday the 13th*? Yes . . . yes, I am.

Jake is grinning.

"What?"

"Your love of horror films is cute."

Is he flirting? Why can't I tell if it's real or not? More on edge, I just blurt out, "Cute was my love of Strawberry Short-cake and Care Bears when I was seven."

"You?"

"Do I not look like a Care Bear lover?" I motion to my virginal white dress.

Am I really giving off "whore" vibes? Why? I want to know if it's something I'm doing, or if I just appear like a quick lay right now.

"It's not about looks," Jake says. "You just seem . . ." He searches for the word, which is driving me nuts in one agonizing second. "Angsty."

"Angsty?"

He tilts his head like it's not the perfect choice. "I would've pegged you as someone who watched R-rated movies in the third grade and had no curfew. You'd be tuning in to *Celebrity Deathmatch*. Hailey is the one who's gentler inside. You're more hard-core."

How does he know that?

Because we let him.

I'm super uneasy now. "That all might be true, too, but I did have a curfew." *Sometimes.*

His lip slowly rises. "I did, too."

"And Hailey likes Nine Inch Nails and Disturbed. Heavy metal is only an acquaintance of mine through her. My music choices aren't hard-core."

Jake looks away in thought, as though searching for Hailey, but he must realize she's already in the theater.

We move up in line, and after another string of silence, I turn to Jake. "You want to know what Care Bear you'd be?"

His smile expands. "Yeah."

"Polite Panda."

His face falls into an eye roll. "Seriously?"

"Seriously."

"And what would Rocky be?"

I stiffen.

He eyes me. "If we're going to date, I figured I should know about your past relationships."

Right . . . my ex-husband.

"He's Grumpy Bear," I say. "Hailey is Funshine Bear, and I'm Give No Fucks Bear."

He drops his arm from my shoulder as we become next in line. "You give plenty of fucks."

Ugh. "Then maybe I am Angsty Hard-Core Bear."

Natural-Born Liar Bear feels more like me, but just thinking it causes Rocky to pop back into my head.

"What about your past relationships?" I ask quickly, wanting to pry a bit. "Any exes?"

"Sure. Three ex-girlfriends. Never married."

"Engaged?"

"No." He shakes his head slowly but strongly. "My mother would've loved if I at least contemplated buying a ring, but I never did."

After bumping into Claudia at the clambake and spilling a tray of champagne, I'm likely her nightmare for a potential daughter-in-law, which is exactly why Jake is dating me.

"How long were you married?" he wonders.

I have this answer, thanks to a marriage certificate and divorce papers Rocky bought from Carter. Since Rocky paid for the fakes, I agreed he could decide how long our marriage lasted. I was a little shocked he didn't go the *high school sweethearts* direction where we would've been married at eighteen.

And then I remembered that Rocky tries to be extremely vague about his age. If we were married young, it might pose more questions about how old he is, and most guests at the country club already believe he's around his late twenties, early thirties.

"Just a year," I tell Jake.

"Newly divorced, I remember you saying."

"Yeah, but time heals all, right?"

He smiles back at me, and we reach the concession counter. I order some chocolate-covered peanuts, a small popcorn, and a Fizz.

He gets a water bottle.

"Boring." I eye his choice as we make our way inside the theater.

"I don't go to the movies much," he whispers. We walk down the aisle, passing Hailey and Erik in the back row, and we sink into our velvety red chairs in the middle section. He quietly tells me how he grew up with two home theaters, and his parents' producer connections sent them screenings of new releases.

I say, "Quite the bougie upbringing."

"You couldn't have been far off if you have a trust fund."

"Had," I remind him. Past tense. In this backstory, my parents took it away.

He nods slowly. "What's the story there? Parents didn't love your husband?"

I think about how my mom *adores* Rocky, but thanks to Oliver, Jake already knows that my mom would wholeheartedly approve of me dating someone prim and proper like Jake Waterford. Which is also true. It's easier to just lean into what Jake already believes than to construct the foundation of a new lie.

So I build off of his belief.

I nod just as slowly back. "Yeah. It was trust fund or Rocky, and they made it *quite* apparent that a divorce wouldn't even earn me back in their good graces. The damage had been done. I chose him."

Jake frowns. "And you lost everything." I hear his sympathy.

I dip my head, more out of guilt that pills at my insides like a knotted blanket. Rocky hasn't taken anything from me. He's been doing more than enough to try to protect my new life with his sister. And I recognize how it's not that smart to mention the truth, but I can't let Jake think the absolute worst of a man who I . . .

The dreaded and vulnerable four-letter word recedes in my brain.

I look over at my fake date. "Rocky isn't a bad person. He's always been there for me."

Jake thinks carefully before speaking. "I can imagine it must be hard . . . to still care for someone but know it's better to be apart. That's why you moved to Victoria?" he wonders. "To get away from him?"

I hate how there is truth in his theory. I should reinforce this belief, too. That this was always about moving on from Rocky.

But I can't. It hurts too much to cement it out loud, especially to Jake. So I say, "It's just a fresh start for me and Hailey."

Jake studies me in the dim lighting of the theater. The screen is blank, and I'm hoping the trailers start soon and shroud my burning face in total darkness.

"Yeah," he says gently, as though not wanting to push too hard. "I hope yours is what you hope it will be." He sounds genuine again, but I know he's hoping my fresh start excludes my ex-husband.

The trailers are starting.

Thank the Lord. I try not to sink in my seat. Lights lower until darkness blankets the rows of chairs. Once the horror flick begins, Jake wraps his arm around me. I know now that he wouldn't be shocked I watched *The Exorcist* at twelve.

My mom said, "If you ever need to pick a movie for a date,

always choose horror, bug. It's so easy to pretend to be interested in them during a jump scare or a slasher scene. Instead of covering your own eyes, lean into them."

The movies never scared me. They still don't.

When Jason kills, I play my role and hide in the crook of Jake's arm. I can feel the low chortle of laughs that rumble his chest. I don't understand, so I dip my head closer to his ear. "Why are you laughing at me?"

He turns his head to meet mine, our lips inches away. My whole body tenses. Real or fake? I don't know, and that uncertainty blisters every part of me.

I don't like being kept in the dark.

His hand cups the base of my neck before he leans past my lips to reach my ear. "I know you're not really scared. You're playing it up. It's cute."

It's cute, again.

Gross.

Rocky would never call me cute. He'd probably tease me for being a big baby and then remind me that I'm fooling no one and my acting is worse than subpar—that he'd give more stars to the actors in a bad porno. And I'd call him a fuck-face. He'd say he's never fucking my face, and I'd tell him he wishes he could fuck mine.

We'd stare at each other. For so long. Until one of us breaks.

Except, we never really break. Because if we did, I'd be on a real date with Rocky and not a fake one with Jake.

My lungs feel full, but I can't expel the deep breath I took. I just replay that imaginary scenario with Rocky over again. And I realize . . . I'd like it. Why would I like it?

Because I'm not attracted to Polite Pandas.

I want Grumpy Bear.

You can't have him.

I ease away from Jake, avoiding his gaze as I shove popcorn in my mouth. Halfway through the movie, I twist in my chair and spot Hailey making out with Erik in the back. *Good for her.* At least one of us is having a decent time.

Jake's phone rings. Not just buzzes. Full on *rings*.

I turn to him with shocked eyes. Who doesn't put their phone on silent in a movie theater? Oh yeah, the guy who has never been to one in his life.

Wait . . . his ringtone.

It's an ABBA song.

Jake is flustered as he digs for his phone.

"Turn it off!" someone yells in the theater.

"I'm trying," Jake politely whispers under his breath. He hits silent, and I get a flash of a number on his phone. No name. "Excuse me . . ." He stands up and slips past me.

I'm about to follow him when he shakes his head at me.

Something is . . . not right. That song was not an angry *I hate you* ballad that he usually awards his family members. But it was important enough to leave the theater to call back?

I spin around in my seat, and Hailey catches my gaze. She looks just as confused, and she nods toward the doors like *go*.

After setting my popcorn tub on the floor and wiping kernels off my lap, I leave the theater. It takes a second to find Jake, sitting on a bench outside the bathrooms. He's texting, and when he sees me, he slips his phone in his pocket.

"You didn't have to come out here," he says, running a hand through his hair. "I know you were looking forward to the movie."

I sit down beside him. "It's okay. I've seen it before, remember?" *Eleven times.* "Who was that?"

"No one, really."

My brows rise. "'Chiquitita' was the ringtone."

He stares at me. "So?"

"So . . ." *How can he not be following?* "I've only heard power *hate* ballads come out of your cell. Who's special enough to get that song?"

He laughs, but it's weak. "You're going to think I'm a rich prick."

"Newsflash, Jake, I already think that."

He takes a breath. "It was my broker. Probably the only decent person in my life." He *seems* genuine, but I haven't been in town with my best A game. I haven't zeroed in on his tells yet.

I don't like that I can't discern if he's lying or not.

It's not good. *Especially* if he's my fake boyfriend. That's what made Rocky and me always work: I knew where the con was at all times. Here, I'm just in the dark.

Twenty-Eight

Rocky

Trouble in fake paradise already?" I grin. I shouldn't gloat, but I'm not one to turn away the chance. Not when it comes to Phoebe.

She stands at the edge of the dock, while I'm up high on my boat. Hammer in hand. No shirt. Threw that off an hour ago during the middle of demoing the galley's cabinets.

Beads of sweat drip down my chest that have momentarily distracted Phoebe's attention. I grin wider and add, "Fake cheating on your fake boyfriend already?"

Her scowl returns to my eyes. "Staring at your ugly chest is not cheating." Her face flushes. "And stop using the word *fake*."

"Why?" I question. "You love that word."

She growls under her breath. "Just . . . help me." She returns to what she said when she first walked up to the sailboat. "I don't trust Jake."

"I never trusted him," I say. "Nothing has changed."

"You don't trust anyone."

"I trust *you*. I trust my sister. My brother. Nova. Oliver. That's a big number of people."

"Five. That's the same amount as a pack of gum," she refutes.

I open my hand out to her like she made my point. "The perfect amount."

She exhales a frustrated noise. "We don't need to worry about your trust issues. You don't have to trust him, but he's cagier than I realized. I feel like he's hiding something." She tells me about the phone call at the movie theater and the ringtone.

I flip my hammer, thinking and glaring out at the sun-reflected water. "What if he's a mole?"

She frowns. "For who?"

My muscles contract in tensed bands, and she slowly shakes her head.

"No," she says. "Our parents aren't spying on us."

"He could be one of their connections, here to feed information back to them," I say. "It makes sense."

"It makes *zero* sense," Phoebe says. "One: they trust us . . ." She shifts uneasily, neck reddening remembering the truth about me confessing my teenage crush to my dad. "At least, I *think* our moms do."

"You don't think they're suspicious of this random *job* in Connecticut? Where none of us have confirmed what it entails. Who the marks might be. Nothing."

Phoebe wavers, then shakes her head. "If they trust us, they wouldn't be too suspicious. We're being vague to protect ourselves. They'd understand *that*."

"My dad has been fishing for details," I tell her, and I wish I could lump my mom and Elizabeth in with him, but they've been largely uncommunicative.

"Have our moms?" she wonders.

I glower and flip my hammer again.

She smiles, her trust in them resurrecting, and I'd never use every tactic in my arsenal to sway Phoebe to hate them. If I did that, I'd be no different than our parents, so I accept her sunny viewpoint while I'm sitting alone in my dark one.

Phoebe gestures to me. "Just think about this, Rocky. They'd have nothing to gain by spying on us." She adds, "We *are* on the same team."

I wipe sweat off my brow with my bicep. *Maybe* . . . I don't know.

All my instincts tell me they're involved somehow. Could this be the first time I have the ability to get *actual* proof of their manipulation?

Phoebe shifts her hips, impatient. "You want to do a trade-off? I'll fix whatever needs fixed in your boat, and in return, you can help me figure out what Jake might be hiding."

"You're not fixing my boat."

"I'm good with my hands." She didn't mean for that to be a come-on, and her glare skewers me. "I'm good with tools."

"Great. You're not getting near mine."

Her gaze drops to my crotch.

Blood runs south, pumping through the veins of my shaft. "I was referring to my hammer, not my cock."

"*You* went there," she accuses.

"Fucking A, Phoebe." I groan, just frustrated. Constantly. "Look, I know you could help me fix the boat, but I don't want your help. I need this." It's my outlet. My thing.

She throws up her hands. "Then what do you want, Rocky?"

I can't even look at her because the answer is *right there*. I adjust my grip on the hammer, rotating the hilt. "I don't need anything in return." I set the hammer down and grab my leather jacket. "I'll help."

She expels a breath of relief. "Thank you."

"Where is Jake, anyway?"

"You can't confront him right now," Phoebe says, wide-eyed. "We have to plot. Make a plan. You don't want him suspicious."

She's right. "Let's call Hailey."

Town streets have closed for Victoria's annual Harvest Festival.

Vendors are set up along the cobblestone, selling warm apple cider, lobster mac and cheese, fresh oysters, and other fall staples. A local band plays somewhat-decent cover songs in the middle of the square, and the pumpkin carving stations contain more adults than children since a cash prize for Best Pumpkin Art is at stake.

Small-town normalcies.

Not here, Hailey has already warned me against confronting Jake at the festival.

I attempt to be interested in connecting two blue pieces of candy on my phone, but while I'm staring at Jake and Phoebe—sipping their apple ciders beside the town's fountain, laughing and chatting like a *happy* couple—the timer runs out.

Shit.

With a tight breath, I shove my phone in my pocket.

My sister is elbow deep in a pumpkin at our table. I haven't seen Hailey smile this much in years. She's already drawn the outline of the Bride of Frankenstein on the pumpkin with a Sharpie, a blueprint for carving. I'm happy that my sister is happy, and I wish I could somehow bottle the essence. Preserve it for her.

But I'm useless on that front. I can't shield her from our parents if they show up. Not completely, at least.

I scoop some seeds and guts from my pumpkin and slap them in the garbage can beside our table. Hacking at this thing with a knife might make me feel better.

I look over at the fountain again.

Phoebe smiles into a fuller laugh at whatever Jake said. He gesticulates with his hand, the one without the apple cider, as if telling a story, and he tries to contain a laugh of his own.

Every muscle in my body twitches.

"The more you stare, the more people notice," Hailey whispers to me, casting a furtive glance to Phoebe, then back to me.

"I don't care," I mutter, wiping the pumpkin guts off my hands and onto a towel. "I'm her ex-husband. I can be jealous."

I *am* jealous.

Locals and caufers (still hate it) meander around the street, partaking in the festivities. And the handfuls of faces I recognize from the country club—I ignore.

Hailey wipes the gooey residue off the pumpkin's skin, just as Oliver strolls over with a tray of coffee and says, "A little early for Halloween to be wearing your costumes, isn't it?" He looks from me to her. "Doom and Gloom."

Hailey lifts her carving knife. "I'm actually happy."

He slips her a smile. "Doom and Raccoon, then." He's referring to her heavy black eye shadow.

"*Procyon lotor*." She lines up her pumpkin and crouches to inspect a smudged Sharpie line. "It's the binomial name of a raccoon."

He intakes a breath. "I love a cute *Procyon lotor*."

My jaw hardens. Jake's laughter is real, genuine. I can tell, even from this far away, and yeah, it bothers me that he's not fake laughing and fake smiling on the outside and for real *cringing* on the inside.

"Their life expectancy in the wild is only one to three years," Hailey tells him.

"Which one are you, domesticated or wild?" Oliver asks, and it's hard to tune in to their conversation while I'm watching Jake tell his story. I bet it's *riveting*.

"Domesticated, unfortunately."

Oliver replies in fluent Dutch, which cuts my gaze to him in warning. He tips his head to me like I'm being unnecessarily paranoid, but him knowing Dutch and being related to Phoebe—people will start asking deeper questions.

Where are the Smiths from?

How do you know so many languages?

Does Phoebe?

Where are your parents?

Who are your parents?

"No one heard." He's quiet while people stroll past us with warm donuts. "And anyway, if they did, I'm the world traveler of the family." *He'll have to be.* He lifts a coffee out of the tray. "A cinnamon latte macchiato for the *Procyon lotor*." He hands it to my sister.

"Thanks, Olly." She takes the cup and inspects her pumpkin.

"Diabetes in a cup for you." He passes me my chocolate chip mocha iced frappé and keeps the black drip coffee for himself.

I force a smile. "You need to go to a dentist, man. Make sure someone didn't pull out your sweet tooth at birth."

"Spending an extra hour at the gym just to work off a milkshake—not an enjoyment of mine, Grey Thornhall." He sips his black coffee.

I'd say Oliver is too concerned about his appearance, but we've all been drilled from a young age to ensure we appear a certain way. Fitting into what society deems "attractive" has been an unspoken rule.

Blowing steam off at a gym is one of the few things that keeps me sane. So I don't mind lifting weights or playing tennis at the club. I can even kill two birds with one stone since they're all social things that help me establish relationships in town.

"Where's your brother?" I ask him.

"Loading up on oysters."

A light wind rattles the trees, and when an orange leaf catches on Phoebe's pink sweater, I think I'm in a new circle of hell.

Jake inches forward and plucks it off her.

"He's touching her hair now?"

"She had a leaf in her hair, too," Hailey says, observing the scene with me. As is Oliver.

"The classic WB drama," Oliver muses, "the upstanding gentleman and the man-whore are fighting over the new girl in town. While her charming older brother stands off to the side and tells you"—he turns to me—"that Jake invited my sister to have dinner with his parents."

I glare. "I know. Thank you and fuck you."

"Guess I don't need to ask how that's making you feel," Oliver says in his *therapist* tone.

The "dinner with the Konings" reminder is more gasoline on the fire raging inside me. Luckily, Phoebe already kept me in the loop.

It's pretend, Phoebe assured.

She also told me that the more time she spends with Jake, the better. The closer she'll come to uncovering whatever he's hiding.

I'm fixated on the fountain. Them. Jake slips a piece of blue hair that escaped her pony back behind her ear, and I can't stand here any longer.

"Rocky, don't," Hailey whispers as I push off in the direction of the happy new fake couple.

Twenty-Nine

Rocky

Hailey and Oliver don't follow, and as I approach Jake and Phoebe alone, I sense heads swerving and eyes rerouting to me. Whispers trail after my dark presence as I cut through the street in a diagonal to reach the fountain.

Jake looks unamused when I come to a stop. He sips his apple cider stiffly. "Enjoying the festival?"

"Not really." I take a bitter sip of my overly sweet coffee.

Phoebe watches the gossipy audience with caution and uncertainty. "Maybe we shouldn't do this here."

"Do what? We're just talking," I say to Phoebe, but I haven't broken Jake's challenging stare.

Skin pinches between his eyes as he feigns confusion. "What'd you say before in the locker room? I think the words were *I'm not interested in her.* Correct me if I'm wrong."

"Not wrong."

I'm more interested in you at the moment and what you're hiding.

His face sobers. "Then what are you doing here?"

Phoebe is shielding her eyes with her hand. There must be a gaggle of people behind me invested in the outcome of this "fake" romantic rivalry. Are pieces real? I can't see whether Jake *truly* is catching feelings or if he's just starting to care about Phoebe's well-being.

"Just making conversation," I say, skating fingers through my hair as the wind blows. "That's what friends do."

"I missed the part where we became friends."

"I'm friends with your girlfriend, and she's not invisible to me."

Phoebe downs her apple cider with a big gulp.

Jake raises his brows. "Clearly, she's not." An insinuation is sitting on the tip of his tongue.

I drill him with a glare. "Continue that thought."

"You've only been stalking—"

"Stalking?" I interject with heat.

"You followed her to *this town* when she tried to get away from you. What else do you call that?"

Are you fucking serious? My eyes flash to Phoebe, wondering if they've had conversations where she's spun them here, or if this is just his assumption. It matters with how I need to proceed next, because I can shoot him down, but I'd rather not discredit her or her story, even if it's one that paints me in the worst light.

Phoebe has no opportunity to send me a signal. Jake steps out in front of her, as though to protect her from my sudden wrath.

Jesus Christ. I rotate slightly as frustration shoots into my bloodstream. And then I cock my head to Jake. "Call it whatever you want."

I hear whispers behind me. "He's going to push Jake in the fountain. Bet you twenty bucks."

Oh, I would love to.

Jake crosses his arms. He stands like a skyscraping brick wall, and I'm not someone who shrinks when men tower. It's just a *tell* to me. A dead giveaway that a man is trying to assert dominance and feels threatened enough to pull the weakest tool out of his weak box. His height.

Congratulations. You're fucking tall.

But continuously seeing him try to protect Phoebe from me is going to send me over the edge. "You're not her white knight."

"You're not her boyfriend," he retorts. "I am."

Fake.

But all I've ever been is the fake thing to Phoebe.

Whispers and mutters catch the wind and hit my ear. He just publicly claimed Phoebe. *Again.*

What was I expecting? *I don't know.* I don't fucking know.

This was a mistake.

Jake suddenly shifts his eyes off me, and I follow to my right and see his mother, Claudia Waterford, and a few of her friends. The well-dressed, polished women are gathered around the craft table where little kids paint pumpkins. The women make no effort to hide the fact that they're watching us.

Claudia's lips are pursed, judgment in her eyes. She's not happy with her son, and she excuses herself from her friends and just leaves in the opposite direction of Jake. Ensuring he sees her disapproval.

His jaw tenses, but this is what he wanted. To stick it to Mommy.

"Grey?"

Fuck.

I barely glance over at the sudden appearance of Sidney Burke. Phoebe freezes behind Jake, likely recalling the boathouse party where Sidney tried to dance with me, but I'm hardly giving the nineteen-year-old the time of day.

For one, I look too old to be entertaining her advances.

For another, her father is at an outdoor patio eating brunch with the other widowers, and he's in view. She knows this, and I'm not about to be used.

Jake is confused. "Sidney? You two know each other?" He motions from her to me.

I frown, more interested in his reaction. "How do you know her?"

Jake can't answer before Sidney speaks. "Grey and I met at the Reynolds' boathouse. Bummer you couldn't make it, Jake. It was a good time." She says that while looking at me with a coy smile. Like we fucked that night.

"She's nineteen," Jake warns me, uncrossing his arms.

The fact that he's buying her bullshit is aggravating. I was actually starting to think he was better than that, but we all have our blind spots.

Sidney is relishing this moment; her smile is off the charts. Jake is feeding into the show she's putting on for her father, and I'm about to embarrass the shit out of her.

Sorry.

I stay on Jake. "Which is one of *many* reasons she's not in my rearview, peripheral, or my fucking windshield, and she never will be. I don't know her. I know *of* her, and that's already too much for me."

Sidney intakes a sharp breath. She's flustered; her cheeks are beet red, and she avoids me and just says a quick goodbye to Jake, then slips away.

Jake glares at me. "You didn't have to be rude."

This guy. I'm so glad he's not a lover I need to please because he's fucking *impossible*. I'd tell Phoebe to have fun with him, but even the thought of them fake together and fake fucking is scarring my brain.

I end up saying, "Sidney hasn't taken the hint when I've been *nice*, so I'm not sorry for being an asshole." His shoulders are squared. He's on guard and not happy. Still, I ask, "Is she a friend of yours?"

"She's my sister's . . . *was* my sister's best friend." His defensive edges start softening at the mention of his sister.

He might feel ten times more brotherly toward Sidney since his sister is no longer alive. Makes sense.

Still hate him.

Behind me, I catch more mutterings: "It's so cute how Jake is protecting Phoebe."

"God, I know."

"Her and Grey are so toxic."

A painful knot constricts in my rib cage. Seeing Sidney Burke reminds me of her father. And how Jake is a better repellent against Weston Burke than I'd been.

Weston Burke hasn't approached Phoebe while she's serving at the country club, not since the clambake. All because she's dating a Koning.

Maybe Jake is protecting her in ways that I can't.

I don't want to believe it. Phoebe doesn't trust him fully. Protecting her from *him* is the reality I'm standing in.

"You done?" Jake asks like he's the valiant hero of this dramatic scene.

I grind my teeth and then force a smile at Jake. "Never. And if you ever hurt her—"

"Really?" He lets out a laugh of disbelief. "I wouldn't dare, but you . . ." He canvasses me up and down. "Who knows what you're capable of?"

A lot.

But not *that.*

"*Jake,*" Phoebe warns quietly. "Please, just let him go."

At the sound of her voice, his posture loosens more, but he hasn't shifted away from my narrowed gaze. "I'm not keeping him here."

"Push him in the fountain!" someone jeers.

"Oh my God, *no,*" Phoebe warns me now. "*Rocky.*"

Jake doesn't stop glaring. I'm shooting an everlasting glare back, but I end up raising my hands in surrender. "Not today, folks."

Some people *boo,* but I hear a lady call me a bastard for even wanting to push their precious Koning boy in the town's historical fountain.

As much as I'd love to lightly drown him, I can't have his family rallying behind him and trying to charge me with assault. So without another word, I just leave the fake couple to do their fake thing, and I return to Hailey and her half-carved pumpkin feeling no better than before.

Thirty

Phoebe

A lump lodges in my throat as I watch Rocky depart like a dark, ominous cloud. Every part of me craves to run after him, to call him back, to share the same torrid air. But I shouldn't want those things.

It'll only fuel the town's obsessions with this warped love triangle—and to be frank, it's already chaos.

Judgy eyes.

Gossipy whispers.

They still linger after Rocky is gone.

Face hot, I take a short breath. Within this chaos, I've gained a semblance of a social standing that I can wedge my feet on. Jake is my boyfriend. People are starting to sympathize with me, and I've even been summoned to a future Koning family dinner. Which I'm told is the equivalent of being handed a golden ticket to the chocolate factory.

But being *summoned* feels nothing like a warm welcome. I'm expecting to be grilled and eviscerated. Jake's mother has been forty feet away all day and hasn't even said *boo* to me.

Luckily, that's the coldest invitation I've received. Mrs. Kelsey asked me to an afternoon tea with her and her twenty-two-year-old daughter. "You'd make lovely friends," she told me. I'm aware that I'm just being used because of my proximity to Jake, and being one degree away from town royalty has its perks.

Those benefits make it easier to keep up the charade and sink into my natural role of pretending. At the festival, I've maintained full focus on Jake.

Until now.

I'm watching Rocky return to the pumpkin carving table by Hailey and Oliver, and my stomach somersaults while my heart volleys in my chest. It's a *fabricated* love triangle, isn't it? Then why do I feel like there is a real loser? Why don't I want that person to be Rocky?

It's impossible to look away from him, even as I sense Jake's intense side-eye on me.

"You still have feelings for him," Jake says under his breath.

I've always had feelings for him. I punt-kick that thought away and avert my eyes to my empty cup. All my apple cider was chugged in one anxious gulp.

Off my silence, his attention travels across the festival. "Come this way . . ." Jake brings me around the fountain, closer to the cast-iron swan spurting water, and I realize he chose this spot because of the ambient noise. The sound of splashing drowns out our conversation from possible eavesdroppers.

Instinctively, I want to glance at Rocky, but I force myself to concentrate on Jake. *What every awesome fake girlfriend would do.*

His fingers glide against my elbow before he gently takes my hand in his. It's featherlight affection that I should try to naturally lean into, but I'm a little stiff. I can see he's doing it for show anyway. And he's good at it.

He's good at pretending. At lying. At hiding *something*.

It unnerves me that I don't know more. That information is gridlocked behind a wall that I can't reach.

Together, we take a seat on the fountain's brick edge, and most of the town's gossipmongers stroll away like the show is *over*. Nothing to see here, people. I swish my cup but remember it's empty.

"What would it take to get over him?" Jake suddenly asks me.

I can't help but laugh. "If I had that answer, don't you think I would've gotten over him already?"

He's quiet until he says, "You think fake dating me will help?"

It hasn't yet. "Do you hope it does?" I question back.

"Maybe," he answers plainly.

"How indecisive of you, Jake."

"Maybe *yes*," he corrects. "Is that better?"

"Maybe," I tease.

He almost laughs. Again, I swish my empty drink. He leans over to pour some of his own apple cider in my cup.

I mutter, "Thanks." *He's sweet.* Yet, my guards haven't collapsed to the ground.

He sips his apple cider, staring at little twin siblings with tiger and fairy face paint. They're trying to play with an oversized chess set while their oblivious parents gab with adult friends.

"I just don't want Rocky to interfere with us," he admits, his gaze flitting to me. "This arrangement is helping me more than you know."

I frown deeply. "There's more in it for you than pissing off your mom?"

"Yeah." He takes a tight breath before saying, "Her name was Natalie Betchel. My last girlfriend."

I watch his brows crinkle at what I assume is a painful memory.

After a beat, he says, "She was stunning, top of her class at Brown, and played doubles tennis on the weekends at the club. She was perfect for my family." He stares off in a faraway haze. "Every girlfriend I've had, my mother *loved*. Obsessively."

I can relate. Kind of. It's not like Rocky and I have ever really been together, but my mother's obsession is there.

I stay quiet. And he fills the silence. "I was with Natalie for two years, and my mother insisted she come to every family meal, attend every charity function, every single thing that warranted an arm hooked to mine or a stand-in for my absence. In my mother's eyes, she was nothing more than a malleable *thing*."

My stomach drops. Okay, my mother is *not* the same. She wouldn't treat my significant other like a chess piece . . . unless they were a mark for a job.

"Why not just tell Natalie to stop listening to your mom?" I wonder.

"I did do that." His forehead is pleated in distress like he's traveling back to that time and place. "A thousand times, *I did*. But she wanted to please my family. All my girlfriends have *always* wanted to please my family. It wasn't long before Natalie's dreams of being a corporate attorney were traded in for ball gowns and afternoon tea. Then my brothers invited her to their parties and after-parties and yacht trips. And I saw her wasting away under three a.m. nights filled with coke and cashed-in dreams. Being around my family any longer would have either killed her or changed her beyond recognition, so I broke things off."

I'm not surprised by the move, but I still ask, "Even though you loved her?"

He stares at his cup. "If I loved her more, I would have never let her enter that world. My family . . . they can be . . ." He struggles for a word before he says, "parasitic." He winces. "I've watched so many innocent things slowly decay in their presence. And they keep pressuring me to find someone new to date. I'm worried any longer and my mother will just match-make me with the first girl she finds."

It clicks. "And you don't want that new innocent person to become another Natalie."

"Or worse," he breathes out.

"So you're dating me instead." I nod along, since I can connect with his intent. "You're protecting a bystander from walking into the insidious webs of your family. So . . . I'm like your shield."

He smiles at the analogy. "If you're my shield, then I'm your crown." He brings the apple cider to his mouth again. "Here to grant you access into the kingdom." He swigs the last of his drink.

I pour mine back in his cup. "According to you, it's filled with vipers."

"I think you can handle yourself." He looks me over. "I don't think you're easily malleable, Phoebe." *Rocky believes I am.* He thinks my mother has been manipulating me. *No . . . there's just no way.* It's still difficult to really make sense of that possibility.

I look up, just as Jake leans in closer. He smooths a strand of my hair behind my ear. Out of the corner of my eye, I suddenly realize we're being watched by Claudia's friends. I'm more caught off guard that I've slipped and forgotten.

"Dating you beats the alternative," he continues in thought, his blue eyes tracing mine with softer affection. He's not too bad at pretending.

"The alternative is what?" I ask. "Being a bachelor forever?"

He nods. "Which I would do, if I had to."

I almost open up and divulge that I, too, always believed I'd be single forever. Living the bachelorette life. But I'd have to explain my upbringing to really dig into those weeds. So I just rest into his side like a real girlfriend. Someone who can have him.

"I need this to work," he breathes, his arm around my waist. "*Us.*" I hear a tinge of desperation. He wants this *badly*. I'm a tool to cutting his mom off from tormenting some other woman who could become Mrs. Jake Waterford. And maybe this is my way of doing some good without fully shedding the things I love. Pretending. Deceiving. The art of a ruse. Only the outcome isn't a boatload of cash but protecting a girl from being Claudia Waterford bait.

Not going to lie, it feels kind of nice to be Jake's shield.

Still, there's one problem.

"I want this to work, too, but you can't keep fighting with Rocky." I lift my weight off Jake and face him more, seeing his scowl. "I'm serious."

He tries to lighten up, but his face pinches painfully. "I don't like him."

"Yeah, no duh. The entire *town* has seen that."

He downs the last of the cider in an aggravated gulp. "The more you defend him, the more I just think—"

"What?" I prickle. "That I'm sticking up for my ex because I'm a battered lover who'll keep apologizing for his abusive behavior?"

His eyes sink into mine. "What should I believe?"

"That he's *never* laid a hand on me. He constantly thinks

about me and my feelings over his own, and he's willing to be a town pariah if it means I'm in a better social standing. He's only following me around because he doesn't trust you, and considering we're in some bizarre fake dating scheme, I don't blame him."

Jake cools off a bit, and I continue, "If you keep provoking him, he might accidentally blow our cover." *Not totally true, but Jake did insinuate that he was worried about him.* "So it'd be better to squash the animosity now and establish . . . something . . . less hostile between you two."

Jake slowly begins to nod.

I try not to act like his acceptance is a defibrillator to my chest. I pick my jaw off the ground. *That was too easy.*

"Yeah," he says softly. "I don't want him to ruin this." He motions between me and him.

"Okay . . . good." I'm ready for this pseudo-war to be over. "You . . . do you realize that means actually having a civil conversation?"

"As long as he meets me halfway, I think I can work it out," he says, his gaze drifting over my features. His fingers skate along the top of my head, and he plucks another fiery orange leaf from my hair.

Those damn leaves. All day they've been attacking me, but it's done a bang-up job of amplifying our romance. I smile at him, my stomach tossing in a weird way.

He whispers, "You hate that, don't you?"

"It's the featherlight touches," I say, still smiling. "I'm more of a hair-grab kinda girl."

"I think if I grabbed your hair in public someone would tackle me."

I tilt my head. "Who said anything about doing it in public?"

Why the fuck did I just say that?

It's a flirt. A come-on. Is it just so natural for me to lean into this like I'm on some sort of "seduce" setting that I can't control? He's searching my gaze for *more*, like he's trying to piece together how real that was.

I don't know.

I don't even know.

Not real! My head is screaming.

I nervously try to tuck flyaway hairs behind my ears. "He's not a bad guy." *Back to Rocky.* Yes, I'm rerouting the Jake & Phoebe Express back to him—even if it means skidding off the train tracks—but luckily, Jake's face doesn't sour at the mention of my ex. "The friends Rocky does have, he'll do anything for. He's *that* kind of guy."

Jake stares off again, lost in deep thought for a quiet second. He tips the cider to his mouth, forgetting he drank the rest, but that breaks his stupor. Now I'm wondering what the hell is churning in the brain of Jake Waterford.

If only mind reading were actually a thing.

"Jake!" Ms. Davenport suddenly swoops into our sphere, breaking our intimate and quiet chat near the fountain. Her manufactured congenial smile and emptied mimosa are putting me on my best girlfriend behavior.

I hold on to Jake's elbow, dutiful and lovesick.

Jake slips on Persol sunglasses and wears a warm smile. "Ms. Davenport. How's the festival treating you?"

"Oh, perfect." Her curiosity zips from him to me, back to him. "Aren't you two looking serious."

Jake smiles down at me. "We are. Aren't we, babe?"

"Mm-hmm." I grin up at him, forcing myself not to search for Rocky and hoping beyond hope that everyone buys our romantic façade.

He naturally slides his fingers along my temple and back behind my ear, the touch soothing and genuine. His eyes carry the same calming sentiments. I'd be a bigger liar if I said the motion wasn't comforting. Maybe he's trying to ease me into this situation where I need to be a fortress against his family.

A shield.

His shield.

Let's hope the crown he's granting me shines like the mother-fucking sun.

Thirty-One

Rocky

*S*hould not have confronted Jake.

That thought has been ringing in my head for a full half hour while I pour my attention into helping my sister fix the Bride of Frankenstein's broken nose. Carving pumpkins with Hailey and Oliver is my only attempt to try and forget Jake and the Burkes. Just for a moment, before something catches the corner of my eye.

I go still.

A familiar figure passes our carving station. Lithe and quiet, the person slips into the crowd like a shadow. My nerves spike, on high alert.

"I'll be back," I tell them and leave the table, following the white guy dressed in an expensive all-black suit with a black button-down. Tailor-made for his lean body. His dark hair brushes the back of his neck.

I watch him weave between bodies like he's made from the sea, water slipping around rock. Closer to the stage, a Tears for Fears song thumps the ground and makes it hard to hear. He uses the opportunity to slip his fingers into a man's pocket.

Wallet in hand for a solid three seconds.

Then he slides it back.

I follow him around the square, observing him as he picks the pockets of seven more locals. His fingers dip into purses. Satchels. Backpacks.

Each time, he returns the stolen wallet, never taking a dime. And then he settles in the long line at the beverage tent.

I stand right behind him, my muscles beyond tensed. He's close to my height, and I bow my head forward to whisper against his ear. "Boo."

He doesn't turn around. "How long have you been following me?" His voice is calm and unsurprised.

"Too long, little brother." Even from behind him, I see the corners of his mouth begin to pull in a smile.

"No one notices me." He's next in line, and we both drop the conversation while he fishes out his wallet and orders. "The hard apple cider." He flashes a fake quickly.

The bartender is busy enough that she barely glances at it. After pouring his drink in a to-go cup, he pays, and we step out of the line together.

He has a slanted smile, and we only face one another when we're under an ice-cream shop's shaded overhang. It's closed during the festival, and fewer people stroll past us.

We can't hug or embrace the way that most brothers would reunite. Not in public. Not until we determine what we are to each other in this town. And I've *wanted* Trevor here—but I didn't know he was coming.

Why now?

How did he even find us?

Stuffing my hands in my leather jacket, I stare at my nineteen-year-old brother head-on.

I remember when he was born—I was only six, and he was the first fragile thing I ever held in my arms. But the older he grew, the more I realized he was as fragile as a viper in a cage.

I have so many questions. Ones I can't ask outright.

"Hey," I say casually, not sure what alias he wants to use.

He takes the biggest swig from the apple cider, two signet rings on each of his fingers. He has a helix piercing in the upper cartilage of his left ear, but his hair is long enough that I can't tell if he's wearing an earring today. He appraises me in a slow once-over like I'm cattle he's considering purchasing for his ranch.

"You let yourself go," he deadpans.

"You're still a twig. And see, one of us is bullshitting and it's not me."

His lip begins to rise. "I feed on misery and despair, so I should be satiated as long as I'm around you."

"Oof." I feign a wince and smile. "Thank God you took all the shithead genes."

Trevor laughs, and I try to be happier that he's here more than I'm on edge. But alarms are *blaring* so caustically in my head, my ears ring.

I nod to him. "You here for long?"

"Long enough." He glances around, catching the eye of a group of young Caufield students who huddle together next to an outdoor heater. A few of the girls ogle him.

Trevor doesn't feed into it and flirt back. He just turns to me. "Where is everyone?"

I lead him past the carving tables where Hailey, Oliver, and now Nova hang out. I signal to them that we're going to my sister's loft and they should follow, and all three make a casual exit from the festival.

The loft is on the same street, and from the living room windows, I can peer down and see Phoebe still on a date with Jake.

So I avoid looking that way when I enter the loft with my little brother, spare keys in my hand.

Trevor, however, fills the frame of the window, the wispy white curtains blowing on either side of him as he observes the festival below.

I curl an arm over his shoulders. "I'm glad you made it."

"Me, too." I hear tension in his voice.

Shit. What happened? I squeeze his shoulder before letting go.

The door bangs shut. Oliver, Nova, and Hailey are here.

Oliver hurdles the couch with his arms outstretched to Trevor for a hug. "Our little psychopath," he greets him affectionately.

That nickname throws me back.

We were all at a coed boarding school in upstate New York for a short period. The six of us would sneak out every Thursday night and meet up at a cemetery a quarter mile from the school to catch each other up. One of those nights, Hailey and Phoebe were drunk on expensive vodka and giggled about how we were a part of some secret club. And we needed names.

We came up with six.

The mastermind.

The seductress.

The silver-tongue.

The chameleon.

The getaway.

And the psychopath.

Hailey, Phoebe, me, Oliver, Nova, and Trevor.

Trevor was the youngest of us. So to get him in the same grade, he had to come to the boarding school as a prodigy. We convinced everyone that he skipped four grades and was actually two years older.

After Oliver squeezes Trevor in a bear hug, my brother's shifty gray eyes flash from Hailey to me to Nova. "We're missing one," he says.

I nod my head out the window.

Trevor rotates back to the festival. "She's with someone?"

"The landlord," I explain, not digging into Phoebe's *fake* business with him.

Hailey has brought her pumpkin, mine, and carving tools with her. *Of course she has.* Nova carries both pumpkins for my sister. And she continues working on the thing on the coffee table.

"Why are you here?" I ask Trevor.

He's fixated on Jake down below. "Is he a Sagittarius?"

That's code for *Is he the mark?* But his casual brush-off of my question only tenses me.

"This is a no fun zone," Oliver tells him, sitting on the armrest of the couch. Nova sips a beer, listening quietly.

Trevor frowns. "How wide is the zone?"

"The whole town," Hailey says, glancing up from her pumpkin.

Trevor looks like he was told Christmas is canceled. "What the fuck? Why?" He looks back to Phoebe at the festival with more confusion. Probably not understanding why she'd be talking to Jake if it isn't for a job.

I'm not explaining that shit in code. It's a jumbled mess.

"I could use your help," Hailey calls over our brother, nodding to my pumpkin. "Rocky quit."

I roll my eyes.

Our brother says, "Sounds like him."

"It does not," I refute.

Trevor picks up the smallish pumpkin and a carving knife. Holding the pumpkin in hand, he starts expertly cutting it without any guidelines. His eyes draw to me. "You're not replaceable, you know."

There it is.

The truth he was reluctant to share.

"I tried to replace you at the Seattle job," Trevor adds without remorse.

And that's why he didn't want to bail on Mom and Dad. He saw an opportunity to be in a role they rarely, if ever, put him in: face-to-face deception and manipulation. In the action, not behind the scenes.

My role.

For many, *many* years, I hoped my brother wouldn't become like me. Bitter. *Cynical.* I never imagined, not once, that he'd want to be this person. I see him claw toward the darkness that I've lived and breathed and suffocated under for decades, and I just want to push him away.

I keep trying.

"How'd that work out?" I wonder.

"Mom wouldn't even let me attempt it."

Good.

"I was done begging, so I came here." He scowls and sets the pumpkin back on the coffee table. Tossing the knife with it. "Oliver was geotagged on social media."

"*Shit,*" Oliver sneers a curse and unpockets his phone, his olive skin flushed at the collar of his button-down.

I groan, raking a hand through my hair. "So they've found us."

Hailey is frowning at Oliver. She crawls onto the couch beside him to look.

"I don't understand how . . ." He shows her, and she cups his phone in her hands. Oliver looks to his brother. "I have no social media presence here. How could I be geotagged?"

Nova is rubbing his forehead. "I need to get Phoebe." He's out the door in a blip.

"One of your clients," Hailey explains to him. "They took a photo of you during a session. Your face is clear. My dad could've done a facial recognition search, and your client tagged her location."

Victoria, Connecticut.

Oliver sees the image. *"Edith,"* he says in displeasure, then to Hailey, "I'm sorry, Hails."

She lifts her shoulders, then meets my gaze. "It was bound to happen."

Yeah, but we all wanted longer for our sisters.

"They'll be here soon, you know," Trevor says at the window. I join him again, hands in my jacket, and Hailey comes over on the other side of me.

"What's soon?" I ask my brother.

"The Seattle job only has two weeks left."

Two weeks.

Jesus.

Everyone is quiet. My brother, sister, and I gaze down at the festival. Vibrant leaves paint the trees, pumpkin juices stain the cobblestone, and bright laughter bleeds into crisp autumn air that I feel seep through the windowsill. A *Harvest Festival* banner hangs high across the streets, and little kids drop pennies in the fountain. Idealistic. Content.

Happy.

"I don't get it," Trevor breathes. "Why is the zone so big?"

"Because of *Mystic Pizza*," Hailey says just as quietly.

Trevor twists his head to her. "Wait, we're not having fun because of your obsession with a Julia Roberts movie?"

It's more than that. I know it is.

But I never learned what happened in Carlsbad, so I just keep my mouth shut with unanswered questions.

"It's not an obsession," Hailey says. "It's a fascination."

"Those are synonyms," Trevor tells her, but they share a small smile, almost like a *hello* and *I missed you.*

Just then, my phone vibrates in my pocket. Digging it out, I recognize Victoria's area code. I answer on the second ring.

"Hello?" *Please don't be my father.*

"Rocky," Jake says hurriedly.

I frown, glancing down at the festival again. I search for Jake, but he's not at the fountain. *Phoebe.* I don't see her. I only find Nova canvassing the crowds and coming up short.

I'm about to ask where she is, but he speaks first.

He tells me, "I need your help."

Thirty-Two

Rocky

It's not an easy stroll down the sidewalk. I drive several miles out of the center of town to a gated property on fifteen acres of land. Along with the address, Jake texted me one thing.

Jake: Meet me at the stables

I called Phoebe right after that text. "I think he's sincere," she said.

"He's sincerely shady," I refuted. "He might as well have told me to meet him behind the dumpster or out in the middle of the woods. You've seen enough horror movies to know how this shit goes down."

"He wants this fake dating thing with me to work out and that means being nicer to you."

"Being nice doesn't involve asking me for help, Phebs."

"But admitting he needs your help for something is an olive branch. Major white flag territory. And anyway, we're more dangerous than him."

Her last statement was what changed things for me. She wasn't wrong. I'm the con artist, and if Jake had a manipulative bone in his body—he wasn't using it well.

She added, "This is the perfect opportunity for you to figure out *why* he's being so shady. Go with it. Keep your phone on. Text me if you run into trouble."

I smiled, feeling like this was a mini-job. Back to our old ways.

Now, I'm parking my sleek black McLaren in front of a large horse stable. No other person in sight. But the security guard at the gate let me in, so Jake should know I'm here by now.

I lean against the hood of the car and take out my phone, a second away from texting Phoebe about how this feels like a setup. *Maybe he does work for our parents.* Jesus, that thought wreaks havoc in my head.

A chill whips through the air, and the sound of crunching gravel stops me from typing. A blue Porsche approaches and slows to a park next to me. Jake exits and zips up his navy windbreaker, his gaze heavy on me.

"Thanks for coming."

I smile dryly. "Coming is only enjoyable when I understand why I'm getting fucked."

"You're not getting fucked, Rocky." He takes a tensed breath, stress clear in every microscopic movement he's making. Down to the shifting of his polished loafers.

"Okay." I hold out my hands wide. "Then what am I doing here?"

"Let me just show you . . ." Worries cinch his brows, like he thinks I'm going to jump in my car and make a quick exit.

But I've made it this far. There's no reason for me to high-tail it out. No offense to Jake, but he's not that fucking scary.

"All right." I follow him to the stable. The closer I get, the more I realize how giant this place really is. Off in the distance, I spot an enclosed riding arena where a horse trots with an older man. Another area has obstacles for equestrian events.

Inside the stable, I count twenty stalls. All are full except the one at the very end.

Jake brings me to a middle stall where a chestnut horse stands poised. The animal has a blaze: a white marking along its forehead and down the bridge of its face. The name *Bowie* is carved on a wooden sign. I tilt my head and scan beneath its torso. *Male.*

I scrutinize the animal quickly. It's been a while since my mom quizzed me on horse breeds, but I just round out a guess. "Warmblood?" I ask.

Jake narrows his eyes on me. "You know horses?"

"Just a little bit. I took some riding lessons when I was younger, but I didn't love it." That's all truth. I give Bowie another once-over. Horses, I don't like. Most animals, I don't like. I can trick them. Deceive them. But it takes more effort than deceiving a human.

Oliver has always been the best with animals.

Jake stares harder at the horse, a sadness washing over him. And then I remember something—a phone call I overheard months ago. My first day at the country club, he was arguing with someone about selling the horse.

"I'm surprised you needed my help, considering our history." We literally just had a public confrontation this morning at the Harvest Festival. The only thing that's changed is his need to ensure I don't ruin his fake relationship.

Jake drags his gaze along the dirt floor, wrestling with his decision to call me. His blue eyes hoist to meet mine. "We got off on the wrong foot."

The wrong foot. "I'd say we got off exactly how the universe intended." Am I going to take pleasure in him asking me for help? A favor?

Yes.

Yes, I am.

I wait for him to speak. Tension coils between us now that it's clear I'm not brushing aside our rift.

Jake takes a tight breath. "Just hear me out."

"It's why I'm here," I say, flashing a smile.

He has to take a second, steadying his breath. Then he says, "This was my sister's horse. My parents aren't sentimental about Bowie, and they're ready to sell him so they can bank more money boarding another horse."

"I'm not seeing the issue," I tell him. "If you're sentimental about him, then why don't you buy the horse?"

His jaw sets, nose flaring as his breath inflates his lungs. Elevates his chest. He holds my gaze so long that I wonder if he thinks I can read his fucking mind. More likely, he's just hating that I'm not bending that easily.

And then he says, "I've *tried*, man. But there's another buyer ready to purchase him in all cash, and my trust fund has its . . . limitations."

I don't ask about his savings. I'm sure they're all tied up in stocks or IRAs or accounts so complicated you'd need three brokers to explain it to you. All these rich heirs are the same.

"So you want me to buy Bowie?" I just come out and ask. It's why he didn't ask Phoebe—he knows she doesn't have the cash.

He nods. "I know it's not a simple request." He runs a tender hand down Bowie's nose. "But Phoebe told me you're the kind of guy who'd do anything for his friends—"

"I missed the part where we became friends," I say sharply, using the exact words he's said to me.

Breath knocks out of Jake like I sucker punched him, but he recovers fast. "It's in you to be one, isn't it? And yeah, maybe I don't see it, but she does."

Talk of Phoebe vouching for my character tenses me in a different way. In my head, I had questioned whether she was shitting on me to Jake at the festival, and now I feel like an ass for questioning her at all.

I shift toward the horse and ask, "How much?"

"He's a hundred grand."

I whistle lowly. "I'm going to be honest with you, Jake. I don't much like horses, and unless this one pisses gold, I'm *not* interested. Maybe take it up with one of your actual friends." I'm about to leave.

"Wait." He jolts forward to stop me.

I pause.

His brows cinch, his eyes troubled. "They all basically said the same shit."

"But I'm the out-of-towner that will take the bait, right?" I stuff my hands in my leather jacket.

He frowns deeply. "This isn't some trick."

I still don't know that.

"It seems fishy," I tell him. "You're so desperate to keep a horse that's definitely not worth the price—all to remember your sister by? It's sweet, sure, but take a picture and frame it. It'll serve the same purpose."

He shakes his head repeatedly like it won't. Like there is no alternative. "I can buy him back when some of my funds become less tied up. You can call it a loan, if you want. With interest."

See, I've been here before.

On both sides.

I've been handed money. Only instead of paying back the "loan," I disappeared with it.

I've handed over money. Only that had a purpose. It was a stepping stone to gain trust, and there's nothing for me to gain here. I don't need Jake's trust. I don't need anything from him, other than to ensure he won't fuck with Phoebe.

He's the desperate one—the person I could so easily screw over in a heartbeat. It's like the universe is dangling a carrot out in front of me, tempting me to just . . . con him.

But easy isn't right.

It's not even smart.

I stare harder at Bowie. He neighs at me, and I cringe. Yeah, still don't like horses.

I tell Jake, "It's just not going to happen." *Sorry, not sorry.*

He blinks hard like I impaled him, and I'm beginning to realize that I was his last-ditch effort. Which isn't shocking at all. He's not fond of me—I wouldn't be first in line for him to grovel to.

Jake rubs his mouth a few times; dropping his hand, he says, "I thought you'd get it because you have a little sister."

"Luckily my sister's hobbies and sentimental memorabilia aren't worth a hundred grand. Throw a paperback at her and she's happy."

He nods over and over in an attempt to stop emotion from splitting apart his face. He loses that battle and runs a palm over his eyes. *"Fuck."* He whirls around quickly and mutters more curses under his breath.

I wonder if his parents chastised him for crying. Made him repress certain emotions. My mom taught me about toxic masculinity when I was little. When to feed into it to be *one with my peers* and when to abandon it because it's not who I should be. And despite that, I'm still bad at dealing with my emotions. I bury everything and let it feed on me.

Jake clutches the stall with white knuckles, and I've been there before. Different situation. Same battle.

"Be real with me, Jake." I step closer. "This is really just about a horse?"

He doesn't reply immediately. He's trying not to cry. "Yeah." His voice fractures.

Even with his genuine emotion. I. Don't. Believe. Him.

Never be seduced by others' emotions. Another hard taught lesson.

"You want me to buy the horse," I say. "Turn off the security cameras." I spotted two when I walked into the stables.

"They're already off." *Interesting.*

"Show me."

He unburies his phone from his slacks pocket, clicking into a security app, and he passes it over. I verify that all the cameras are down, and then I put his phone face down on Bowie's gate.

Jake waits.

"Beg me," I tell him.

He blinks. "What?"

"I want to know how badly you want this horse," I say. "So *beg me* for it."

He glowers. "You're a fucking asshole—"

"You've never thought I was a *nice guy*," I retort. "Yet, you called me. You asked me for a favor, knowing that I am a fucking asshole. So if you really, *sincerely* want this horse, you're going to drop on your goddamn knees and you're going to show me just how much you appreciate my act of kindness."

Jake is full of blistering anger, his scowl hardened. "Fuck you."

"How much is your dignity worth? Is it worth your sister's memory?" I say, driving in the knife deeper.

His hands clench at his sides, a nerve struck. "Is this because of what I said at the festival? Or because I'm fake dating your ex-wife?" Jake snaps. "Is this your sick, twisted way to get back at me for that?"

Yes . . . and no.

"She deserves to be with someone who's not weak," I tell him. "You're a pathetic piece of shit who's crying over something so damn trivial—"

"Shut up," he grits out.

"Boo-hoo, son of one of the richest families in the country can't buy a horse—"

"I said stop!" He's a second away from lunging at me. Rage scorches his eyes.

"I guess you're just going to have to bury that memory of your dead sister."

"She's not dead!" he screams, and instantly Jake's face breaks in surprise like he's shocked he even said it out loud.

I control my body not to blow backward, but I'll be honest, I didn't expect that. I go so still, my muscles cramping. My mind reels in a million directions.

His sister didn't die. So he what—lied about her death? Orchestrated her disappearance? Every theory leads to the same gnawing thought.

I didn't peg Jake Waterford correctly. From very beginning, my read was wrong. I saw him as too uptight, too ethical, too moral to deceive even a stranger. Has he been pulling the wool over his entire family? Or are they in on this, too?

"Shitshit*shit*." His hands fly to his head.

Pushing buttons to surface the truth—not my finest moment. Usually, I couldn't give a shit when I go this far, but usually, I go this far with the bastards of the world. The seemingly untouchable men who treat Phoebe like she's nothing more than a warm body at night.

Jake isn't one of them.

It doesn't feel right breaking good men.

A biting sensation eats away at my core, and I have trouble looking at him. Because it feels like Jake is where I should be. And I'm no different than the men I've always hated.

Disgust with myself—what a new wretched feeling. Guess it'd catch up with me in time.

I'm still motionless. Watching.

Jake crouches, breathing harder. "You can't tell anyone. You can't tell anyone." His wrought gaze strikes me. *"Rocky."*

I run my fingers over my sharpened jawline. *Fuck*. If the Waterford family is behind this . . . I'll be bought off to keep my mouth shut? *At best*.

Threatened to leave town? *Second best*.

Followed and stalked and possibly killed? *Worst*.

Except, he's begging me. He's not spinning the knife in my direction.

"I don't even know what I'm agreeing to, Jake." But I see his earnestness, and a raw honesty that's hard, if not impossible, to fabricate.

With another exhale, he stands. "Let me explain," he pleads, hand outstretched. "Can we take a walk?"

"All right. Lead the way."

We end up among a thicket of trees, walking along a wooded horse trail, and through all this, I think about Phoebe and her horror movies. "Don't murder me, yeah?" I ask Jake casually.

"That's not in me." His gaze dips to me, wary. "How about you don't murder me?"

"Deal," I reply.

We're on a trust teeterboard. Going back and forth with having confidence in each other.

We keep a slow pace, and Jake starts talking. "Our parents were hard on Kate. The only girl of the family. She was pushed at every moment."

"They planned her whole future?" I'm guessing. I've seen it before among affluent families. They place their hopes and dreams on one specific child, and it's suffocating.

He nods once. "Her life was dictated to the smallest degree." He lets out a tight laugh. "My mother had a weekly schedule for her, and Kate never even had time to eat lunch. Dance recitals, morning tutoring, after-school French lessons—once she mastered that, then Dutch and Swedish. Equestrian events, charity galas, tennis, book club—the list never ended. If there was a minute untouched, my mother touched it."

I look over at him, a pressure rising in my chest. *If there was a minute untouched, my mother touched it.* I understand what it's like to be used.

Smothered with backhanded affection.

Trapped.

It's easy for me to feel for Kate, but even easier to feel for Jake. The depth of his empathy for his sister is . . . relatable.

I hate that it is, because again, *never be seduced by others' emotions.*

Thing is, he's not trying to play me. Or outwit me. I believe he's just being frank. Candid and truthful. And I'm just the cynic afraid to lower my guard.

Jake stares ahead, emotion barreling through him. "Every year, I saw her get *smaller* and *smaller.* Sadder and sadder. And then one day . . ." He takes a beat, his eyes welling and reddening. "I caught her in the stables with Bowie. She'd taken a whole bottle of our mom's Vicodin . . . I got her to the hospital in enough time." He gazes out at a large oak tree. "I thought . . . things would change for her after that. I thought our parents would change for her."

Our shoes crunch fallen leaves, and Jake comes to a stop near a babbling stream.

He twists around to face me, more resigned than angry. As though he's accepted what his parents are, and I'm not even there when it comes to my own parents.

Fury isn't dormant in me. It's living, breathing. Awake at every step, every turn. But I've mastered the art of control, just so it won't consume me.

Jake holds my gaze. "Nothing changed. When Kate got home, they just went back to their normal routine like it never happened." He skims my features. "You don't seem surprised."

"These social circles aren't foreign to me," I remind him, since I'm supposed to come from Manhattan. Raised in New York. "Your parents were more afraid of the social repercussions of admitting their daughter almost took her own life than they were of losing their daughter. I'm not shocked they didn't want to self-reflect and question whether they could've been at fault. Because even *if* people want to look in a mirror, sometimes they spend their whole lives convincing themselves there are no flaws."

I've never wanted that to be me.

I intake a breath. "And I appreciate the backstory, but how did that get you *here*? To where your sister isn't actually dead?"

"We were out riding one day. A trail farther north." He points in the direction. "And we came across some old remains. A battle in the American Revolutionary War was fought around here, then the War of 1812. The bones could've been that old, I wasn't sure at the time." He pauses. "But once I saw them, I saw an opportunity for Kate to leave town and get away from our family for good."

"*You* staged her death?" I question, unable to be impressed since I'm stunned it wasn't a ploy concocted by his entire family.

It was just Jake.

He nods. "They were *bones*. Not the body of a girl who had died a week or month ago. So she had to disappear. I bought a little cabin in a remote area . . ." He trails off, deciding not to share the location, and I respect that. "I drove her there. She stayed, and I came home alone to the fallout. There were search parties. It was even in the news. 'Daughter of Koning Beer Empire Goes Missing.'"

"I saw," I say.

"You looked me up?"

"You're my sister's landlord and now my ex-wife's fake boyfriend—if I didn't dig into your family, I'd be a fool."

Jake wears a weakened smile. "After a year passed with no news of Kate, I made sure another search party went out in the right direction." We both look to the north. "They found the remains, which turned out to be from the late 1700s, but I paid the coroner to say it was my sister." He winces. "I'm *paying* the coroner."

"That's where some of your money is tied?"

"Yeah, but I always told Kate I'd get Bowie back to her. I just . . . I needed more time."

Too many feelings churn through me. I run both of my hands through my hair, feeling the soft strands slip between my fingers.

I must look skeptical because Jake sighs out, "I know it seems impossible."

Not impossible.

Faking a death? Child's play.

Done it three times.

But I can't tell him that. Can't even say that I didn't think he had it in him.

Jake touches his chest. "I love my sister. I'd do anything to make sure she's still on this planet. Do you get that?"

I take a pained breath. "Yeah, I get that." But I can't buy into words. I need proof. "Can I see your phone?"

He pulls it out.

"Show me her number."

He scrolls down to a number, no contact info. I hold out my hand, and he passes it to me. I text her: Call me. It's important.

I wait.

Jake waits.

And then an ABBA song plays. "Chiquitita." *Little girl* in Spanish. I answer the call. The line is quiet, so I look at Jake.

He speaks. "Kate, everything okay?"

"Yeah, you're the one who texted me." She sounds young, her voice having a breathy cadence that's so distinct, I recognize it from the interviews on YouTube. The ones with her and her family, praising the Koning beer.

I hang up on her and hand Jake his phone back. It's becoming hard to hate him. Even harder not to brush aside the deepening crater of jealousy.

Jake Koning Waterford is everything I can't be.

He's a good guy who pulled a con to *save* his sister.

He's done what I could never do. What I've never tried to do. I've only pulled cons for my own gain—or my family's gain. Any altruism is a side effect, not the main cause. I've never convinced myself I'm a vigilante with a moral backbone. I know what I am, and yet . . . here he is.

I want to hate him.

But I want to be him more, and that scares the shit out of me. I've never wanted to change. Never hated myself to warrant it. And I don't dislike who I am—I don't.

But could I be better?

"I'll buy the horse," I say.

Shock pierces his face. "What?"

"I'll buy Bowie. You can pay me back later."

He shakes his head over and over. "I don't understand. Why?"

Because maybe a path exists where I can be good. Maybe I want to keep him close because he could be useful down the line—and I have so much blackmail I could fill a landfill with it.

Or maybe I think his friendship would be good for me.

Maybe it's all those things.

"I don't know," I whisper out. "I just am."

Thirty-Three

Phoebe

Pacing back and forth in my bedroom, I stare at a piece of paper in my hand. I've replayed what Rocky said happened at the horse stables a million and one times.

Oh wait, he said *nothing*. That's right. Rocky has been withholding the *one* piece of information I asked him to help retrieve.

I mimic him and his stupidly gruff voice. "It's a lot, Phebs. Just give me a sec." I exhale a pissed breath. "*Lies*. You had to go flee town for a stupid cash grab."

After the horse stables, he immediately packed his bags and left for Rhode Island. He even took Oliver with him. Something about needing a large chunk of change quickly.

I didn't have the chance to see them go. He called from the car. *I'll tell you everything when I get back. I don't want to do this over the phone.*

"It hasn't been just a sec," I mutter hotly, still pacing. "It's been two awful weeks."

And it's been the worst two weeks since I arrived in Victoria. Not because of my job. Katherine has removed her claws from my shoulders. Mr. Burke barely acknowledges my existence. Guests at the country club chat with me like I'm heir adjacent. All because I'm dating Jake, and his social status has boosted mine into a glittery stratosphere.

Hailey and I even found an *honest* path to cover rent for the rest of October. We parted ways with our matching diamond bracelets, gifts from our moms when we were twelve. And the family dinner with Jake's parents was postponed after Mr. Waterford came down with the flu.

These two weeks should've been the best ever. Easy job. No big financial concerns. No interactions with Jake's influential family.

No Rocky.

I hated it. I hated that he wasn't here. I hated that I missed him every time I thought about him and my heart clenched. I hated wishing for his stupid comebacks and eye rolls. I hated how each day passed, and I just hoped and hoped that each day would be the day he'd return.

"He shouldn't have left," I say, my lungs on fire. *I need him.* "I don't need him." I want to pace, but I'm glued to the floor, the paper crumpling in my tight fist. *I want him.* "I don't want him." My eyes burn. "I'm not a needy bitch. I'm . . ." I swallow a rising lump.

What is wrong with me?

"I just want answers about Jake," I tell myself.

I know, I know . . . I'm lying.

Unfurling the crinkled paper, I try to focus on other problems. The clip joint job in Seattle ends today, and since our parents know we're in Victoria, they could show up tomorrow, two days from now, a week, a month—we have no idea.

Hailey and I have been trying to prepare a list of what we'll say to them.

I uncap my pen with my teeth, and resting the paper on my dresser, I scribble a second point beneath my first.

I'm twenty-four. I can choose what I want to do with my life.

If you ever need my help, I can only do it through honest means. I won't pretend to be someone I'm not.

Yeah, this is a recipe for disaster. My mom might think she failed me somehow and even blame herself.

I already hear her response and see her saddened eyes. *Someone you're not? Bug, you've never been anyone other than who you are. This is you.*

"This is me," I mutter to myself, not disagreeing since I literally went to the movie theater to establish my fake relationship, but I haven't been miserable in Victoria. I've liked knowing we're not packing our bags and fleeing. I like trying to make *one* life work instead of reinventing myself every time I arrive somewhere new.

I never knew I'd enjoy being rooted to a place, but I haven't wanted to abandon this town.

I've just wanted Rocky to come back to me.

Folding up my paper, I go to the kitchen barstools where Hailey is working on her list. Trevor is camping out on the couch, scrolling through Netflix like he owns the place. He tinkers with a wooden box on his lap.

His presence here is a ticking bomb, counting down the seconds until our parents arrive. He's also made that couch his bed for two weeks. And no—Jake has no idea we've sufficiently lit his favorite *no extended guests* rule on fire.

"How's it coming?" I ask, sliding onto the barstool beside her.

"I have a few things."

She has more than twenty bullet points, but over half are scratched out. I watch Hailey chew on her thumbnail. Concern balls in my ribs.

I should tell my mom that this is about the life I'm supporting for Hailey. The future my best friend wants, and the one I've started growing to like, too.

My mom would do anything for Addison, and Addison would do anything for my mom. They should understand they raised two girls who are unfailingly loyal to each other— who'd go to great lengths to see the other happy.

I recap my pen. "We're burning these later?" I ask Hails since we don't like keeping things documented on paper.

"Yeah, but not yet." She crosses out another line, deep in concentration.

"We'll figure it out," I encourage. "I know we will." Except these are only words, and I'm not a better planner. If I could magically transform into a logistics mastermind right now, I would. For her, I would. This is falling on her shoulders, and I wish I could power-lift all the weight.

It hurts knowing I can't.

Hailey nods repeatedly and forces a smile for me. Her confidence is fading. "We've got this. Don't worry."

We're both extremely worried.

I nod and swivel on the barstool. Facing the living room, I see Trevor picking an HBO show, and he continues to tinker with his box.

Every time I ask him how long he'll be here, he says, "Until I'm needed elsewhere."

I check my phone. No missed calls. No new texts. Last night, I received one message from most likely a burner phone.

401-555-2013: be back tomorrow. All good there? 🕷

I knew it was Rocky. When he was eighteen, I'd told him he needed to choose a better emoji as an identifier.

"What should I be, then?" he'd contested.

"You have tons of options. A wolf, a snake, a fox—a venomous scorpion. Doesn't that sound more like you?" Everyone in our family could be considered a spider. I just figured he'd want to stand out.

He tapped his phone and sent me another spider. And then another one. And another. Until spiders flooded our text message thread. He stood up from my bed, and I still remember how he dipped his head to me. How little pieces of his hair brushed his lashes. How his gray eyes pulsed with fervor.

And very quietly, he said, "It's the reign of spiders. This is exactly what I'm supposed to be."

He never wanted to be different than the rest of us. He's made it clear that he'll always be loyal to our families, even if he'd like to carve out our parents and chuck them into another galaxy.

Last night, I texted him back: we're fine here 🕷

I'm staring at my dumb strawberry emoji on my phone. Wondering if I can manifest a new text with my eyes.

Hailey peers up from her paper and studies me and my new phone obsession. "He'll call."

I click out of the texts. Tap into the recent phone calls. Back into the text threads. "Call," I whisper to my cell.

From the couch, Trevor watches me with raised brows. "Hailey, come collect your friend, she's losing it."

I shoot Trevor a glare. "King of the Hypocrites." I look to the box on his lap. "I thought your parents said no more money boxes?"

Trevor fabricated a box that prints counterfeit bills. It works ten times before being useless, but the marks he sells them to never know that.

"What they don't know won't hurt them," Trevor sing-songs in-key, and he glances from his sister to me. "Isn't that the golden motto in this town?"

I regret letting Trevor know about our "new start" here in Victoria because he cackled like we needed to be sent to a traveling circus. He thinks we're clowns. Now he's mocking us.

"The golden motto is don't be an ass," I snap.

Trevor blows out a breath in a mock wince. "Ooh, I think you might have already failed that one, PG-13."

PG. Phoebe Graves.

"Clever," I say dryly.

He rattles the money box. "What's clever is this box, Wannabe NC-17."

"Ooh," I make the same sound he made. "You're so *edgy*."

"Edgier than you," he refutes. "The edgiest thing you've done is pretend to be a stripper. And you weren't even good at it."

Hailey whips toward him. "Don't be mean, Trevor."

"You don't need to stick up for her, Hails," he says. "Phoebe doesn't have a sensitive bone in her body."

I set my phone down on the counter to flip him off with both hands.

"Point made," Trevor says. He returns to his box, and I go to pick up my phone when it buzzes on the counter.

My heart almost jumps from my chest.

Hailey leans into my side and reads over my shoulder.

Rocky: You both free to grab dinner at the Lure? 5 p.m.?

He's back on his regular phone, which means he's already in town.

I quickly text back: Yeah, we'll meet you there. How are you and Jake?

I've wanted this answer for a while. Especially since I've asked Jake about his chat with Rocky, but he just brushes me off.

Rocky: Peachy. Jake and I are BFFs

Hailey frowns. "That's sarcasm, right?"
Confusion furrows my brows. "I'm not sure."

Thirty-Four

Phoebe

On our walk to the seaside bar, my phone buzzes.

Laurie Strode: Send me your coordinates, bug.

My stomach somersaults. "Hailey?" I show her my phone. "Doesn't she already know where we are?"

Hailey frowns. "It might be a test."

A test? Of loyalty?

I've been so withdrawn that she must be questioning where I stand. *Not good, not good.* It's my fault. Maybe I should've made a better effort so she knows I wouldn't betray her.

By the time we're seated on the outside patio of the Lure, I still haven't figured out how to respond to the text, and Rocky is late.

We opt for a table close to a family of four. The parents are more preoccupied corralling two toddlers than eavesdropping on our conversation.

Where's Rocky?

I keep checking the time. The waitress serves us warm crab dip and the best fried clam strips I've had, and I shift the patio heater closer to Hailey as the sun begins to drop.

Finally, Rocky arrives, eighteen minutes past the time *he* set.

He shows up in a sexy sport coat, his black hair artfully windswept. And as soon as he seizes my gaze from across the patio, he doesn't let go. He walks to the table still clinging on to me, and my expression isn't necessarily inviting.

I'm a little aggravated he's late. And I'm mad that my pulse is skipping, and my heart has practically catapulted to my throat.

Rocky looks me over, as though ensuring I've been fine in his absence. Does he want me to be fine when he's gone? Would that make him happy?

I drop my gaze first and check out the menu. We've only ordered apps.

When he sits down, he already starts digging into the crab dip like he hasn't eaten all day.

I glare. "Hello. How are you? I'm doing great, too, thanks."

"We need to talk about Trevor," he says after swallowing a mouthful.

I frown. "I thought we were here to talk about Jake?"

"That, too." He wipes his hands on a cloth napkin. "But Trevor is more like an impending doom. Jake is taken care of."

Hailey narrows her eyes. "Did you kill him?"

He gives her a look. "Hailey."

She eases back. "Just checking."

"What about your annoying brother?" I ask, grabbing a pita from the dish.

"As you both know, he comes with baggage."

He means *enemies*, but he's trying to be discreet in public. Trevor is a liability that my mom is sometimes afraid to have around, so they place him in shadows and dark corners. Over time, he's angered the wrong people with the money box scam. There've been a few instances where Nova has seen men tailing him.

"The longer he's here, we'll need to be careful about any photos he's in so he's not geotagged."

Hailey nods. "Can do."

"Same. Is he for sure staying?"

"I don't know. But I think he'll still be around when our parents show, which could be soon."

My stomach nose-dives at the mention of our parents. I remember the text, and I drop my pita on my plate. Appetite gone.

He watches me with a frown. "What happened?"

I fish my phone from my pocket and hand it over.

He reads the text quickly, eyes darkening, and then passes the phone back. "She's testing you?"

"That's what Hailey thinks. I kinda believe it, too. She has reason to mistrust us. We haven't exactly been forthcoming."

Rocky just expels this rough, heavy breath. "What are you going to reply?"

"I know what you'd want me to reply," I say. "Coordinates to the Arctic. Send them to the North Pole to live with the penguins."

"Penguins are in the South Pole," Hailey tells me.

Rocky smiles at me like I've been successfully burned. Au contraire, I love my best friend's helpful facts and corrections. I become smarter by association.

"That's not what I'd do," Rocky argues. "I'd tell her it's none of her business. I'm working my own job, and I'll see her in time. Until then, we can shoot the shit about literally anything else."

"Sounds not cagey at all," I say dryly. "I have no reason to lie to her. I've never been at odds with my mom."

"Then just tell her where you are, Phoebe. It's not like she doesn't already know. And if you want her to believe that you trust her, because you clearly still do, then maybe it's the right move. But it's not my move to make. It's yours."

I don't know if I can resist falling into a big con if she's around, and I can't fail Hailey. I can't screw up this life we've built.

I don't want her to come here. Not yet.

It's all I know for sure.

So I send a text: Trevor said that you all have our location. We're doing really great. Everything's going well. We'll meet up somewhere else.

She's quick to reply.

Laurie Strode: I'll talk to Everett about it. Didn't know he got your location. See you sometime soon! Miss you, bug.

Everett has been keeping her in the dark? Why would he do that? I'm not exactly opening giant lines of communication with my mom right now, so I fight the urge to pry deeper about Hailey's dad. I send one more message about missing her, too, and I show the thread to Hailey, then Rocky.

Hailey's legs bounce underneath the table. "I-I'm not ready for them to come here. I can't . . ."

"Hey, Hails." I hug my friend beside me.

Rocky goes rigid, concern pinching his brows.

"We're going to be there," I remind her. "I'm not leaving you alone." It's what I keep telling her.

She goes sheet pale. Her black lipstick and eye shadow a

darker contrast against the stark white of her skin. "Maybe we should talk about Jake."

"Maybe we should take a walk," Rocky suggests, waving over the server. None of us order entrées, we just pay the bill and then hike down to the beach, carrying our shoes as our feet sink into the brown sand.

Wind is fiercer closer to the ocean, and in October, fewer people stroll along the water in the chilly evening. Squinting, I can distinguish a dog and an older person in the distance, tossing a Frisbee into the shallow waves. Otherwise, no one is around.

In this moment, it feels like the beach is ours.

Orange hues from the setting sun paint the horizon. It's pretty, but I'm only really looking at my best friend.

"What's wrong, Hails?" I find myself whispering, even though there's no reason to be quiet.

Her eyes are already bloodshot, restraining tears. "They'll see what I see when they get here." She peeks back at the seaside bar at the top of the hill.

"Which is what?" Rocky asks.

"I've been here for two months, and I've come up with about a hundred different jobs. Not meaning to, really. It's just habit." She looks sick to her stomach. "But even if I don't share any of my proposals, they'll make their own. And they're going to want to stay and pull one . . . and I can't convince them not to. I don't know how. I-I've never . . ."

I drop my heeled boots in the sand and reach out to console her, but she inches backward, avoiding my gaze. It crushes me, but I swallow hard and just nod. Maybe she needs space.

"So leave," Rocky tells her . . . and me. He's looking at me. "Go on the run. Keep your normal lives."

Will you come with us?

It's the first thing that I think. Too mushy and vulnerable. I grind the thought away. "How?" I ask him, crossing my arms and balling the sleeves of my pale pink sweater in my fists. "We can barely make ends meet here, Rocky. How are we supposed to do that jumping from place to place without . . . ?" *Conning.*

We weren't given proper life skills to have normal lives, and adding *runaway* to that makes it infinitely harder.

And I really want to live this one life *here.* Not a million lives out there. Setting down roots has been my favorite part of this whole experiment.

"Then this doesn't work. And you two need to pull the cord because as soon as they know they've lost their pawns, they will do everything to reel you back in."

"We're not their pawns." I shake my head.

I may have slight doubts in them—mainly in Everett—but there's still love between my mom and me. I know that.

Hailey intakes a big breath. "It's going to work." Her voice is strangely high-pitched. "I'm going to explain the situation when they get here. Phoebe and I are done. They'll understand. They have to understand."

"This is a *delusion,*" Rocky says in an intense whisper. His eyes are pleading with us to just wake up. I want to stay in this dream just a little longer.

One more day.

One more minute.

One more second.

It's a feeling I've had before. The grip-on-tight, not-wanting-to-leave feeling—because most good things in my life have been painfully short-lived.

"They will come here," Rocky says slowly, "and they will go straight for the Waterfords, for Jake. Am I wrong, Hails?"

Hailey rotates on her heels, distraught. Water laps against the sand near our feet, and I feel the rush of the cold against my ankles.

I frown at Rocky. "When have you cared about Jake?"

"He's your boyfriend, right?" He waits for me, maybe, to say *no*.

"Fake," I correct.

"Fake boyfriend." His voice is rough. "I care by association to you."

He cares about me. It's a truth, but one that's more said in action, less in words.

It's hard to look at him. Do I really want to leave Victoria, just to do another job where I'm seducing more men and Rocky has to watch? I'm not sure my heart can handle that. But I'm not sure my heart ever has been able to truly handle it.

More than myself, I am doing this for Hailey. Our pact. It's her dream that I've adopted as my own.

Rocky must see that in my eyes because he spins to his sister and says, "I know you want your *Mystic Pizza* life. And I wish, from the bottom of my soul, I could give that to you. But I can't. You can't have that life without the approval of our puppeteers. They're not ever going to give it to you, Hails."

Her face breaks. "Rocky—"

"It's a town. A silly fucking town. *Please*, you can't be this attached—"

"I'm not doing it for me!" Hailey yells with full-blown tears. She's dropped her boots, her hands pressed to her chest. "This isn't about me, okay?! I *love* my job. I love what we do. You think it was easy for me to stop?" Tears cloud her vision.

I'm pummeled backward, my pulse lodged in my throat.

She points out at the ocean. "I've wanted to go back about ten *hundred* times."

My body stills.

I blink past a glassy film. "What?" I whisper, not understanding.

Rocky looks just as stunned, his hand clamped strongly over his mouth.

Hailey points at the sand, tears streaming down her cheeks. "You two *don't* have a patent on protecting people. Other people can protect you, you know that? Other people can try." Her chin quakes. "And maybe I haven't done a great job of it—maybe it won't last like I've wanted it to, but I've *tried*." She pinches her eyes, choking on a sob.

I fight between the urge to comfort her and to prod for a clearer answer.

She wipes at the creases of her eyes, mascara already smudged.

"Hailey," I say, choked. "I don't understand . . ."

Her watery, splintered gaze hits mine. "Do you really think I could've let you go back after what happened in Carlsbad?"

Oh my God.

Rocky's hand that's clamped on his mouth suddenly combs through his hair, and when he looks at me, my world is overturned. Swallowed whole by his sheer tidal wave of concern.

I struggle to speak, and I just focus on Hailey. "I was doing this for you," I whisper, my voice broken.

"And I've always been doing this for you. You're my best friend." She rubs at her runny nose. "I love you, Phebs, and you've protected me my entire life. It was my turn to protect you."

Inertia. Why did I think she invoked the word for herself?

Why did I never consider she could've had other reasons to quit conning—when the first time that I surfaced our pact, it'd been for Hailey? And all along, when she said the word in Carlsbad, it'd been for me.

Tears have built in my eyes, my throat swollen closed. I don't know what to say, so I just come forward and put my arms around her. She hugs tighter, and my wet tears fall into her blonde hair.

She touches the back of my head and whispers, "I know . . . I know I can't force you to quit for good. But I tried . . . I had to try."

"I know," I breathe.

I know.

"It's up to you what you want to do next, Phebs. It's your choice."

My choice.

Hailey's not the one grounding us here anymore. She never has been. It's always been about me and that night in Carlsbad.

Thirty-Five

Rocky

Phoebe says she needs to think on everything and hightails it back to the loft. I see the panicky look in my sister's eyes. "Go with her," she pleads.

I'm not sure I'll make things better. I'm still shell-shocked from my sister's confession. I've known the depth of which Hailey and Phoebe love each other, but I never considered the lengths Hailey would go to protect Phoebe. I figured she knew that I would be there for her friend. That she could rely on me, instead.

You two don't *have a patent on protecting people.* She was speaking to me, too.

"Why won't you tell me what happened?" I ask Hailey. "I would've—"

"I couldn't. I couldn't, Rocky." She rubs her reddened nose, then picks up her sandy boots. "Please, just go."

"You can't just tell me about Carlsbad yourself?"

"She needs you." Hailey nearly starts crying again. "Don't leave her alone, *please.*"

I hate leaving either of them like this. "Call Nova or Oliver."

She nods.

Right now, I don't feel comforting. More like raw wire ready to slice open anything I touch. I want answers so badly that I could dig through hardened clay to reach them.

So maybe I need Phoebe more than she needs me in this moment. I unearth my heels from the sand and head to Phoebe's loft, unlocking the door with my spare key.

Her bedroom door is ajar, and I push it further open.

She's tucked in on her queen-sized bed, watching *A Nightmare on Elm Street* on the TV in the same jeans and sweater from the beach. She doesn't acknowledge me.

I lean a shoulder against the doorway, eyes on the screen. "My sister was willing to quit her whole life, piss off our parents, and lie to us both."

I turn to Phoebe.

She doesn't take her gaze off the movie, but she hugs a white pillow to her chest, her jaw cementing in a struggle not to cry.

"And here I am thinking, what could have possibly happened to make her go to such lengths to protect you? What could have been so *bad*? You want to know what I'm thinking, Phoebe? Because in my head I'm painting real vivid pictures of that night."

My pulse isn't steady. I'm swallowing a mountain of emotion, and the only way not to burst at the seams is by concentrating on my breathing. On the fire that fills my lungs with every searing inhale, every anguished exhale.

Phoebe tosses her pillow aside and swings her legs off the bed. While she comes toward me, I shut the door. Trevor is on the couch in the living room, and I couldn't see whether he was asleep or not.

As I walk deeper in her room, Phoebe meets me near the foot of the bed. She faces me with toughened eyes. But it's a front. I see the pain simmering beneath. I can practically feel it tearing through me.

She asks, "You want the truth?"

"From you. Always."

She takes a step closer, her chest rising and falling in heavy breaths. "The truth won't solve anything. It's going to hurt you, and the last thing I've ever wanted is to hurt you."

Now I'm scared. I search her eyes for something more. "Did you kill someone?" I ask in a breathy whisper.

She shakes her head. "I wish I did."

Jesus Christ.

I run a harsh hand through my hair, trying not to jump to any conclusions. "I need answers, Phoebe. I'm asking for them. I'm telling you to fucking hurt me. Because *this* . . . this is *obliterating* me." I want to touch her. Hold her.

She swallows hard, her throat bobbing. "Rocky." Her voice quakes.

I push closer, cupping her cheek in my hand. She hangs on to my wrists like we're falling, and I breathe, "Hurt me." I hear that movie playing in the background. "Do your worst, little nightmare."

Her eyes flit to mine and they steel. "It was the Fiddle Game." She tells me first what I know. The basics of the con.

Hailey played the role of a small-town girl living in California for the first time. Phoebe was her rich socialite friend who convinced her to fly out to the West Coast to pursue modeling. They both attended a party at a multimillion-dollar beach house with a hundred other guests.

Among them: Jeremy Leeds, CEO of Aquarius, one of the biggest fashion brands in the country. He was the mark.

"It started out fine," Phoebe tells me, my palm on the nape of her neck. She's clutching my forearm, and I wonder if she feels my pounding pulse like I feel hers. "I was just introducing Hailey, also known as Faye, to Jeremy and telling him that she's new and getting her feet wet in the industry. Then she left for the bathroom, and she gave me her purse to hold on to. Her phone, wallet, everything inside."

"That's when I called."

She nods.

I remember that phone call. It was the last contact I had with them until after the con. I haven't wanted to replay the call in my head. I didn't want to think I had any part of something going bad. But I have mulled it over. And now . . . for the hundredth time, I recollect it again.

Phoebe "drunkenly" answered her friend's phone and put me on speaker.

"Faye?" I asked over the music. "Are you at a party? You do realize, you have a photo shoot with Dior tomorrow? This is a two-hundred-grand campaign on the fucking line. The agency is not going to be happy about this. Faye, are you there?"

Phoebe probably pretended to be stunned and then she hung up on me.

"I put on a show of complete remorse," she says. "I told Jeremy that I shouldn't have answered the call. That you must have been her agent. I kept telling Jeremy not to tell Faye. That I had no idea just how successful she's been in California, and I didn't want to fuck it up for her."

I know how this con is supposed to work. Jeremy should have realized the fiddle (Hailey/Faye) was actually worth more than Phoebe knew. Add in the fact that Jeremy Leeds hates Dior, and he should've offered Faye more money than Dior to get her in his Aquarius campaign instead. But all of this relies on Jeremy being greedy enough to screw over another brand.

"It didn't work?" I ask.

"He was already kind of drunk," Phoebe says, staring straight ahead. Past me. Off in the distance in remembrance. I skim her, careful not to move. Her grip is tightening on my forearm.

"When Hailey returned," Phoebe says gradually, quietly, "he told her that he found out what she was worth, and he'd be willing to double it and bring her into the Aquarius campaign in exchange for sex."

My heart quickens, now seeing where this is going. Muscles tensed, I don't make a sound. Don't want to startle Phoebe into stopping the story altogether.

"Hailey was against it, of course," Phoebe murmurs. "And I was the principal on this—so I tried my best to course correct. I told Jeremy that Hailey wasn't that kind of girl, but if I could get a slice of the deal, I was willing to sleep with him as long as he agreed to wire the money beforehand."

I don't go numb.

I'm torched. Burning the fuck alive. I can barely breathe, barely move. Barely see anything other than red. I blink. Because I need to see. I need to see her.

Phoebe grits down on her teeth, and her eyes flash up to me. "How many times had I been in that situation before? And how many times had I talked my way out of it?"

Sickness churns in me. "Too many times," I tell her, fury and torment making a home in my body. "But you should have never been in that position in the first place. You should have bailed—"

"I couldn't!" she screams at me, battling tears. "I can count on my hands the number of times our moms gave Hailey and me two-person cons. If I failed *once*, it'd never happen again. And I've never failed before. On *any* con. I couldn't imagine disappointing my mom in that way, and I thought . . . I *believed* in myself enough that I could get out of it." She blinks back more emotion. "Would you have not believed in me?"

Pain infiltrates like a ten-inch gash. I struggle to keep my shit together. "I would have," I tell her the truth. I would have let her go like I've always done. "But I wouldn't have left you alone with him for long. You know I *never* would have left you—"

"It's not her fault!" Phoebe screams, her voice threatening to crack. She catches my other forearm and brings both of my arms to my sides. Causing my hand to slip off her neck. And I don't fight her. She doesn't release her hold on me.

"I'm not blaming my sister. I'm not blaming you," I say with an inferno in my lungs. It hurts—every single breath *hurts*.

"Hailey tried to get in the room," Phoebe says with amassing tears. "She *tried*. Really hard."

This is gutting me.

"But it was being blocked," Phoebe explains. "They even took her phone." I grind my jaw, breathing through my nose, and she takes a long beat, gazing over at a crumpled dress thrown across the ottoman at the foot of the bed. "I told her it was okay beforehand. I wanted it to be okay. And afterward, I tried telling her it was fine. The sex was all right, a little rough, but not the worst thing in the world. I thought I played it off cool, but obviously not if Hailey devised this whole thing . . ." She looks around the room, taking it all in.

She's still holding on to me. Her nails are digging into my arms. I can hear my heavy pulse beating against my eardrums. I try to simmer my rage to be comforting, but how can razor wire embrace anything without slicing it open?

Her reddened eyes lift to mine.

"Give me the truth," I tell her.

"About the sex?" Her voice isn't small despite the tension splitting it.

"Yeah." My muscles are flexed scalding bands, and my hands clench into fists. "How was the sex? Truthfully?" Never in my life have I wanted Phoebe to tell me how another man rocked her world. Lit her up in the most mind-blowing orgasm alive. But I'm hoping to hear it now. Anything other than what I think happened. How he hurt her. Abused her.

Her breath staggers, and then she swallows hard. "I was just . . . an object to him. A plaything. He was rough—and I mean, I like rough, but . . . his rough was . . ."

I run my tongue over my back molars, fighting a thousand emotions that boil inside of me.

"It was like he didn't care if he split me in five pieces that night." Her eyes meet mine again. "It wasn't good, Rocky."

"I'm going to kill him," I say, coldness in my voice.

She sniffs hard. "You aren't. Because I need you here and not in prison."

My breathing deepens like each inhale is a struggle for oxygen. "That's it?"

She nods, but I can tell there's still more.

The pressure in my chest won't relent. "Phoebe?" I lean my forehead down and press it against hers. "Phoebe, please." I try to lift my hands to her cheeks, but she's still imprisoning my arms at our sides.

"I can tell I've already hurt you," she whispers, closing her eyes, and a tear tracks down her jaw.

"I said do your worst," I tell her. "So fucking do it."

"His friend came in and asked if he could pay for an hour. It didn't feel like a question."

Jesus fucking Christ.

She releases my arms like a dam rupturing, the worst wounded sound I've ever heard her make escapes her lips—and I clutch the back of her neck, drawing her against me. Her hands cling at the button-down under my jacket, fisting the fabric.

My other arm curves around the small of her back. I tuck her close to my chest like I can protect her from the past. *You can't*.

I stare down at her, watching Phoebe slowly gather her breath. She tries to speak. "The saddest part . . ." She looks off. "Is I felt nothing. It was like my body wasn't mine. And I kept thinking: Has it ever been mine? Have I ever felt like it belonged to me while anyone was touching me?" Her watery gaze meets mine. "And the answer was yes. The answer was you."

My hand slides up to her cheek, our eyes crashing into each other. "I love you," I tell her through a swollen throat. "I'm sorry I couldn't protect you."

Tears slip down her cheek and over my hand. "That's not your job."

"It's always been my job," I breathe. "Loving you, though, that wasn't a role I was given, Phoebe. Loving you has been the most authentic and natural thing I've ever done in my life. And I don't protect you just because I'm told to. I protect you because I'm yours. You've had me since I was five."

She's crying in my arms.

And I'm done—I'm done giving a shit what they'll do if they find out we're together. I never thought I had a breaking point. I believed I was made to withstand everything under the sun. But I've found my limit—and I can't do this another day. I just fucking can't.

She lets out a shaky breath and fear hits her eyes. "Don't pity me, Rocky."

I hold her gaze. "I've never pitied you a day in my life."

"Then why are you saying that now? After my sob story—"

"If you think I heard a fucking sob story, you're mistaken," I say strongly. "I heard a story about a girl that was raised to be manipulative, self-reliant, and brave. And when she was put in a position to save herself and someone she loved, she took it. It backfired. I heard a story about parents who manipulated this girl into thinking her worth came from a job and not from *this* . . ." I place my palm on her heart.

Her eyes search mine in wanting.

God, I want her. I've always, always wanted her.

The door suddenly opens, and I'm cursing myself for not locking the damn thing.

"Hey, Rocky—" Trevor freezes, and Phoebe spins her tear-streaked face away from him.

I'm still holding her against me. "Get the fuck out," I tell my little brother, pointing at the doorway he stepped through.

"PG?" Trevor frowns, then looks to me in confusion. "Is she crying?"

"Close the fucking door, Trevor," I tell him like he's being obtuse, and my brother is many things, but he's not an idiot.

He hesitates, a phone in the pit of his hand. He's not in pajamas. Black slacks, snakeskin belt, black button-down with gray swirls and gold buttons—he dresses like an immortal vampire with thousands of years of accumulated wealth.

"I would," he says, "but I have a problem. And I need your help, Rocky."

Phoebe rubs her nose, and I can feel that she's about to break away. So I ask him fast, "It can't wait?"

"It's Boyd Delacey. According to his socials, he's in Connecticut. I think he followed me."

Shit. I scrape a hand through my hair, and Phoebe inches

away, quickly wiping her face. I crave to draw her back, but she speaks to me. "If Boyd tailed him here, he shouldn't leave the loft."

Trevor cracks his neck, tension building. "See, this is why I need someone's help, so I'm not a hostage in this loft." He turns to me. "You call him. Tell him he won a trip to Bermuda, Bahamas, Antigua—I don't care. He has to collect it at a port in Miami."

Phoebe asks, "You think he'll fall for that? He was already big-time scammed. By *you*."

Trevor glares. "Can you tell me something I don't already know?"

"Phoebe's right," I interject. "It takes a certain kind of mark to fall for telephone sweepstakes scams. He's going to hang up unless you open with something familiar and actually give him the trip." I'll have to pretend to be his distant relative. "You want to pay for Boyd's vacation?"

"Away from me, yes." Trevor nods. "So you'll help?"

Do I want to leave Phoebe right now? Fuck no. But if Boyd is already in this state, he might be closer to Victoria than we know.

"Yeah, I'll help. You have a gun on you? In case he finds you while we aren't at the loft?"

Trevor reaches in his pocket and displays a switchblade. With the flick of his wrist, the double-edged blade opens from the hilt. "You know I don't like carrying guns."

"You should keep mine in the living room," Phoebe says to me. "Just in case."

"Where is it?" I ask her.

She points to the top left drawer of her dresser.

I'm closer and reach the thing. It's in her panty drawer. *Of course it is.* I shift aside her lacy pink thong, her white panties, baby-blue panties, red mesh lingerie, and as I comb through more and more pastel-colored panties, a new type of heat gathers in my veins.

Frustrated on two counts, I turn my head back to her. "It's not in here."

"Oh, that's right." Her arms are crossed. "I forgot it's in the drawer next to it." She doesn't hide the subtle lift of her lips, a smile peeking.

I nearly smile back. "You're so full of shit."

"Takes a liar to know a liar."

I do know Phoebe, and I'm not complaining that she led me into digging through her panties. I flip her off while I open the other drawer.

Through the mirror above the dresser, I see her smile growing behind me. I also see it flickering in and out.

The gun is beneath an old journal, the cover faded and creased with a bright pink strawberry on the front. I push aside a pink tin with strawberry-flavored mints and her Strawberry Shortcake pens. Once I have the Glock, I press the release and pull out the magazine. Ten rounds. I push the mag back. It clicks, and slowly, I draw back the slide and check the chamber.

"It's fully loaded," I tell my brother, about to hand him the weapon.

"You take it."

Jesus. "Fine. I'm putting it on the bookshelf behind the fern." Gun in one hand, I grip the doorframe with the other, and Trevor is gone. But I linger and glance back at Phoebe.

She's climbing on her bed. Remote in hand, she rewinds some of *A Nightmare on Elm Street*. As I shut the door behind me, it takes so much in me just to walk fifteen feet away.

Thirty-Six

Rocky

After learning about Carlsbad, one of the last places I want to be tonight is in the back booth of a 24-hour donut-scented breakfast diner—but here I am. The things I do for my brother.

I thought it'd be better to let Phoebe have her loft to herself and not deal with the messiness of a potential stalker there. So I left with Trevor and walked down the street to this local place. It's taken *all* of my energy not to peel my ass off this booth, give a finger to Seaside Griddle, and go back to her.

If she'd given me permission, I would've been on the first flight to California. Gun in my bag. I would've hurt those entitled *sick* fuckers who hurt her. Made them pay in ways they didn't. In ways they should've.

I still feel like doing it.

Still feel like inflicting sheer pain on someone else, and that darkness tries to burrow further and further inside me and make a home in my core.

A small con might be the perfect distraction from my

homicidal thoughts, and anyway, ignoring Boyd's presence in Connecticut would be a major mistake that I'm not going to make.

I rub at my swollen eyes, the light from the laptop starting to wear on me. Sitting on the same side of the booth as me, Trevor clicks through Nathan Deering's social media profiles. Prep for a sweepstakes scam isn't usually this intensive, but since Boyd is a repeat mark, we need to be extremely careful.

"This isn't half bad," Trevor says, stopping on a YouTube video of Nathan. In the clip, Boyd's second cousin reviews a new postapocalyptic video game. I hear him talking through the right earbud of my headphones. Trevor's wearing the left.

I mentally catalog some of his frequently used words. *Dude. Like. Whatever. Dope.*

The audio quality is the best we've come across in two hours. "Run it through the program," I tell my brother, and then I stab my fork into a stack of double chocolate chunk pancakes.

I smell hash browns and hear the sizzle of oil. The staff consists of two college-aged girls, and according to them it's been a slow night. They've only had to serve us and an older man at the bar. Pete Morris, a calc teacher at Victoria High. Made small talk with him when we entered. He said he has insomnia.

I wish trouble sleeping was my biggest problem.

Trevor clicks a couple buttons and opens a new window on the laptop. He rotates the screen more toward himself. Away from me and Grace, the young waitress who meanders over to refill our coffees.

"Can I get you anything?" Grace asks Trevor. He hasn't ordered food yet.

Without looking up from the computer, he says, "The sweet potato pancakes."

"That's a good choice," she tells him, then slips me a friendly smile before leaving our booth.

I glance over at him. "And here I thought you didn't eat food. You just feasted on the souls of the damned."

"There's not enough damned souls to consume when I'm in a no fun zone." He taps another key.

"Mine's not enough for you?" I quip and take a swig of coffee.

"You're not damned." He's typing. "You're just emo."

I mess his hair. "That's what I let numbskull little brothers believe."

He lets out a laugh, then slips me a shadowy smile. "You are more melodramatic than Machiavellian these days." I'm about to tease him back, but as he trains his gaze on the screen, he says, "PG rubbing off on you?"

Mention of Phoebe locks my shoulders in place.

Trevor picks up on it. He scans me like he's casing a locked safe. "I sense tension."

"You sense me dropping this subject," I snap. "Just plug in the recording."

"I already did. I have to wait for it to process."

With enough high-quality recordings of Nathan, the voice-changing software can alter my ingoing voice to sound like Nathan on an outgoing call. Technology has made duping people infinitely easier—it's what my dad always told me. Even the rise of the internet created more pathways for people to be deceived. But in the same breath, there are more ways to get caught.

Trevor's attention hasn't left me. "So . . ." He flips over a sugar packet, watching me.

I'm staring at the screen. *He's not going to let this go.* "I'm doing you a favor right now—" I start.

"I've never seen her cry like that."

I grind my jaw, pushing back an avalanche of gnarled feelings. "Just drop it, Trev."

He overturns the sugar again. "Is she okay?"

"Yeah." I tell him what Phoebe would want me to say. "She's fine."

Trevor rips open the sugar. "She's fine but she's bawling in my brother's chest when I've never seen her sob like that in my *life*." He's killing me, and he's frustrated that I'm not giving him details after seeing Phoebe cry, which must've disturbed him, but it's something I'm not repeating. Even if I could claw out the fucking words, it's not for me to share.

He adds, "Clearly she likes you." It snaps my eyes to him. "In the most kindergarten way."

"You never went to kindergarten," I remind him. "How would you know?"

Trevor reaches for his coffee. "You never went to law school and you still believe you're the judge of everything."

"I'm only judging your cologne, shithead."

He almost smiles. "It's vintage."

"It smells like burnt sage and ass." I don't let him quip back. "This isn't relevant right now."

"You mean Phoebe," he deadpans.

"Yeah." *Boyd. Stalkers. Sweepstakes scams.* This is the path we need to be driving down. "Let's just stay on fucking track." I squeeze his shoulder to show I'm trying to be here. For *him*.

"Fine." He nods and sips his coffee slowly before gently setting down the mug. He goes rigid. "Shit." He shoots forward to the screen and taps a key.

"What?"

"We're only at fifty percent recognition."

We need another audio recording. Maybe two more. I run a hand through my hair and then glance at my watch.

Fuck, it's late. Any hope of going back to the loft before midnight flies out the window. We'll also need to call Boyd at a reasonable time. It's unlikely he'll pick up a three a.m. phone call from his distant cousin.

Taking out my cell, I shoot Phoebe a quick text.

This is taking longer than I thought. Sorry.

She's quick to respond.

Phoebe: no rush.

I grimace and reread the two words. Part of me wishes she would've asked me to hurry back, but that's not Phoebe. I'm not even shocked at her next text. Just fucking dejected.

Phoebe: going to sleep now, see you tomorrow or whenever I do.

My eyes burn the longer I reread it. All I can do is type out a similar casual-toned response.

Sleep well. I'll stop by tomorrow.

Phoebe leaves me on read.

It's not that unusual. My text was basically an endnote to our conversation, but my lungs are tight. The only thing keeping me focused is my brother beside me.

He scours the internet for more recordings and finds a

couple five-second clips from Instagram. Still not enough to hit a hundred percent, but it's progress.

I try and come up with a vague idea of what I'm going to say. Not a script. That'd be stilted. But the wording also has to be authentic to Nathan.

"Hey, dude," I whisper under my breath, sounding it out. I'll probably say something about it being a while since we've spoken. Keep it vague since I don't really know how long it's been, besides their interactions on socials. "I had this all-inclusive trip planned to Cancún, but I can't make it. There's snorkeling and cave tubing. It's pretty dope."

I wince.

Trevor also winces. "You're going to have to do better than that."

"Give me a fucking second," I snap. I don't like impersonating *real* people. I like being someone new. Someone molded by me. This . . . this is going to take time.

"You have a second," my brother says. "You have five. Ten. However many you need, Rock, just make sure he believes it."

"I'm trying," I say dryly. "But I'm not God." And this is *exactly* why we don't have repeat marks. It complicates everything.

Trevor studies me. "Once upon a time, you could have made me believe you were." He goes back to his coffee. "I was five," he deadpans. "So keep your ego in check."

"My ego is still right where I left it . . ." I taper off, skimming Nathan's socials again and figuring out his mutual friends with Boyd.

Trevor takes my silence as doubt, but I'm not that afraid. "I'm dead serious, Rocky. He *has* to believe it." The urgency. It's something I won't get used to from my brother.

"I know," I tell him. "I know."

After the prep is done, pancakes eaten, and voice recognition complete, we pay the bill and return to the loft. Quiet in the living room, we're on the couch where he's been crashing. It's one a.m.—almost too late to make the call, but both Boyd and Nathan regularly post photos on Instagram around this time, so there's a chance he might be awake.

I have the burner phone to my ear, but the end of it is plugged into the laptop to run my voice through the software in real time.

The phone rings and rings.

Pick up, Boyd.

He answers. "Who's this?"

"Hey, dude, it's Nathan. I got a new phone—sorry, I know this is out of the blue. How have you been?"

Trevor's leg jostles, and I clamp a hand on his knee to stop him. I mouth, *Get out.* He glares, but he can't make any noise and like hell am I putting this on speakerphone so he can listen.

Boyd starts talking. "Pretty good . . . Is this about Trish?"

Trish. Their mutual brunette friend. I only know they all went to some line dancing club together five years ago.

"Nah, nah, nothing like that." I keep it casual, but Trevor is unblinking and too intense, probably internally freaking the fuck out—so I stand up with the laptop and move to the window. Away from him. "Funny enough, I have, like, this thing I booked, and I can't go."

"No shit?"

"Yeah." I sound bummed. "It's super dope. All-inclusive to Cancún. Leaves soon. There's snorkling and shit."

"Huh . . ."

I hate his skeptical *huh*, but I try not to linger on the sound.

"It's nonrefundable, and I didn't want something like this to go to waste. I've, like, been going through my list—"

"And I'm on it?"

"Yeah, but come on, you're not that high up."

He laughs.

That's good. "Everyone else can't make it out but I thought, *Like, this might be a Boyd thing to do*. Take a trip at the last second. Seize the moment or whatever. It's not a cheap cruise either. So you want it or do I need to go ask Randy?" *Boyd's brother.*

"No, I'm interested," he says fast. "Text me the details."

"Sure, but there's documents and shit. It's not easy to text."

"Okay, email me at . . ." I memorize the address and quickly rush to Hailey's notebook on the kitchen counter. I jot down his email while we're saying goodbye.

Once I hang up, Trevor asks, "And?"

"Good chance he'll take the cruise."

Trevor eases back against the couch, hands laced on his head like his scrawny ass just completed an Ironman Triathlon with no training. I tell him to rest easy tonight. He thanks me, and as I get ready to leave for the boathouse, I stop at Phoebe's room.

Her door is ajar, and I peek inside. She's sound asleep beneath the comforter, her TV off. I battle the urge to wake her and say and do so much more, but I can't fucking destroy the kind of peace she's in. So I close the door and go.

Thirty-Seven

Phoebe

Late-morning light filters into my bedroom. I haven't heard from Rocky since our texts last night, but running a sweepstakes scam on Boyd wouldn't be a fast task. I don't have work until this evening, so I'm in no hurry to completely self-eject from the comfort and luxuries of a foam mattress.

I'm not against a sloth-like lounge day, even if I've already showered and jumped into jeans, a T-shirt, and a bra—and you know what, maybe I deserve this time to myself. My swollen eyes would agree.

Just me, my bed, and sinister deeds on my TV.

Leaning on the fluffed pillows against my headboard, I scroll through Netflix on the mounted TV, looking for another horror movie to dive into. For some reason, I keep going back to *A Nightmare on Elm Street*. I didn't finish it last night.

I'm about to press play, but I glance at my shut door. Is Rocky going to stop by before I leave for work? Or will he just show up later at the country club?

Rocky.

His name causes an onslaught of vivid memories from last night to gush forth, but one thought overtakes every mental image.

He loves me.

My heart swells, but then I remember . . . he won't ever be with me. Won't ever sleep with me.

Has anything really changed?

It stings a little, and I try to accept the agreement we've had in place for two years. Pining after him—not my favorite hobby. At least speaking about Carlsbad—sharing that night with him—has removed the heaviest weight from my body; this morning, I feel lighter than I have in a while.

I always thought the truth was *my* ten-ton burden, and I didn't want anyone else to carry it. Hailey was enough. But I realize that I wasn't passing weight to Rocky.

He helped throw it off me, catapulting that night into the clouds. Shrouded and out of sight. Floating further and further away. Maybe one day it'll even begin to fade.

There is no rewinding and altering the bad course of events. Only moving on. Sometimes I believe my job makes it easier to deal with what happened. Pretending to be someone else gives me nice little cupboards to fit horrible nights into. Then again, I wouldn't have been in that position if it weren't for my job.

A conundrum of epic proportions.

I raise the volume a little and then sink against the pillows. Settling in to watching the horror movie, I try to focus, but my mind keeps drifting to Rocky.

The strong cut of his jaw. How his masculine hands encased my cheekbones. The way he stared into me like I belonged to him. Like he would rip through every circle of hell just to reach me.

I picture his lips dipping toward mine, the warmth of his

breath ghosting over me. A rush of heat pricks my body, and a long-built need throbs my pussy.

"Fuck," I murmur in a frustrated breath. Shifting my legs and arching my back, I'm wrestling with an escalating desire. Honestly, satiating this craving sounds too good to kick away.

I begin to rewrite my reality into a fantasy. I imagine Rocky didn't run out of the room last night.

Instead, he stayed.

He pushed me down on the mattress where I currently rest. Oxygen jettisoned out of me, and his hands—he planted them on either side of my face. His gaze dripped with deep longing and carnal, filthy need.

Yes.

While I paint this hot visual, pretending he was on top of me, I unzip my jeans and slip my hand below my pink panties. With my other hand, I pat the bed and find the remote. Muting the movie, I tangle up in my thoughts and close my eyes.

Reigniting the picture of Rocky. He's not completely naked yet, but I fast-forward to him being shirtless.

His hard, bare chest presses against me, the length of his erection digging between my legs but confined behind his slacks. *I'm going to do what I dreamed of doing a thousand times,* he tells me in a husky breath. His lips hovering over my ear. *I'm going to fuck you, my little nightmare.*

Little nightmare.

When he said that to me, it unfastened every chain around my heart. Now, it's lighting every nerve ending in the *best* way.

I'm baking in arousal on the bed, and I kick down my large white comforter. I'm panting, and my fingers slip against wet heat, my clit swelling as I circle the bundle of nerves.

"Rocky," I whisper in an aching moan. *"Please."*

My legs twitch and hamstrings flex, sweat beading up on my skin. I imagine his teasing hardness, the almost-there, drawn-out tension, and dying thirst that has never, *ever* been fully quenched.

He pins me. He pins me so hard, I can't escape. I chew on my bottom lip. *Oh God.* I don't want to escape. I want him to always have me, and I need him. Deeper, inside . . .

"I need you," I whisper out loud.

You have me, I imagine him saying.

"Phoebe?"

My eyes shoot open.

Oh . . . *fuck.*

Rocky is here.

Rocky is here?! It fully jars my brain into total alertness. I go absolutely still.

He's standing an inch inside my room with narrowed eyes, piecing everything together. Quickly, he slips farther in and shuts the door. It's not hard to figure out what I'm doing with my hand stuffed down my jeans and panties. *Should've locked the door.* But it's not like I intended to masturbate.

We lock eyes, not breaking.

Not moving.

He won't come over here and satiate me. He's made it clear we'll never be together, and maybe all I'll ever have is this. My hand. My imagination.

Maybe he deserves to watch and see what he's missing.

I return to rubbing myself, keeping my eyes fixed on Rocky.

"Phoebe," he breathes out, a frustrated groan clinging to his throat. *"Christ."*

"Tell me to stop," I say through a ragged breath. Wetness slips between my fingers as I quicken my pace.

He watches my moving hand, and his nose flares. "I can't."

"Then leave," I snap coldly, thinking he's mad I'm pleasuring myself in front of him. "Because I'm not stopping. I'm going to come whether you're here or not."

He runs a stressed hand through his hair.

I knead around the sensitive bud, and my breath hitches into a short moan.

"*Phoebe,*" he says my name like he's scolding me, but he's striding over to me.

He's coming to the bed with a scorching, powerful gait, and I'd think this was another fantasy. Another dream. But when he grabs my ankle and yanks me flat on my back, I know this is real.

Holy fuck. My lips are parted as oxygen flees, and I start to pant, "You're just going to tease me—"

He grips the denim of my jeans and rips them down my hips. Off my legs. Watching him throw my pants to the side, I'm breathless.

The hunger in his eyes devours me. "I'm going to do so much more than just tease you," he says in a throaty, husky breath. "And by the end, you'll be begging me to never pull out." He sheds his leather jacket.

Does this mean . . . ? My mouth keeps falling open. "I don't believe you," I say, almost in challenge.

"You'd be the first not to." He unzips his slacks, our eyes glued to one another.

The anticipation of what he could do, what he *wants* to do, is a fiercer thumping need between my legs. Once his pants are gone, I fixate like a starved animal on his hard length that bears against his charcoal boxer briefs. I've seen his cock before. He has been *very* blessed. Almost too blessed.

I've imagined him nestled deep inside of me. But I've never felt him go that far.

Rocky moves the ottoman away from the foot of the bed. More in the middle of the room. *What's he doing?* I prop myself on my elbows, my heart beating out of control, and I like it. I really fucking like it.

Is he actually going to do anything to me, though?

There's just no way . . . *Ohhh, God.* He's hot. After he undoes the buttons of his shirt, he grabs the fabric by the back collar and sheds it over his head.

I hate that he's this hot. That I'm so attracted to him, I can't help but wedge my hand back down my panties.

"Impatient?" he says, like I'm too needy.

"You're too slow," I taunt, and we share a flicker of a smile.

He climbs back on the bed, kneeling between my legs. Swiftly, he catches my wrist and pries my fingers out from the lacy band of my panties. And then Rocky pulls my white T-shirt over my head, my hair falling back down on my bare shoulders.

I thought I'd be gawking more at his sculpted muscles. I thought he'd be so obsessed with my tits, he wouldn't stare elsewhere.

But we're looking more into one another—like our souls are the most beautiful things we've ever shown.

His knees spread me wider and wider, and the stretch and his musky scent and closeness causes a strange, aching noise to leave me.

Rocky pauses.

How he's feasting on my arousal is so, so sexy.

I'm really wet, and my cheeks flush as he brings my wrist up and over my head. His abs flex as he bends over my body. Bearing his weight down on me. Our eyes never break apart.

As if one glance away will disrupt this. A caustic tension spindles between us.

All these years, we've fought against this. Giving in to it should be easy, but it's anything but.

His lips skate above mine, the warmth tingling me. My toes curl in anticipation, and I clutch his carved bicep with my free hand, holding on to the moment. We've never kissed for real.

And once this happens . . . there's no going back.

His forehead presses to mine, emotion tangling with our breaths, and as his lips descend to my lips, we are a crack of lightning. A tsunami crashing into buildings. A cyclone touching ground. Destruction bursting together. His kiss is vicious and loving, and I taste his hunger against my mouth. His tongue melds with mine, and I claw at his back while he pins my other wrist overhead.

"More—" My raspy voice is cut short with his kisses, and fuck, *fuck*, his hand slides down my panties. I'm throbbing, swelling around his fingers that slip and tease inside me. His electric touch, his penetrating eyes, his building warmth—it's making me feel so alive. "*Rocky.*" I roll my hips against his palm.

"*Fuck.* Phoebe." He grunts into a deeper groan. "Stay still."

I want him all over me. To overwhelm every inch of my body. To make me stay very fucking still himself. In protest, I arch my back and spread my legs wider.

Rocky reads my eyes, my body. He lets go of my wrist to clasp my face. Forcing my head still, I look right at him while his fingers pump inside me.

The intensity of us staring at one another is shooting pure adrenaline in my veins.

He finds my G-spot, and spots dance in my vision the more

he teases. My lips break apart, breath shallow. "R-Roc . . ." I struggle against him, pushing at his biceps and chest, my legs writhing into the bed, and he bears more of his weight into me. Pinning me with his build.

Yes, yes, yes.

As soon as his fingers curl into my hair and he yanks, I moan and my eyes flutter. *"Oh my God."*

He suddenly releases.

What? "No, no."

Rocky stops finger-fucking me. "Safe word. Pick one. Now."

I blink, my mind whirling. "Is that . . . ?"

"Yeah. It is *necessary*." He dips his head down, his lips against the pit of my ear as he whispers, "I'm going to fuck you exactly how you've dreamed of being fucked."

I try to layer on a glare. "You don't know what I like." I sit up on my elbows. "You've never been inside me." There's still a part of me that believes this will end before we have sex. It will stop short.

It will all fall apart.

Rocky shoves me down, and when he comes down on my lips in a sweltering, clawing kiss, my whole *being* melts beneath him.

Ohh, *yes*. I whimper against his mouth, and he combs my hair back, his fingers scraping my head in a melodic, intense rhythm. His touch is power, and the vulnerable bits of me yearn to relinquish to the way I come undone in his hands.

He breaks the kiss with a graveled noise. "I'm starting to figure it out." *What I like*, he means.

"Does it turn you on?" I pant.

Rocky lifts off me and tugs the elastic band of his boxer briefs. Slowly, he frees his erection. *Holy . . .* I pulsate. I've never seen him that hard or swollen. He looks bigger. *Erect.* He is very . . . erect. His cock stands at mind-altering attention, and all I can do is imagine him filling me.

He speaks the minute our eyes crash together. "It turns me on." As he leans over me again, his scorching closeness is welcomed and protective and everything to me. His whisper hits my ear. "The thought of railing your pussy from the front and behind and on the bed, against the wall, until you only see stars—that also turns me on."

Yes, God. I'm soaked.

He unclips my bra and rips it off. His thumb circles my perked nipple.

I moan and arch my hips, grinding against his length.

"*Fuck,*" he grits out, his arousal flaring his nose. I reach out to touch his cock, but Rocky catches my wrist and pins it again.

He rests his forehead on mine, his free hand diving back between our pelvises, and he toys with my clit. I squirm beneath him, and he breathes against my lips, "Pick a safe word, Phoebe."

"Ahh, *fuckfuck.*"

"Not that one."

"*Rocky.*"

"Or that one."

I hold on to his bicep and feel for his large hand that's between my legs. "I'mgonnacome. *I'mgonnacome.* Please, please. I need . . ." *More.* Him.

He stops.

Again.

Ughhh. "Rocky." I glare.

He climbs off me. Off the bed. My heart just drops. Until he says, "Where do you keep your condoms?"

My heart floats higher than before. "My dresser."

He goes to my dresser, buck naked, and his ass—God, he has such a perfect ass. As he angles toward me to open a drawer, I see the muscles of his waist that tease my eyes toward his cock. So much heat bathes my face and body, and I think about taking off my panties.

But I kinda just want him to.

Rocky checks a couple drawers before finding the right one. He inspects the *two* boxes. "This is it?" he asks.

"Yeah." There's plenty. I'm really confused. "Do you plan on coming twenty-four times in one night?"

He shoots me a look. "I'm not talking about the fucking quantity." He reads a black box, his brows pinching.

"The size?" I ask. He's holding a box with *XL* on the front.

"I don't like this brand." He examines the other box without the *XL*. "This one is too small. And I hate the feeling of thicker condoms. Or any of this *warming* shit."

Who knew Rocky was particular about condoms? Definitely not me. We're both learning new things about each other.

He's unconcerned when he deserts both boxes. No condom?

"I've been off birth control since the move here," I warn him.

He picks up his crumpled slacks and looks right at me. "I'm not raw-dogging you." A breath catches in my lungs, lit up with one single deep-throated phrase, and he eyes my split legs, my ragged breath, and he grins.

"Fuck. You." I groan and throw a pillow at him.

He dodges the pillow and fishes out a wallet from his slacks. "I already knew you like dirty talk, Phoebe."

"You did not," I refute in a huff, but now I am wondering when and where and how he figured that out.

Rocky procures a couple condoms from his wallet. He keeps condoms in his pocket?

I arch my brows. "Who were those waiting for?"

"You, apparently." He gestures to the boxes on the dresser. "Who were those waiting for? Because clearly not me."

"Sorry, I didn't know your condom preferences."

"You're not sorry." He goes and locks the door.

I like watching him strut around the room naked. Usually I'm in those positions, and the role reversal is swelling a greater affection in me. "No, I'm not . . ."

He reaches across the bed and grabs the remote. "Trevor is already awake in the living room." Again, I'm confused at what he's doing and why he mentions his brother until he unmutes *A Nightmare on Elm Street* and raises the volume to an obnoxiously loud level.

I, also, do not want his little brother to hear us. So I'm not protesting.

"What condoms do you prefer?" I ask over the movie as Rocky rips the packet. He's still standing beside the bed, and I can't see the tiny words on the foil.

"Ultra-thin or extra-thin."

Hmm. "Should I take notes?" I quip, but honestly, I'm still nervous this might not happen *once*. I can't even think about *next time*.

Rocky rolls the condom on his shaft with ease. "No."

No?

Before hurt punctures me, he adds, "I buy the condoms." He's on the bed. Kneeling again, he has my hips in his strong clutch. "I'm the rich bitch. Remember?" He yanks my panties straight down my legs, off my ankles and feet. *Ohhh wow.*

I'm completely bare.

Pleasure sizzles beneath his hands as they return to my hips and ass. I murmur, "It's . . . ringing a bell." His gaze is diving so deep inside me. I already feel like Rocky has entered me.

Bracing his forearm beside my face, he lowers down on me. The thump of his heartbeat pounds against my body, and his erection bears between my legs. He hasn't slipped in me.

Instead, he cups the inside of my thighs and splits them wider. I hook one leg around his shoulder, and he grabs my calf in the air. "Safe word," he demands.

"Fuck me."

"Cute fake safe word. Pick a real one."

I wet my lips to keep from smiling. "Why don't you pick?"

"Because I'll choose a word you won't want desecrated in bed."

"Strawberry?" I'm guessing.

He raises his brows.

I'm right. "Yeah, no, don't ruin my wholesome love of strawberries." If I have to use a safe word, then it means I'm scared and I want to feel protected. I look at him as it hits me. "Miami."

He's not perplexed, but he stares into me for a solid moment. Likely recalling our time in Miami. We've lived in so many cities, it'd take me hours to name them all, but my time in Miami with Rocky was adrenaline-fueled, messy, and a vivid, fond memory.

"Miami," he repeats, the word rough in his throat. "That'll work."

And this is the magic green light. Rocky holds my face, his hand diving into the sweaty tendrils of my hair, and as he descends on my lips with a crushing, aching kiss, he grinds against my pussy. Teasing. Still just teasing.

Until he's not. Our kisses leave my lips swollen, and he fastens his eyes onto mine as he thrusts into me. His guttural noise and my sharp breath electrify my senses, and he holds my face steady while he flexes deeper into me, pumping. I take more of his length little by little, the pace tantalizing and hypnotic, and the feeling of Rocky filling me carefully and completely is shaking my limbs.

"I . . ." I moan, not even sure what I planned to say. "Oh . . . my God." *He's in me. He's in me.* I cling on to his biceps, unable to even arch my hips and reciprocate the movement. His deep penetrating thrusts take total control of me, and I bask in the essence of being this close and intimate with Rocky.

His jaw muscles tic, gritting down on a groan, and he pries my hands off his biceps. Pulling my arms overhead and nailing my wrists to the mattress, he clutches my face with his other hand, and my legs are helpless, just a quaking, shuddering mess on either side of his waist.

His firm, glistening chest welds with my soft skin, and I'm so lost inside this moment. To the way he traps me beneath him, like no one else will ever reach me or touch me but him. To the way he pounds my swollen pussy, jostling my body upward with each plunge inside me, and we're bound together, rocking to the stormy waves of our love.

Our grunts and moans and throaty approvals of pleasure are all I hear. The horror movie, though loud, is shot so far out of my brain.

"Rocky," I whimper, tears wetting the creases of my eyes. *I'm going to come.* Holy . . . I shudder again beneath him.

His hot, agonizing breath ghosts my lips, and he stares into me. "You think your cunt can keep taking me? Because I'm not stopping. I'm never fucking stopping."

True to his word, Rocky does not stop.

I'm sent over the cliff as soon as he thrusts and whispers exactly what he's doing to me in graphic detail.

I cry out, my fingers curling while his grip tightens on my wrists, and my hips buck in an explosive, earth-shattering climax. An orgasm ripples out of me in pulsing waves, and my entire body trembles like the aftershocks of an earthquake.

Rocky sits up on his knees and clasps my hips. Pulling me against his groin, he continues the eternal fucking, and I see him slide in and out of me. *Holy fuck*. My lips split apart, and I'm unable to catch my breath as he begins to build me up again.

When he slips fully out, he's still so hard, and though I'm breathless, my energy isn't near depleted. We're steam engines. I should've known our first time would be as inexhaustible as we are.

I climb off the bed, locked into his hunger as he stalks after me, but I walk backward and pretend like I'm finished. "Thanks for the climax. It was good. Middle-of-the-road. Like a soft handshake."

"Is that what it was, you little liar?" He reaches me, his palm on the small of my back. He's guiding me to the wall, but I jerk away from him. Rocky catches me around the hips and pushes my front so hard against the wall with his build seared to my back.

Holy shit. I ache between my legs. The feeling of being pressed so forcefully against the wall by him is doing a number on me. I can almost sense Rocky drinking in the way I'm melting.

Turning my head to try and see him, I rasp, "I'm done." I don't really mean it. If I did, I would've used the safe word.

He pauses, gauging my expression. "You're not done." He draws my hips a little backward into him, his cock brushing against my ass, and when I try to reach around for his arm, he confines my wrists above my head. And then, he pushes inside my pussy again.

I'm in love with this. *I'm in love with him*, bleeds deeper like indelible ink on my heart.

Rocky bites back a groan. *"Fuck,"* he curses hotly, and keeping me trapped against the wall, he fists a handful of my hair. *Yes, yes, God, yes.*

I'm dizzy. The heady rush weakens my knees, but Rocky slams into me with the vigor of a celestial demon. I guess he's always been more of a fallen angel.

"Is this middle-of-the-road?" he breathes against my ear.

Not at all.

"Yes," I taunt in a slight moan. "I want it . . . rough." With my cheek on the wall, I meet the longing in his eyes. "Do I have to . . . spell it out for you?"

He thrusts deeper.

Ohhh fuck.

"Please do," he whispers and bites my lip before kissing me with loving aggression.

When he lets up, I start, "R."

His hand curves around my sweaty hip. I jerk as he touches my sensitive clit. *Fuck.*

"O," I cry out.

He's fucking me senseless. I'm unable to finish spelling; the friction of him lights up my core. I've never felt anyone go this deep in this position, and pleasure shoots through each nerve ending.

"C," he tells me in a ragged breath. His muscled arms flex as he braces one near my face. He's taking me harder. "K." He lets out a grunt. "Y."

That fucker spelled his own name.

The name I gave him.

Arousal swims through me like a riptide. And when I come again, he hasn't met his finish line. Before I descend off a peak, he spins me around and cups my thighs, hoisting me up against his chest. I barely have the strength left to hook my legs around him.

We kiss like we're fighting for oxygen, and Rocky brings me to the ottoman. Lying my back across the long, tufted bench, he fits right between my legs.

Once he pushes back into me, I clutch the back of his neck, and he slows his thrusts to a sensual, hypnotic pace. So deep.

Our eyes are latched, and he whispers against my lips, "I'm inside you." It wells up in me. "I'm making love to you." Tears leak, and he brushes the corners of my eyes. "I'm never letting go of you, Phoebe. *Never.*"

I hang on to him.

He holds on to me.

We're both overwhelmed. Overcome, and with three more deep flexes inside me, Rocky grunts out a curse, his muscles contracting, and my legs shake and toes curl again, just seeing him come. He rakes a cool hand through his sweaty hair.

He doesn't pull out yet. I love him right there. I always want him this tormentingly close, and I clutch on to his biceps to keep him still.

Rocky places a sweet kiss on my lips, and as he inches back, his smile rises. "Believe me now?"

"Yes." I really, really do.

Thirty-Eight

Rocky

First time you had sex during a horror movie?" Phoebe asks while we rewind *A Nightmare on Elm Street* again and watch on her bed. Sweaty sheets are tangled around our equally sweaty, naked bodies, and her bare legs are intertwined with mine. Her question is more curious than taunting.

"Yes, actually." I unwrap an Almond Joy, a giant-sized bag of assorted Halloween candy between us.

"Hmm," she muses.

I look over at her, wondering what the hell that *hmm* means. She smooths her lips to hide a burgeoning smile. *She likes that I'm doing new things with her.*

I begin to smile into a bite of coconut and chocolate. Finally having sex with Phoebe blew every image I'd constructed into a thousand smithereens. It was inconceivably better. Greater. A) Because it was real, and B) because the depth of how compatible we are stunned me. We just fit. I could've predicted how much I'd completely, undeniably *love* being that close to Phoebe, but the raw, overwhelming emotion and power that came with detonating years of volatile, built-up tension—that was unpredictable.

Phoebe munches on an M&M, her smile fading as I reach over and brush candy wrappers off the bed. She asks, "When did I do that?"

"Do what?"

"That." She points at my forearms.

I barely glance down, knowing the sore reddened fingerprints exist, and they'll likely turn black-and-blue tomorrow. Her nails also cut into my skin, and I wish she didn't ask about it because I'm afraid to darken her happiness.

"Earlier," I say vaguely.

Her frown bunches her thick brows. "I don't remember . . ."

Fuck. I just look right at her, the answer in my serious expression.

"Oh." She goes still. "When I was telling you about . . . right." *Carlsbad*. She shakes her head, wincing. "So I emotionally and physically hurt you. Great. Awesome."

"I wanted it." I slide my arm across her bare shoulder and place a kiss on her temple. "I'm glad you did." I press another kiss.

Phoebe looks up at me, seeing how gravely serious I am, and she eases with a big exhale, then burrows more against my chest.

We relax into the normalcy of this time together. Naked after the best sex of my life. Watching one of her favorite movies.

I like horror okay, but definitely not as much as Phoebe.

"Freddy, no!" Phoebe chastises Freddy Krueger a half hour through. She tears open her fourth bag of mini M&M's. "Just one more," she tells me, or maybe she's convincing herself. "We'll still have enough for the little kids next week."

"Or here's an idea. We don't pass out candy." I eat another Almond Joy.

"Halloween Scrooge," she combats, dumping the M&M's into her palm.

"You shouldn't insult the guy who just made you come four times." I crunch on the fun-sized candy bar.

She lets out a long breath, blushing and slightly glaring. Her body is splayed a little over me right now, and she's gorgeous. Flat-out, drop-dead *gorgeous*. But I fell in love with so much more than her tits and ass and the curve of her hips. Though, God, I love her wide hips. They're the perfect crook for my hands to rest while I take her.

I raise my brows. "I only speak the truth."

"I'm not denying it," she says hotly, then sits up more against the headboard. Her blue hair cascades along her collarbone. "I was just thinking . . ."

She takes forever to finish that.

It's killing me.

"Was there a thought there?" I retort.

"Now who's impatient?" she snaps back.

Me. I take a frustrated bite of Almond Joy. I'm on edge while she withholds her tortured thought. I say *tortured* because her face contorts and brows wrinkle.

"Can I help you?" I ask her. "You want me to guess?"

"No, no," she says, more softly. "I was just thinking that sex makes things more complicated. Are we . . . what is . . . ?" She trails off.

Okay.

I pick up the remote to pause the movie. I've been waiting for this talk. Phoebe rotates fully to face me and hugs a pillow to her bare chest. I'm only thankful because her breasts would be incredibly fucking distracting right now.

"What are we?" I clarify what she tried to ask. "We're together. Fuck everything else. I want to be with you, Phoebe. I told you I wouldn't have sex with you for any other reason than because I love you." I watch her contemplate this with a short breath, and my muscles tense. "Isn't that what you want?"

Am I wrong to think this? Are we not on the same page?

She tucks a strand of hair behind her ear. "I want that." Her eyes lift to mine. "To be together outside of a con, I've always wanted that, Rocky."

"Then what's wrong?"

Phoebe is quiet in thought.

"Our parents?" I question.

"'Fuck everything' means fuck them, right?" she asks. And when I nod, she says, "Then fuck them." She picks at a feather poking out of the pillow. "I mean, of course I'm still nervous how involved my mom will be if we tell her. I can't just shut that off." She looks to me. "We are telling our parents, right?"

"Yeah. I wasn't planning on keeping this a secret from them."

I knew that once I crossed the line and slept with Phoebe—that was it. I'd be opening the door to have our relationship manipulated and used by them. But I'd rather roll those dice and find ways to come out on top than stay in the hellhole I've been living in.

She smiles a little bit, but it fades in another thought.

Phoebe. I wish I could read her mind right now. "You're not just hung up on our parents?"

"There are so many messy parts to this." She sighs, but quickly adds, "It's worth it." Her eyes say: *you're worth it.* My chest rises in a deeper breath, and I nod her on. She tucks hair behind her other ear. "How do I tell Hailey? She doesn't even know I like you like *this.*" Phoebe gesticulates to my naked body.

"Why is that?" I wonder. "Afraid she'd run and tell me?"

"No, I was afraid she'd want us together."

That surprises me. "Really?"

"I didn't . . . I didn't want her to be like my mom and hope for another Tinrock-Graves union. Now I'm actually more afraid she'd hate us together." Phoebe's neck reddens. "She's adamant we'd be terrible for each other, and I have agreed with her. A lot."

"Yeah," I say with understanding. What we've been to each other has always been complicated, and I can't foresee whether my sister will get it. Let alone Phoebe's brothers. "Your brothers are more of my concern," I admit, "but it's not going to stop me. I'd rather tell all of them than have to sneak around."

"Me, too." Her voice is quieter. "How do we break the news that we're together? Because in each version in my head, it feels so preplanned, like another con." Her face breaks. "I *want* this to be real. But I don't even know how to announce it without it sounding fake."

"So we don't plan anything," I tell her. "We just let them figure it out or tell them casually when it feels right. We don't need some elaborate setup, Phebs."

She thinks this over, popping another M&M into her mouth. "Okay."

"Okay." I hold out my hand. She pours three candies into my palm, and I toss two back, crunching. "You're forgetting another messy part to all this."

She frowns.

"You're fake dating Jake Waterford."

She winces. "Shit." Apologies fill her eyes. "Sorry."

"No apology necessary," I say. "The fact that he's a forgettable piece of your life makes me rock-hard."

Her eyes dip to my crotch. Hidden by a sliver of the white

sheet. She bites down on the chocolate. "I'll break up with him."

"Obviously," I say.

"Obviously," she combats roughly like that word was unneeded. The heat in her eyes makes me want to take her again, but I've delayed too many conversations already.

I throw back the last M&M, crunching harder. "I can't do this without your permission, but if you'll let me, I'm going to tell my mother to give you a larger cut of the Fiddle Game earnings."

"Don't," Phoebe immediately says. "I know it might piss you off that I didn't see the money—"

"Four hundred grand, Phoebe," I say with heat in my chest. "What'd you get?"

"It was always supposed to set up Seattle," she refutes. "It was going toward reestablishing our lives in a new city. That's what *every* big payout at the end of a job does."

"We didn't go to Seattle," I remind her. "Which is exactly why you and Hailey deserve more—"

"I don't want it," Phoebe snaps. "That con wasn't about the money for me. It was about not failing the team, and if I take more cash, then it just makes me feel like I prostituted myself that night more than I guess I did."

I put my hand on her knee, intaking a boiling breath, and I nod a few times, respecting her decision and dropping it. She's tense, and I reach out and bring her closer.

Phoebe lies against my chest, and once her pulse slows, I breathe, "Speaking of money. I bought a horse."

"What?" She shoots back up and spins to face me, knocking over the bag of Halloween candy. "You? The guy who curls his lip at Seabiscuit and Black Beauty and Flicka—"

"We get it—"

"—bought a horse?"

"Jake's horse," I clarify.

Realization widens her eyes. "The horse stables." What I haven't told her about since I've been gone for two weeks.

"Actually, it was his sister's horse."

Her mouth keeps dropping. "What?" Her eyes grow again. "That's why you needed a big chunk of change. To buy his sister's horse?"

"A hundred grand." Could I have swung that without leaving? Eh, it'd put me closer to a financial hole, and I hate even stepping toward one. It was smarter to leave town and make the cash the immoral way.

Phoebe straightens up in anticipation. "So what'd you find out?"

"'Chiquitita.' He wasn't calling a broker."

She gasps. "I knew it."

"He was calling his little sister."

She goes still. "The one that died? How . . . ?"

"She's not dead."

I tell her everything I know about Jake. How his sister is still alive and how he staged her death. How I'm the proud new owner of a warmblood named Bowie. She snorts when I say *proud*, which makes me grin, truthfully.

I end by saying, "It's weird. Jake's the first guy I've ever known that I don't want to con—but he's primed for conning."

She frowns. "Is it because you like him?"

I glower. "I don't *like* him."

"Not sexually." She glares back. "But I guess I'm just thinking it'd be easy to like him now that you know he's capable of deception. That's a trait most people scorn, but you've always seen it as a sign of capability."

Maybe.

"I do envy him," I say. That admission feels good.

Her brows shoot up. "Really?"

"Yeah, he was able to deceive his own parents, and there's no chance in hell I'll ever be able to do the same." I unwrap another Almond Joy, a tension winding its way through the room. Just because we're together now doesn't mean we've suddenly joined sides on the issue about our parents.

We can agree to disagree and still love one another. She doesn't need to believe in everything that I believe in. It won't make me care any less about her.

She takes a deep breath. "I still really love my mom, Rocky."

"I know," I say into a rougher sigh and then smile dryly at her. "We all have our flaws."

She tosses an M&M at my face. I catch the candy in my mouth. Crunching on the chocolate, I say, "As long as we're on the same page with *us*, I don't really care if we disagree about them."

"Same," she says.

I look her over. "Have you decided if you're going to stick with this 'honest' lifestyle?" Hailey put the ball in her court.

She shakes her head. "I'm just taking it day by day."

I nod slowly.

Day by day.

That's all we can do at this point in our fucked-up lives.

She tells me, "First order of business: break up with Jake."

That—I'm going to love to watch.

Thirty-Nine

Phoebe

Y ou want to break up?" Jake asks behind the pool bar. Erik called in sick this morning along with four other servers who went to the Gulp Seafood & Lounge last night. They all ate the oysters, and now they're probably making best friends with their toilet bowls.

I was a little bummed I wasn't invited to the staff outing. Now I'm flying on cloud nine for dodging food poisoning. Since the club is short-staffed, Jake has been the fill-in bartender. Only there's just one guest on this cloudy fall afternoon.

Carla Evans sips on her mojito and reads a book on an e-reader at the edge of the pool.

She's way out of earshot unless she has bionic hearing like Wonder Woman. Wait . . . does Wonder Woman have bionic hearing? I file that question away to ask Nova later.

I tell Jake, "Yes, I would like to break up with you and end our fake relationship."

"It's only been a month." He frowns deeper and wipes some

martini glasses with a rag. "You're supposed to have dinner with my parents the second weekend of November."

Ah, the reinstated Waterford family dinner. Not high on my to-do list.

But Jake reminds me, "Breaking up with me before then won't win you points with my mom."

"Right," I say. "So you should probably break up with me."

He shakes his head vigorously. "No, she'll love that."

"One of us is going to lose out on this scheme."

Skin pleats between his brows. I've been getting used to Jake's thinking-too-hard face. "Why do you want to break up, anyway? Is this about Rocky?"

Hearing his name causes a thousand butterflies to flap their annoying wings in my stomach. "It's about me," I say, not wanting *this* to be the way I profess my first real relationship. "And I'm just done lying."

That feels right.

It feels . . . good?

Jake thinks this over. "Yeah, I get that. Lies can weigh on you." He watches me, and I bet he's waiting to see if I react suspiciously. To see if Rocky confessed about his own con.

I tilt my head. "You say that like you have experience in lying."

He pauses. I make zero show of playing dumb. His eyes flash hot. "Rocky told you."

"We don't keep secrets from each other."

He curses him out under his breath, and then his worried gaze veers to me. "Phoebe."

"Your secret is safe with me," I assure him.

Jake lets out a long, agonized groan, my words not offering an ounce of comfort to him.

"I think it's sweet what you did for her," I tell him. "Really."

His squared shoulders begin to unbind a little. "Okay."

"Okay?"

"We can break up," he confirms, though the idea looks painful for him. He was not expecting this so soon, that's for sure. "At the pool party on Thursday."

He means *on Halloween*. I'll be serving at the country club on my favorite day of the year. I would be more bummed, but I'm used to being preoccupied with a job during nearly every holiday.

"I'll pencil it in." I smile over at him. "It'll be the most epic breakup of your life. You'll remember it forever."

He groans even harder. "Let's not take it to the extreme, okay? For your sake and mine." I try not to hang on to the foreboding tone of his voice.

Forty

Rocky

I have a front row seat to the breakup of the year. I've posi-
tioned myself at the poolside bar; black streamers and a
cocktail list of only dark-colored spirits outfit the event tonight.

"It's a farewell of sorts," Valentina explained to me this
morning when I ran into her at the tennis courts. "The club
closes the pool on October thirty-first every year, and it's the
official last night members can use it. Oh, and you *must* wear
black."

So they're holding a funeral for a pool that will be risen
from the dead next spring.

It's one of the silliest excuses I've heard to throw a party.

But I'm not complaining that hard. The death of one annoying fake relationship happens tonight. And that's good
enough to celebrate.

This event is a favorite with caufers (still hate it). College
students mingle in Gothic dresses and tuxes, and the ones
wearing swimsuits soak in the heated waters, illuminated with

orange lights tonight. Fog and steam skim the surface of the pool.

Since the club has been short-staffed for Halloween, Jake is swamped behind the bar, and Phoebe and Hailey are busy scrambling to take orders at a packed iron table at the end of the pool.

I wave down the second bartender, a girl with a streak of white in the front of her hair. She looks like Rogue from X-Men, and thanks to Nova's raging hard-on for the super-hero, I unfortunately have that fun fact stored in my head. I wouldn't be surprised if he spent his teenage years jerking off to the cartoon.

I flag Lola down. She's rarely ever bartending when I'm at the club, so I only know of her.

She stops near me. "Grey, right? I'm Lola."

"Nice to meet you, Lola."

"What would you like?" She splays her palms on the bar with a flirty smile.

"Margarita."

She grabs a glass from underneath the bar. "I'll have to put activated charcoal in it to make it black. That okay?"

"Disgusting, but I'll survive."

She smiles until she notices a struggling Jake Waterford as he fumbles with some sort of black vodka concoction. "Hold on . . ." She goes to his rescue just as Phoebe slips beside me.

"It's a madhouse," she says from behind the bar. "I have fifteen orders, and I can't read half of them." She hands me the slip of paper she wrote on.

I can't even decipher her chicken scratch.

"I was trying to write shorthand like Hailey."

"First mistake," I tell her. "Never try to imitate Hailey." It's led many astray.

We're both watching Jake mop up a vodka spill on the other bar, and Phoebe whispers to me, "I told Jake he could push me in the pool, but he said he'd never do that."

I roll my eyes. Of course he wouldn't.

Does that make me feel worse, knowing that I've pushed Phoebe in a pool plenty of times during cons? Maybe . . . I don't know.

It doesn't send warm fuzzies through me that Jake has lines he won't cross that I've clearly vaulted over with no question or problem.

"You should push Jake in the pool," I tell her.

"Funny."

"Not a complete joke . . ." I trail off as my phone vibrates in my pocket. I take out my cell, and Chelsea urgently waves at Phoebe from across the patio.

"I'll be back," Phoebe tells me. She's quick to respond to Chelsea's SOS.

As she leaves, I glance down at my phone. It's my brother. He should be holed up at our sister's loft. Last we heard, Boyd didn't reach the port and board the cruise ship as planned. For whatever reason, he didn't accept the free vacation that Trevor paid for. Either he didn't buy into the scam or his desire to be in Connecticut right now won out. So my brother should be spending Halloween eating the remaining fun-sized candy and keeping the door *locked*.

"No trick-or-treaters," I told him before I left. "Promise me. Don't answer the fucking door. The only people allowed inside are the ones with keys."

"I promise, Rocky," he said.

I didn't believe him.

There was a look in his eye, and I knew he was lying to me. But I left him anyway. Because he's nineteen, and what am I supposed to do? Babysit him all night? He's not a kid anymore . . . but he is my little brother.

Dread seeps into me just seeing his number on my phone.

"Hey?" I answer quickly.

"*Rock* . . ."

I'm on my feet in seconds flat, slipping my arms through my leather jacket—and I speak low into my phone. "Grab the gun on the bookshelf."

"I'm not . . . there." His voice sounds choked.

He's not at the loft. Fucking Christ. I push through college students and older club members.

"Grey!"

"Hey, Grey!"

Their voices recede the second they see me tearing out of the patio and to the parking lot. I climb in my McLaren and start the engine. "Where are you, Trev?" I don't leave yet. If he's somewhere closer to the loft, parking will be a nightmare tonight and it'll be faster for me to walk.

"Trevor?"

". . . help, *Rock*." His fractured voice is one full of fear. An emotion I've never heard from my brother. In my entire life. He'd fallen from a tree when he was eight and stared at a bone poking from his calf. He didn't even cry.

"Where are you?" I almost shout, fisting my phone against my ear.

He doesn't say anything, but my phone beeps and I check it quickly. He sent me his location via pin drop. My pulse skyrockets. We don't send our locations like this.

He's close.

Abandoning my car at the country club, I start into a sprint. Cold October wind whips against my face, and as I run, I check the map on my phone to ensure he hasn't moved. *He's still there.* The town's main street is alive with late-night trick-or-treaters, mostly teens, and adults attending costume parties at the restaurants and bars. Kids in Ghostface masks from *Scream* whack each other with pillow sacks of candy.

Purple and green streamers tied to lampposts blow in the chilly night. Witch cackles and tiny screams echo around me, and my pulse races as fast as my feet.

"Ahghgh!" A bloody soccer player tries to scare a cheerleader as I pass.

"You're not funny, Vincent!"

I never slow down.

Halloween remixes pump from the nightclub as I close in on a darkened alley behind the Gulp Seafood & Lounge. And I spot a crumpled figure on the cobblestones beside a dumpster.

It can't be . . .

But I know it's him.

The gray zip-up jacket, black pants, and sneakers should throw me off—so should the hockey mask—but I recognize my brother's tall, lean frame and the dyed black hair that touches his neck. He's dressed as Jason from *Friday the 13th.*

I slide onto the ground next to his body, and immediately, I pry the mask off his face. He's shivering, his face ghostly white. Urgency pummels me, and I waste no time searching for a wound. "What'd he do?" *What'd he fucking do?*

His hands tremble near his abdomen, his fingers stained with blood. I finally spot his switchblade lying near his thigh and another knife I've never seen before.

Trevor's teeth chatter. "He . . . got me once . . . I got him better. But he . . . ran."

I can already tell he's lost so much fucking blood, and I swiftly take off my jacket and apply pressure to his stab wound.

"I . . . I wanted to end it." He gulps for breath. "I was . . . so tired . . ."

Of being followed. Of being hunted. I pocket both knives, and I send a cryptic text to the people I trust most.

We loved with a love that was more than love. 🦇

And then, I collect his mask.

Tears leak out of his eyes. "I thought . . . Halloween . . ." He takes a shallow breath. "He wouldn't notice me coming . . ." He winces into another pained gulp. "No one ever notices . . . me."

His eyes flutter.

"Hey, stay with me." I grab his cheeks. "You hear me? Stay. Awake."

He blinks hard, and fear slowly contorts his face. "I-I don't want to die . . . *Rock*."

"You're not dying." It's the biggest lie I've ever told my brother, one I hope he believes. He needs a hospital. I know this. But there are a million and one reasons running through my head why I can't take him there. Why I shouldn't. "I have to put this back on you, all right?" I slip the mask back on his face, and I lift my brother in my arms, cradling him against my chest.

And I run.

I run down the main street carrying my slowly dying brother. Tendons scream in my legs, my lungs blistering with each short breath in the frigid night. My pulse is a jackhammer against my temple.

People are oblivious. It's Halloween. He's Jason. They're either drunk or in their own celebratory world, and I'm scraping through real horror. Real terror.

Slowing at the apartment door next to Baubles & Book-ends, I struggle to fish out my keys while holding Trevor.

"Grey!"

Sidney fucking Burke.

She comes up to me in a red minidress and devil horns, pull-ing away from her tipsy friends. "I thought you'd be at the pool party." I'm a challenge to her, so telling her off at the Harvest Festival was temporary. Her curiosity descends to the hockey-masked boy in my arms. "Who is that? Is he okay?"

"He had too much to drink. You know how it is?" I widen my eyes. "Halloween." I sound bitter that my night has driven me here. "You mind helping me? I'm trying to get my keys."

"Yeah." She begins to grin. "Which pocket?"

"Left side. Front pocket."

I watch Sidney slip her fingers in my front pocket. Feeling around, she purposefully takes too long, and I bite back a glare when she caresses my shaft. *What a fucking night.*

"Find it?" I ask.

"Yeah . . ." Her lip quirks, and she dangles the keys.

I motion with my head to unlock the door. She does, then I let her drop the keys back in my pocket. "Thanks."

"See you around, Grey."

My back to her, I roll my eyes, and I slam the door shut after entering the stairwell. "Trevor?" I whisper to him.

He doesn't answer.

"Trevor?" I'm about to drop him and check him on the stairs.

"Ughh . . . yeah . . . yeah." He groans behind the mask. "Who was that?"

"A girl pretending to be a devil." I carry him quickly up the flight of stairs, biceps burning, and while I'm unlocking the loft door, Nova arrives.

He bolts up the stairs and helps me carry Trevor into the loft. We place my brother on the couch, and I whip the hockey mask off his face and cup his cheek, my fingers bloodied.

Trevor winces. *"Fuck . . ."* His hands still rattle near the stab wound.

"Concentrate on staying awake, okay?" I apply pressure while Nova races into the kitchen. All I can think is, *He's not going to die.* This isn't how my brother goes out, and between Nova and me, we have enough skills to help him.

If I didn't believe we did, I wouldn't have risked bringing him to the loft.

"Yeah . . . yeah. I can do . . . that," Trevor chatters, fighting consciousness.

"No hospital?" Nova asks, returning with a blue canvas trauma kit.

Trevor grimaces. "No . . . hospital. Just . . ." He shivers, and I rub his arm.

I look to Nova. "He hasn't made a new alias yet." I can't be sure which IDs in his pocket are tied to what con, and if he dies because I'm trying to protect the families—it's on me.

It'll always and forever be on me.

He's not dying.

I won't let him die. I can't let him die.

I just can't.

Nova crouches beside me. His costume distracts me for half a second. *What the hell is he wearing?* Purple chest armor and a long trench coat complete what I'm guessing is an obscure superhero.

"Captain Underpants?" I ask.

His jaw tics. "Gambit. X-Men. Everyone knows him but you."

"That's definitely not true." I keep pressure on my brother's wound.

"You're going to have to back up, Rocky." Nova snaps on gloves from the trauma kit. We've all been trained in first aid, but Nova has the most experience delivering urgent care, since he was in EMS academy when he was eighteen.

I shuffle back and give Nova my position.

"I can already tell he's gonna need a blood transfusion," Nova says as he starts an IV in record time. "He's lost way too much."

Blood transfusion. I touch my wrist to my forehead, my palm bloody. I want to say that I can give him my blood, but I hesitate. "Do any of us know our blood types?"

Nova shoots me a tense look.

That'd be a *no.*

"Fuck," I curse and dig out my phone and do a three-way call.

"Rocky?" Phoebe says, sounding panicked. "We got the message. Hails and I are on our way."

"It's Trevor?" Hailey asks since I used the bat emoji.

"I'm almost there," Oliver says, out of breath like he's running.

I tell them, "Whoever's closest to a drugstore, we need a blood-typing kit. Steal it."

"Oh my God," Hailey mutters in the background.

"Ah, I just passed one." Oliver breathes hard. "I got it."

"Where's Nova?" Phoebe asks.

"He's with me," I say.

"He'll be okay, Hails," Phoebe whispers. "You want me to drive?"

We all hang up after Oliver says he'll be here in less than

five minutes. Returning to the couch, Trevor blinks hard, his lips losing color and beginning to turn blue. "Just . . . sit down." He winces. "And . . . play some Candy—" He coughs.

"Nova," I say hurriedly, and I help him apply gauze on Trevor's abdomen. While I add pressure to the gash, Nova starts to stitch the wound.

"It looks longer than it is deep," Nova says in the quiet. "I don't think he hit an organ."

So much blood coats his gloves, the couch, the floor. I'm just hoping we have time for the blood transfusion—that it's not too late.

Hope.

Belief.

It's driven my entire life. But I manufacture belief for others. I create false hope and fake promises, and in a jarring second, I question if I'm tricking myself into believing we can help him. I've always trusted the confident voice in my head that whispers, *I have this. Trust me. Everything. Will. Be. Okay.*

My head is on a turntable. Whirling at high speeds.

Trevor trembles but stays conscious. I hold his hand in mine, using the other to stop the bleeding as Nova works on a portion of the long gash.

"Annabel Lee," Nova says quietly while threading a needle through the wound. "Who came up with that? Do you remember?"

He's referring to the message I texted everyone. It's a line from an Edgar Allan Poe poem. *Annabel Lee.* It's our biggest SOS signal. And we all know to meet at the safe location—which everyone already agreed would be the loft.

"Hailey did," I say. "We were young. I can't remember . . . nine or ten?"

The six of us created signals and codes outside of our

parents. It's just what we as kids did. Hide from the adults late at night with secrets of our own.

I tell him, "She felt like we all 'loved with a love that was more than love'—she thought it was beautiful." I watch as Trevor focuses on my voice, so I keep talking. "How the man lamented over a dead woman. I think it's morbid." I glance at Nova's stitches. "Perfect for fucked situations."

Nova fishes the needle in flesh. "We should've gone with the Tinrock-Graves family motto."

"Which is?"

"'Believe nothing you hear, and only half of what you see.'"

Also Poe.

The door opens with abrupt force. "I have it!" Oliver rushes inside with a blood-typing kit. He's dressed as a pirate with a frilly white shirt and deep red vest. Panting, he rips open the box and fumbles with the contents.

"Give me the directions." I hold out a hand.

"I'll read them. Your hands are bloody, man." Just as he says it, Hailey and Phoebe storm into the loft, the door banging loudly behind them.

"Is he . . . ? Oh my . . ." Hailey careens backward.

"I'm . . . fine," Trevor says, no longer shivering. His eyes are heavy-lidded and try to close. "Fine . . . it's fine . . ."

Phoebe searches through the trauma kit and snaps on gloves, and our gazes slam together with so much emotion that my throat swells closed.

"I'll take over, Rocky," she says. "You do the blood transfusion."

Nova looks to his sister. "We don't know their blood types yet."

"He's probably a match," she refutes. "Or Hailey is."

I back away and let Phoebe press on the gauze.

"Hailey." Oliver hands her the contents of the kit, and while Oliver reads the directions out loud, Hailey and I follow the instructions. I wash Trevor's blood off my hands in the kitchen sink, and then my sister and I both prick our fingers and drip blood onto the card.

Phoebe uses a pipet from the trauma bag to suction drops of Trevor's blood for the test.

Oliver reaches the bottom of the directions and shifts his weight.

"What is it?" I ask him.

"It'll take ten minutes."

"Just give him my blood," Hailey says, not thinking this through.

"We don't know our blood types, Hails," I interject. "We don't even know Mom's—"

"She's O negative," Hailey says. "She told me."

To your face?

My doubt reeks like five-week-old garbage, but I'm not releasing the stench in the room. They likely already smell it on me.

Especially as Hailey feels the need to clarify. "She was telling me a story about how she used to donate blood a lot when she was young. Before this whole lifestyle became her everything. She's a universal donor."

Believe nothing you hear, and only half of what you see.

I'm not thinking straight.

Everything is muddled as hell in my brain.

Where's the lie?

There is no lie. They wouldn't tell us our blood types because they'd have no reason to. Just like we have no social security cards, no identification that could incriminate us.

Or incriminate them . . .

Am I lying to myself?

There is no lie.

What do I want to believe? What do I want to see?

And is what I want even the actual truth?

I sit on the coffee table. Waiting for the timer to buzz. Lost in a pool of belief and disbelief.

Oliver turns to my sister. "Hails, if your mom is O negative, then he could be O negative, too. And then that means . . . ?" He finds the answer in his head. "He can only receive O negative?"

"Yeah." She rips open another kit. "You, Nova, and Phoebe should also do a test in case you match him."

The triplets prick their fingers.

Ten minutes.

Turns to five minutes.

Turns to two minutes.

"Trevor." I snap my fingers, his eyes drooping.

"Still . . . here." He's drifting.

The timer vibrates my phone. I check my kit. "I'm B negative. *Shit*," I curse.

Hailey examines her results. "I'm O negative." *The universal donor.* Thank God. Quickly, we push the coffee table closer to the couch, and Hailey lies on the surface while Nova taps her vein and starts an IV line.

We don't need to check Trevor's blood type, but it's nagging me.

The doubt.

The unknown. I eye the results on the ground near Phoebe and the trauma bag.

Don't look. I shouldn't look. I should be like every mark and just live with rose-colored glasses. Seeing exactly what I want to see.

I've never wanted that to be me.

Right as I go toward my brother's results, a timer beeps on Oliver's phone. The triplets. Their tests are done.

Oliver checks them on the kitchen counter. He says nothing.

He's not shocked by whatever he sees. He just moves away from the bar and watches blood flow through the narrow tube out of Hailey's arm and into Trevor.

"What are yours?" I ask him.

"All A positive."

Okay.

Okay.

I can't trust myself right now. Our parents haven't been tricking us—maybe they never have been. Maybe I've been wrong. This entire time.

I've just hated my father, and that resentment piled so high inside of me that I couldn't see beyond the mound of hatred.

I saw what I wanted to see.

I'm just the cynic. The pessimist. I'm made to disbelieve.

With a deep breath, I comb a hand through my hair and try to focus on the dull throb of my finger that I pricked.

Phoebe sees Trevor's results near her knee, and she picks them up. Glancing at them, she says, "He's AB negative."

Hailey props herself up on her elbows and peers at the test in Phoebe's hands. "Run it again."

I go still.

"Why?" Oliver asks.

"Th-that has to be Boyd's blood," Hailey stammers. "Run it again."

Tension slips through the room like a coiled snake. No one argues, and Phoebe pricks Trevor's finger this time instead of pipetting blood around his wound.

While we wait, I ask quietly, "What does it mean, Hailey?"

Blood slips out of the IV that Nova hooked on a coatrack—his makeshift medical IV pole. Oliver wedges a pillow under her head, but she's staring dazed at the ceiling.

"It doesn't mean anything," she breathes shakily, "because it can't be right."

"But if it is right?" Phoebe asks. "What does it mean?"

"It's impossible for someone who's O negative to have a child who is AB negative," Hailey whispers like she's reading a fact she remembers from a book she read ten years go. "If the test is right, Trevor isn't Mom's kid."

I don't know what to think anymore.

The air hums with a heavy current. My first feeling isn't even surprise. Dread is covered in remorse and uncertainty.

"It's wrong," Nova says. "The test is wrong. There's a lot of blood here. It's contaminated."

"Phoebe just pricked his finger," Oliver tells his brother. "She didn't take it from the opened wound. We'll just wait."

We wait.

No one says anything except to ask Trevor how he's feeling. He's in and out of consciousness. I keep my fingers on his pulse.

"He'll be okay," I tell Hailey.

She's so pale, and it's not from the lack of blood. It's like she's seen a monster.

Oliver's phone rings shrilly, and Phoebe jolts. "Fuck."

He shuts off the timer, and Hailey crunches upward to check the test. As soon as she sees it, she buries her anguished face in her palm. A pained noise like a fisted sob comes out of her.

Phoebe looks. "It's AB negative."

"No kidding," Oliver says with a short breath. "I just thought she looked gutted because we're out of candy kisses." His eyes flash to me.

Phoebe turns to me.

Like they'll expect me to chime in and say, *I told you so.*

But if Trevor isn't Addison's son, then this is deceit on another level. I almost . . . I almost can't believe it, and that scares me, too. There is actual proof sitting in front of us. So that means, regardless of my aversion toward our parents, I don't want to believe that my brother isn't my brother.

I don't want to believe that our parents could've done worse than what I imagined.

I don't want to believe my entire life could be a sham.

I've been fooled.

We've been fooled.

"She was pregnant," Nova tells everyone. "We all saw Addison *pregnant.*"

That's true. I have memories of my mom with a big, round belly. I was six at the time. They were all five.

Are those even our real ages?

My stomach churns, and Oliver says what I'm also thinking: "Did any of us see Addison's bare stomach? No shirt covering her belly."

"How would any of us remember that?" Nova questions. "We were five."

Hailey is lying flat on the table, her hands pressed to her face. If she remembers, the answer is she never saw.

"She could've been pretending," Phoebe says, her brows bunching with the pain of this theory.

"Pretending to be pregnant?" Nova says with traces of skepticism.

Oliver is wincing. "She could've faked her pregnancy with

a fake belly that both Hailey and Phoebe have worn before, and she did it to convince all of us that Trevor was hers. How is that not in the realm of possibility, Nova? We've all pulled bigger cons than that."

Silence.

"When have they *ever* pulled a con on us?" Nova questions all of us.

It sits in the room for a long minute.

Until I whisper, "From birth."

Oliver starts laughing, his face twisting. "This is classic . . . a classic. They wanted another little child with little hands when we got too old, so he could be the cute little innocent kid, and so they what—steal Trevor?"

My brother's pulse thumps beneath my fingers.

Trevor has a similar eye color to mine and Hailey's. Except flecks of blue lie inside his grays. And Hailey—does she even look like me? She has a thin nose, one that our mom said she got from Grandma Nellie.

A grandma we've never met.

I grit harder, my jaw clenching.

"What about us?" Phoebe asks her brothers. "We're triplets. You can't fake that."

It's also true—they're very clearly related, even being fraternal.

Hailey drops her hands, her cheeks blotchy with mascara. "You'd be good shills. The *perfect* shills." Her voice carries a tremor. "If the three of you look undeniably related, none of us would ever question our parentage."

Oliver freezes in place. "Rocky wasn't old enough to remember our mom being pregnant."

"How convenient," I mutter.

"What if they're not our mothers?" Oliver questions with

outstretched arms. "What if they're not our fathers?" He's saying what everyone is contemplating. Not one looks surprised by his declaration.

"There are no pictures," Phoebe realizes. "There are no pictures of any pregnancies. Not Addison with Rocky. Not Addison with Hailey. Not Elizabeth with us."

"They couldn't incriminate themselves," Hailey says quietly. "That's what they always told us . . . but is that even the truth?" She looks to me. "Rocky?"

I shake my head. "I don't know."

That's my truth.

I have no fucking clue.

Nova finally stands up from beside Trevor. "Would they even tell us the truth if we asked?"

"No," most of us say.

"That's what I thought." Nova sighs out and drags his gaze, snapping gloves off his hands. He catches my eyes, holding for an extended beat.

We've been on opposite sides for so long—clashing when it comes to our mothers, my father—and I never thought he'd question them, not for anything.

I was wrong.

"'Believe nothing you hear, and only half of what you see.'" Nova nods to me.

I nod back to him. "Should I stop calling you Winchester?"

"No." He disposes of the gloves. "Only because Dean *is* the cool one."

I let out a short laugh.

"Your brother is going to make it, by the way." He pauses, as though considering what he called him. "Trevor, your . . ."

"He's still my brother." Fury begins brewing again. Toward

our parents. "He'll always be my brother." I don't care what they did.

That's going to stay true.

"What do we know?" Phoebe wonders. "Like, what do we know as fact?"

Hailey is the one who says, "Trevor isn't related to Addison. That's it."

"That's not all," Nova says, zipping up the trauma bag. "We know that we can only trust everyone in this room."

For the first time, I'm not alone in this.

Forty-One

Phoebe

I give Trevor my bed. He's already woken up, but he's weak. No one has told him what we found out yet, but Oliver's been tasked with keeping a steady watch of his vitals tonight. Rocky wanted to do it, but Trevor kept complaining that Rocky was staring at him with "Bambi eyes" like he'd already died.

So now Rocky is helping me clean the living room floor. Blood has stained the hardwood. We're on our hands and knees scrubbing.

Hailey is fast asleep in her bedroom, wiped from the transfusion, and Nova left to clean the droplets in the stairwell. *Fake blood*, he's planning on lying to anyone who asks.

Halloween, my fav, came through in the clutch tonight. Then again, Trevor only risked leaving the loft *because* it's Halloween.

I'm just going to disregard that.

Just like you're disregarding your mom's deception, Phoebe.

No, *no*, that is right in my face. If Trevor isn't Addison's son, then that means she had it in her to possibly steal a kid from another mother. My mom wouldn't be partners in crime with someone like that if she didn't have it in her, too.

I don't want to believe it's true, but that doesn't mean it isn't.

To know for sure, we'd have to take a DNA test, but we can't risk having that information on file in some lab. We're supposed to be anonymous, invisible, off-the-grid.

Imagining my mom stealing me and my brothers is sickening enough to send me to the toilet. I did yack privately in the trash.

I think only Nova saw.

"This isn't coming out," I say, my fingers raw from scrubbing with a Brillo pad. The stained couch is the least of my concerns. We can throw that in the dump.

Rocky sighs heavily and tosses a sponge into the soapy water bucket. "Fuck it."

"Fuck it?" I frown. "There has to be something we can do. What about replacing the floorboards?"

"That is definitely not in your rental agreement," he says with a dry smile.

He's joking—kind of. But he is right. Jake would know and ask questions and definitely wouldn't be happy.

"Fuck it . . ." I mull over those words again.

"I'm done with all this shit, Phoebe. Just tell Jake the truth," Rocky says in almost a defeated, exhausted voice. "My brother got stabbed. He bled a lot. Done."

"He's going to ask why we didn't take him to the hospital," I reply softly. "You want me to tell him we're awful people?"

"You can tell him it was my choice. I don't care what he thinks of me." He leans back against the couch. I look around at the disarray. The bloodstains. A garbage bag of Trevor's bloodied clothes and used blood-typing kits.

All right.

I crawl next to him and toss my Brillo pad into the soapy water bucket. "Fuck it," I say with certainty now.

He wraps an arm around me, and a wave of guilt festers in my stomach. "Rocky," I whisper. "I'm sorry I didn't believe you sooner."

Rocky clutches my gaze. "I'm glad you didn't, and truthfully, I'm glad you *all* didn't."

I frown, a pain in my heart. "Why?"

"If you were all easy to sway, I think I would've questioned how much I influenced you. How much I was just tricking you into believing what I wanted you to believe. I never had any doubts because you all constantly challenged me."

That's good to know. I exhale a little, and I love leaning into Rocky and how he brushes hair off the nape of my neck.

He holds me close. "And there should only be one hardcore cynic among us."

"Jake thinks I'm hard-core angsty."

He rolls his eyes. "Jesus. He's a little soft-core bitch . . ." Rocky trails off seeing my glare, and his brows jump. "Protecting the fake ex-boyfriend?"

I stiffen. "I thought you liked Jake?"

"*Like*? No. But I don't completely hate him . . ." He's trying to read my face. "What's wrong?"

I just come out with it. "I didn't break up with Jake."

His wince plunges a sharp dagger in my gut.

Hurriedly, I add, "I was going to, but then you left the pool party, and I was looking around for you and then you sent the text—"

He puts his arms around me, hugging me into silence. "It's all right." His voice is tender affection.

"It's *not* okay. I'm fake dating Jake Waterford when I'd rather be fake *and* real dating you."

"I know that, Phebs," he whispers, and his loving gaze bathes me. "You don't have to convince me. I know . . ." He looks me over in a heavier sweep. "I know you."

My heart swells, and our love is an unspoken light between us, radiating among the darkness of our many lives and lies.

It has always been unspoken. Rocky has never needed words to see how much I love him. He's never asked for them. But he deserves to hear them. He's already said them to me. He's told me, verbally, he loves me.

But I haven't . . . and this is the time.

This is it.

To tell him how much I love him. To tell him *exactly* the depth of what I feel. I open my mouth, and as his fingers brush against my cheek and our lips near, those three words completely escape me.

Something else replaces them instead, and very softly, I whisper, "I'm your Phoebe."

The purest emotion brims his eyes. "I'm your Rocky."

Forty-Two

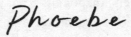

Phoebe

Jake. Jake. *Must. Find. Jake.*

And thoroughly *break up* with Jake.

Unfortunately, I was going to call in sick to work like Hailey, but Chelsea begged me for the extra hands since half the staff are no-shows and likely nursing hangovers from Halloween parties last night.

Two birds, one stone: I told Jake to meet me at the country club.

I'm an hour into my shift, and I haven't seen any sign of the Konings' third heir. I'm antsy as a lady with pearl earrings peruses the drink menu, keeping me hostage.

"I'll give you a minu—"

"No, no, no," she refutes with the wave of a hand. "I just about have it."

She does not.

Patience. I inhale a little breath and remember Ms. O'Neil is a sweet older woman who spends most of her time doing crossword puzzles. I'm being prickly, and she doesn't deserve that.

"Can I help make it easier?" I ask her. "What are you looking for?"

"That drink."

This time, her vagueness makes me smile. "A tea? A spirit? A soda—"

"It's a soda."

Great. One step forward. I try to subtly scan the dining room for Jake. It's packed this afternoon, nearly every chair occupied, and Chelsea is practically sprinting from table to table.

"My daughter was talking about it yesterday. It's new."

"Pepsi? Coke? Fizz?"

"Fizz!" She catches my wrist, remembering. "That's right. It's called Fizz Life."

I frown. What? "Uhh, I know we have a lot of Fizzle products stocked, but I'm not sure if I've heard of Fizz Life."

"It's new," she assures me, letting go. "My daughter said it's healthier than the diet stuff. I'll take one of those."

"Okay, I'll check to see if we have it." *Doubtful.* "Can I get you anything if we don't?"

"Just the Fizz Life, dear."

All righty then.

With this, I spin on my heel, and what do you know—Jake is leaning against the dining room bar and chatting with Katherine, of all people.

At least he's here.

At least he's right next to the bar where I need to be.

Without wasting another second, I hightail my ass to the bar, and as I approach, Katherine air-kisses his cheeks in a polite goodbye. She side-eyes me on her way out, and it's disturbingly familiar to Jake's side-eyes.

I let it go and try not to come in super hot. "Do you know anything about Fizz Life?" I ask him, resting an elbow on the bar like him.

His brows crinkle. "You mean Diet Fizz?"

"Nooo, Ms. O'Neil was adamant there's a drink called Fizz Life and that we have it."

Jake takes out his cell. "I'll look it up."

So I think we should break up, like, today. Now. Right now. That shouldn't be a tough request considering our breakup fell through yesterday.

I'm nervous about his reply since he seemed . . . *relieved* when I left the pool party last night and our fake relationship was still intact.

"She said it's new," I tell him.

He scrolls on his phone. "It's an aspartame-free soda."

Holy shit. "It exists?" I peek at his phone. He's reading a news article.

"It's not being unveiled until January," he explains. "She must've heard about it through her social circles."

"So we don't have it," I realize.

He pockets his phone. "No. Not unless you have a time machine."

Dammit. I round the bar and open the fridge. Grabbing an ice-cold Diet Fizz, I pop the can, but before I pour the drink into a glass, I stop myself.

She won't know the difference. It's not like she's ever tasted Fizz Life.

The deceit sits more strangely. After Hailey brought me here for a reason, after the doubt surrounding our parents and what they could've done, I realize I still want to try and live a more honest life.

For myself, this time.

I set the soda down.

That also means ending my fake relationship. "Jake." I face him across the bar.

"Yeah?"

I motion him closer, and as he stretches over the bar, women in the club seem to watch us with rapt fascination, as though Jake and I are sharing flirty secrets in the corner. My face burns. Thankfully, we've yet to share a fake kiss to establish credibility. I'm *very* glad we're ending things before taking the next physical step in this pretend relationship.

"We need to wrap this up. You and me," I say in a hushed breath. "Like, now. You can yell at me, storm away—I don't care. We just need to rip off the Band-Aid."

Jake tenses. "About that . . ."

I read the hard lines of his face. "No, we're not delaying—"

"I just need this to go on for another month."

"A month?" I try not to yell. My heart is skipping beats. "Jake—"

"The family dinner, *Phoebe*." Urgency is all over my name. "You don't understand. I really need you there for that." He drops his voice to a whisper. "If I don't bring you, my mom will invite Mrs. Kelsey's daughter, Julia, as my date. That's her plan, as of right now. She blatantly told me this morning."

I've met Julia at an afternoon tea. Best part: the teeny-tiny cucumber sandwiches. That I didn't have to pay for—thank you, Mrs. Kelsey. What I learned: Julia is shy and lets her mother do most of the talking. His fears aren't exactly unwarranted. I can see Julia being overly agreeable to Claudia's requests and demands, but I don't even know exactly what those are.

It's not like I've had a formal sit-down with Claudia. She treats me like a literal skunk, not just an outsider with the cutesy (slightly demeaning) town nickname.

I frown. "If this is just about Julia, you could warn her— tell her *don't come*."

He lets out a laugh like that's an impossible ask. "I warn her, but her mother pushes her to go. Who do you think she'll listen to?" His blue eyes cradle my gaze with tenderness. "I'd rather you come with me. We're already together."

Fuck, *fuck*. "We were supposed to break up *last night*," I whisper, careful of the watchful eyes around us.

"But we didn't. Everyone believes we're still a couple, and let's let them." He adds earnestly, "Julia is only twenty-two. She's never been around my brothers—"

"Neither have *I*," I cut in. *And I'm only two years older.*

"If you can handle your ex, you can handle them." He has the utmost confidence in me, but it's mildly disturbing that he's comparing Rocky to his brothers. He places a comforting hand to my wrist, and his touch should feel heavy, burdensome—but it's become familiar and reassuring.

Still, I waver.

He sees. "It doesn't have to be forever."

"Jake—"

"*Please*. Just a couple more months."

"Now it's two more months?"

"One month," he amends fast. "One month."

I shake my head. "I can't—"

"I'm begging you here—"

"*I can't.*"

"Please—"

"I'm with Rocky," I whisper-hiss, and my face is on fire. This is *not* how I wanted to tell anyone my real relationship status, and I can't believe Jake—of all freaking people—is the first to know the truth.

His face freezes. "You're back with your ex-husband?"

Okay, he also knows some lies.

I nod tensely. "It just happened . . . recently."

He's unenthused, but I never thought he'd throw confetti seeing me reunite with a guy he believes is bad for me. Plus, I think he really hoped I'd get over Rocky by dating him.

I clear my throat, adding, "And if you want our fake relationship to extend past five minutes from now, I need to call him." I can't let this go on without Rocky knowing. If our positions were reversed, I'd be crushed.

Jake takes a tense breath. "Let me talk to him."

"Fine," I say. "You talk to him . . ." My voice tapers off as a slender fortysomething woman dripping in Chanel approaches the bar.

Stella Fitzpatrick. She's the kind of person who demands attention when requested. Her son, Archer, a professor at Caufield, was at the boathouse party months ago.

I think she's headed for Jake, but she zeroes in on me. *She must want a drink.*

I'm about to ask what I can get her.

"Phoebe, sweets."

Sweets?

She's only ever called me *you* and *hey*. Even after I started dating Jake. It's no secret she's Claudia's best friend and firmly against me dating a Koning boy.

"Yes?" I say, hoping this'll be a quick flyby for her.

"I need to chat alone with you for a moment. Jake won't mind if I steal you for a bit."

Jake starts, "Actually—"

"Oh please." She swats him with a playful smile laced with arsenic. "It'll only be a moment. You can spare your girlfriend that much."

I detect her slight cringe at the word *girlfriend*.

Jake turns to me. "You okay with that, babe?"

We really are prolonging this another minute, aren't we? "Yeah. That's fine." I'm a teensy bit curious what Stella actually wants, but I'm praying this isn't a curiosity-killed-the-cat situation.

With reluctance, Jake begins to leave me at the bar with his mother's friend, but not before he warns Stella, "She's not an enemy. Remember *that much*." He doesn't offer her the chance to reply.

I'm a little impressed, but then again, I haven't seen Jake in the upper-crust wild among his brothers and mom before. Maybe he isn't such easy prey.

As he exits the dining room, I'm hoping he's taking this opportunity to call Rocky.

Stella examines the bottles behind the bar. Her dark hair is center-parted and slicked behind her ears to flaunt teardrop diamonds. "I'll take a mimosa."

Okay. I swallow a snarky retort as I find the carafe of orange juice and bottle of Pommery champagne. "Is that all you wanted?"

"Hardly, sweets." She rests her rouge Chanel clutch on the bar counter, and I frown, wondering why she's still pretending to be semi-nice when Jake isn't here anymore.

"Then what?" I start to whip up her mimosa.

"You've made quite the stamp in Victoria."

She wants me to leave?

She's going to pay me to break up with Jake?

She's going to pay me to skip out on Jake and this town?

A handful of theories buzz through my brain, and I say nothing as I splash orange juice over the bubbly champagne.

She examines me, like she's searching for a crack. "Let me ask you something important, Phoebe."

"I'm an open book," I lie, sliding the mimosa over to her.

She neglects the drink. "How much do you care for Grey?"

Grey? My pulse skips; I wasn't expecting her to surface Rocky. "He's my ex."

"That's not what I asked." She angles fully toward me, as though blocking out the rest of the dining room. "Your *tempestuous* relationship with your ex-husband has been the talk of the town for some time now, but even I can see there is love there."

I have feelings for Jake is the lie I should fling to reinforce our fake relationship. Maybe even, *I love Jake.* Yet, the words stick cruelly and painfully to the back of my throat.

I haven't said them to Rocky, and I feel sick at the idea of saying them about Jake first. And, of course, she's wielding Team Grey flags. She'd likely be the largest benefactor of Rocky's fan club if it meant he'd pry me out of Jake's clutch.

I'm walking such a strange line right now.

I've just started a real relationship with Rocky.

I'm temporarily fake dating Jake.

And I'm not supposed to implode the fake dating scam yet.

"I'll always care about my ex," I say. "Jake knows this, and really, my relationships are none of your business."

"You're dating a Koning, sweets. If you can't handle being daily gossip, then you can't handle being with Jake." It's a warning.

"Understood," I say tightly. "But I can handle everything just fine."

I mop up a nonexistent spill beside her mimosa.

She pinches the stem of the flute. "There are those of us who feel it's worth saving." I don't understand until she adds, "Your marriage."

I shift my glare to the wall, not knowing the best way to bail myself out of this sinking ship. Staying quiet is likely the smartest avenue, and so I keep my lips shut.

"What if I told you there's a way we can help you?" Stella asks, practically oozing over the bar.

"I'm not interested in your help."

"Don't be prideful, sweets." She straightens. "We all need a little help now and then, and you should take ours."

I don't ask who "*ours*" entails. I'm guessing her bestie Claudia is partially behind this ploy. "Again, I'm not—"

"You care for Grey," she cuts me off. "You likely even love him, but you can't move beyond the baggage and the past. We can help you. Come." She waves her fingers at me like I'm a poodle.

"I'm busy."

"You aren't. *Come*." It's an order, and from across the dining room, I catch Katherine staking a *you better not piss off Stella Fitzpatrick* glare at me.

For my job, I obey the command and abandon the bar.

This better be quick.

Sipping her mimosa, she guides me toward the crackling fireplace. "There are people in the business of love, soul mates, fixing marriages, matchmaking—that type of field. I know anyone who's a big deal, and I only want the best for you, Phoebe."

"I'm sure you do."

She hears my dry tone and stops me in the middle of the dining room, a strict hand to my elbow. "Look, I understand why you wouldn't want to listen to me or even Claudia. But if they truly believe your relationship with Grey is worth rehabilitating, then you should at least listen to them. They're unbiased and professionals. They've likely dealt with worse issues than yours."

I try not to roll my eyes.

Who the hell did she hire? A freaking prestigious marriage counselor? I cast a glance back at the exit, hoping to see Jake.

No sign of the Koning boy.

Great.

I face forward again, and as two women rise from chairs like larger-than-life figures, my soul leaves my body.

I recognize her honey-blonde hair first. With the fire behind her, she looks ready to take the whole town by storm. Mustard-yellow blazer, matching flared pants, white blouse, and small gold hoop earrings—she could have so easily stepped out of a magazine.

But so could the woman next to her, encased with the same powerful wealth.

White turtleneck, off-white slacks, tortoise glasses, and a fancy taupe leather belt. Her brown hair is tucked behind her ears and flows pin-straight down her back.

Addison.

And my mom, her blonde hair perfectly curled in loose waves, ones I used to run my fingers through as a little girl.

Self-preservation wipes my face of all emotion, even though I know them.

My mom's radiant, charming smile and dazzling brown eyes dance over me. "Phoebe, is it?"

When Stella introduces them as the professionals, her voice fades like an echo in a tunnel.

They finally found us. I can't move as I stare deeply at the two women I trusted, I loved—I still sort of love. Thoughts crash against me in searing waves.

Why didn't you warn us you'd be here?

Why didn't you loop us into what you're doing now?

Am I really your daughter?

Did you kidnap all of us?

How can I ever believe anything you say?

Hi, Mom.

"Yes, it's Phoebe," I say softly. "Phoebe Smith."

Acknowledgments

When we were fourteen, we wrote a very rough book (but very beloved between the two of us and the walls of the bedroom we shared) called *The Reign of Spiders*. It currently lives on a floppy disk in a tin box, and throughout the years, we've re-read our childhood story, for nostalgia. It needed so much work to meet the world without us panicking about ALL of our writing insecurities, but the core concept was something we often revisited in our talks about "What do you want to write next?"

The answer this time: a spicier, messier romance about those two con artist families we've always loved. Truly the only thing that has stayed the same since our childhood is the concept, but if we had time machines, one of the first things we'd do is tell ourselves, *We did it*. And we'd tell our parents right after. But luckily, and very fortunately, we don't need a time machine to tell them now. Thank you, Mom and Dad, for giving us the tools as kids to write stories and for believing they could exist outside our bedroom.

Thank you to our mastermind agent, Kimberly Brower, for championing us and these dysfunctional characters. Outside of our family, you were the first to read about Phoebe and Rocky, the Graves and the Tinrocks, and all the complicated, tangled webs they've woven—and your love for this romance meant so much to us from the very start. You always have a way of making our books *better*, and we can't thank you enough for your input!

Thank you to our brilliant editor, Kristine Swartz, for truly helping us discover the best story possible. You've given us these amazing "ah-ha!" lightbulb moments where we think you just might be our Hailey Tinrock, and we are so grateful to have this experience to work with you and shape this series to be the best it can be! Likewise, thank you to the rest of the Berkley team: Mary Baker, Kristin Cipolla, Jessica Plummer, Kim-Salina I, the copyeditors, proofreaders, and everyone in between—we feel incredibly lucky to have you all in our corner. Thank you for making Phoebe and Rocky's story all it can be.

Thank you to the longtime readers who've believed in us and rooted for us for so, so very long. You all, we're here together! Thank you for still believing in us enough to read this one. Thank you for never giving up on us and for wanting to read what's next. We love childhood romances possibly because of the enduringness of them, and it's a love we often feel beyond romance. We feel it with our family, and we've felt it with all of you.

And that goes to say, thank you to our friends Jenn and Lanie. You created the Fizzle Force and it's become what we call our beautiful, magical, kind, and loving group of readers. Thank you to Shea for joining them not too long after. We love you three like Phoebe loves her strawberries (definitely all the ones she keeps and treasures!). Thank you to more beautiful friends we've made along the way: Haley, Alyssa, Juana, Andrea, Andressa, Margot, Em, Laura, Marie, Sarah, and so many more—you all are extraordinary people in our eyes.

Thank you to Ashley, our best friend, the Hailey to our

Phoebe. Thank you to our big brother, Alex, for all the sibling adventures that've filled our creative wells!

Thank you to our amazing patrons on our Patreon, who were a reason we could continue writing and living our dream. We'll never stop being grateful for your love and support, and we always hope our Patreon can be a happy place for you.

Speaking of support—thank you to our significant others for constantly being shoulders we can lean on. Even on our saddest, most doubtful days, you both are there with pom-poms and ready to remind us of who we truly are. Muggles! Just kidding, we know you both find us pretty damn magical.

Saving the best for last!

Thank you to you. The reader. For taking a chance on us and Phoebe and Rocky. This isn't the end of them. Just the beginning of their chaotic, messy adventure. We hope to see you again.

—xoxo, Krista & Becca

TURN THE PAGE FOR A
PREVIEW OF THE FIRST BOOK
IN THE ADDICTED SERIES

ADDICTED TO YOU

AVAILABLE NOW!

One

I wake up. My shirt crumpled on a fuzzy carpet. My shorts astray on a dresser. And I think my underwear is lost for good. Somewhere between the folds of the sheets or maybe hidden by the doorway. I can't remember when I took them off or if that was even my doing. Maybe *he* undressed me.

My neck heats as I take a quick peek at the sleeping beauty, some guy with golden hair and a scar along his hip bone. He turns a fraction, facing me, and I freeze. His eyes stay shut, and he groggily clings to his pillow, practically kissing the white fabric. As he lets out breathy snores, his mouth open, the strong scent of alcohol and pepperoni pizza wafts right towards me.

I sure know how to choose 'em.

I masterfully slip from the bed and tiptoe around his apartment, yanking on my black shorts—sans panties, another pair gone to a nameless guy. As I pick up my ripped gray tee, tattered and practically in shreds, the foggy image of last night clears. I stepped through the threshold of his room and literally tore my clothes off like the raging Hulk. Was that even sexy? I cringe. Must have been sexy enough to sleep with me.

Desperate, I find a discolored muscle tee on his floor and manage to tug it over my shoulder-length brown hair, the straight strands tangled and greasy. That's when I find my woolen hat. Bingo. I smack that baby on and hightail it out of his bedroom.

Empty beer cans scatter the narrow hallway, and I stumble over a bottle of Jack Daniel's, filled with black spittle and what looks like a Jolly Rancher. A photo collage of inebriated college girls decorates the door to my left—thankfully not the room I exited. Somehow I was able to dodge that Kappa Phi Delta horndog and find a guy that *doesn't* advertise his conquests.

I should know better. I swore off frat houses after my last encounter at Alpha Omega Zeta. The night I arrived at fraternity row, AOZ was hosting a theme party. Unaware, I stepped through the four-story building's archway to be met with buckets of water and guys chanting for me to rip off my bra. It was like spring break gone awry. Not that I have much in the upstairs department to show off. Before I convulsed in embarrassment, I ducked underneath arms, wedged between torsos, and found pleasure at other places and with other people.

Ones that didn't make me feel like a cow being appraised.

Last night I broke a rule. Why? I have a problem. Well, I have many problems. But saying *no* happens to be one of them. When Kappa Phi Delta announced that Skrillex would be playing in their basement, I thought the crowd would be a mixture of sorority girls and regular college folk. Maybe I'd be able to land a normal guy who likes house music. Turns out, the demographic centered on frat guys. Lots of them. Preying on anyone with two boobs and a vagina.

And Skrillex never showed. It was just a lame DJ and a few amps. Go figure.

Deep, *male* voices echo off the marble balusters on the balcony and staircase, and my feet cement by the wall. People are awake? Downstairs? Oh no.

The walk of shame is a venture I plan to avoid all four years of collegiate society. For one, I blush. Like intense tomato red. No cute flushed cheeks. Just rash-like patches that dot my neck and arms as if I'm allergic to embarrassment.

The male laughter intensifies, and my stomach knots at the nightmarish image spinning in my mind. The one where I stumble down the stairs and all heads whip in my direction. The look of surprise coats their faces, wondering what "brother" of theirs decided to hook up with a flat-chested, gaunt girl. Maybe they'll throw a chicken bone at me, teasing me to eat.

Sadly that happened in fourth grade.

Likely, I'll sputter unintelligible words until one of them takes pity on my flaming red leopard spots and shuffles me out of their door like unwanted garbage.

This was such a mistake (the frat house, not the sex). Never again will I be forced to hoover tequila shots like a vacuum. Peer pressure. It's a real thing.

My options are limited. One staircase. One fate. Unless I happen to grow a pair of wings and fly out of the second-floor window, I'm about to face the walk of shame. I creep to the balcony and suddenly envy Veil from one of my newer comics. The young Avenger can vaporize into nothingness. A power I could surely use right now.

As soon as I reach the top step, the doorbell rings and I peek over the railing. About ten fraternity brothers are gathered on leather sofas, dressed in various versions of khaki shorts and collared shirts. The most lucid guy nominates himself for door duty. He manages to stand on two feet, his brown hair swept back and his jaw intimidatingly squared. As he answers the door, my spirits lift.

Yes! This is my one opportunity to dash out unseen.

I use the distraction to glide down the steps undetected, channeling my inner Veil. Halfway to the bottom, Squared-Jaw leans on the doorframe, blocking the entrance. "Party's over, man." The words sound cottony in his mouth. He lets the door swing shut in the person's face.

I hop over two more stairs.

The bell rings again. For some reason, it sounds angrier.

Squared-Jaw groans and yanks the knob hard. "What?"

Another frat guy laughs. "Just give him a beer and tell him to piss off."

A few more steps. Maybe I can really do this. I've never been a particularly lucky person, but I suppose I'm due for a dose.

Squared-Jaw keeps his hand planted on the frame, still blocking the passage. "Speak."

"First of all, does it look like I can't read a clock or further-more don't know what *daytime* looks like? No shit, there's no party." Holy . . . I know that voice.

I stay planted three-quarters down. Sunshine trickles through a tiny space between the doorframe and Squared-Jaw's tangerine-orange polo. He clenches his teeth, about ready to slam the door back in the other guy's face, but the intruder puts his hand on it and says, "I left something here last night."

"I don't remember you being here."

"I was." He pauses. "Briefly."

"We have a lost and found," Squared-Jaw says curtly. "What is it?" He edges away from the doorframe and nods to someone on the couch. They watch the scene like a reality re-run on MTV. "Jason, go grab the box."

When I glance back, I notice the guy outside. Eyes right on me.

"No need," he says.

I sweep his features. Light brown hair, short on either side, full on top. Decently toned body hidden beneath a pair of faded Dockers and a black crew-neck tee. Cheekbones that cut like ice and eyes like liquid scotch. Loren Hale is an alcoholic beverage and he doesn't even know it.

All six foot two of him fills the doorway.

As he stares at me, he wears a mixture of amusement and irritation, the muscles in his jaw twitching with both. The frat guys follow his gaze and zero in on the target.

Me.

I may as well have reanimated from thin air.

"Found her," Lo says with a tight, bitter smile.

Heat rises to my face, and I use my hands as human blinders, trying to cover my humiliation as I practically sprint to the door.

Squared-Jaw laughs like he won their masculine show-down. "Your girlfriend is a skank, man."

I hear no more. The brisk September air fills my lungs, and Lo bangs the door closed with more force than he probably intended. I cower in my hands, pressing them to my hot cheeks as the event replays in my head. Oh. My. God.

Lo swoops in behind me, his arms flying around my waist. He sets his chin on my shoulder, hunching over a little to counter my short height with his tall. "He better have been worth it," Lo whispers, his hot breath tickling my neck.

"Worth what?" My heart lodges in my throat; his closeness

confuses and tempts me. I never know where Lo's true intentions lie.

He guides me forward as we walk, my back still pressed against his chest. I can barely lift up a foot, let alone think straight. "Your first walk of shame in a frat house. How'd that feel?"

"Shameful."

He plants a light kiss on my head and disentangles from me, walking forward. "Pick it up, Calloway. I left my drink in the car."

My eyes begin to widen as I process what this means, gradually forgetting the horrors that just occurred. "You didn't drive, did you?"

He flashes me a look like *really, Lily?* "Seeing as how my usual DD was unavailable"—he raises his eyebrows accusingly—"I called Nola."

He called my personal driver, and I don't begin to ask why he decided to forgo his own chauffeur that would gladly cart him around Philadelphia. Anderson has loose lips. In ninth grade when Chloe Holbrook threw a rager, Lo and I may have been discussing illegal narcotics that were passed from hand to hand at her mother's mansion. Backseat conversations should be considered private among all car participants. Anderson must not have realized this unspoken rule because the next day, our rooms were raided for illegal paraphernalia. Luckily, the maid forgot to search in the fake fireplace where I used to keep my X-rated box of toys.

We came away clean from the incident and learned a very important lesson. Never trust Anderson.

I prefer to not use my family's car service and thus embed myself further in their grips, but sometimes Nola is a necessity.

Like now. When I'm slightly hungover and unable to drive the perpetually drunk Loren Hale.

He has knighted me as his personal sober driver and refuses to shell out money to any cab services after we were almost mugged in one. We never told our parents what happened. Never explained to them how close we were to something horrible. Mostly because we spent that afternoon at a bar with two fake IDs. Lo guzzled more whiskey than a grown man. And I had sex in a public bathroom for the very first time. Our indecencies became our rituals, and our families didn't need to know about them.

My black Escalade is parked on the curb of frat row. Multimillion-dollar houses line up, each outdoing the last in column sizes. Red Solo cups litter the nearest yard, an overturned keg splaying sadly in the grass. Lo walks ahead of me.

"I didn't think you were going to show," I say and skirt past a puddle of barf in the road.

"I said I would."

I snort. "That's not always accurate."

He halts by the car door, the windows too tinted to see Nola waiting in the driver's seat. "Yeah, but this is Kappa Phi Delta. You screw one and they may all want a piece of your ass. I seriously had nightmares about it."

I grimace. "About me getting raped?"

"That's why they're called *nightmares*, Lily. They're not supposed to be pleasant."

"Well this is probably my last expedition into a frat house for another decade or at least until I forget about this morning."

The driver's window rolls down. Nola's deep black curls caress her heart-shaped face. "I have to pick up Miss Calloway from the airport in an hour."

"We'll be ready in a minute," I tell her. The window slides up, blocking her from view.

"Which Miss Calloway?" Lo asks.

"Daisy. Fashion Week just ended in Paris." My little sister shot up overnight to a staggering five foot eleven, and with her rail-like frame she fit the mold for high fashion. My mother capitalized on Daisy's beauty in an instant. Within the week of her fourteenth birthday, she was signed to IMG modeling agency.

Lo's fingers twitch by his side. "She's fifteen and probably surrounded by older models blowing lines in a bathroom."

"I'm sure they sent someone with her." I hate that I don't know the details. Since I arrived at the University of Pennsylvania, I acquired the rude hobby of dodging phone calls and visits. Separating from the Calloway household became all too easy once I entered college. I suppose that has always been written for me. I used to push the boundaries of my curfew and spent little time in the company of my mother and father.

Lo says, "I'm glad I don't have siblings. Frankly, you have enough *for* me."

I never considered having three sisters to be a big brood, but a family of six does garner some unique attention.

He rubs his eyes wearily. "Okay, I need a drink and we need to go."

I inhale a deep breath, about to ask a question we've both avoided thus far. "Are we pretending today?" With Nola so close, it's always a toss-up. On one hand, she's never betrayed our trust. Not even in the tenth grade when I used the backseat of a limo to screw a senior soccer player. The privacy screen was up, blocking Nola's view, but he grunted a little too loud and I knocked into the door a little too hard. Of course she heard, but she never ratted me out.

There's always the risk that one day she'll betray us. Cash loosens lips, and unfortunately, our fathers are swimming in it.

I shouldn't care. I'm twenty. Free to have sex. Free to party. You know, all the things expected of college-aged adults. But my laundry list of dirty (like *really* dirty) secrets could create a scandal within my family's circle of friends. My father's company would not appreciate that publicity one bit. If my mother knew my serious problem, she'd send me away for rehab and counseling until I was fixed up nicely. I don't want to be fixed. I just want to live and feed my appetite. It just so happens that my appetite is a sexual one.

Plus, my trust fund would magically vanish at the sight of my impropriety. I'm not ready to walk away from the money that pays my way through college. Lo's family is equally unforgiving.

"We'll pretend," he tells me. "Come on, love." He taps my ass. "Into the car." I barely stumble on his frequent use of *love*. In middle school, I told him how I thought it was the sexiest term of endearment. And even though British guys have staked a claim to it, Lo took it as his own.

I scrutinize him, and he breaks into a wide smile.

"Has the walk of shame crippled you?" he asks. "Do I need to carry you into the threshold of the Escalade, too?"

"That's unnecessary."

His crooked grin makes it hard not to smile back. Lo purposefully leans in close to tease me, and he slips a hand in the back pocket of my jeans. "If you don't unfreeze yourself from this state, I'm going to spin you around. Hard."

My chest collapses. Oh my . . . I bite my lip, imagining what sex would be like with Loren Hale. The first time was too long ago to remember well. I shake my head. *Don't go there*. I turn around to open the door and climb in the Escalade, but a huge realization hits me.

"Nola drove to fraternity row . . . I'm dead. OhmyGod. I'm dead." I run two hands through my hair and begin to breathe like a beached whale. I have no good excuse to be here other than I was searching for a guy to sleep with. And that's the answer I'm trying to avoid. Especially since our parents think Lo and I are in a serious relationship—one that changed his dangerous partying ways and reformed him into a young man that his father can be proud of.

This, picking me up from a frat party with the faint smell of whiskey on his breath, is not what his father has in mind for his son. It is *not* something he'd condone or even accept. In fact, he'd probably scream at Lo and threaten him with his trust fund. Unless we want to say goodbye to our luxuries from our inherited wealth, we have to pretend to be together. And pretend that we're two perfectly functioning, perfectly well-kept human beings.

And we're just not. We're not. My arms shake.

"Whoa!" Lo places his hands on my shoulders. "Relax, Lil. I told Nola that your friend had a birthday brunch. You're covered."

My head still feels like it'll float away, but at least that's better than the truth. *Hey, Nola, we need to pick up Lily from frat row, where she had a one-night stand with some loser.* And then she'd look at Lo, waiting for him to explode in jealousy. And he'd add: *Oh yeah, I'm only her boyfriend when I need to be. Fooled you!*

Lo senses my anxiety. "She's not going to find out." He squeezes my shoulders.

"Are you sure?"

"Yes," he says impatiently. He slides in the car, and I follow behind. Nola puts the Escalade in gear.

"Back to the Drake, Miss Calloway?" After years of asking her to call me anything, even *little girl* (for some reason, I thought that would entice her to drop the whole act, but I think I only offended her instead), I gave up the attempt. I swear my dad pays her extra for the formality.

"Yes," I say, and she heads towards the Drake apartment complex.

Lo nurses a coffee thermos, and even though he takes big gulps, I'm certain that the caffeinated beverage does not fill it. I find a can of Diet Fizz in the center cooler-console and snap it open. The dark carbonated liquid soothes my restless stomach.

Lo drapes an arm across my shoulder, and I lean into his hard chest a tiny bit.

Nola glances in the rearview mirror. "Was Mr. Hale not invited to the birthday brunch?" she asks, being friendly. Still, anytime Nola goes into question mode, it jostles my nerves and triggers paranoia.

"I'm not as popular as Lily," Lo answers for me. He has always been a much better liar. I blame it on the fact that he's constantly inebriated. I'd be a far more confident, self-assured Lily if I was downing bourbon all day.

Nola laughs, her plump belly hitting the steering wheel with each chortle. "I'm sure you're just as popular as Miss Calloway."

Anyone (apparently Nola, too) would assume that Lo has friends. On an attractiveness scale, he ranges right between a lead singer from a rock band you'd like to fuck and a runway model for Burberry and Calvin Klein. Although, he's never been in a band, but a modeling agency did scout him once, wanting him for a Burberry campaign. They retracted the offer after seeing him drink straight from a nearly empty bottle of whiskey. The fashion industry has standards, too.

Lo should have lots of friends. Mostly of the female kind. And usually they do come flocking. But not for long.

The car travels along another street, and I count the minutes in my head. Lo angles his body towards me while his fingers brush my bare shoulder, almost lovingly. I make brief eye contact, my neck burning as his deep gaze enters mine. I swallow hard and try not to break it. Since we're supposed to be dating, I shouldn't be afraid of his amber eyes like an awkward, insecure girl.

Lo says, "Charlie is playing sax tonight at Eight Ball. He invited us to go watch him."

"I don't have plans." *Lie.* A new club opened up downtown called The Blue Room. Literally, everything is said to be blue. Even the drinks. I'm not missing the opportunity to hook up in a blue bathroom. Hopefully with blue toilet seats.

"It's a date."

Silence (of the awkward variety) thickens after his words die in the air. Normally, I'd be talking to him about The Blue Room and my nefarious intentions tonight, making plans since I am his DD. But in the censored car, it's more difficult to start R-rated conversations.

"Is the fridge stocked? I'm starving."

"I just went to the grocery store," he tells me. I narrow my eyes, questioning whether he's lying to play the part of a good boyfriend or if he really did make a Whole Foods run. My stomach growls. At least we all know I didn't lie.

His jaw tightens, pissed that I don't know a fib from a truth. Normally I do, but sometimes when he's so nonchalant, the lines blur. "I bought lemon meringue pie. Your favorite."

I internally gag. "You shouldn't have." *No, you really shouldn't have.* I hate lemon meringue. Obviously he wants Nola to think he's an upstanding boyfriend, but the only girlfriend Loren Hale will ever treat well is his bottle of bourbon.

We stop at a traffic light, now only a few blocks from the apartment complex. I can taste freedom, and Lo's arm begins to feel more like a weight than a comforting appendage across my shoulders.

"Was this a casual event, Miss Calloway?" Nola asks. *What? Oh . . . shit.* Her eyes plant on the muscle tee I snatched from the frat guy's floor. Stained and off-white with God knows what.

"Umm, I-I," I stammer. Lo stiffens next to me. He grips his thermos and chugs the rest of his drink. "I-I spilled some orange juice on my top. It was really embarrassing." Was that even a lie?

My face flames uncontrollably, and for the first time, I welcome the rash-like patches. Nola gazes sympathetically. She's known me since I was too shy to say the Pledge of Allegiance in kindergarten. Age five and timid. Pretty much sums up my first years of existence.

"I'm sure it wasn't that bad," she consoles.

The light flickers to green and she redirects her attention to the road.

Unscathed, we make it to the Drake. A towering chestnut-brick structure juts up in the heart of the city. The historic thirty-three-story complex boards thousands and teeters into a triangle at the apex. With Spanish Baroque influences, it looks a cross between a Spanish cathedral and a regular old Philly hotel.

I love it enough to call it home.

Nola offers a goodbye and I tell her thanks before hopping

from the Escalade. My feet no sooner hit the curb than Lo clasps my hand in his. His other fingers run over the smoothness of my neck, and his eyes trail my collar. He sets his hands on the openings of my muscle shirt, touching the bareness of my ribs but also concealing my breasts from Philly pedestrians.

He observes me. Every little movement. And my heart speeds. "Is she watching us?" I whisper, wondering why he suddenly looks like he wants to devour me. *It's part of our lie*, I remind myself. *This isn't real.*

But it feels real. His hands on me. His warmth on my soft skin.

He licks his bottom lip and leans closer to whisper, "In this moment, I'm yours." His hands run through the armholes of my shirt and he settles them on my bare shoulder blades.

I hold my breath and immobilize. I am a statue.

"And as your boyfriend," he murmurs, "I really hate to share." Then he playfully nibbles my neck, and I smack him on the arm but fall victim to his teasing.

"Lo!" I shriek, my body squirming underneath his teeth that lightly pinch my skin. Suddenly, his lips close together, kissing, sucking the base of my neck, and trailing upward. My limbs tremble, and I hold tightly to his belt loops. He smiles in between each kiss, knowing the effect he has on me. His lips press to my jaw . . . the corner of my mouth . . . he pauses. And I refrain from taking him in my arms and finishing the job.

Then he slips his tongue inside my mouth, and I forget about the fakeness of his actions and believe, for this moment, that he's truly mine. I kiss back, a moan caught in my throat. The sound invigorates him, and he pushes closer, harder, rougher than before. *Yes.*

And then I open my eyes and see the absence of the

Escalade on the curb. Nola's gone. I don't want this to end, but I know it must. So I break the kiss first, touching my lips that swell.

His chest rises and falls heavily, and he stares at me for a long moment, not detaching.

"She's gone," I tell him. I hate what my body eagerly aches for. I could so easily hike a leg around his waist and slam him against the building. My heart flutters in excitement for it. I am not immune to those warm amber eyes, the ones that a functioning alcoholic like Lo carries. Endearing, glazed, and powerful. The ones that constantly scream *fuck me!* That torture me from here until eternity.

With my spoken words, his jaw hardens. Slowly, he peels his hands from me and then rubs his mouth. Tension stretches between us, and my very core says to *jump*, to pounce on him like a little Bengal tiger. But I can't. Because he's Loren Hale. Because we have a system that cannot be disrupted.

After a long moment, something clicks in his head, and he's horrified. "Tell me you didn't blow some guy."

Oh my God. "I . . . uh . . ."

"Dammit, Lily." He starts wiping his tongue with his fingers and dramatically takes what's left of his flask and swishes it in his mouth, spitting it out on the ground.

"I forgot." I cringe. "I would have warned you . . ."

"I'm sure."

"I didn't know you were going to kiss me!" I try to defend myself. *Or else I would have found toothpaste in that frat's bathroom. Or some mouthwash.*

"We're together," he says back. "Of course I'm going to fucking kiss you." With this, he pockets his flask and aims his sights on the entrance to the Drake. "I'll see you inside." He spins around, walking backwards. "You know, in *our* apartment.

That we share, as a *couple*." He smiles that bitter smile. "Don't be too long, love." He winks. And part of me utterly and completely crumbles to mush. The other part is just plain confused.

Reading Lo's intentions hurts my head. I trail behind, trying to unmask his true feelings. Was that pretend? Or was that real?

I shake off my doubts. We're in a three-year-long *fake* relationship. We live together. He's heard me orgasm from one room over. I've seen him sleep in his own puke. And even though our parents believe we're one small step from engagement, we'll never have sex again. It happened once, and that has to be enough.

Photo © Kelley Raye

Krista and Becca Ritchie are *New York Times* and *USA Today* bestselling authors and identical twins—one a science nerd, the other a comic book geek—but with their shared passion for writing, they combined their mental powers as kids and have never stopped telling stories. They love superheroes, flawed characters, and soul mate love.

VISIT KRISTA AND BECCA RITCHIE ONLINE

KBRitchie.com
🄾 KBMRitchie